SKINS GAME
A Billionaire Sports Romance

By: Blair Babylon

A spicy sports rom com with a billionaire CEO, an impossible wager, and a salty engineer with a long ponytail who will fight him all the way, but he can't keep her out of his mind.

My stupid, drunken bet last New Year's Eve is going to financially wipe out me and my friends, the only family I have, but it led me to Nicole Lamb, so I guess we'll have to call it even.

Just as soon as she stops shaking that golf club at me.

On a bet, I was forced to buy a company and turn it around. I purchased Sidewinder Sports, which came with a stellar reputation for high-end sporting equipment, a mountain of debt that its former owner had snorted his way into, and **one feisty, curvy, absolutely maddening engineer.**

Nicole is the genius behind the aforementioned high-end equipment who will not budge a dang inch on every policy and manufacturing change I'm making to save the company under her delicious little feet.

She's shouted at me that she will fight for Sidewinder forever.

I don't have forever. I have less than a year, or else I'll lose the bet and go bankrupt.

But if my fiendish plan works out, I'm betting on forever with her.

Get notices of new releases,
special discounts, freebies, and
deleted scenes and epilogues
from Blair Babylon!

Go to:
https://blairbabylon.com/emailbx
On your favorite browser.

Published by Malachite Publishing LLC

PRAISE FOR BLAIR BABYLON

PRAISE FOR UNDER PARR, LAST CHANCE, INC. #1

"Under Parr was a pleasant surprise! **I am an addicted fan of Blair Babylons, but I am not a golfer** and was afraid that I wouldn't find Under Parr as exciting as all of her other works. Boy was I wrong! **Under Parr was exciting, funny, romantic, and touched on some very real social issues; I walked away feeling enlightened and totally satisfied.** And like all orher books by this amazing author, **once I picked it up, I didn't put it down until I was done.**" Renaye, Amazon Reviewer

"**Totally enjoyed this PARR-fect story !!!** I thought that this book was **extremely accurate** on a lot of instances that people of color have to navigate in this country that we live in. The way her parents were , are how my parents are in a lot if ways too !! Also , how Europeans healthcare and child-care is so different then here. **How Tiffany felt in this story is how I have personally felt in a lot of ways. I thought that the chemistry between these two was terrific !!** Her family was funny and so were his friends !! But there was an under-standing of how things can happen , and the tough uphill battle that is a daily situation for many in this country.

[T]his book was brilliantly written and look forward to the next in this series !!" *Serena B, Amazon Reviewer*

~~~

PRAISE FOR TWISTED, TRISTAN BOOK #1

"I loved Twisted. It's a **definite five star read.** While it's a Billionaire in Disguise novel, it's the first in it's series of books. If you like **seriously tall, really smart men, with a serious side of Daddy Dom this is the place.**

This is a **seriously hot hot hot read. It has kink.** Blair knows how to write unique voices for each of her characters. Twist has a very unique voice giving you best of both sides of the Atlantic. Colleen is such a nerdy, sweet, and reliable woman with serious self-esteem issues. Which is so **relatable.** If you're already a fan, this is an excellent new book. **If you haven't read Blair before this is an excellent new book to try.**" Meghan K. Books2Read Blog

PRAISE FOR ROGUE, MAXENCE BOOK #1

"**Maxence is everything I love in a romance novel** - a whipsmart man with an anguishing call to serve that conflicts with his love for Dree. I was spellbound!" - New York Times bestselling author Julia Kent

"**What a wild and sexy race through Paris!** Rogue masterfully combines nail biting suspense with high steam for the ride of your life with Maxence and Dree." ~ USA Today bestselling author JJ Knight

"**Another masterpiece from Blair Babylon, who I am convinced keeps getting better and better.** Max is not at all as I'd imagined him, and really it's no wonder, since he has been forced to repress who he is. The real Max keeps popping up his head, doing real-Max things that the other Max wishes he wouldn't do. He struggles with his inner demons to be a Godly man, but he hasn't quite figured out how to balance the different parts of himself, and as a result, tortures himself. He is a man searching for himself, impeded by too many bad guys who wish him harm. It's hard to focus on self-actualization while trying to simply survive without getting yourself killed." -- E.C., Goodreads Reviewer

"Blair's stories have always been hot but this one might be the hottest yet." -- Xtreme Delusions Book Blog

"I just couldn't stop reading! This book is addictive!" -- Kat, Goodreads Reviewer

"Rogue is a phenomenal romantic suspense that is sure to delight and entertain as it holds your heart and mind captive. Nothing can prepare you for the roller coaster ride that is Maxence. He will take you unawares and leave you completely breathless and wanting. If nothing else, you will learn why he is so addicting to the women that he meets." -- Words Are The Breath of Life Book Blog

"Good gosh! Author Blair Babylon is a master at building suspense. I have been eagerly awaiting Maxence's story for YEARS. Finally it arrives and I am practically salivating as I tear into the book, excited that I will finally learn the truth about the elusive Maxence. As I am reading, I am finding that Maxence's unveiling is happening at the rate of an excruciatingly slow strips tease. The end of "Rogue" finds me with almost as many questions regarding who Maxence is as the beginning of the book-- but I promise that slooowly he is starting to be unveiled. **One thing that is made abundantly clear is that Maxence lives two** polar opposite lives and this results in my finding myself even MORE intrigued by him. Now THIS is what I consider phenomenal writing!" -- Lil Miss Reads A Lot Book Blog

PRAISE FOR ONE NIGHT IN MONACO

"Holy Maxence! Max hotness! Max suspense! Max everything! Follow your favorite book boyfriends Casimir and Arthur as they try to figure out WHAT the hell happened to Maxence in Monaco, with all the opulence and lavish lifestyle you'd expect from Blair Babylon's Runaway Billionaires. This series starter is hot, hot, hot!"
~~ USA Today bestselling romance author JJKnight

"Blair!! LOVED it! A fun, sexy, fast-paced read that had me on the edge of my seat wanting to know what happened that night!"
~~ Pippa Grant, USA Today BestsellingAuthor

"What I love about Blair Babylon books is the worlds she creates, and One Night in Monaco is no exception. Luxury, power, wealth - all of it beyond your dreams - is a backdrop for our very human, very vulnerable, and often extremely alpha characters who show us how uniquely human we all are -- but Maxence? He's one of a kind. And hot. Whooooo boy."
-- New York Times bestselling author Julia Kent

"Addictively entertaining and full of escapist goodness,this stylish page-turner left me breathless and begging for more!"
~~New York Times bestselling author Annika Martin

"Friends, Casimir, Arthur and Maxence, will do anything for the other. Max is missing...His friends fear the worst, when they look for Max, always coming up empty handed...Until Genoa Italy happened. Maxence, always the gentleman and rescuer, was needed by Simone. He would do anything to help get her home, where she will be safe. I want to thank, Blair Babylon, for bringing Max's story to life. I can't wait until the next episode. This most definitely gets 5 stars."
-- Goodreads Reviewer

PRAISE FOR BLAIR BABYLON'S BOOKS

"The book oozed heart and passion from every page, it was as if it was traveling through my fingers to touch my very soul - I'm gobsmacked at how I feel about it! It showed more than I thought I was going to get it gave me *love and passion in absolute bin loads and moreover it was full of desire, hope, longing, honesty and devotion* - not just from the characters but from the author also because her devotion to her craft was clearly evident in this book - she nailed it!!" *-- Books Laid Bare Blog, (Every Breath You Take, Rock Stars in Disguise: Xan)*

"*Every Breath You Take* was an absolutely stunning and creatively passionate exploration of two lost and lonely people finding the missing part of their heart and soul in each other. What a breathtaking journey filled with unwanted hope, unwavering love, and unexpected devotion! This series is continuing with such a brilliant depth of heart and soul that I just can't get enough of. I am definitely looking forward to more of these ground-breaking stories." *--Shadowplay Book Blog, (Every Breath You Take, Rock Stars in Disguise: Xan)*

"The writing is great, as usual, and the characters are so well developed. **Author Blair Babylon has extreme talent here.**"
-- *Sammy's Book Obsession Blog, (Every Breath You Take, Rock Stars in Disguise: Xan)*

"This book brings together two of the author's series, Billionaires in Disguise and Rock Stars in Disguise. Prior to this book, the two were entirely separate. If you haven't yet read any of the books in these series, then what are you waiting for? **You do not need to read them to understand this book, but reading them will give you a broader understanding of the incredible canvas Blair is using as her background. She has basically created these worlds and characters from scratch, and what a world it is.**" *~Fictional Men's Page for Book Ho's*

"**This was one incredible story.** I can't wait to continue with this series." *~Books and Beyond Fifty Shades*

"**Let me first say WOW... I am seriously addicted to Blair Babylon's books** her imagination whether it be Crime, Rockstar or Billionaire. **She creates a world where you are immersed with colourful and diverse characters and situations that you don't want to escape from.**" *~Kat's Book Promotions*

"What a pair! This story had me clutching my chest. **I loved Tryp. His damaged and broken soul tugs at your heart strings.** His need to spiral down into the darkness to escape his past will have you wanting to comfort him and just whisper sweet nothings in his ear. The unlikely friendship was definitely the perfect route for this story. It takes a special kind of person to handle all of Tryp's darkness. Elfie definitely proved herself worthy and I loved her determination and strength even though she has a past of her own that she is desperately trying to run from. **Blair Babylon delivers a truly emotional story that had me on one helluva emotional rollercoaster.** I am definitely looking forward to reading more from this series." *~Jennifer's Book Obsession, (Somebody to Love, Rock Stars in Disguise: Tyrp)*

"Just believe me when I say you DON'T want to miss this one." *~Jo's Book Addictions (Somebody to Love, Rock Stars in Disguise: Tyrp)*

"This was my first Blair Babylon book and I was on a rollercoaster. **Tryp and Elfie need to read by all, a raw story of friendship and love.** Truly only the strong survive. I want more of these two."*~Romance Bytes (Every Breath You Take, Rock Stars in Disguise: Xan)*

"The chemistry Wulf and Raegan have is amazing and the fact that they are both so stubborn makes their relationship funny at times. The series covers everything from finding out about the good, bad, and ugly of each other to meeting the family. There are raw emotions in these books." *~~Random Musesomy Book Blog*

"Blair Babylon knows what she is doing. **This is some of the best romance I have read, hands down.** It's got a little bit of everything, for everyone....the story was so well written, infused with sex, humor and drama, that **I would gladly read it over and over again.**" *~Contagious Reads Blog*

"If I could give 10 stars I would! I adore this book, I have

read it two times completely and many times parts of it."
~*Katrina's Books Blog*

"**AWESOME!** When I first started reading this book I thought it was going to be your regular romance book and I thought, what kind of spin could possibly be put on this kind of relationship. Don't get me wrong, I am the first person to admit that I love a good relationship. I think it's hot but I was still waiting for a new refreshing spin on romance novels, and this was it for me. So of course you still had the typical kind of damsel in distress and then that sexy as hell man coming to save her. **Well the twist is something that you wouldn't expect....** Wulf also has a secret, and when I mean secret, it's a big secret. No, it's nothing that you might be thinking, like he is married or he is gay. **I mean huge, I was in complete shock when I found out.** That is one of the things that I loved most about this novel, **everything that I thought was completely wrong and it kept me intrigued the entire time.**" ~*Fictional Book Ho's Blog*

"**The writing was great** and **I loved the way the author "peeled away" the layers** of them and let us really get to know them gradually. I loved the mystery in the characters backgrounds and personalities. **I loved the suspense and action thrown in the story also!**" ~*Sammy's Book Obsession*

ALSO BY BLAIR BABYLON

Somebody to Love (Tryp)

The Rock Star's Secret Baby (Cadell)

Santa, Baby (Peyton)

All I Want for Christmas (Epilogue) Get it FREE HERE.

https://blairbabylon.com/epilogues

<u>Billionaires in Disguise: Xan Series</u>

"Alwaysland" (Prequel) Get it FREE:

https://blairbabylon.com/alwaysland

Every Breath You Take

Wild Thing

Lay Your Hands On Me

Nothing Else Matters

"Dream On" and "Keep Dreaming" (Epilogues) Get them FREE
HERE: https://blairbabylon.com/epilogues

"Small Miracles" (Epilogue) Get it FREE HERE.

https://blairbabylon.com/epilogues

<u>Runaway Princess Series</u>

Once Upon A Time ~~~ OUAT Audiobook

In Shining Armor ~~~ ISA Audiobook

In A Faraway Land ~~~ IAFL Audiobook

At Midnight ~~~ AM Audiobook

Happily Ever After ~~~ HEA Audiobook

<u>Billionaires in Disguise: Maxence Series</u>

Rogue ~~~ Rogue Audiobook

Order ~~~ Order Audiobook

Prince ~~~ Prince Audiobook

Royal ~~~ Royal Audiobook

Reign ~~~ Reign Audiobook

Twisted Billionaires

Twisted Billionaire (Book #1)

Tangled Billionaire (Book #2)

Conning the Billionaire (Book #3)

Tempting the Billionaire (Book #4)

Stolen by the Billionaire (Book #5)

Saved by the Billionaire (Book #6)

Last Chance, Inc. Billionaires

Under Parr (Book #1)

Match Play (Book #2)

Skins Game (Book #3)

Sand Trap (Book #4)

Dragon's Den Paranormal Romance

Dragons & Magic

Dragons & Mayhem

Dragons & Fire

Check for New Releases by Blair Babylon

https://blairbabylon.com/books/

skins Game

LAST CHANCE, INC.

A *Billionaire* SPORTS ROMANCE

To my readers. I love you all.
And thank you for reading.

CONTENTS

NEW YEAR'S DAY
KINGSTON MOORE

The Museum of the Inquisition in Carcassonne, France holds hundreds of iron implements of torture, including spiked iron bands to pierce a heretic's eyeballs, racks to dislocate every joint between bones, funnels to force burning oil down the throat to the stomach, and skull vises.

All of these were applied at once to Kingston Moore in his dream, but when his eyelids parted to the laser-edged rain of white light like he was suspended in the heart of a star, the pain didn't stop.

He managed to lift one arm and touch his head, finding only his own thick hair slipping through his fingers, no metal device, no blood.

His hair hurt.

This was—brutal. What the hell had happened?

He was worth a lot of money those days. Kidnapping for ransom? Had he been down in Central America or Mexico and been abducted by narco cartels? Lately, his business had been real estate and venture capital, not the less legal endeavors of his early career, but the past can ride into your life, brandishing a baseball bat.

Voices.

Men's voices, talking quietly.

Not screaming at him to wake from being knocked out during the kidnapping.

His arm could move normally, unencumbered. He wasn't tied down.

As a matter of fact, the couch under his back and against his face was buttery-soft leather, not the usual wooden pallet of drug cartel kidnappers.

He rubbed his eyes, scrubbing the acid sand away. Foul slime coated his teeth and tongue.

Maybe they'd drugged him instead of beating the crap out of him during the kidnapping.

His stomach cramped, clenching in an attempt to vomit. Sweat needled from his pores.

Gasping deep breaths of the cool air around him trickled enough oxygen into his blood that he stopped the expulsion before it started.

He opened his eyes again, and the blinding light subsided, dimming, until he could see empty bottles on a coffee table, glistening and winking in the sunlight.

Tito's. Macallan. Pappy Van Winkle. Cristal.

Jesus, this was a *hangover*? He hadn't been this poisoned since his freshman year of high school when he'd weighed about seventy pounds.

A man's voice said, "What could we have done that is so horrible?"

Kingston recognized the flat tones. Morrissey Sand, one of his three closest friends and business partners, was speaking.

Had Morrissey been kidnapped, too?

No, kidnappers didn't toss their victims on soft leather couches like under the side of his face and leave them untied.

He waggled a foot.

Yes, definitely not tied up. His feet were also free.

Gingerly, he drew his palms up beside his shoulders and rested his fingers on the couch cushions for a moment, gathering strength and courage, and he pushed his torso up and did his best to look around.

Morrissey was struggling to lift his head from where he lay curled in an armchair with an ottoman and squinting at the two shadows over on other couches.

Kingston swallowed hard, traces of toxic saliva running in rivulets down his cracked throat. He tried to ask what was happening, but no sound came out of his mouth.

Mitchell "Match" Saltonstall, another of Kingston's lifelong friends-slash-business partners, gasped, *"What did we do?"*

Maybe kidnapping would've been preferable.

If Kingston laid right back down on this couch, maybe he would wake up in his own bed after a weird remnant of a dream.

Or maybe he would die. Whatever.

Jericho Parr, the last of the foursome, asked, "I say, Match, what have you got there?"

Match said, *"We're in trouble."*

The horror in Match's voice alarmed Kingston right down to his maybe-bleeding toenails. He writhed on the couch, flipping over to get a better look.

Match was holding trembling leaves of paper, maybe full-size photographs, and staring at them.

Jesus, what could they have done that was *so bad?*

Snapshots of them with hookers and blow wouldn't

matter. They were venture capitalists. If they'd lived in the eighties, a *lack* of snapshots with whores and cocaine would have shocked potential investors.

So, *dead* hookers? Drunk driving arrest warrants? What the hell were the papers Match was holding?

Oh, Jesus is Lord. He hadn't *married* one of those debutantes who'd been on the hunt last night, had they? The cream of the New York ton, carefully coiffed and cut into pastiches of the ideal female form, had swarmed the party with their parents the night before, hunting rich bachelors. Had he been set up and roofied? He could probably get an annulment for that.

Morrissey rubbed his face again, grumbling, "We spent New Year's Eve at an exclusive country club in Rhode Island, not the casino in Monte Carlo. Surely, we haven't gotten ourselves involved with international arms trafficking or Bitcoin speculating at one of the oldest, stodgiest, most boring parties on the face of the planet."

Match covered his mouth with his hand and stared at the pages, flipping them back and forth as he studied. "Jesus, it's notarized. How did he get somebody to notarize this thing in the wee hours of the morning at a country club New Year's Eve party?"

Notarized? Probably not a marriage certificate, then. Also, that was a lot of paper for a marriage certificate unless the girl or girls had come complete with a no-prenup contract.

Kingston swallowed harder, trying to hold his gorge down and himself together. Nothing fucking rattled him. His element was bedrock stone. He needed to damn well act like it. He croaked out, "Considering the types of business deals that have been closed in this room over the past century, I imagine several of the staff are also notaries public so that contracts can be finalized and deposited before the signatories have a chance to rethink and back out."

Whatever it was, whatever had happened, Kingston would rectify the situation.

He was sharp, aggressive, and ruthless as fuck when it came to business and especially to safeguarding Last Chance, Inc., the venture capital firm that he and those three hungover corpses around him had built over the past few years.

The four of them had been friends since high school.

Morrissey, Jericho, and Mitchell had been there for Kingston when he'd had *no one* else.

Kingston would be their sword and shield and *destroy* this situation, whatever it was, no matter who he had to ruin, murder, or blackmail to do it, and no matter the cost to himself.

He stretched, lengthening his overbuilt arms over his head. Waking shivers ran through his broad shoulders and thick arms, stiff from sleep. He needed to get to the gym to sweat this poison out of his muscles. "What did we sign?"

Match shuffled through the document, hesitating.

Jericho asked him, *"What did we sign,* Match?"

"It's a bet," Mitchell finally said. "Was Gabriel Fish here last night?"

Jericho rubbed his face. "I saw him early in the evening. He had a model fresh from fashion week in Milan on his arm and said he was in town because his grandfather was tottering near the edge of his grave. Was *The Shark* in on the bet?"

Match nodded.

Kingston winced inside. Gabriel Fish, the mythological shark of their high school, must have been at the party the night before. The Shark crashing a party was like playing a neighborhood pick-up basketball game for a couple of C-notes, and your nemesis's old buddy LeBron James wanders over and slides onto the other team.

But The Shark never made a bet for mere hundreds of dollars.

Kingston had watched Gabriel Fish financially ruin people in their industry for the hell of it by yanking projects that he could afford to overpay for out from under them when they had contracts already signed. He'd misrepresented who and what he was to responsible organizations and then pulverized them.

In the world of venture capital, where pirate tactics were the norm and mass layoffs were standard, Gabriel Fish gave VCs a bad name.

Jericho asked, "Who was stupid enough to make a bet with The Shark?"

Match whispered, *"All of us."*

Jericho leaped to his feet and bobbled, catching himself as he almost fell over, and then wrenched himself around to stare at Match. *"What?"*

Match sucked in a deep breath and said, "We *all* signed this, *all four of us,* plus Gabriel Fish. It's *a five-way bet.*"

So Kingston was on the hook.

And so were Mitchell, Jericho, and Morrissey.

He spun his legs off the couch, the sick in his mouth and knitting needles rammed through his temples less important now that his entire life was on the line.

He leaned forward, his elbows on his knees, and Morrissey and Jericho did the same as they watched Match sift through the contract he held.

Morrissey said, "Well, it can't be that bad. How much could we have bet?" His shoulders were hunched, and he wasn't smiling as he whistled in the dark.

Match shook the paper he held. "A hundred million dollars each."

Holy shit. Kingston's fingernails bit into his knees through his blue suit slacks.

Match continued, "Winner take all. Whoever wins, the other four saps have to pay him a hundred million dollars *each.*"

Jericho staggered off the couch like an earthquake had shaken him off. "Are you serious?"

Though Kingston was usually solid as hell, he slapped his hands on the old wood of the coffee table. The empty bottles rattled their glass shoulders against each other. "If the four of us lose, we'll owe Gabriel Fish four hundred million dollars. That would bankrupt Last Chance, Inc."

And break up the only friends he had in his life.

The only brothers he had in his life.

The only *family* he had.

Morrissey shook his head, and his breath rasped in his throat. "We were drunk. We were not of sound mind when we signed that contract. It's not enforceable."

The rays of sunlight slicing through the windows high above the long lounging room turned to glimmers of hope. Morrissey had graduated tip-top of his class in law school and been admitted to the New York State bar. He could get them out of this stupid sucker bet.

Except that Match shook the paper at them. "It's got *two* notarized sections. One is us agreeing to the contract. The other one states that we were of sound mind and body. *Ten witnesses* co-signed and attested to it, including *Justice Marissa Otis.*"

Morrissey grabbed another copy of the contract from the stack on the coffee table and started going through it.

Jericho raised his hands as if they were being held up,

which they were. "Gabriel got *a Supreme Court justice* to witness the document stating that we were of sound mind and body when I can't even remember what happened?"

At least Kingston wasn't the only one who'd drunk himself stupid the night before, though that was cold comfort in the light of them ruining their lives with one night of sordid inebriation.

Morrissey stared at the document and finger-combed the dark waves of his hair away from his face. "It'll take years in litigation to break this contract, and I don't know if we could ever do it with *Otis* as one of the signatories." He flipped to the last page. "Who else?"

Match said, "AG Lydia Dickman witnessed it, and so did Senator Harkness."

Jericho sat back down on the couch like his knees had given out.

Kingston leaned back on the couch and stared at the dark beams of the white plaster ceiling three stories above, daring it to cave in and bury them in rubble and snow.

Jericho asked, "The Shark got a Supreme Court justice, a sitting senator, and *the Attorney General of the United States* to witness his contract with us?"

He'd tied it up like a fucking Christmas present, ribbons and all.

No wonder The Shark had shown up at the stodgiest New Year's Eve party on the planet. Gabriel Fish had been trolling for suckers, and where better to find willing victims who would get drunk and sign their lives away than a New England, old-money soiree?

Kingston Moore sure as hell wasn't old money, though, far from it. His parents hadn't been posh enough to be serving staff at a place like the Narragansett Country Club.

Like always, he was just a hardscrabble guest of his high society friends the night before.

Jericho asked, "What the hell was the bet?"

Kingston cocked his head, listening.

Match flipped the papers in his hands and read from the document. "It says, 'The five wagerers will each purchase a golf venture and strive to increase its value. The golf venture with the highest net percent increase of value will win the bet, and the four losers will pay the one winner one hundred million dollars *each*.'"

Golf? The bet was *golf?*

Kingston knew the world of fuckin' golf like his own neighborhood. If the bet was golf, he would damn well *decimate* The Shark.

The world brightened.

But his eyeballs still hurt.

Yeah, maybe Kingston was a little sunny-side-up when it came to his own abilities, but someone had to be. "This is a cinch. Only *one* of us has to beat him. We can write a side contract amongst ourselves to work together. I mean, *jeez*, guys. *We own and run a successful venture capital firm.* This is what we *do*. We can outplay The Shark if we work together."

"Nope," Match ground out through his clenched teeth as he continued to read. "The contract states that 'No wagerers may work together, nor give aid, comfort, advice, or information to the other wagerers upon pain of forfeit.'"

Random spikes shot through Kingston's temples again. They had well and truly fucked themselves, and they had only themselves to blame.

Themselves and the empty liquor bottles littering the coffee table, which had also been a choice.

"So, we can't work together," Morrissey said as he

scanned the paper sheaf, "and we can't help each other. We can't even tell each other how we're doing."

Match continued reading to them, "'The wager will end one year from this date on New Year's Eve when the four wagerers will meet back here at the Narragansett Club with financial evaluations of the golf ventures.' And then he specifies financial firms and accounting standards because The Shark wouldn't leave that to chance."

Bile soured the back of Kingston's tongue again.

Dammit, he'd worked his *ass* off, and he'd *had* the cash when the three other guys had asked him to invest and work with them.

Idiot. He was a stupid, drunken idiot, getting wasted around Gabriel Fish or, really, any of those Founding Family snakes who thought Kingston was just another poor they could fleece.

Because he was.

"And we've only got *one year* to do this," Jericho repeated. "Most of our developments don't start paying out for at least two. We're not a pump-and-dump firm. Did he put something in the tequila? Is that why we were all so stupid as to sign this?"

Yeah, maybe they'd been roofied. *Figured.*

If only there were some way to replay last night.

Kingston always had his phone in his hand, taking pictures and notes, documenting.

He tugged his phone from his hip pocket and swiped through his photos, finding way too damn much from the night before.

Even without the sound, the tiny images of all four of them gathered around the coffee table, each bending to scribble on white paper, were damning. "Oh, no. I have a video."

The others lurched over, obviously just as destroyed as he was, and they crowded around Kingston's phone to watch.

Each moment of the video was worse than the last, all of them laughing, the people around them laughing and toasting, and each one signing their damned lives away with each stroke of their pen on five separate copies of the contract.

Above them, the windows were white with blowing snow, and a fire blazed in the enormous hearth that could burn old-growth tree trunks as logs.

Jericho said, "At least it *looks* like we held our liquor pretty well."

Morrissey nodded. "One of the benefits of going to boarding school for thirteen years is an iron liver and an impressive ability to hide how drunk you are, especially during class."

Jericho sighed. "I think my liver's gotten flabby. I'm not doing well this morning."

Mitchell sat on the couch and held his head between his hands, a picture of how miserable Kingston felt but would not let on.

All right, they had a year.

That year started *today*.

Thus, they needed to sop up the poison in their systems and get a damn move on.

Kingston hoisted himself off the couch, stretching the stiff muscles that wrapped his arms and thighs, and wandered over to one of the staff members to ask for four glasses of ginger ale and if it was possible to get some dry toast.

The staff person trotted into the kitchen at the back.

Poor guy, working on New Year's Day. Kingston hoped

this overpriced country club was paying him at least double. They could damn well afford it.

As Kingston wandered back, Mitchell's head wobbled on his neck like it was about to fall off. "You guys know that Gabriel Fish is going to win this, right? He never makes a bet that he doesn't know he will win. The Shark will tear us to pieces, and Last Chance, Inc. will sleep with the fishes."

Not unless Kingston was dead at the end of the year.

Jericho said, "There are four of us and only one of him. We have an eighty percent chance of winning this."

Mitchell shook his head. "I took macroeconomics at Le Rosey with that guy. You guys were in the other semester. He won the *Weimar Republic Simulation.*"

That made them all shut up.

Le Rosey's extensive business curriculum included a semester of macroeconomics during their junior year of high school. Every semester, that sadistic econ instructor designed a new unwinnable scenario to test the students' steely character and the ice-cold nerves required to recover at least some assets in an impossible situation.

No one ever won.

The underlying point was to keep Le Rosey alumni from jumping out of the skyscraper windows when the stock, bond, and real estate markets crashed simultaneously, as they sometimes did.

Mitchell's semester had been dealt the Weimar Republic Simulation, a scenario that still lived in infamy at the boarding school as a particularly fiendish test, but the professor hadn't called it that, of course. She'd made up some stupid name for her fictional country, so they hadn't known it was based on Germany between the world wars.

Morrissey asked, "How the hell did The Shark do that? It's not on a computer, so you can't reprogram it and cheat."

Mitchell said, "Gabriel knew his history better than the rest of us. Dr. Barney devised something devious every year, but the Weimar Republic year was the *worst*. At the very beginning, the rest of us hadn't figured out that the fake country of Sardoninnica was actually the Weimar Republic, and our savings and capital were about to die a horrible death in the grip of hyperinflation. We thought she was doing the 1929 US stock market, so we put our money in bonds and lent it at interest, which is what you do in a bear market. The Shark borrowed money at set interest rates from everybody else and *bought gold*."

Ah, gold, the suckers' bet in every economic situation except the rare, almost singular instance of hyperinflation.

Mitchell continued, "When everybody's notes came due at the end, he sold ten percent of his gold and paid us back with the worthless, inflated money. Basically, he borrowed a hundred dollars when a hundred dollars was worth something, invested it in stuff that inflated along with the market, and then paid everybody back a hundred and five dollars each but kept *millions*. He *was* the Weimar Republic, paying First World War reparations to France and England with hyperinflated dollars that weren't worth the paper they were printed on, and the rest of us were German citizens who got suckered into using our retirement savings to buy a loaf of bread."

Just as The Shark had destroyed his classmates during the simulation, he would do it again, but this time with real money.

Mitchell said, "If we work together, we lose. If we don't work together, he'll beat us. He's as ruthless and relentless as a tiger shark, and he just suckered us all."

Morrissey stood up and clenched his fist. "We *are* going to lose if we just roll over and take it. We may not be able to work *together,* but we can at least consult on each other's ventures and make sure we maximize each one of them. Surely, one of us can beat him."

Mitchell shook his head. "You didn't see him in that macro class. He made us all think that we were the smart ones, loaning him money at a guaranteed interest rate because we all thought it was the 1930s stock market crash like it had been the year before."

"So that means he's a con man," Jericho said, scratching his beard. "Swindlers make you think *you* are stealing from *them.* They can't hustle you if you play the game with ethics and morals. You can't trick an honest person. So that's how we'll play it. Each of us will go out and buy a 'golf venture,' and we'll run it to the best of our abilities. We're going to invest and create value, and we're going to be the best damn businessmen we can be. We've got a great track record with Last Chance, Inc. We've taken five companies from deep red balance sheets to profitability in the five years we've been running it. There's no reason why *one* of us can't win."

Kingston wasn't convinced. They'd vetted hundreds of companies and picked *five.* And they hadn't been limited by the type of businesses they'd selected.

Mitchell grumbled, "Golf. Why does it always have to be golf?"

Match had never taken to the sport like the rest of them had, like Kingston surely had. Of the four of them, he had the lowest handicap and the most contacts in the golf industry.

As a matter of fact, he knew of several golf-related companies that were ripe for the picking.

Morrissey said, "Jericho's right. This is what we're going to do. We've been practicing for five years while running Last Chance. If anybody can beat The Shark at *this* game, it's one of us. And only *one* of us has to beat him. We can sign a side contract between the four of us that if one of us wins, the holdings stay within Last Chance, Inc. *And,* if one of us wins, Last Chance gets an infusion of a hundred million dollars of capital from Gabriel Fish. That way, we can save the company we've been pouring our blood and sweat into. We can do this."

That was an attitude Kingston liked.

He slapped his knees and stood. "Deal. I'll call Last Chance's contract attorney and have them draw up a side contract for the four of us. We can keep working on Last Chance as usual, and then we'll each have our side project to make sure that at least one of us beats The Shark."

Kingston would beat The Shark.

He had to save Last Chance, Inc. and keep his friends from splitting up.

Their friendship wouldn't survive the bankruptcy of their company and mountains of personal debt, he knew.

His whole life had been cut away from him before, and he'd be damned if he'd let it happen again.

Everything was shit.

SIDEWINDER GOLF
NICOLE LAMB

Nicole Lamb waited outside the glass doors of Sidewinder Golf in the cool California April breeze, watching the skinny palm trees sway in the parking lot's xeriscaped islands, her computer backpack heavy on her shoulders.

Any minute now.

7:29 AM.

You'd think that Sidewinder's chief engineer would have a key to the dang building or at least the code to deactivate the alarm system that locked the place down precisely at six o'clock every weekday.

You'd think a company whose motto was "Nobody engineers golf clubs the way we do. Period." would trust the person doing *the actual engineering.*

But maybe the motto was right.

To Sidewinder Golf and its owner, she was just Nobody, an interchangeable and untrustable cog in the Sidewinder machine who did the club engineering, and that's why she was standing outside the front doors, waiting until exactly seven-thirty when the cubic building's impregnable security system would *finally*—

Whirr, click.

The door came loose in her hand, swinging outward.

—open the dang door.

Nicole walked inside, passed the empty receptionist desk in the front office, and headed straight into the hallway to the elevator and then up to the top floor to her lab.

Her lab.

Her gleaming white and steel lab had a main room for simple proof-of-concept experiments, a clean room, and a manufacturing mock-up for production testing. The tech's break room was in the back so they didn't have to scrub out whenever they needed a cup of coffee or a bio break.

Tall windows surveyed her domain, or at least the parking lots and surrounding beige office buildings of the industrial park around her domain.

Nicole's materials science lab was tiny compared to those at the big golf companies like TaylorMade or Karsten Ping. Still, she could have designed and tested a rocket ship in her research facility if she'd needed to.

But she didn't need to.

Nicole imagined and designed golf clubs, not rocket ships.

Far more people's lives would be improved with a better golf club than the launch of yet another billionaire's vanity rocket ship.

As always when she got to her lab, she left her backpack in her office off the main room, dumping it in her office chair behind the desk with a giant curved screen for CAD, and shoulder-brushed one of the swords hanging on the walls and steadied it before heading to the break room to make a pot of coffee for everybody when they rolled in.

Even though it was April first, she didn't want to fool her lab staff by denying them coffee. The pranks would start soon enough. Knowing those clowns, she hoped no one got hurt in the explosions.

Chemistry labs and mat sci labs are dangerous places on April Fool's Day. When people can use their work materials to manufacture bombs or weapons, you've got to watch your back.

Nicole was pretty sure the first prank was already in motion. The HR admin had texted last night to ask if Nicole could give the new club fitter/sales guy they'd hired a tour of the office that morning.

The "new guy" would either be a complete psycho or dumb as a rock, because that was the joke.

Seriously, what kind of a stupid name was *Kingston Moore,* anyway? They should have come up with a better fake name like Dylan Waverly or Berkeley Tran if they were going to fool her. Nobody was named *Kingston Moore* in SoCal.

Nicole prattled along in her head, a list of previous years' pranks scrolling through as she measured out the ashy-smelling grounds and spring water for the catering-size coffeemaker. Her mental chatter was a cloud of cicadas buzzing in the forest of her head: conversations about metal alloys in golf club heads replaying themselves, theories connecting dots about what was *really* going on in her favorite dragon-based series, and debate points coalescing for the argument with her landlord about whether she could keep *that many* plants on her balcony.

Hey, she hadn't manufactured the seven-foot towers of forty-two overlapping pots each. She'd just bought ten of them.

A *lot* of zucchini were growing just outside her glass sliders.

It wasn't her fault that they were sucking up a lot of water, and the apartment complex had chosen to include utilities in the rent. She was going to have home-grown tomatoes that summer.

The babble swirled in her head so thickly—would Xylan survive being turned into an evil wizard vernin, and could Zennifer find a way to turn him human again?—that Nicole didn't notice the email icon on her phone, or the Teams notifications flashing, or even the phone call from her head tech buzzing her silenced phone across the table.

Nope, she just held three separate conversations with herself, happily analyzing and scheming and thinking up zucchini recipes, until Arvind flung open the break room door and screamed, "Why don't you ever answer your phone because *we've been bought!*"

She looked over her shoulder at him from watching coffee stream into the glass carafe. "What?"

Spittle flew from Arvind's mouth as he over-enunciated, "That old *goat* of an owner *sold* us to the highest *bidder!* And it's *venture fucking capital!* We. Are. *Doomed!*"

The worry quivering in her heart froze into crystallized dread at the horror in Arvind's hazel eyes, and the possible futures of Sidewinder Golf—fifty-percent layoffs, eighty-percent layoffs, *liquidation*—landed like boulders in the streams of thoughts in her head. *"No."*

"It's true." Arvind pulled out a chair and collapsed into it, holding his head in his hands. "If it were TaylorMade or Titleist, we'd have a chance at keeping our jobs. But VC... holy shit. They're going to *savage* us. They're going to wring every bit of value out of the company and then sell us for parts."

Nicole scrambled after her thoughts, trying to keep up as more and *more* scenarios poured through her mind until one very important thought turned and smacked her in the face, and she laughed, yelling, "April Fools!"

Arvind looked up at her, his jaw slack and one hand tangled in his graying hair. "No, Nicole. No, it's not April Fools. We've been bought."

"Of course, it's April Fools. Look. if you want to play this out, I won't tell anybody. But it's obviously April Fools."

"It's *not,*" Arvind said, his voice breathless. "I know it's April first, but this isn't a joke. Check your damn phone."

Nicole turned back to the coffee pot, making sure the coffee was properly draining into the carafe and not over-flowing the basket. "Yeah. Sure."

"Nicole! I'm serious! We're in trouble, and we need a *plan!*"

The panicked soprano notes in Arvind's voice despite the fact that he was six-two and over forty convinced her to pivot to face him. "You swear you're serious."

"I am." He held up his right hand. "I swear to gods, I am *not* pulling some bullshit April Fools."

Nicole plopped down in another chair. "Well, *darn it.*"

"*Yeah.*"

"Which venture capital firm?"

He consulted his phone. "Last Chance, Inc."

"Sounds stupid."

"Yeah."

She shook her head. "This sucks."

"Yeah, it sucks. What are we going to do?"

Nicole gritted her teeth. *"Fight them until we can't anymore."*

THE NEW GUY

KINGSTON MOORE

A t ten o'clock that morning, Kingston drove his rented BMW into the parking lot of Sidewinder Golf, looking for red flags in the business that hadn't been apparent on the balance sheet.

It almost didn't matter now because the deal was done, but Kingston wanted to know if he'd bought a lemon. His strategy might change.

If he walked into Sidewinder like, "I'm your new owner, I'm your new boss," the employees would cobble together a dog-and-pony show to exaggerate Sidewinder's profits and prospects because they wanted to keep their jobs.

Understandable, but not what Kingston needed.

He needed to know *exactly* what he'd bought, all the faults and cracks, all the liabilities.

And thus, the ruse.

While Kingston and the previous owner had been haggling, he'd convinced the guy to notify Sidewinder's HR that a new sales guy had been hired and would be arriving that morning, a tragically comic situation considering the company had just been sold. As the supposed new sales guy, Kingston could figure out how the company stood.

The cubic white and glass building was a standard industrial park rental among the biotech and genAI startups in the other buildings, which meant their R&D was probably onsite.

Good. He'd been counting on the hope that Sidewinder Golf had new products in dev that they weren't talking about yet. Trade show season had already started, and he'd pulled strings last night to make sure Sidewinder had booths for summer shows and a gigantic display for the PGA Show in December in Las Vegas.

The other Last Chance guys were making smart plays for their golf-related investments.

Jericho had bought a down-on-its-luck private country club with a golf course, but trying to pivot a large investment like that was like trying to flip a U-turn in an aircraft carrier. It would probably increase a decent percentage in value, maybe thirty to fifty percent.

Mitchell had bought a bankrupt tee times app that was a little risky but would surely make a good profit with an infusion of cash for advertising. He could probably increase the value of that company by two or three times.

Morrissey hadn't found an investment yet, but it didn't matter.

With Jericho and Mitchell's solid investments, Kingston could shoot for the moon.

And he would need to because Gabriel Fish had probably had an investment lined up when he'd made the bet, and it was probably a whopper. At least a fifty-fold increase. Maybe a hundred times his money.

So Kingston needed to blow Sidewinder Golf sky-high, and if he needed to use the more common ruthless venture capital tactics to make sure the company increased in value, he would.

Pump and dump, baby. Pump and dump.

Because Last Chance, Inc. wouldn't survive losing the bet, and his friends would drift away.

A kernel of sheer terror burned deep in Kingston's gut.

He plastered a salesman's plastic grin on his face as he walked through the warm California spring morning and into the building, the shift to air conditioning like walking through a sorcerer's portal into a wintery landscape.

The receptionist glanced up at him and tossed her long hair behind her shoulder as she turned on a bright West Coast smile and tilted forward. "Welcome to Sidewinder Golf. How can I help you?"

He placed one hand on her desk and leaned in, stretching his face into a bigger smile that would never have flown in Connecticut. "Hello! I'm the new guy. Kingston Moore, club fitting and sales. How're you doing?"

She blinked at him, her lush eyelashes sweeping down. "Hello, Kingston Moore. I'm MEREDITH, front desk, obviously. Well, I've got to warn you, it's been a heck of a morning. You didn't already move to California, did you?"

Kingston didn't feel the need to torture anybody. "I'll be working the Northeast territory, so I'm remote. I didn't have to move."

Her shoulders lowered, and she looked down at her desk. "Oh. That's good, I s'pose, that you won't be moving to this area when everything is so up in the air."

"But I'll be traveling to the office a few times a month," he told her.

She looked back up at him, her eyes lifting and smile returning. "It'll be good to *see* you around the office."

"So, what happened this morning?" Kingston asked because he wasn't supposed to know about the deal.

"Oh! A venture capital firm bought Sidewinder in some back room deal, and we are *just now* learning about it *in an email from the new company*. Our chicken previous owner didn't even do a videocall or a town hall or anything."

Considering the circumstances, that wasn't surprising even though Kingston had given Joe Flanagan the opportunity to tell his people about the sale. "That's too bad."

She nodded, her smooth skin creasing between her brows. "Everybody's upset. People don't know whether to go home and update their resumes or prepare for tech transfer to China."

Getting a company sold out from under you is always traumatic, but Kingston was there to make a profit.

She continued, "If I were you, I wouldn't make any long-term plans. The situation is fluid, to say the least."

Kingston had written that last sentence about the situation being fluid in the unsigned email he'd sent from a Last Chance's company account the night before. "I'm not too worried, and neither should you be. Companies always need good sales personnel and receptionists."

She looked up and to the side, while her lips lifted in the middle. "That's true."

"Is someone around to give me a tour? I'd love to see the product and your set-up before I head back east. Maybe a sneak peek at anything new you have up your sleeves?"

"Oh, sure. I think Bob said Nicole Lamb was going to be around—"

A woman's low voice said, "Nicole Lamb is right here."

In the hallway behind the receptionist's desk, a curvaceous woman stood, one hand on her hip as she rested her weight on one leg, her other leg extended and toe pointed like a dancer. Her dark brown hair was falling out of the bun on her head and waving in the air conditioner's breeze like banners calling Kingston to war, and she was looking somewhere behind him like she was distracted.

Kingston skirted the front desk, his hand extended to shake. "Hello! I'm Kingston Moore, the new guy in sales. I heard it's been quite a morning around here."

As he moved, she looked him up and down, evaluating. "*Yeah, right.* You're the new guy, Kingston Moore, *right.* I'm sure you're *absolutely* who you say you are. *Totally* in sales."

Her sarcasm was an icy blast to his face.

Had she hacked Last Chance and figured out who Kingston was?

Like most engineers, people in materials science often have a background in computer science. She might have doxxed him.

Nevertheless, just in case, he played his part. "I've loved Sidewinder's golf clubs for years, but I never managed to get off the waiting list. I'm working here so I can qualify for the employee's discount and finally get my own full bag."

She stared at him, nodding as if placating an absolute lunatic. "Okay, *fine.* I'll play along. Come on, *Kingston Moore.* I'll give you a tour of Sidewinder Golf, because *sure,* you're *totally* going to be working here. You're totally not going to get fired along with the rest of us by the end of the week."

She turned and led the way into the white corridor behind her.

Nicole Lamb knew something about him.

Kingston trotted a step, but with his long legs, he was beside her in an instant. "I just heard that Sidewinder had changed owners."

"Yeah, I *guess* that's real," she said. "Sucks to be you, showing up on *your first day,* and the company just changed hands."

"It must seem odd that I'm still interested in working here after the acquisition. I admit I took the job for the employee benefit of getting a set of clubs, so it's worth the risk."

She stopped in the hallway, planting both her feet on one of the floor tiles.

Kingston strode another few steps before he stopped himself and turned back. "Are we going on the tour?"

"It's April Fool's Day," she ground out, her teeth clenched. "I don't like being fooled."

He looked around, expecting a jump-scare, but the corridor was empty except for them. "I don't get the joke."

"*You're* the joke. There's no way a new guy just happens to start on April Fool's Day. Like, I'm going to waste my whole day showing you around but you'll be dumb as asphalt or something, and everyone will laugh at me."

"Oh!" He chuffed a laugh. Thank Jesus, he wasn't found out. "It's not an April Fool's prank, just abysmal timing on my part. I am Kingston Moore, the new salesperson for your company that just got sold to a venture capital firm."

Everything except that part about him being in sales was true.

For a venture capital guy, that was more truth than usual.

"Well, your timing sucks, and I'm sorry you got mixed up in this." Nicole paused, sucking her lips inside her mouth and staring at the gray-flecked tile under his loafers and her hiking boots. "Are you sure this isn't an April Fool's joke?"

"It's not," he assured her.

"Because I'm an easy sucker for jokes. I believe everything and go on like it's real, and then everybody laughs at me, and then I have to laugh, too. But I don't like practical jokes. They're mean."

"Hey." He ducked his head, trying to catch her eye. He didn't want to invade her personal space because he didn't need an HR incident on his first day of owning the company, but he stroked his fingers along the soft skin under her chin and tipped her chin up, raising her eyes to meet his.

Her eyes were dark, shining polished mahogany with a film of tears.

Oh-no flooded him. The urge to stop her crying, to *fix*, crested. "Don't be upset. This isn't a joke. I am who I say I am and will be working with Sidewinder Golf." He didn't want to lie to a woman on the verge of tears. "I'm not an April Fool's joke. No one's going to laugh at you for believing me."

She blinked at him, surprise replacing turmoil.

"And if they do laugh," his voice dropped into his chest, "you tell them to come talk to *me* about it."

Her blinks increased, and her elbows tucked in by her body, protecting her ribs.

His fingers were still under her chin, near the smoothness of her throat, just where they'd be if he'd raised her face to kiss her.

Her full lips began to part in the middle.

Kingston dropped his hand and stepped back. "I apologize if I overstepped."

She looked toward the floor, her head snapping to new positions like she was trying to accommodate a new thought. "I—*no*, it's okay."

"But I assure you, I'm not an April Fool's Day joke. I'm exactly who I say I am."

Mostly.

"Okay." She was still flustered, and without looking at him, she began walking.

Kingston followed her hourglass form swaying in the sterile, white hallway toward the elevators.

He wasn't altogether composed, so he hung back, checked himself, and then caught up to her. "Are you the head engineer?"

"Yes," she hissed.

"Because I asked to see the head engineer, and I've been pawned off on techs so many times that I can't keep count anymore."

"I'm *not* a *tech.*"

"As we established."

"Do you change jobs so often that you have a protocol?" she asked.

Oh, perceptive, this one. "Only when the company gets sold out from under me on my first day, and you'd be surprised how often that happens."

"Betcha I wouldn't," she grumbled and thumb-pointed toward a door they passed. "Anyway, downstairs break room, administration and HR offices, and sales offices are on the other side of the building. We'll come back that way after we tour upstairs."

"And what's upstairs?"

"My domain."

He grinned at her. "Ominous."

Her sly glance from the corners of her eyes up at him seemed like she was beginning to relax. "Maybe."

He was chuckling as the elevator doors slid open.

As they walked inside, Kingston assumed the standard elevator-riding position: facing the doors, feet shoulder-width with weight evenly distributed, hands clasped in front, and silent. If the elevator had been crowded, he would have sorted himself into a staggered row.

The elevator lurched and jiggled, then began laboriously dragging itself upward, hand over hand, swaying as it jerked.

The stairs would've been faster.

Nicole leaned against the side wall, facing him. "So, where are you from?"

Unease washed through him, but he was in the West. Even complete strangers lounged in the elevator, looked straight into each other's eyeballs, and held entire conversations within the enclosed, forced intimate space.

Shocking, really.

Kingston softened his face with a small smile and turned to look at her. "I live in Connecticut now, near Bridgeport."

"You sound like you're from England."

"I've spent a lot of time overseas as a child."

"I was born and raised here in SoCal, in Oceanside," she said. "I live in an apartment complex just a short drive from work. My landlord is being rude about a few plants I'm growing on my balcony."

All right, so they were talking in this closed coffin of an elevator.

He softened his stance and angled toward her. "I'm sorry to hear your landlord is being a dick."

"Yeah, but I pay my rent on time. He can't do anything about it."

"That's good."

Nicole had stuffed her hands in the front pockets of her jeans, and her lush body bent at the waist as she gazed up at him. The air conditioner blowing even in the elevator brushed the curling tendrils of her hair around her face.

Her face was sweet, Kingston noted. Her cheeks were soft, rounded, and her dark eyes seemed luminous, glowing with the light of a dark sun. Her blinks made him think of shyness.

He could crowd her back against the wall of the elevator, pull that elastic loop thing out of her hair and let it tumble over her shoulders, and kiss the daylights out of her right there.

His lips warmed with the mental image of being pressed against her mouth, her throat.

She asked him, "Where have you lived other than Connecticut?"

He forgot his role as a nondescript salesman. "I attended boarding school in Switzerland from the time I was eleven through high school. I've lived in Paris, Zurich, and London, among shorter stints elsewhere."

Her eyes widened as she stared at him in wonder. *"Wow."*

Had he phrased it quite like that just to elicit that response? Did he want to pique her interest in him?

He shouldn't. He was lying to her about too much. A smart woman with significant computer acumen, which Nicole Lamb most assuredly was, would discover that he was an owner of Last Chance, Inc. far too quickly. His social media profiles weren't hidden.

"I've never been to any of those places," she said.

I'll take you, was on the tip of his tongue. *I'll show you the world.*

He swiveled back to stare at the elevator doors and watched the number *3* finally light up. "You should go. They're nice."

The doors parted, relieving Kingston of being in a cramped space with Nicole Lamb, and he strode out.

She bustled out beside him. "The third floor, which is

the top floor, is R&D. We are a soup-to-nuts organization, from the conception of new golf clubs through design to commercialization and production. Actual manufacturing is off-site, of course, but everything else is under this roof."

"And what's your purview?" he asked, feeling his vocabulary become more British, practically arch, as he tamped down untoward inclinations toward the pretty, vulnerable Nicole Lamb.

He wasn't at Sidewinder Golf to hunt for a date. He was here to inspect his acquisition, determine its potential, and discover redundancies in personnel or entire departments that could be outsourced.

Even the delectable little Nicole Lamb wasn't safe from his cost-cutting scythe.

She said, "My team oversees the pipeline. We brainstorm dev with sales and the executive branches for high-level product ideas and blue-water industry niches. After that, we design products in CAD and IRL modeling, then cast or forge prototypes, and then produce the product for commercialization, and then we put it on the train."

"A literal train?" Trains were inefficient.

"Metaphorical. It's just the phrase that means we send the plans to the manufacturing plant to start producing it. If anything, we should say we put it on a slow boat to China."

"That sounds like an extensive process."

She shrugged one slim shoulder. "One time, we overhauled a wedge and took it from conception to the first manufacturing shipment in four months. That was the Scimitar Edge fifty-degree wedge, a blockbuster for Sidewinder."

Nicole Lamb had produced the Scimitar Edge from concept to production in *four months?* Most golf products took three to five years to hit the shelves.

Kingston's attention was a blazing spotlight beam on her.

The Scimitar Edge was a powerhouse of a golf club with excellent feel. Kingston had managed to finagle one for his set. It was so good that it felt like cheating.

Every time he'd played golf with his Scimitar Edge, he'd had his hands wrapped around her craftsmanship.

His palms grew sensitive, almost a tingle.

Kingston paused outside the door to her lab. "Four months? That's astonishing."

Nicole shrugged both shoulders this time, and her smug smile was cute as heck. "Just doing my job."

"Why a wedge?"

"Because it's a golf club, and we make golf clubs."

"No, I mean, why not a driver? Everyone goes to trade shows looking for the magic driver, not another wedge. Some people already have four in their bag."

"Your driver determines how high you score. Your wedge and putter determine how *low* you score."

Because a miss-hit with a driver meant hacking a ball out in the woods and destroying your score for one hole on that bad luck, but the finesse shots around the green with wedges and putters were where you saved shots on every hole. "Drive for show, putt for dough."

"Yeah, sure, if you want to put it *that* way."

"So we could conceive of a new product as late as early August and have commercial stock on hand for the PGA Show in December."

"Ugh, *shows*," she said, rolling her eyes. "Shows are for sales people, not R&D. You'll be traveling with Gia Terranova to the shows and stuff. She'll be your boss."

Something in Kingston's chest went *thud*. "Right, my *boss*."

Kingston also needed to remember that *he had a boss* for as long as this farce lasted.

He hadn't had a boss in years.

After Kingston had finished his MBA, he'd worked in finance, jetting around Europe's cities, negotiating and wooing, until Morrissey had one day written in their group chat, *We should start a VC.*

So they had.

Nearly bankrupting himself to put up the capital to join Last Chance had been the best decision he'd ever made. Every day, he flew around the world, making deals and making money, or he went into the office and hung out with his three best friends, his only real friends, the closest people Kingston had to family, and he had no *boss* except himself.

"Yeah, Gia is the head of trade shows and does a great job with the booths."

"You don't go to them?" he asked her.

"Oh, dear God, no." A shiver shimmied her clothes. *"Never."*

"But you'd pick up valuable information at those shows. Trends. Niches."

She badged them into the lab area. "Yeah, *no.* I'd be too busy hiding under the tablecloths to listen to anything. Gia and the other guys give me the scoop after they get back. There are too many people at those trade shows. I don't like peopling."

"You don't like people?" he asked, amused.

"I like people fine, a few at a time. When they gather in herds, they look like they're about to stampede. I hang out in the lab all day, talking science with my friends. I love my job."

The door opened to a tiny room with white fabric on the

walls, and the scents of hot metal, bug zappers, and icy cold air flowed into the hallway. "This is the antechamber where we garb for the working lab."

Kingston followed her example and donned hooded white Tyvek coveralls over his suit trousers and white shirt, then covered his face with plastic safety goggles and a surgical mask.

His voice was muffled, and the mask vibrated on his face when he asked, "You work like this every day?"

Papery white protective clothing and a blue square of a mask cocooned her, only her dark eyes visible beneath her plastic glasses. "Absolutely. We're grinding and smelting heavy metals in here. You don't want to breathe dust or fumes or get shavings in your eyes. Everything is OSHA-compliant around here. We never get violations. Glove, and then let's go."

He followed her into her lab as she pointed out lathes, kilns, and crucibles, feeling like an animated oak tree shambling along after a lithe elf who danced through the wilderness.

She shoved open a glass door and led him into a hallway off the central lab, where she paused to shove her safety glasses up to the top of her head and drag down her surgical mask, then unzip her suit halfway down her chest, a sultry move that Kingston couldn't quite look away from.

"Our tech break room is down this hallway, so we don't have to ungarb and go downstairs to get a darn cup of coffee, and here's my office." She flipped her hand at an almost-closed doorway as she paced by. "And down past here, that's where our—"

The only personal office in the hall did indeed have a nameplate reading *Nicole Lamb, PE*, but when Kingston pushed the ajar door farther open, it wasn't so much of an office inside as a medieval armory. *"Whoa."*

The swords hanging on her walls shone in the morning sunlight filtering through the slats of the horizontal blinds. Silver-steel glistened. Black leather wrapped the grips, and glass or jewels sparkled on pommels and guards.

The little engineer had a violent streak, or at least a taste for weapons.

"Oh, yeah, *those*," Nicole said quickly, walking back toward him. "Come on. We're doing a tour. Just down this hallway are our golf simulators, where we test prototypes. We've got the latest ones from SkyGolf. Playing them is like standing on the eighth tee box at Pebble Beach. You can practically smell the sea breeze in your hair. *Come on.*"

Kingston pushed her door open farther. "Are all these swords yours?"

"Yeah."

Her monotone voice signaled disgruntled thoughts.

He turned back. "Do you not want to discuss them?"

Her arms were crossed tightly over her chest. "Depends on how you want to discuss them."

"Can you give me a tour? Tell me about them?"

Her arms drooped a little, and she turned her head warily as if waiting for a blow. "What do you want to know?"

"About them. Did you make any of them?"

She brightened a little and moved toward him. "Some of them. Just a few, really. Maybe half."

Ah, yes. This collection was how he'd get her to open up and tell him anything he wanted to know about Sidewinder.

Everyone had a vulnerable spot.

"Tell me about that one," he said, pointing to a slim, curved specimen halfway up her wall.

"Good eye," she said, walking back toward him and into

her office. The Tyvek coveralls blended out her form, but the loose swing of her arms was more relaxed. "That's a katana, a two-handed, single-edged sword. This one's an antique, at least a century old."

She reached up and took it down from its hooks.

Kingston vaguely wondered if he should fear for his life because some people didn't take kindly to venture capitalists raking over their employers, even though they remained employees.

Oh, but wait. He was the new sales guy, not their venture capitalist overlord.

He leaned against the door jamb as she reverently held the katana with two hands. She said, "It's a beautiful specimen. I bought it in Japan a few years ago."

"So you have traveled?"

She lifted her shoulders again, and each shrug was cuter than the last. "I had the deal all ready to go, and I went with Gia and some of the guys to a trade show. I met the dealer in the hotel lobby and followed Gia and the boys afterward."

"Traveling with friends is the best."

She flicked a glance up at him and then away. "Yeah."

"Which sword is your favorite?" he asked.

Yes, he was interrogating her, but most people like to talk about themselves.

She hung the katana back in its place and lifted another sword from the wall, another curved blade but more delicate. "You picked out my favorite, but this scimitar is a great piece, too."

"A scimitar? Like the Scimitar wedge?"

She turned it over carefully, gingerly keeping her fingers away from the blade. "Exactly like the wedge. I forged this one a few years ago, working with a master blacksmith who showed me how to carbonize the iron and fold the steel."

Her elfin grin at him while holding the deadly blade was the first absolutely genuine smile he'd seen from her, an enchanting mix of delight and shy pride, and she took his breath away.

She said, "It's a wicked blade."

The steel gleamed in the sunlight from her window, picking up the fine striations on the razor-thin edge. "Is it sharp?"

"Grab a paper from the printer, and I'll show you."

Kingston slid a blank page out and held it taut between his hands.

"Nah," she said. "That's too easy. Just dangle it from two fingers."

"You're not going to cut my fingers off, are you?" he asked as he switched how he held the paper. "That would mess up my golf game."

Nicole was holding the sword en guard, the tip weaving in the general direction of his eyes. "Maybe you should worry that I'll run you through."

He shrugged and held out the paper with two fingers. "Friends of mine would not be surprised that a woman killed me with a sword. They would assume I'd had it coming. Show me what you've got."

With delicate flicks of her wrist, Nicole carved easy slices in the paper, the sword tip so sharp that the steel parted the paper rather than nudging it away.

In seconds, Kingston was holding fringe. "That's amazing!"

Her smile broadened, genuine mirth showing through. "Learning how to forge it inspired the wedge design."

"Was it?" Kingston asked, keeping her talking and not looking away. He didn't think he could blink.

Nicole admired her blade, twisting it in the sunbeams.

"Humans have only been casting and forging golf clubs for a little over a century, but the human race has been making weapons of war for millennia. Our institutional knowledge is in *weapons,* not sporting equipment."

"That seems like an indictment of humanity, that our effort over thousands of years has directed toward warfare."

Her sharp smile up at him was a warm caress, an acknowledgment that they were both talking about the same thing. "Sports are warfare. We pick our tribes and scream in triumph or howl in defeat for our chosen champions. Of course, we look to weapons for inspiration for the tools."

"That's quite a sociological view, Ms. Lamb."

The prim press of her lips was a sly agreement, but she turned away and hung the scimitar back on the wall.

"Are you working on any other sword-inspired golf club designs?"

Her glance at the upper corner of the room was an unintended flash of information for Kingston.

She said, "Maybe. We'll have to see how they pan out. We should probably finish the tour."

"Yes," Kingston said, ridiculously rapt at her discussion of swords. "By all means, lead on."

She walked past him and out of her office.

He spun on his heel and stepped to follow her, but she'd stopped in his path.

He jumped back, saying, "Oops!" He'd almost plowed her over.

"So," Nicole said, wiggling with nerves. "There's a meeting after work, just an impromptu gathering to talk about how that VC company bought Sidewinder and what we all think about it. It's nothing official, but it's food and drinks at a bar and grill down the street called The Meeting

Ran Late. I guess you're an employee now." She twisted one leg, digging her toe into the industrial floor tile. "So, if you want to show up, some people will be there at six o'clock."

Meet Nicole Lamb at a bar for drinks and discussion? *Absolutely.*

"Six o'clock? Yeah, I think I can make it," he said.

4

THE MEETING RAN LATE
NICOLE LAMB

A t six-ten, Nicole stood on a curved-back chair and clinked a spoon against her thick pint glass, yelling, "Okay! Hey! Can I have your attention, please?"

Fifty or so of Sidewinder Golf's employees had taken over the back room of the bar. Wait staff roved between the tables, delivering appetizer baskets and burgers to people spouting, "This is bullshit!" and "So that's how Joe Flanagan wants to do it, huh? Just an email out of the dark, no notice?" and "I've already got my resume out to three different companies," and "I've got a party this weekend where I'm going to network like a bat out of Hell."

The new guy, Kingston Moore, had found a seat over with the rest of the salespeople he'd met that afternoon after she'd finished the tour. Gia Terranova was hanging on his shoulder, holding her beer out for him to tap in response to whatever she'd toasted.

Whatever.

Nicole clinked the spoon harder against her pint glass. "Hey! One moment of your time please!"

Everyone simmered down and turned, shuffling their chair legs on the cement floor.

Nicole had planned ahead of time with her lab people and some admin friends to commandeer the big, round table in the middle of the room. Thus, she was now, spatially speaking, the center of attention.

Even Kingston Moore had turned away from Gia and the other sales crew and was watching her, his gaze as sharp and unyielding as when she'd been putting on a show with the swords.

"Thank you for coming tonight," she called out, uncomfortable as heckers with taking over the room. Everyone else was dithering about what *they,* in the singular sense of *they,* were going to do as an individual.

And since no one else had stepped up, Nicole would take over and lead.

She continued, "As we all found out in a darned email this morning, a venture capital firm named Last Chance, Inc. bought Sidewinder Golf for an undisclosed sum and considerations, whatever the heck that means."

The jeers and cheers felt supportive, so she went on. "In the words of Benjamin Franklin, 'If we don't hang together, we will surely hang separately.'"

Laughter.

Good.

"So, whatever happens the next few days or weeks, we can influence the outcome. We can make sure that we're all on the same page when we talk to this evil VC firm, and we can hang together!"

With raucous laughter and a smattering of applause, Nicole climbed off her chair while Arvind steadied the back, but Kingston Moore was holding onto the back when she looked up.

"That was quite a speech you gave," he said, smiling.

His smile was really something to behold: charming crinkles surrounding his blue eyes, white teeth showing, seemingly on the verge of a genuine laugh.

"Yeah, well, people were freaking out today," she said, her shoes finally resting firmly on the slightly sticky bar floor. "You almost walked in to find an empty front desk and no one in HR to do your paperwork, let alone anyone in the lab to work on the new designs."

"New designs?" he asked, leaning in.

Nicole continued, "And so I organized this get-together to keep everyone from literally walking out of the company today. I don't know how long I can hold Sidewinder together. The fact that we haven't heard jack-shoot from our new VC overlords is messing with people's heads."

Kingston looked upward at the wagon-wheel chandeliers hanging above the chattering, noshing crowd. "Good point."

"These Last Chance folks are some *dumb* evil venture capitalists—"

"Evil venture capitalists, you say?"

"Yes. Evil. And dumb. They should know that the most qualified people will bolt first, leaving their new acquisition short-handed and with a drawer full of the dullest knives."

"That is an excellent point," Kingston said.

"Yeah, well, I figure they've got until tomorrow at noon to get their act together and start *communicating* before there's a mass exodus."

Kingston nodded, then said, "I'll have to watch for that email while I'm on the plane back East tomorrow morning."

Gravity dragged at Nicole's shoulders and pressed on her neck, and fighting it to move her feet felt too difficult to contemplate. "Oh. I didn't know your stay would be so short."

His gaze found her eyes again. "I'll be back soon."

Sure, but not much. "Most of the remote sales guys only come into the office once a quarter or so."

His soft smile was slow, and he held her gaze the whole time. "I'm not most guys."

5

HE WROTE THE EMAIL
KINGSTON MOORE

The next morning, a ping from Kingston's phone indicated that his Sidewinder company email account, the one with the address k-moore-sales@sidewindergolf.com, had received an email. When he checked the email, it was indeed from Last Chance, Inc., the evil venture capitalists, contacting their new employees and discussing their future.

Kingston had made a brand new Last Chance email account to send it from, last-chance-c-suite@lastchanceinc.com, and triple-checked that he was logged into *that one* and not his own name before pasting the text and clicking the send button.

It was only eight-thirty in California, somewhere behind the tail of the private jet soaring eastward into the burgeoning morning sun.

Nicole would see the email any minute now, unless she was garbed in her enveloping white paper coveralls or smacking range balls with a prototype club on Sidewinder's first-class golf simulators. It might take a while until she read it.

He probably didn't need to sit in this leather chair and stare at his phone any longer. She might not even email or text him about it.

Why would she contact *him,* really? He was just the new guy in sales. She'd probably discuss the email with her friends and co-workers who had been with the company for the four years she'd worked there, as he'd noted in her HR file.

Kingston should stop staring at his phone and waiting for Nicole to contact him.

He stretched and slid out of the chair, leaving his laptop on the table with the three empty chairs, and walked to the back of the plane to get another cappuccino, extra sugar.

The private plane's air hostess person smiled at him. She was pretty, in a probably-didn't-own-swords way. "Do you want breakfast, Mr. Moore?"

"Sure," he said and sipped the coffee.

"The captain noted that there might be a little turbulence over the Rockies. Also, you can ride in the cockpit with her if you'd like. Mr. Saltonstall prefers to."

So Mitchell rode in the front when he took the company plane, huh? Interesting. "I have work to do, but thank her for me."

When he returned to his seat, Nicole still hadn't contacted him about the email.

Two hours elapsed, and Kingston was somewhere over Nebraska when he could not wait any longer and emailed her, *Wow, how about that email from the new boss, huh?*

An hour later, she emailed him back.

The hit of dopamine from the ping dissipated as he read, *Yeah, can you believe the nerve of those assholes?*

6

CALLING THE NEW GUY
NICOLE LAMB

N icole and the techs gathered in the lab conference room.

She shook her phone, a gesture she hoped everyone would understand as a reference to the mass email they'd all received from Last Chance, Inc. that morning. "The heck! The actual *heck!*"

Much grumbling from Arvind and the other techs around the table told her that she was not the only one riled up by this email missive from their new corporate overlords.

She shook her phone again. "Did they think *this* would placate us?"

Her phone in her hand pinged, and she caught a quick glance at an email from Kingston Moore, probably in reply to her what-the-hell email to him.

He'd written, *I didn't think it was that bad. As a matter of fact, I thought it was quite reassuring. Those Last Chance guys said that they weren't currently planning any layoffs.*

Oh, Nicole hoped Kingston wasn't one of those corporate stooges who believed anything that anyone in authority told them. Surely, he was more independent than *that*.

Well, no time like the present to suss things out.

She tapped the phone number in Kingston's sig file at the bottom of his email, and her phone rang once before the call clicked. Kingston's voice asked, "Nicole?"

"Yeah. I'm in a meeting with the other lab members, and I thought you might want to sit in as a new employee of Sidewinder Golf."

"Well, that's very open of you," he said.

"We are all going to have to work together to have a viable company on the other side of this."

"I'm glad you put it that way. As a matter of fact—"

"I'm putting you on speaker so you can participate." A grinding roar emanated from her phone's speaker as she tapped the button. "Are you on a plane right now, Kingston? You shouldn't be talking on a cell phone on an airplane! It interferes with the radar or something, plus it's *rude.*"

"Oh, no. I'm not on a plane," he said.

The roar sounded like he was on a plane, like maybe he was sitting on the wing. "There must be a lot of wind or something."

"Yeah, it's wind. I have a layover in Chicago, and they don't call it the Windy City for nothing. It's wind. Chicago wind."

"Did you go outside the airport or something?"

"I wanted to get outside and walk around for a few minutes, so I'm in the airport's outdoor smoking area for fresh air. Even though I don't smoke."

"But it's not fresh air because you're standing around with a bunch of smokers, right?"

"I'm upwind. And like I said, it's windy. And you can probably hear the planes taking off out on the runway. That's why it's so noisy. Wind. And airplanes. In Chicago."

"Okay, it's your health, I guess. Anyway, we were just

talking about the email that Last Chance sent this morning. What a bunch of bull hockey."

Airplane-engine roar filled his long pause. "Tell me why you view it like that."

Nicole sure as heck told him, and she added in the comments that her techs yelled out while she was talking.

- Last Chance obviously had no idea what it's like to be a working person in today's marketplace in California, where there were way more high-tech job openings than qualified people.
- Companies were expanding and needed experienced admins, HR, accounting, etc., too. Anybody at Sidewinder Golf who wanted another job could network, go through the HR process, and start their new job by Monday, probably with a signing bonus.
- Those Last Chance venture capitalists must've thought they were being cute by trying to reassure Sidewinder's employees that there would be no layoffs "this month," but again, people have car payments and mortgages. People aren't going to stick around for "maybe layoffs next month."
- Being coy about people's jobs and livelihoods was *not* reassuring.

"I didn't think it sounded coy," Kingston said on the speaker. "To me, it sounded like Last Chance was trying to be genuine and honest. Transparent, even. But also not promising something they couldn't deliver."

"They're venture capitalists," Nicole told him. "They're never honest or genuine about *anything*."

"Do you think it's fair to pre-judge people like that?"

"Venture capitalists never have the company's best interests at the top of their agenda. Their whole agenda is to make money and nothing but make money. For everyone else involved, a venture capitalist buying your company is a tragedy."

Kingston didn't speak for a few beats after that, and then he asked, "Are you going to tell our people that they should quit and go to other companies?"

"As a high-level manager, it's my duty to tell people the truth. If somebody has an opportunity with a different company that isn't owned by a venture capital firm, I would tell them to seriously consider the offer."

"That's—very honest of you."

"What else could I say? These are my friends." She gestured to the eight people sitting around the break room table, even though Kingston couldn't see her. "This new venture capital company hasn't done anything to earn my loyalty, and Joe Flanagan lost our loyalty to him because he sold the firm without even notifying us until after the deal was done. This is so *shady.*"

"You're right," Kingston's voice said. "That's an interesting way of looking at it, and it's valid."

Heck yeah, it was *valid.* "I'm glad you think so." She tried to keep the snark out of her voice but probably failed miserably. "I just wish there was some way that we could tell the guys at Last Chance, the evil venture capital firm, how we're feeling."

"You should write an email," Kingston said. "You should say all this to them so they can rectify the situation or address people's concerns."

She rolled her eyes, and the other people around the

table laughed out loud. "Jeez Louise, Kingston. Are you trying to get me fired?"

"Not at all," but he chuckled. "However, it sounds like these guys might be a little clueless, and maybe if they had this feedback, their emails could consider Sidewinder's company environment when they craft emails or policy."

"That still sounds like a spectacularly bad idea," Nicole said. "The nail that sticks its head up gets hammered first."

"Make sure you reply directly to *that* email address on their previous email, not to any other email address you find online. I've heard that's the best way to make sure that the person you want to talk to gets your email. And of course, make sure you don't reply-all. I hope whoever sent it was smart enough to send it BCC, but you never know what will happen if you click the wrong button on an email app."

"That's the truth. Reply-all is the bane of my existence. Are you sure this isn't a ploy to get me fired?"

"I promise it isn't. If anyone tries to fire you for this, I'll go up the line of command and make sure everything's okay. This is an important set of circumstances that corporate needs to know."

All this time, the wind roared behind his voice like a hurricane. "It sure is windy in Chicago."

"Oh, yes. Terribly windy."

When they hung up, Arvind and Caitlin Moffett were looking at each other and then at her.

"What?" she asked.

Everyone around the table started shrugging extravagantly, and finally, Caitlin said, "Interesting that you dialed the new sales guy into a closed-door lab meeting call. That's all."

"He's a new hire. The sales department is cliquish and weird. They probably aren't letting him inside the circle of trust yet, but he deserves to know what's going on because he works here."

"Right," Arvind said, nodding.

"Right, what?"

He sucked both of his lips inside his mouth and looked at everyone else at the table, who all looked up at the ceiling or at their laps.

"What?" Nicole asked.

Arvind shrugged. "You like this guy?"

"No," she said. "I have terrible taste in men. If I like him, he's probably a cheater or an embezzler. I am a perfect negative indicator."

Caitlin asked, "Do you want to date him?"

"I—what? *No.* I'd have to think about it."

7

SECOND SHOT
KINGSTON MOORE

Kingston didn't wait for Nicole's reply email before starting to draft another company-wide missive for Sidewinder's employees.

Yeah, some days, Kingston could be out of touch with the people who worked for the companies owned by Last Chance, Inc.

Jeez, that singular thought conveyed the whole issue. Too many layers existed between Kingston and the people who worked for him.

The whole corporate structure was like shouting through fifty layers of asbestos insulation. No wonder the message was muffled.

And no wonder Sidewinder employees were now holding war councils and deciding whether to abandon ship.

If Sidewinder's staff simply packed their desks and left, taking their institutional knowledge, sector expertise, and product ideas with them, Kingston's chance to win The Shark's bet would evaporate in his palms.

Intellectual property companies like Sidewinder were

only as good as their innovators and pipelines. They were essentially idea factories, and half-finished projects were worthless.

Any generic company could cobble together a lump on the end of a stick that approximated a golf club and sell it for cheap on the internet. The precise metallurgy in Sidewinder's golf club heads and the specific fiberglass composition of their clubs' shafts made them special, and special made them sought-after, and sought-after made them expensive.

And all that made the company profitable.

Kingston needed to staunch the bleeding of employees at Sidewinder quickly.

And yet, as Last Chance's private jet streaked through the sky and he stared at the blank page on his laptop screen, no matter what he wrote, it sounded like what Nicole would call "more venture capitalist bull hockey."

He stared at the glowing rectangle, deleting anything he dared write, as they flew over Indiana, Pennsylvania, and New York and then landed at White Plains, a regional airport in Westchester County, New York, that was friendly to the private planes belonging to those who worked in New York City or affluent western Connecticut, both less than an hour away by car.

As he disembarked down the staircase to the tarmac, he yelled back to the pilot, "Has the plane been reserved for tomorrow?"

The shout came back, "No, sir. The schedule is clear until next week."

"Turn it around. We're going back to California tomorrow morning. Schedule take-off for six."

Kingston did not acknowledge the leap of his heart at the thought of seeing Nicole Lamb, bantering with her, standing close to her in elevators or the anteroom of her lab so soon.

He especially did not look at the fact that he was gleaning information from her about her friends as he pretended to be someone other than the evil venture capitalist who'd bought her company and held all their livelihoods hanging from a puppet string between his fingers.

8

THE RATTLER LINE
NICOLE LAMB

The following day, Nicole had a meeting with the sales department at two o'clock to update them on new golf club models that would be commercialized in time for the summer golf show season a month hence, so she de-garbed and stopped at the first-floor employee lounge on her way to get a candy bar because the sales folks' vendoland was much better than the slim pickings in the tech break room.

So she was shoving a Snickers in her pie hole as she juggled a tablet computer and a bunch of slippery paper with her notes, and her hair was sticking out like a pine needle compost heap where her goggles strap had snarled it and the humid Tyvek coveralls had made her whole body sweaty, when she walked into the conference room with the long table.

Kingston Moore was sitting at the foot of the table, looking sharp as lasers in a dark blue suit with an open collar.

Yeah, Nicole thought the new guy was kind of hot, sitting

there with his bright blue eyes and dark hair, even though she had very little chance with him and no time for pursuit.

But why did the universe conspire to embarrass her, too?

Nevertheless, she had a meeting to run. "Hello, sales team. How is everything going, down here on the first floor with the good air conditioning?"

Laughter from the rest of the sales team, and Kingston wrote something on a pad of paper in front of him.

The sales team, other than the hottie lurking down at the other end of the table and staring straight at her, was a panel of people who looked like they'd been crafted by AI to sell exorbitantly priced items to straight white men.

Two nubile white twenty-something women with probably plastic surgeon-crafted boobs and definitely bleached-blond hair were at the top of the table near Nicole's right hand. She might have mentally dismissed them except that Morgan and Meagan asked the best questions, took sharp notes, and could play the vapid airhead at golf shows right up until a customer wanted specs. Then they could both reel off the numbers and explain their importance, becoming the cool girls who liked sports.

They sold *a lot* of golf clubs.

The other five people at the table were Ben and Andy, who looked like junior country club pros into all the latest tech and gadgets, and Rich and Ron, who appeared to be grizzled country club pros with decades of sun damage and had seen golf fads come and go but would set you right with the perfect set of clubs for you.

And then there was Kingston Moore, sitting at the end of the table with his hands folded on his paper, leaning in and peering at Nicole like she was prey.

He didn't fit any of the roles.

Maybe they'd hired him to act like the club champion

who vouchsafed the secret for his sudden drop in handicap to you, which would be his new clubs, which you could buy for the low-low price of—

Just kidding. Sidewinder didn't have a value line. Cheap crappy clubs were antithetical to the company's primary mission.

Still, Kingston Moore was—*disconcerting.*

Nicole didn't understand the machinations in Human Resources, and that's why she was in tech.

She announced, "Okay, let's start with the specs on the Mojave short iron series that we just put on the train for production. We expect the commercial product to be ready for wholesale orders in a month, with delivery in three." She tapped a button on the control panel on the table, and the lights dimmed as her slides projected on the screen behind her. "The Mojave is an extension of our flagship line of clubs, the Rattler line—"

She expounded on the benefits and discussed the specs in detail. She'd worked on the data for hours.

The cool girls and the young pros took notes and asked questions. The grizzled pros cracked jokes about the colors it came in.

And Kingston? His steady gaze alternated between the slides and her eyes.

When he stared into Nicole's eyes, even from across the room, she forgot what she was saying and why golf clubs were important because she was caught, stuck to the wall behind the screen by the weight of his gaze.

Nicole looked back to her notes full of chicken scratch and meaningless numbers and sucked in a deep breath before she looked at the slide, back to her notes, at the slide, her notes, and didn't look up at Kingston's mesmerizing gaze again.

Part of her brain laughed at herself for being so easily distracted even while she reeled off digits and explained graphs. If she was going to be *this* weird, she might as well crawl under the table and run the meeting from there, her hand occasionally snaking up to the surface to slap the button and advance the slides.

Another part of her brain warned her off.

Nicole had terrible taste in men. He was probably a cheater or a trash fire if she liked him.

Somehow, Nicole survived and answered questions from the sales team. They all asked questions except for Kingston, who seemed to watch how she answered more than listening to the data itself.

Finally, at three o'clock on the frickin' dot, Ron stretched and announced, "Good meeting!" before standing and walking out, leaving the handouts Nicole had distributed on the table.

The others gathered up their handouts—the young pros having written down some numbers, the blondes with copious notes—and chatted for a few minutes before exiting the conference room, leaving Nicole alone with Kingston Moore.

He was leaning back in his chair but still watching her.

"Did you have any questions?" she asked him.

He paused, and the still air in the conference room gathered around Nicole, squeezing her, until he said, "So, you said the Mojave is the latest in the Rattler line."

Words flopped off her tongue. "Yes, right, uh-huh."

His gaze flicked to her, pinning her like a dead butterfly against the projection screen. "So what line is the Scimitar Edge in?"

"That's, um, the marketing people haven't named the line yet, in case it's a one-off."

"Is it a one-off?"

"Not if I have anything to say about it."

"And so, what *should* the line be named?" he asked.

"That's not my job."

'That's not what I asked."

She paused that time, watching him as he lounged in his chair at the far end of the conference table, utterly at ease with waiting. "The Legendary Line."

"Interesting. And what do *you* call the line in the lab?"

"Stabby McStabberson," she admitted.

He looked down and chuckled. "Yes, marketing might not go for that. Why 'Legendary?'"

"Because it's a great name."

"It is. I've heard several people say the Scimitar is like 'magic.' What's the *next* one in the line?"

"R&D has not released any prototypes of further designs."

"Again, that's not what I asked."

"There's no use even discussing concept models until we get to early prototypes." She swiveled and flopped into a chair. "Probably eighty percent of models that we mock up on CAD don't even get to the late prototype stage, so flapping our gums about them is a waste of air."

"So there are models. More than one?" he asked.

"Yeah. We've got three in early dev and one more in the middle stages. The problem is that if the club's engineering fails, it won't matter. We don't want to produce a club head that shatters after a month of playing. It would ruin Sidewinder's reputation."

Kingston stood and picked up the handouts. "Let's go look at them."

"There is zero percent chance that any of them will be

available for sale this summer," she told him. "That's your job, *sales,* right?"

"Oh yes, but I'm interested in understanding where new golf clubs come from."

The sarcasm rose strong. "Well, when a mommy golf club and a daddy golf club love each other very much—"

He rolled his eyes, his really blue eyes that seemed to draw her attention even in the dim room. "Oh no, you aren't going to send me pictures of your knobby-headed drivers, are you?"

Nicole clutched her chest as if he'd stabbed her in the heart. "My designs are never *knobby.* Sidewinder clubs are sleek and aerodynamic. *Never knobby.*"

He laughed out loud at her faux outrage, and the superiority of being the funny one stirred in her. Nicole wasn't usually the funny one, as her jokes ran toward golf puns.

"Right, and just for fun, let me see these future designs. Even though I understand that they will not be ready for commercialization by summer, the Vegas PGA Show isn't until early December." He inclined toward where she stood. "What *could* be ready for Vegas?"

"Again, *I don't know* that because *I don't know* how the design and metals are going to work together until we *do it,*" she said slowly.

Kingston prowled toward her, a looming silhouette in the still-darkened conference room. "Show me what you've got."

This conversation was getting weirdly double-entendre-y. "Dude, I don't know what you want to see."

"I know what I can sell, but I want to see what's coming," he said. "It's imperative to sales morale to know that innovation is always coming down the pipeline."

Okay, that wasn't a double entendre. That sounded like a

sales dude trying to sell a golf club. "None of the other sales staff care about what's in design until we have a release date."

He was standing near her, looming over her, menacing in the darkened room. "I'm not your average salesperson."

"*Right,* I got that," she grumbled and shuffled backward. "This is so *irregular.*"

Kingston leaned back and blinked, then spun out a chair and sat. "How about you give me an in-depth tour of your *possible* future directions? I promise to keep in mind that these are early concepts in the developmental process. In return, I will take you out to dinner to discuss anything other than golf clubs or sponsor lunch for your lab. Pizza. Subs. Whatever you want."

Nicole had been in college recently enough that turning down free food for her lab felt like a betrayal. "Okay, but you must understand that *none* of these concept clubs might make it to production. Or maybe some kludged-together Franken-club version of several of them might be produced. We came up with probably two hundred concepts last year, and *one* went to commercialization. *Capisce?*"

"I understand," he said, smiling. "Lead the way."

"What, like right now?"

"No time like the present."

"It's already past three o'clock."

"Come on. I'll buy you supper *and* do a lab lunch."

Two meals? With her student loans sucking her finances away every day, Nicole couldn't pass that up. "Okay, but we have less than three hours, and there are a lot of concept clubs."

"Let's go."

9

6:01PM

KINGSTON MOORE

Nicole Lamb's lush form swayed in front of him as she walked, leading the way to her lab.

His skin practically crackled with energy as they neared the lab. Here, he would find out if the succulent Nicole was as attracted to him as he definitely was to—

No. He was going to look at Sidewinder's future products, *and that was all.*

That was the reason he'd goaded Nicole Lamb into taking him upstairs.

That was the reason he was in California and Sidewinder Golf in the first place, to evaluate the company so he could win the damn bet.

Being distracted by a pretty face and an hourglass figure and a cute sense of humor and a shared passion for golf was the last thing Kingston Moore needed.

So he kept his eyes to himself as he trod behind her. He intently watched the elevator floor numbers flicker when they were in the confined space where in two steps he could have her up against the wall with his mouth on hers and his hands in her hair, and then he followed her down the corridor to her lab where she once again badged him in.

Again, they donned the crackling Tyvek suits, plus the masks, goggles, and gloves that protected them from flying metallic debris and the prototype clubs from the oils on their hands and other detritus from their bodies.

He'd thought that once Nicole was swathed in a papery burka, he'd be able to ignore his rising infatuation a little. Still, every time she flashed her dark eyes full of intelligence and humor at him, even from behind plastic safety glasses, he didn't want to look away.

She looked at him when she straightened from bending over, sliding the blue gauze booties over her shoes, and his focus wrapped his mind around her gaze. "Okay, you asked for it. I've got to warn you, though. This is all just pie in the sky cogitating, not actual clubs for release," she said.

"I understand," Kingston said, arrested where he stood by her, looking at him and himself staring back at her. "I just want to see."

No, he just wanted to touch.

But he *must not.*

"Okay!" she said, her voice as perky as a pixie. "You're paying for it. Let's go look at these golf clubs that don't exist and probably never will."

Kingston hadn't meant to dawdle, but every club on every computer-driven lathe might have been the magic wand that boosted Sidewinder's sales into the stratosphere.

At Last Chance, Jericho Parr had his spreadsheets where he divined a company's worth from digits like tea leaves. Mitchell Saltonstall was a showman who could sell oil to Saudis.

But Kingston was good at finding sociological niches that needed a product.

He didn't mean taking a square product and hammering it into a round population niche, but looking at a group of people, figuring out what they wanted, and then giving it to them.

Kingston loved golf. He loved the challenge and the mechanics of it.

He knew everything that golfers needed.

He was looking for what they would want.

Nicole stopped at every machine in her lab and prodded her introverted techs into talking to Kingston.

"This is—well—it's not done yet," the first guy said, a lanky fellow with graying hair.

"Yes, Arvind, I *understand* it's not done," Kingston said. "Tell me what you *think* about it, though."

Those poor techs must never have anyone genuinely interested in their jobs. Once they understood that Kingston was serious in his inquiries, they snapped open like popcorn and told him everything in their heads.

It's a good thing Kingston wasn't an industrial spy for Titleist. The Big T would have scooped Sidewinder's lines for the next five years with all the information, theories, and strategies these techs were vomiting out at the slightest provocation.

Nicole, meanwhile, hung back once she'd gotten them talking and watched, her dark eyes never missing a thing behind her bulbous safety glasses.

The way she'd crossed her arms over her chest, plumping up her breasts even under her paper jumpsuit, distracted Kingston.

The techs were talking, telling him exactly what he needed to know. He had to *concentrate.* "Yes, and if you had *one club* you would stake the company on, which one would it be?"

Out of the corner of his eye, he watched Nicole slip her cell phone from her pocket and swipe, texting or writing something.

She kept it in her hand, obviously working hard, furrowing her dark eyebrows behind her goggles and tapping on the screen as she edited.

At four-thirty, while Kingston was deep in discussion with Caitlin, passing a prototype club back and forth and peering down the shaft in turn and commenting on its superior straightness that extended to the microscopic level when Nicole nodded at the phone in her hand and tapped it one last time.

An instant later, his own phone in his front trouser pocket chimed and buzzed under his Tyvek coveralls, the vibration a little too close to his dick's half-mast bell-end for comfort.

Nicole's sharp eyes were right on him, examining how she'd sent an email to the Last Chance, Inc. email address, and he'd received one at precisely the same time.

Lying to her about who he was made his skin crawl.

As soon as Caitlin finished her dissertation on the perfect straightness of the golf club, she said her farewells and headed for the lab's exit.

Yes, it was a quarter past five o'clock. These technicians should have left work a few minutes before.

Hourly and salaried employees leave when the work day was over.

Owners stayed longer, and Kingston was used to twelve-hour work days.

After making the rounds of all the techs, each one expounding on their golf club-related specialty, Kingston and Nicole ended up at the corridor leading to her office and the break room in the back of the lab.

"So, that's all the new clubs we have in the works," Nicole said, her voice muffled from her mask and Kingston's Tyvek hood over his ears. "I guess we're done."

They were withholding information. Kingston could smell it. "Is that everything?"

"Everything to speak of."

Oh, that was waffling. He'd used that one himself. Obviously, projects existed that were not to be spoken of. "Is it?"

"Sure."

She was holding out on him.

Should he pull the *I'm-really-your-boss* rabbit out of his hat yet? Pulling rank seemed like a douche move, as was the reveal of the hogwash he'd been peddling.

Instead, he went with, "Well, those are some *amazing* clubs. Really *innovative*. Truly *game-changers.*"

He put his heart into it, too, raising his eyebrows in enthusiasm and shoving all the sarcasm right down into his shoes.

Her sharp sideways glance from behind her safety goggles looked like she wanted to contradict him.

Good.

The new clubs she's shown him weren't innovative game-changers. They were, at best, incremental improvements on technology already incorporated into Sidewinder's Rattler line or, at worst, cosmetic marketing gimmicks.

Golf clubs' shafts don't need to be *straight* down to the molecular level. They need greater consistency when they bend from the angular momentum of the swing.

Kingston looked directly back at Nicole, lifting his cheeks and crinkling his eyes so it looked like he was smiling behind his mask, a skill everyone learned during the Covid pandemic that came in handy when garbed in protective clothing.

And then he waited.

Nicole's shoulder twitched first, and then she cocked her hooded head to the side, and then she broke eye contact and looked away. "Yeah."

"Those clubs will change the face of the company."

"*Sure.*"

Which was what Nicole said when she was fibbing. She did not disagree nor confirm.

Kingston sucked in a deep breath through the blue surgical mask over his face and said, "Those Mojave clubs you showed me are definitely enormous improvements. You should be so *proud* of them, and they'll be blockbuster additions to the Legendary line."

"Oh, they're not for the Legendary line," she said quickly.

Of course not, because the Legendary line was her baby. "Oh?"

"These are definitely Rattler series clubs."

"Really?"

"Oh, yes."

"So, where are the clubs destined for your Legendary line?"

Nicole looked down at her feet. "Those aren't even in pre-*pre*-production. It was a miracle that I managed to push through the Scimitar Edge."

Kingston leaned down, watching Nicole's eyes through the scratches on his plastic safety glasses. "Why is that?"

"Because Joe thought innovation like the Scimitar was too risky, and its manufacturing is different than any other club. Nothing in the head is cast. We don't pour molten metal into a mold and glue it together with plastic like every other golf club on the market today. It was *barely* accepted by the PGA as a legal club—"

"But the professional golfers *can* use it in PGA Tour events?" he asked, checking to make sure.

"Oh yeah, its coefficient of restitution is compliant, but it took *an extra month* for them to approve it. Three extra rounds of testing. Joe didn't like the uncertainty."

"*Joe* doesn't own the company anymore." And Kingston needed to stop talking right there.

"*I* don't like the uncertainty," she said.

"You don't own the company, either."

Sometimes, an owner has to roll the dice to make gains.

Arvind, the tall, lanky guy whose arms moved like flopping ropes under his white coverall passed them on his way out of the lab, striding for the anteroom to change out of his gear.

He nodded at them.

Kingston and Nicole nodded back.

Arvind left.

And Nicole still stood in the hallway with her arms folded in front of her like a locked computer while Kingston tried password after password, trying to get her to open up. He said, "Those clubs are truly the next step in golf technology."

"Maybe. Sure."

The little tech who'd talked to him about metallic alloys on the club faces bounced by on her toes, her papery coveralls whispering as she walked past them, said, "See you tomorrow!" to Nicole.

Kingston said, "Those were definitely *some clubs.*"

"They definitely were," Nicole said.

This wasn't working in the slightest. "Can I talk to you *privately?*"

Yet another white paper-swathed technician—how

many techs did Sidewinder employ?—walked past them and left the lab.

Nicole watched them walk out the door to the garbing room, and two other people shoved their coveralls in the waste bin and left, heading toward the stairs. "I don't know if this is a good time."

Because everyone was leaving, and she would be alone with Kingston in her office.

Yeah, Nicole Lamb would probably pick the bear rather than sequester herself with him in an out-of-the-way office as other Sidewinder workers left the building for the night.

Logical, really. He was just some guy who, for all she knew, had passed a cursory employment background check that was probably skewed toward finding financial crimes, not violent ones.

Thus, he did the crinkly thing with his eyes again and joked, "I don't know if I'm comfortable being alone with you in your office. You aren't going to run me through with one of your swords, are you?"

She cocked her hip to the side and placed one blue-gloved fist on it. "Are you asking to see my big, thick, pointy swords?"

He winked at her, exaggerating it behind his safety glasses. "Now, if I would've said that, HR would've had to get involved."

Nicole huffed one chuckle. "Okay, come on, but let's make it quick."

Oh, the entendres he could double on that one. "HR would definitely have something to say about that."

Her low chuckle wafted back to him as she badged them into the back corridor, where she shoved her paper hood back off her mahogany hair, tugged her mask strings down to let it dangle, and unzipped her coveralls with a groan.

Her throaty sound caught Kingston off-guard as he loosened his protective gear. Yes, it was sound of pleasure and relief, and deep in the animal part of his brain, he wanted to make her make that sound again, and more, and deeper.

He needed to get a grip on something other than his dick because he needed information, not to get laid.

He needed that, too, but that wasn't his goal that night.

Was it?

Nicole badged them into her office and shut the door behind them, closing them in the small room bristling with swords shining on the back wall. "Okay, what is it you wanted to know, *really?*"

How you taste, rose in Kingston's mind, and he shoved *that* thought straight back down into the murky caveman depths from whence it had come.

Instead, he went direct, if slightly sideways from the actual truth, as he sat in one of the chairs before Nicole's desk. "Look, I heard through the grapevine," that grapevine being the due diligence discovery spreadsheets when he'd bought her company, "that Sidewinder Golf was a few weeks away from bankruptcy, and *that's* why Joe sold it. If Last Chance hadn't bought you, Sidewinder might not have been able to meet payroll on May first. A sign on the door that day would have told everyone that you weren't getting paid and not to come back."

Nicole was standing across the office from him, and she grabbed a filing cabinet as she leaned back, resting against it. "*What?*"

"Yeah. It's *that bad,* and that's why I'm *really damn interested* in whether there's an undiscovered blockbuster in this place that we can leverage to profitability *real soon.*"

"I—I did not know it was that bad. Heck, I didn't know it was bad at all. I mean, we're selling clubs as fast as we can make them. We have a backlog that is longer than our year-to-date sales. People are screaming to get *on* the waiting list."

"Yes."

"Why are you looking at new clubs, then?" she asked, looking straight at him. "We need to expand manufacturing so we can deliver the clubs we've already taken deposits for."

"Yes, and we—" *Be careful, Kingston! Jeez!* "Not *we*, surely. I mean *they*, the people at Last Chance, Inc., are already looking at additional manufacturing capacity to fulfill the backlog."

"Where?" she asked, still staring straight at him.

God, that direct eye contact was so sexy that he could feel his body flinch, trying to rise from the chair, stalk over to where she stood, and pin her against the wall to kiss her senseless.

Butt in chair, asshole.

"China, of course," he said.

"Most manufacturing capacity is located in China. Which site, though?"

"Dali Manufacturing, in the western part of China, near the Myanmar border."

"Dude, *Dali?* It's *awful!* First of all, goods have to travel eleventy billion miles to the coast for shipping, and secondly, it has a dirty reputation for stealing patented secrets. If we send our specs there, you can plan on *a million* knockoffs of Sidewinder's clubs hitting the online shopping sites for a *tenth* of the price by next year."

"But, by then—" Kingston didn't finish his sentence. He'd almost said, *By next year, Last Chance can win the bet, dump this turkey, and get out of the position.*

"We *can't* let them infringe on our patents like that," she said. "Really, the intellectual property of what's in

Sidewinder's clubs and how we make them *is* the company. We can't lob it out there willy-nilly, especially if we have anything truly innovative and revolutionary up our proverbial sleeves."

"And what do we have?" Kingston asked, honing in on what she obviously wanted to tell him.

"What do we have *what?*"

"Anything innovative and revolutionary?"

She shrugged, *finally* breaking eye contact with him, which he felt like someone snapped off the spotlight dazzling his eyes, and she studied the corner of the ceiling. She said, "All companies have concepts they haven't acted on yet."

"What's yours?"

She fell silent, staring at the upper corner of the room.

Kingston followed her gaze.

The sword in the uppermost part of the room near that corner was a long, thick weapon, its steel burnished, hanging by its pommel with the blade pointing down as if to fall and stab the Earth.

He asked, "Is it that one up there?"

"Is what which one?"

He pointed to the oversized knife on the wall. "Is that the sword your next magical concept club is based on?"

Nicole looked down and away. "I don't know what you're talking about."

"Your design for the club that other people call 'magic,' the Scimitar Edge, just happens to be named after your favorite sword. Now when we're talking about your next design, you can't stop looking at that sword up there. What kind of sword is it?"

"A broadsword."

"Sounds massive."

"Oh, it is. Broadswords are huge. I barely wrestled that one up onto the wall. Those hooks have six screws each into the studs."

"Are you going to name the club after it?"

She snorted a laugh. "We were joking that we should design it for women, for the LPGA, because—get it? A *broad* sword?"

"Oh, no-no-*no*. You are not roping me into an HR complaint with that opening." But he was grinning, and so was she. "What are you *really* going to call it?"

She sucked one side of her lower lip between her teeth as she smiled at him, obviously debating.

Kingston raised his eyebrows and leaned back in the chair, smiling harder at her.

Keeping up the grin wasn't tough. She looked like a mischievous little kitten over there, practically wiggling its butt, convinced that you didn't see it ready to pounce.

Nicole said, "Excalibur."

Marketing strategies lit up Kingston's mind. "That's *fantastic*, and that's why you want to call it the Legendary line."

"Yeah."

"Are there any other magical sword names that aren't under copyright?"

"The Vorpal Sword from Lewis Carroll's poem 'Jabberwocky.' The copyright on *Alice in Wonderland* expired."

"Oh, that's a good name."

"Angrvaðall from Norse mythology, which has letters that shine brightly in battle but dim in times of peace."

Kingston's grin grew until his cheeks ached. "Hologram lettering that reflects in the sunlight. Brilliant."

"Khanda, a sword that represents wisdom cutting through ignorance in Hindu mythology."

His heart fluttered. "The marketing just writes itself. What else?"

"It really doesn't matter what else because we don't have the manufacturing capacity to make them," she said. "Sending the specs to Dali Manufacturing is like flushing them down the toilet. There are a lot of other manufacturers in China, you know. Dali isn't even one of the bigger ones."

"Yes, but they have room," he told her. *"I heard* that Joe Flanagan tried to have club heads produced by the same manufacturer as Titleist, but they didn't have the capacity."

"How about the original equipment manufacturer Taylormade uses in Vietnam? Taylormade's specs are never leaked."

"They don't have room for another client, either. If we want additional inventory this year, it's Dali or nothing."

She frowned like a frustrated bunny. "Surely, some OEM has to have room for—"

From somewhere outside Nicole's office, a buzz sounded, and then a *thump.*

"Oh, no," she gasped.

Kingston looked around again. No fire alarms. No more thumping or buzzing. "What?"

Nicole covered her mouth with one hand while she looked at the clock on the wall, which read six-oh-one. *"No!"*

10

STUCK TOGETHER IN THE BUILDING

NICOLE LAMB

T*hump.*

The building had locked down.

The digital clock on Nicole's desk read 6:01pm in glowing red letters.

Nicole's Apple watch slipped on her wrist as she flipped over her arm, praying that the clock was wrong, and read 6:01pm on her watch, too, which meant Sidewinder's stupid impregnable security system *had locked down the building.*

Nicole grabbed her purse from her desk and ran out of her office. *"We have to get out!"*

Behind her, Kingston's heavier footfalls chased her. "What's the matter?"

Nicole slapped her dangling mask over her face as she sprinted through the lab. Then, not bothering to take off her paper coveralls, she rushed through the anteroom to the stairs. She flung open the stairwell door and trotted down the stairs, hitting most of the steps but jumping the last few of each flight, and then she raced flat out for the building's front doors.

The hallways were empty. The receptionist's desk was empty. The whole building was *empty.*

She slammed against the glass doors, flailing her whole body as she yanked the door handles, but the doors did not budge.

They didn't even rattle.

"No!" she yelled at the darned ceiling.

Kingston jogged up beside her. "What's wrong?"

"We're locked in!"

Kingston unzipped his Tyvek coveralls and rummaged inside his trouser pockets, finding his phone. "So we'll call the security company to let us out."

"They can't get us out!" she shrieked, yanking on the immobile doors like a toddler dragging on her mother's leg. Jeez, she needed to regain her composure, but *they were trapped.*

"Who can't get us out?" he asked.

"The security company! Joe Flanagan made them set a timer so that *no one,* not even *the security company,* can disable it!"

"What? Why would he do that?"

"I don't know! Industrial spies or people wanting to be paid for overtime? How should I know?"

Kingston glanced at the ceiling, his eyes bunching with worry. "This place isn't going to release poisonous foam or call the police to swat us, right?"

"No, it just locks down, but we can't get out!"

"So, nothing bad is going to happen, right? We're just stuck here for the night."

"We're going to be stuck in here *all night!"*

"Yeah, tomorrow's Thursday," he said. "You people work on Thursdays, don't you?"

"Of course we work on Thursdays!"

"You never know. This is California. But those doors should unlock tomorrow morning to let everybody in, so we can leave then."

"Yeah, but we're *stuck* in here all night!"

"Is there somewhere you're supposed to be? Doctor's appointment or something? Hot date?"

"No. I mean, my plants will survive one night without being watered. But this building is holding us prisoner. It's not right!"

"Then we'll stage a sit-in. Protests always work."

She spun around and glared at him, "Why aren't you freaked out that we're locked in here all night?"

Kingston shrugged and fished around inside his coveralls and then his trousers pocket for his phone. "Let me see if I can get this sorted with a phone call." He tapped his phone screen a few times and then spoke into it. "Joe? What's the code to turn off the security system in this building that used to be yours?"

Nicole gaped at him. "Seriously, you have *Joe Flanagan* in your contacts? What, is he your buddy or something?"

Kingston held up a finger while he listened, and his eyebrows lowered in a frown. "What do you mean, there's no way to turn it off?"

Yeah, just like she told him. Maybe he'd believe it now that a man told it to him.

"Won't the security company see us on the surveillance cameras?" He looked up, his head swiveling wildly as he stared at the corners of the lobby. "You had an eighty-million-dollar-annual company, *and you didn't put in security cameras?*"

Totally on brand for Joe Flanagan, like his buying million-dollar couches for the lobby but not offering vision care coverage on the employee insurance plan.

"There are *no* surveillance cameras in this *whole damned building?*" He paused and grabbed his hair on the top of his head like he was pulling it. "Oh, outside, watching the bushes. That's goddamn useful. *What the hell?*"

Good thing Joe was Sidewinder's *former* owner. Otherwise, Kingston Moore would probably be looking for another sales job.

Weird, though, that he was talking to Joe like an equal, instead of like an employee.

Kingston called across the lobby. "Nicole, is the building's security system tied into Sidewinder's business operations intranet?"

She shook her head. "Different companies. Different networks. Our work laptops are walled gardens. We can access the business operations and research web from them, but nothing else. We can't even watch streaming TV on them. Only those company laptops can access the company's system for security. You can't log in from a personal computer."

Kingston went back to talking on the phone. "Your security system isn't tied into your intranet, so your master password isn't going to help me with the security system or get us out of here. And by the way, that's a stupid master password. I'll be changing that tomorrow."

The conversation grouping of couches and coffee tables was in her way, and she paced around them while she watched him on the phone.

Kingston scowled. "What, did you cheap out *again* and get the no-technical-support option? What the hell were you *thinking?*"

At least someone had finally said that to her former boss. It had needed to be said.

Nicole waited, her hands on her hips. The Tyvek coveralls trapped her body heat inside, and she was beginning to steam like she was being baked *en papillote*.

Kingston's glower deepened as he talked to her former boss, so Nicole unzipped her coveralls all the way down the inside of her left leg and started peeling them off. The last thing she needed was to develop a rancid case of B.O. when the only bathing facility in the building was the lab's chemical safety shower that had flooded the laboratory and the entire floor below it that one time Caitlin had accidentally pulled the cord.

As she fought her way out of the papery material that was clinging to her arms and legs like wet tissues, Kingston kept glancing at her out of the corners of his eyes and then hurriedly looking back at his shoes or the opposite wall.

By the time Nicole had gotten the stupid coveralls off, the paper was half-shredded, and she had tweaked her ankle while hopping on one foot and yanking the leg over her dress slacks and navy blue leather Chelsea boots.

When she was free and looked up, Kingston was staring at her while listening to a tinny whisper-babble on his phone.

Nicole blew a random strand of hair out of her eyes and demanded, "Did you enjoy the striptease?"

He instantly looked away, closing his eyes and weaving a bit on his feet. "Joe, I'll have to call you back." To her, he said, "I was wondering if I should catch you if you tripped yourself and fell over. Also, that's a good idea, I'm roasting in these coveralls."

Nicole gathered her hair back into its customary ponytail while Kingston more elegantly pulled his coveralls off like he was removing a camel hair coat at a country club.

Yeah, she was a slob, but she was a darn fine engineer. "So, did Joe tell you *exactly* the same thing that I told you?"

He was folding his coveralls as if they weren't disposable. "I was hoping the previous owner had access that employees didn't."

Okay, that was actually logical.

"But he didn't," she sighed.

"No, he didn't. I cannot believe how cavalier he was. Sidewinder's intellectual property *is* the company, especially with its super-elite marketing strategy. Anyone could have just broken into the building, walked out with the design specs, and started their own knock-off company with the *exact same clubs.*"

"Oh, no," Nicole told him. "The computer system is locked down tight. Joe and I are pretty much the only ones with access to the specs because I don't put them on the intranet here. I keep all the important data and specs on my hard drive. And Joe should have been locked out when he sold the company. Being onsite wouldn't make any difference."

"That's reassuring," he said, grumbling.

"But he did tell you we're hopelessly locked in here, didn't he?"

Kingston shook his head. "Yeah, but I'm not out of ideas yet."

Nicole paced the length of the lobby back and forth while claustrophobic panic condensed into words and rattled around her brain.

At the far end, Kingston held up a wall with one hand and made phone calls. "Matilda? I need the name and home phone number of the CEO of Hammerhead Business Security Solutions. Their security system locked me in one of their customer's buildings."

Nicole tried to shove the nervous crazy into her feet as she paced. They were going to be locked in there all night.

They were never going to get out. She was locked in this building with a guy she didn't know who might be a serial killer for all she knew, and she couldn't *get out of the building.*

This was a horror movie happening to her.

Kingston said into his phone, "Lisa Monro? This is Kingston Moore of Sidewinder Golf. Nice to meet you. Your company built and maintains the security system for our building here in Carlsbad. I need the back-door emergency override code for after the building locks down for the night and the location of the keypad." He paused. "What do you mean *there isn't one?* That's got to be an OSHA or fire code violation."

Nicole stayed on the other side of the lobby from him, even though he hadn't made an untoward move in the very short time she'd known him. Being around somebody in a crowded place of business was entirely different than being isolated and locked in with them.

Kingston dialed someone else. "Arthur, my old chum? Yes, I know it's really late there in London. I'm really sorry to call you. I am locked in a commercial building in Carlsbad, California. Is there any way you can hack the alarm system so I can leave?" Another pause as Kingston ran his fingers through his dark hair. "No, I wasn't doing anything like that. It's, uh, that venture capital firm we know of, Last Chance, bought Sidewinder, and I just happened to be hired by Sidewinder right before the deal went through." Another pause as Kingston rolled against the wall, holding his dark hair in his grip like he might be pulling it out. "All right, thanks for trying."

"No, I assume?" she asked.

"Connections aren't helping. Let's try—*breaking us out of here!*"

Nicole sucked air to yell in horror as Kingston angled his

tall body and his leg shot out in a powerful side kick to the glass of the building's front wall.

His foot bounced off.

"Don't!" she shouted as the ricochet force of his kick knocked him backward, and he flopped to the floor.

He rolled over on his side. *"Ow.* That always works in the movies."

She ran over to him because that's what one does when someone gets knocked down. "Are you okay?"

His scowl at the people on his phone had shifted to the vacant gaze of someone stunned. "That door should be made from shatterproof glass like a car windshield. I thought it would break up into little cubes."

Nicole squatted down beside him. "It's bulletproof glass."

"Why would Joe put *bulletproof glass* in an office building?" he gasped.

She rolled backward and sat cross-legged on the floor beside him. "He was *really* paranoid about industrial espionage. Are you okay? You didn't break your leg or anything, did you?"

Kingston rolled up to sitting and glared at his leg, then gingerly probed his ankle. "Definitely didn't break it. I *went* for that side kick, though," he grumbled. "I thought I would be a hero and rescue the fair princess from the locked dungeon."

She chuckled at him. "Okay, hero. Let's get you up and walking around."

"I'm fine." He brushed off her hands and tottered to his feet.

Getting all those long bones stacked vertically must be hard. Nicole wasn't tiny for a woman, but there was just so much more *length* to every part of Kingston that balancing all those long blocks on top of each other looked unlikely.

But then he was standing up, very tall above where she sat on the floor, and testing his ankle with his weight. "It's a little gimpy, but it's fine. My ego may have suffered a mortal blow, though."

She grinned up at him. "Just goes to show, don't be a hero, right?"

His eyeroll mocked himself. "Looking at all those Asgardian and Arthurian swords inspired me to stupidity."

"Many swords and golf clubs have inspired awesome feats of dumb."

He glared at the front wall. "You think the fire department could get through that glass?"

"No. It's probably ax-proof, too."

Kingston's sharp look held worry in his blue eyes. "What if this building catches on fire? People wouldn't be able to get out."

Nicole shook her head and waved her hand. "If the fire alarms go off, all the doors supposedly spring open, even if it's locked down."

"*Supposedly?*"

"That's what the manual said."

"I am *not* reassured."

"Right? Seems kind of like the Triangle Shirtwaist Factory."

Kingston glanced at the ceiling. "Yeah, it does. I was going to suggest setting one of those chairs on fire to activate the fire system and call the fire department." He gestured toward the blocky blue conversation set on the other side of the glassed-in lobby. "But I don't think we should risk burning to death in case the manual was wrong."

"Yep. That manual was sketchy as heck."

"Oh, that does it. That lockdown system *will* be disabled tomorrow morning. This is *unsafe,* and no employee of *muh* —" Here, he coughed. "—of *Sidewinder Golf* should be endangered by the damned building."

Nicole laughed at him. "The new owners are venture capitalists. They don't care if we live or die. They might even burn down the building for the insurance money. Joe might have even had it scheduled and forgotten about it in the deal."

He looked around the lobby like he was scanning for arsonists. *"What?"*

"It's just a joke. I'm sure they won't burn it down," she sort-of lied. Probably not *right then,* anyway.

"Yeah," Kingston said, but he was still watching. "Okay, nothing we can do about it tonight. I would offer to order supper in, but I don't see any way the delivery person could get the food in here. There isn't even a mail slot in the door for them to shove French fries through one at a time."

Nicole hadn't even thought about food. "We can just smash the glass of those vending machines and take anything we want. Really, who's going to stop us?"

"I like the way you think. As we don't seem to have a choice in where we are camping out tonight, it seems like we can either pound on the glass of the front wall until our fists are bloody, or we can turn it into *A Night at the Museum.*"

She raised an eyebrow at him. "You mean the golf clubs will come to life and attack us?"

"I mean we can eat candy for dinner and then play with golf clubs in the simulators until we get tired, and then we can crash on the couches until the stupid alarm system turns itself off tomorrow morning."

"The downstairs break room has better candy in their

machines than up in our tech room. Let's start there, but I think there was only one Snickers bar left."

He offered her his hand to help her up off the floor, so Nicole reached up and clasped his fingers with hers.

The palm-to-palm touch was a smooth ripple of a shock up her arm and over her skin to the back of her neck, like maybe the stupid security system had electrified the floor and their hands had completed the circuit.

As she stared up into his Mediterranean Sea-blue eyes, his gaze was perfectly level, like he hadn't felt anything.

She was just imagining things. There couldn't be any other explanation, right?

A trace of a smile curved Kingston's lips. "Ready?"

"Uh-huh."

His strength lifted her off the floor so fast that a tiny part of her brain conjectured that the wind had blown her to her feet, but Kingston helped her settle and said, "Let's go forage for M&Ms."

"Sure."

And yet she was entirely discombobulated and couldn't figure out what to do.

She was still holding Kingston Moore's hand, his warm fingers wrapped around hers.

"You steady? You bobbled there," he said.

"Um, yeah?"

She was still clinging to his hand because she—she—*she liked it.*

He frowned and tilted sideways to look at her legs. "Did your feet fall asleep while you were criss-cross-applesauce?"

"No, I'm fine."

He straightened and regarded their hands, where she was still hanging onto him. "You're sure?"

Her body wanted to flow toward his like he was giving off gravity waves.

But she was still clinging to his hand like a weirdo.

Nicole opened her hand like she was flicking goo off her fingers. "Thanks for the help up!"

Kingston looked at his hand like maybe she'd crushed it. "I'll arm-wrestle you for the last Snicker bar."

Hold his hand and strain against his strength, even if she was going to lose the arm-wrestling contest in a flash? *Yes, please.* "You're on."

11

THE SNICKERS

KINGSTON MOORE

The downstairs break room had three round tables beside the kitchen countertop and four huge vending machines.

Kingston perused the possibilities. "Pop-Tarts?"

From behind him, Nicole said, "Absolutely. Should I get the ax from the fire emergency box?"

He straightened and looked back at her. "We don't need to go ragtag anarchist. I can just use a credit card and buy whatever we need. I'll put it on this month's expense report."

She flopped at one of the tables. "Yeah, better to rob those evil venture capitalists for our supper. Do that."

"Besides, these machines don't even belong to the evil venture capitalists," Kingston said, choking a little because deception had never really been his strong suit. "The sticker in the corner says they belong to and are stocked by Vend-O-Land Limited."

"Oh, well, they might be a small business, then. Sure. I'll take some Pop-Tarts and a package of sunflower seeds."

Kingston tapped his card against the machine's sensor and started dropping candy into the bin at the bottom. "I don't think I've ever eaten a supper like this in my life, but it's never too late to learn."

"What, you didn't eat supper out of the library vending machines at college when you were cramming for your calculus final?"

"Didn't take calculus in college," he said and dropped every package of nuts, corn nuts, and granola from the machine's metal coils, as well as several candy bars.

"I'm sorry. I just assumed—I hang out with nerds way too much, and I have a big mouth. Um, tell me about yourself?"

Kingston gathered the packets from behind the flap and carried several dozen over to the table. "I majored in sociology. So I crammed for a stats final, not calculus."

"Oh, stats. Yes." She nodded gravely. "Very difficult. Much cramming."

He knew when he was being patronized. "You had to take the three-semester calc with analytical geometry sequence, didn't you?"

"Well, I was in the College of Engineering, so yeah. Calc with geometry is a core class."

"All right. For that bit of preciousness, you do have to arm wrestle me for the Snickers. Elbow on the table, Ms. Professional Engineer." He rolled up his sleeves with flips of the silk fabric and set up, bracing his elbow and tucking his other hand behind it. "Let's go."

Nicole grabbed the lone Snickers bar from the middle of the table, even though she'd had one for lunch, too. Snickers was her favorite candy bar. "It's mine now."

"Hey, that's not fair! We were going to arm wrestle for it."

"I outsmarted you, and possession is nine-tenths of the law."

He shook his empty hand that was waiting for her to wrestle. "Stand and deliver."

Nicole eyeballed his forearm. "This is ridiculous. There is no way I could even start to arm wrestle you. You can have the Snickers."

"Set up, little lady."

She hung her mouth open at him and then said, "You obviously work out *a lot,* and I obviously *don't.* Your forearm looks like a python is wrapped around it."

"Aw, you're just saying that."

"I am not just saying it. Is that even real? Do plastic surgeons do forearm implants?"

"That's a question you would only hear in California." He pinched his arm. "I can assure you, that's a hundred percent beef."

"Great, if the doors don't unlock tomorrow, it's reassuring to know that I could fry you up for dinner."

"Surely we don't have to resort to cannibalism the first night. Come on, what do you have to lose?"

"Evidently, my Snickers bar. Why do you even want to go through with this preposterous arm wrestling?"

Because he wanted to hold her hand again.

Because holding her hand while he'd helped Nicole up and steadied her and pretended that there must be some reason why he was still holding onto it had blistered through him like lightning.

Picking up a woman in a bar for sex paled in comparison. He'd looked into Nicole's eyes. Her fingers had wrapped his, and his attention hadn't wavered every second their palms and fingers had been intertwined.

He said, "Because we agreed to arm wrestle for the Snickers."

"Fine." Nicole slapped the contested Snickers bar on the

table and sat across from him, examining how he had braced his arm and fidgeting as she figured out how to copy him like a kitten choosing its angle of attack. "This farce should be over with in one second, anyway. *One-two-three-go.*"

Aw, she'd tried to trick him. So darn cute.

As she tried to shove his arm over, Kingston locked his muscles and held her arm straight upright.

And enjoyed holding her hand again.

Nicole was straining, leaning in her chair as she tried to find leverage to push his arm over, but he held her hand vertically.

Yeah, he went to the gym a lot. He wasn't even pushing back. He was just stopping his arm from moving.

Her eyes were clenched shut, but she sneaked a peek at him.

Kingston screwed up his face like he was working hard.

"You're just toying with me!"

Nope, just enjoying it. He wondered if he could make himself sweat to look like he was working harder than he was. "I assure you, you are a formidable opponent."

"This is stupid."

She leaned back in her chair and tried to flick her fingers away from his, but before Kingston knew what he was doing, he'd flipped her hand around, grabbed her fingers in his, and brushed his lips over her knuckles.

He hadn't meant to do that. Human Resources was going to be pissed at the owner making a pass at one of the employees.

Then again, there were no surveillance cameras to catch him doing it.

But when he looked over Nicole's hand into her eyes, her pearl-pink lips were parted, and she didn't pull away.

12

KISS, MARRY, KILL

NICOLE LAMB

Kingston Moore kissed Nicole's hand.

It was a chaste kiss, a soft brush of his lips and a whisper of breath, but it was as courtly as the swords in her office and his valiant if dumb attempt to save her from imprisonment.

No one had ever kissed Nicole's hand before. She hadn't even realized it was on her bucket list.

When Kingston looked up at her over her knuckles, his fiery blue eyes and steady gaze were a challenge.

Accepted.

She leaped to her feet. The stupid wire chair tumbled over behind her. She scrambled across the table, climbing on it with her hands and knees, toward him.

The table tipped under her knees. As she reached for Kingston's shoulder, he wrapped his arm around her waist and dragged her the rest of the way, pulling her up to her knees and her mouth to his.

The first seal of his lips to hers was a sear that broiled through her mind, shivered down her arms, and reverberated through every cell in her body like a blast wave. His arm around her waist crushed her against his chest, and he stroked up her throat and splayed his hand over her face, then cradled the back of her skull.

Nicole wrapped her arms over his shoulders and hung on while he kissed her, slanted his lips over hers and devoured her, his tongue tasting, teasing, then wrapping hers as she opened and pushed back, trying to feel all of him.

She was short-circuiting, his lips on hers and his hand in her hair and the steel band of his arm around her waist, a pandemonium of sensation.

And then it was lessening, lightening, and he was pulling away.

Either an earthquake was rattling the hell out of the building, or Nicole's legs were jelly as she gasped.

The fluorescent lights were too bright, haloing his dark hair, and she held onto his neck as she panted.

Wow, she'd been half-ready to flop backwards on the table and grind against him until their pants came off, just from a kiss.

Like, wow.

Kingston's breath was harsh in her ear and warm on her neck, and his temple pressed hers. "The HR department is not going to like this."

A few neurons connected in her head and sparked, but only a few. "Then let's not tell them."

He huffed a chuckle. "Those barracudas will find out eventually."

"Why is that a problem? You're not my boss. You're in an entirely different department, so there's no chain of authority problem. Considering you're the new sales guy, low man on the org chart, there's every possibility that they'd consider me to be *your* boss."

"Yeah, sure," he said, his voice rough.

As he straightened a little, she swung her legs around to sit on the edge of the table. "You worry about HR a lot. Have you had problems with them in the past?"

Was she snogging a notorious company 'ho? Is that why he'd left his previous job?

Kingston braced his arms on either side of her, leaning over. "Never. I've always been careful *not* to have problems with them. It's like stopping for red lights. It's a good rule, keeps everybody safe, and prevents getting T-boned."

Nicole couldn't help herself. "Heh. You said *boned.*"

His chuckle escalated. "Oh, you are dangerous, little miss engineer. I think you won the arm wrestling contest. To the victor goes the Snickers bar."

He picked it up, peeled the wrapper, and broke off a piece, which he held out for her.

And again, his blue-fire stare above his hand was an offer and a challenge.

She could reach over, pluck it from between his fingers, and toss it in her mouth.

Instead, Nicole leaned forward and took the bite between her teeth from his fingertips, locked in eye contact with him.

The dark circles of his pupils expanded in his blue eyes.

Without changing his intent focus on her or looking at the candy bar, he broke off another bite and held it out.

With that bite, she grazed his thumb with her lower lip.

His gaze bored into hers solid like a fist, and he stepped toward her and held out another piece just below her mouth, a chunk of chocolate and peanuts at the bottom of her peripheral vision.

A tiny part of her brain was an indignant old auntie, standing with her hip out and arms crossed, asking what

Nicole was doing by leading this guy on or accelerating the problem because they were trapped in the building together.

But a much larger part of her mind wanted to see what Kingston would do.

She was playing with fire, not to tame it, but to see how much she could burn down.

Thirteen long hours stretched before them until the front doors unlocked.

"Last bite," he said, holding out a chocolate cube.

Nicole sucked it from his fingers with just a kiss on his thumb, not too slutty, not discouraging in the slightest.

Kingston dropped the wrapper in the trash. "What do you want to eat now?"

Just how much did she want to escalate this?

Thirteen hours was a long time. They literally had all night.

Nicole picked up a bag of sunflower seeds and tore it open.

Kingston backed up a step, a half-grin curving his mouth, and snagged a bag of trail mix. As he ripped it open, he sat in the chair beside her legs and poured some into his mouth.

She grinned back at him and tossed more crumbly seeds into her mouth.

"I've got to admit, I did not see that coming," he said.

"What, that?" Admitting to it seemed too much.

"Yeah, in the game of Kiss, Marry, or Kill, I would've put my money on you running me through with a sword."

"The night is still young."

He laughed. "I suppose it is. I never got to play with those high-tech golf simulators you have up on the third floor. You just pointed to them, and we moved on. After we eat all this junk food, do you want to show them to me?"

"Sure. What the heck? We've got all night."

His slow smile was more sultry than she'd expected. "Indeed, we do."

The casualness of his smile made her think that maybe forgetting about the time and the security system hadn't been an accident.

"Did you do this on purpose?" she blurted.

He bounced a palmful of granola like he was funneling it before tossing it in his mouth. "Do what?"

"Get us locked in here together?"

His sideways head tilt and rueful grimace looked embarrassed. "No, and I had dinner reservations for us for eight o'clock at the restaurant in my hotel. I should probably cancel those."

The timeline clicked in her head. "But you didn't ask me out to dinner until after the sales meeting that ended at three."

He shrugged.

She raised an eyebrow at him and plucked a package of peanut M&Ms from the pile of crap food. "So you just assumed I would go back to your hotel with you?"

He looked at her and tilted his head. "I only said dinner. It sounds like you had more in mind."

"I can't say what I had in mind."

His smile rose on one side. "Well, I wouldn't have said no."

She hadn't meant—she'd only meant that she—"What hotel are you staying at?"

"Any reason you're asking?"

Oh, the snark. "The sales guys usually stay at the La

Quinta down the block, so we don't have to rent them a car while they're here."

He laughed a sarcastic *hah*. "I'm not staying at the La Quinta."

"Then where are we putting you up?"

His sharp, blue-eyed gaze turned back to her. "You'll have to go to dinner with me to find out."

She rolled her eyes at him. "Transparent."

"I've already told you I'm not playing hard-to-get."

"But what about HR? Aren't you worried about Human Relations anymore?"

He shrugged, still grinning. "Like you said, you're probably my boss. It's rather alluring, having your boss crawl across a table and kiss you."

Horror struck her like walking through a spiderweb. "Oh my God. You aren't going to *tell* anyone, are you?"

Kingston blinked and grimaced. "I'm not one to kiss and tell. Are you?"

"*God,* no. None of their business. And how excruciating."

His naughty smile returned. "Excellent."

13

PEBBLE BEACH
NICOLE LAMB

The simulator room was the size of an oversized two-car garage with dual wide bays hung with projection screens. A conversation grouping of a couch and chairs stood between the door and the first simulator.

"Nice set-up," Kingston said, pivoting in the middle of the room as he scanned the space.

Nicole was too busy watching him. His white dress shirt accentuated the breadth of his muscular shoulders that tapered to his narrow waist and long, *long* legs in his navy-blue suit pants. He looked like a superhero in disguise standing there, fists braced on his hips, shockingly hand-some even in the fluorescent ceiling lights lining his jaw and strong cheekbones with bright lines.

Nicole stood beside him and powered up the computer. " Yeah, I think Joe Flanagan wanted to schmooze prospective investors in here, but instead, it became the technicians' playroom."

Kingston looked down at her. "No other investors were

listed as owners, just Flanagan and the banks that loaned him operating capital. Are there other owners?"

"Nah, he didn't actually *do* anything about schmoozing other investors. He built this area so he could, if he ever got around to it. That's probably why Sidewinder was going bankrupt."

"Indeed. What course should we play first, Pebble or Augusta?"

"Guest's choice," Nicole said, firing up the software.

"Pebble Beach."

Projectors hanging over the bays glared electric blue light onto the screens. Nicole squinted as she clicked through the windows to load the golf courses.

The lush green golf course of Pebble Beach Golf Links flashed into view on the screens of the right-side simulator.

"Wow," Kingston whispered and walked inside the glowing cube.

Most golf simulators are just a flat screen that the struck golf ball smacks into, and then a virtual simulation of the ball continues into the image as the real ball drops to the Astroturf mat.

Sidewinder's simulators included the room's sides, and above it, a bright blue sky scudded with clouds.

He turned back to look at where she was standing at the computer. "This is unreal. Actually, it's *very* real. It's like I'm standing on the first tee, except there's a portal back to the office behind me."

"Yeah, Joe wanted to put a rear screen with a door on it, too, but that seemed excessive," she said. "And not conducive to schmoozing."

He squinted up at the sky. "That's, what, forty feet up there?"

"Thirty. Optical illusion."

"It's a good one."

"There aren't any real corners, either. It isn't four separate films. It's one huge wraparound video image, so you don't have the problem with jiggling or discrepancies in the corners that make some people carsick."

He turned his back to her again, looking down the course. "The first hole is three hundred eighty yards, par four, dogleg right. This is amazing. I can see every grain of sand in the fairway bunkers to the left of the bend and all those traps right around the green. It's like standing on the tee box." He swiveled and looked back at her. "Do you have loaner clubs? Mine are in my car, but you know."

Yes, their cars were as out of reach as pizza delivery. "Flanagan stocked this room with sets of every high-end club known to golf: Titleist, TaylorMade, Krank, PXG Black Ops, Honma Five-Stars, Bentley Centenary—"

"*Wow.* Bentley only released a hundred of those sets."

"Yeah, so one percent of the world's stock of them is sitting in this room, gathering dust. We also have prototypes of some of the newer clubs we're working on."

"I'd love to play with your prototypes."

She laughed. "HR will totally get you for that one."

"Come on," he said and winked. "Let me play with your clubs."

"That should be my line." She'd led him over to the racks of golf clubs lining the wall and selected one. "The Mojave set I was talking about at the sales meeting this afternoon is over here. We can start with that."

"The Mojave line, huh? No real prototypes? No Legendary clubs that you're still working on?"

It was kind of gratifying that he was so interested in her work. Most guys didn't care about the design's elegance and how hard she worked on them. "Luckily, I just made a couple of sets in the usual men's shaft variations of the Mojaves for the trade shows in May. Righty or lefty?"

"Righty," he said.

"How tall are you?"

He towered beside her and looked straight down his chest, like standing under a tree as the crown bent at her in a high wind. "Six-five."

"Oh, so you have a *long* shaft."

Kingston snapped his head up and looked at the wall. "The HR violations just write themselves."

She laughed at him. "Seriously, though. You're right on the dividing line. Half-inch or a whole inch extra for the golf club's length?"

"Regular-long shaft, not extra-long, even though I'm right on the cusp." He waggled his arms like a scarecrow. "Long arms and legs, so my wrist-to-floor measurement is right under forty inches."

"Ah, okay. And regular shafts or...stiff?"

"Stiff," he muttered.

"I'll bet, what with—" She glanced up at him, deciding just how far to go, and she chickened out. "—your *long arms,* you probably have a high swing speed."

They both paused while Nicole waited for him to say something dirty, but Kingston just raised an eyebrow at her.

Finally, he said, "So, yes. My clubs are fitted with *long, stiff shafts.* Where are those Mojave clubs you mentioned?"

She cracked up and hauled a golf bag off the rack, checking one of the bands just below the club heads to make sure she'd grabbed the right ones. "Here you are. You're the first to play with these."

He tilted his head and asked, so innocently, "So, the clubs are a virgin set?"

She snorted and grabbed herself a women's regular-regular set off the rack. "Yeah, the *clubs* are."

He laughed behind her in the dim light as she turned and flounced back toward the simulator.

She asked over her shoulder. "Those clubs are the *only* virgin things in the room, *right?*"

"I went to boarding school for secondary. I assure you, the clubs are the *only* virgins in the room. Hey, let me carry those for you!" he called from behind her.

"It's right here. I'm already—"

The bag lightened in her hand and floated, and then the handle snaked from between her fingers. "Hey!"

"Wouldn't want to appear unchivalrous to the woman with the swords," he said, holding her bag in his hand and his back with the strap over his other shoulder. "You still might run me through. The night is young."

She rolled her eyes and stalked over to the simulator.

Inside the brightly lit cube, they stood on the Astroturf floor, the tee box of the first hole of Pebble Beach all around them, even the bushes rustling in the wind from the ocean and waves roaring in the distance.

Kingston set their clubs over on the side. "I can almost smell the sea breeze."

She went back to the computer. "Yeah. I wouldn't put it past Joe Flanagan to have scented oil sachets just for the ocean courses. What tees do you play from?"

"The blues."

"Yeah, *of course,* you would play from the back tees." And now, she would discover whether he had earned the right to play from the tips or was just a hacker faking it. "I play from the women's, so it's the greens for me."

"So, you do play," Kingston said.

"Well, I hack around the course. Some days are better than others. But why wouldn't I play?"

Seriously, why not?

He said, "You're a mat-sci engineer. You don't need to play the game to optimize the material science specs on a club. You can design a car for Lamborghini but drive a BMW or ride a bike."

"No, I play."

He smiled. "I see that now. Would you like the honors?"

"Sure, I'll tee off first."

Nicole clicked on the green tees on the computers and grabbed her driver, the longest club in her bag, settling a ball on the tubular range tee.

The heady mixture of chocolate, sugar, and sexual attraction sped through her veins.

With a quick check to make sure Kingston was standing back far enough that she wasn't going to uppercut him with the driver and knock out all his teeth, she swung *hard* at the ball.

She ripped it, all right.

But it was a fat banana-slice to the right. "Oops."

"Mulligan," Kingston said. "Breakfast ball. Drop another one."

She did, and she sliced it again. "Um, rats. You go ahead and hit while I think about this."

He went back to the computer, changing the settings so that the fairway on the screen stretched a hundred more yards, and then he brought his driver into the simulator. "It's like walking out a door into a summer day, but with air conditioning. And no marine layer. The last time I played Pebble, the fog was so thick, we had to use orange balls."

"Right?" Nicole stood back and away from him, twisting

her body and looking at her backswing for whatever the heck she was doing so very wrong. "It's fun."

Kingston teed up a ball and ripped it—nay, *smashed* it—dead-center down the middle of the fairway, and it landed just an easy chip from the green. He said, "Sure is."

Okay, she needed to remember to keep her eyes on her own game, and that golf is a game you play against yourself, not against the other players, because evidently Kingston was going to beat her as badly in golf as he had in arm wrestling. "How many strokes are you going to give me?"

He half-turned and looked back over his broad shoulder. His voice was low, sultry, as he asked, "How many strokes do you want?"

Nicole's whole body flushed hot as if the bright sun on the screen above had turned to an August-summer sizzle. She'd *meant* it in a golf way, but now she couldn't get the image of his hands on her bare skin out of her mind.

"Two per hole," she choked out. "Eighteen per side."

He laughed. "Fine. So what is *really* different about the Mojave clubs?"

She explained it to him, eventually clicking out of the golf sim software so she could sketch equations. "And that variable right there, *that's* the whole reason you get five extra yards *and yet* they're more accurate."

He grinned at her. "That's really amazing."

She drew herself up a little. "Yeah, I suppose it is."

"It's astonishing that all that math is necessary to design a better golf club. It's golf club design, not building a nuclear submarine."

She felt slightly patronized-to, like he thought her job wasn't important enough to use advanced math. "Yeah, the value of the golf industry is eleven-point-one times the size of the nuclear submarine industry, so I guess we get to use the math, too."

"That's an oddly specific number."

She shrugged, switched the computer back to the golf sim software, and then proceeded to hack her way around the first hole. "I'm a materials science engineer. I had offers from Sidewinder Golf and Electric Boat when I graduated, among others. The nuclear submarine market is nine billion dollars. Golf is over a hundred billion. I went where the money is."

"You didn't want to work at EB?"

She threw him a sharp glance. Usually, only people who worked there used the acronym. "What do you know about *EB?*"

"I live in Connecticut. Electric Boat sails its new subs down the Thames River when they're launched. It's a big deal. Why Sidewinder instead of EB?"

She shrugged. "I like golf better than nuclear war."

"Okay, valid. But Sidewinder? How much money can this place be making?"

"Oh, a *lot.*"

"And yet it very nearly went bankrupt. This isn't really a money laundering operation for a cocaine cartel, is it?"

She chuckled. "As far as I can tell, as long as I've been working here, we make golf clubs and sell them for an exorbitant amount of money. Joe just kept buying ridiculous 'investments' like these golf simulators. Besides, if Sidewinder was a cocaine money laundering operation, it would have *made* more money, and the lab and simulators would never have actually been built."

Kingston nodded thoughtfully, staring up at the ceiling. "Money laundering is generally thought to be a profitable business model. Okay, it's probably not a mob business, then."

They stepped onto the second tee box at Pebble Beach Golf Links, seven hundred miles north of Sidewinder Golf. The insanely long par-five had a waste area before the green that Kingston shot over just fine. After three hacks, Nicole finally overrode the software and electronically kicked her ball onto the green to putt out.

She hoped she didn't die of embarrassment while they were locked in the building. Kingston might have a hard time explaining her corpse to the police the next day.

Her postmortem grimace of mortification might save him, though. Every golfer would recognize that pathetic hangdog expression after you shank every shot out of bounds.

Okay, every hit of the golf ball was a new game. She just had to stop sucking so much.

Yeah, she'd like to—

No, no. She was not going to think about Kingston in that way. They were locked in for the night, and hankering after something and some*body* she should *not* have was just a recipe for frustration.

Nicole stepped up to the tee, calmed herself down, breathed slowly, and smacked another ball directly off the side of the golf course.

Her game didn't get better from there.

Kingston chatted about golf and club design while Nicole deeply considered breaking every darned club over her knee and throwing the bag off the digital cliff and into the electronic ocean beside the fourth tee box. Maybe the software would catch the bag and show the stupid thing falling onto the rocks far below.

After four agonizing holes in which Nicole shanked

every single shot way off the course into the rocks and deep grass, and Kingston knocked each of his hits onto fairways and greens and then tapped a few short putts, scoring pars and one birdie, he asked her, "Would you like a tip or two?"

She wanted more than just the tip.

No. Nicole was *not* going to get involved with the new sales guy who, it had been confirmed, was *not* moving to California but staying in Connecticut.

Long-distance relationships were always doomed to heartbreak.

She didn't need any more heartbreak.

Not that he was offering her anything, really. All golf terms just sounded dirty.

But when she turned around to look at him standing back by the computer, the mischievous glint in his blue eyes made her laugh.

14

THE TEMPO OF A GOLF SWING IS A WALTZ

NICOLE LAMB

Kingston was still watching her, a smile growing on his lips.

Nicole sighed hard. "I don't know if a few tips would even help. I have been to all sorts of coaches and classes that Sidewinder brings in. I'm way better at designing golf clubs than I am at the game, and I knew that when I took the job. I thought I might get better while I worked here, but I was delusional. I'm hopeless."

He inclined his head and bit his lip for a moment, obviously calculating what he would say next. "You don't really have a lot wrong with your swing. It's just that each minor variation from the classical club path—"

"Variation? Is that what we're calling the *massive flaws* in my swing?"

He continued, enunciating precisely, "—each minor deviation is multiplying the effect on the club head path and angle."

"That is the nicest way I've ever heard someone tell me that my swing sucks." He must really want to have sex with her.

"Some deviations can compensate for each other, like in Jim Furyk's swing. I heard an announcer once say that his swing has more movement than an octopus falling out of a tree, and yet he shot a *fifty-eight* at the Hartford Open. That was a miraculous day."

They both stood in reverent silence for a moment at the pinnacle of golfing prowess, the holiness of the perfect round of twelve-under par, ten birdies and an eagle, no bogies.

Kingston continued, "I think just a few tweaks would vastly improve your results."

Nicole shook her head. "Joe brought in pros every week to work with us so we would understand the game better, and every one tried to fix my swing. I made one guy cry. Surely, one of those PGA professional golf instructors would've picked up on 'a few tweaks.'"

He shrugged. "Too many instructors try to force everybody into the same classical swing. Most people can't do it. Let's try something else."

"I'm willing to try *anything,*" she grumbled.

Kingston retrieved his driver, the longest club in his bag, and stood directly across from her. "Assume the stance."

He ordered people around really easily for a sales guy.

Nicole braced her legs and made a triangle of her arms, holding the club like she was ready to hit the ball. "How's this?"

"Fine." Standing across from her, Kingston held his golf club at the wrong end, wrapping his fingers around the bulbous head, and gently rested the foam grip on her head. "Now swing."

She looked up from under his club lying on her skull. "But I'll hit you!"

"There is no way you can hit me. At the bottom of your

swing, your club should hit the golf ball, which is three feet in front of my shoes."

"But if it bounces off the toe of the club—"

"I'll take my chances."

"Okay. Your funeral."

"No more arguing. Hit the ball, Nicole."

Considering where he was standing, if she mis-hit this golf ball off the toe of the driver, it would more likely be his *nut shot* than his funeral, but okay.

She screwed her eyes closed and flailed into her backswing.

With Kingston's club's handle resting on the top of her head, her shoulders rotated instead of her torso swaying. Even with her eyes shut, the sharp *tick* of her club head meeting the ball sounded better.

His low voice said, "Good girl."

When she opened her eyes, the white trail soared above the fairway on the video screen and still leaned to the right, but the ball landed barely in the rough instead of far into the trees. "That sucked significantly less!"

Kingston was holding his club to the side and watching the flight of her ball on the simulator screen. "There's one more thing we can work on."

Nicole was so jazzed by her lack of complete ineptitude that she almost squeaked. "What's that?"

"Assume the stance."

Nicole did. "Okay."

"This time, *relax.*"

She laughed out loud at him. "I can't *relax!* I'm about to screw this up and launch my ball into the ocean!"

"Nah, come on." He strolled around behind her, looking her over like she was a car he was thinking about buying.

"You're so worked up that you're stiff as an iron rod. Your shoulders are up around your ears."

Nicole listened to his footfalls on the plastic grass mat behind herself. "No, they're not."

"They are." Warmth and gentle weight pressed her shoulders, and he whispered, "Relax."

Her shoulders dropped incrementally with a jitter like they'd clicked down a flywheel.

His chuckle behind her head was friendly like she was cute. "No, *really* relax. Don't just pretend to relax because that's what you've been told to do."

"Dude, get out of my head."

His deep voice was closer. "Are you a firstborn or an only child?"

"First," she whispered.

"Yes, and you got excellent grades in school."

"I'm an engineer from a UC engineering school. So yeah, I took calculus my junior year of high school, and my grades were stellar."

"Yes, you've mentioned calculus." His hands stroked the tops of her shoulders from her ears to the joint. "Is this all right?"

His fingers gently smoothed the cricks and crackling from her neck to her biceps, a slow squeeze that milked the tension away. "It's *fantastic.*"

His thumbs caressed from her skull down the back of her neck, draining the stress from her spine. "None of this matters," he whispered.

"Okay," she breathed.

"You don't have to be perfect. You just have to relax and swing."

"But the club head has to be at maximum speed and squared up at the point of impact—"

"*No.* Nothing matters. You can relax now." His arms slid around her, his hands caressing down her arms to her fingers gripping the club. "Relax your grip. You're strangling it."

The warmth of his large body against her back and around her arms felt like he was cradling her.

"Nothing matters." He stroked the backs of her hands clenched around the club with his strong fingers. "You're just going to move, to twist, to dance in my arms. Got it?"

The warm air around Nicole's face felt too thick to breathe, like she needed to gasp. "Sure."

"It's like sex," he murmured, his voice lower and his breath feathering her ear. "Just relax and feel me. Let me hold you and make you move in my arms."

Her lips felt swollen, and she nodded.

His hands guided her arms and twisted her shoulders as he moved the club up to the three o'clock position in her backswing, then back to the ball. "We go back, and we're relaxed. We come back to the ball, and nothing matters. And again. And again."

It was like dancing. He was leading her, holding her, his arms around her. "Okay."

"A little farther. Relax everything. Feel my hands holding you."

Oh, she did.

"The tempo is a waltz. You move on *one,* and the top of your backswing is the next measure. Ready?"

She nodded, the back of her head rubbing his strong shoulder.

"All the way through now." He guided her hands back and forward through the swing. "*One*-two-three, *one*-two-three."

Crack.

Nicole turned her head and watched the white trail of the golf ball arc gently into the video of the immaculate emerald lawn covering the black-rock peninsula jutting out into the sea, waves crashing on the boulders and spraying salt water into the air.

The ball dropped onto the fairway, bounced, and trickled to a stop near the center of the field. *"Oh, wow."*

"Yes," he whispered near her shoulder, his arms still around her. *"Wow."*

His lips grazed the side of her neck.

A shiver swept from that so-sensitive place on her neck over her body, trembling in her legs.

His weight and warmth withdrew as he stepped back.

Nicole dropped her golf club, spun in his arms, and stepped with him.

A slow smile lifted one side of his mouth.

She was lifting her hands to his shoulders when his arms tightened around her, and he dipped his head. His lips found hers.

Kingston kissed her like he was famished, crushing her against him. One of his hands clutched her cheek in front of her ear, and the other wrapped around her waist and pinned her against his body.

The ocean crashed on the rocks below, a roar in her ears as loud as her pulse. He traced her waist to her hips and wrapped her arm there, lower, pressing her against him.

His body was hard against hers, steel cords of muscle wrapping around his waist and legs, and a hard ridge pressed in the front of his pants.

Nicole pushed herself harder against him, rubbing his body with an undulation of her hips.

With a quick kick, he swept her feet out from underneath her and grabbed her as she fell, following her down to lay her gently on the mat and hold himself above her.

"Oh," she said, because everything was going so fast.

"Relax," he murmured against her ear. "You are perfect. Just being here with me, you are perfect. Feel my hands holding you. Be with me."

His words drugged her, turning the chocolate and sugar in her blood to passion as heady as wine. Heck, yeah, it was fast.

He kissed down the side of her throat, and she stretched to let him. With one hand, he popped open one button on her blouse, and he kissed her collarbones while his warm breath slipped lower over her skin.

His hands caressed her, held her.

Nicole relaxed into him, her skin attuned to his strong body above hers.

He wound her ponytail around his hand and used it as leverage to turn her head away so he could mouth her neck. "This could be fun. This could be very fun."

Awareness drowned Nicole that she was playing with fire, that all sorts of things could happen that night because they were locked in the building together.

Under Kingston's shirt, she could feel the rocky ripples of his torso, the boulders of his chest and shoulders, and she unbuttoned his shirt.

First, just one button popped open under her fingers, and then two more popped open. She slipped her hand inside his shirt, rubbing her palm over the smooth expanse of his pectoral muscle.

He groaned against the skin between her breasts, and his thumb gently rubbed over her nipple, sending a streak of pleasure through her.

God, she was up for anything.

Everything.

Nicole wasn't like this. She'd had a few "serious" boyfriends but no one-night stands. No sultry affairs.

She was the girl who went home and did her homework, not trolled the bars.

And yet, under Kingston's expert hands and mouth—and she could sure as heck discern that they were *expert*—to heck with it.

To heck with being the good girl.

To heck with being first in her class in high school and then at UC San Diego and never having any fun.

Never going to the beach with the poli sci majors.

Never going to the hills with the English Lit kids.

Nicole wrapped her leg around Kingston's hips, grinding him against her.

That ridge she'd felt earlier—his *male part*—fit against her even through their clothes, pressing against her clit and rocketing sensation up her spine to her head. Her gasp echoed in her head.

"That's right. Good girl," he whispered. "Feel me."

He was only rubbing against her a little, and she was already tightening inside.

A tiny part of her brain set itself aside from the maelstrom revving up in her flesh, observing. She didn't usually react this strongly to men. This kind of response usually took a long date and romantic stuff and *lots* of foreplay.

Interesting.

Kingston flipped open the buttons on her blouse, dragged the fabric and her bra aside, and captured the top of her breast in his mouth.

The deluge of sensation swamped her, lifting her back off the floor as she wrapped herself around him, *feeling* what he was doing to her.

Her body smacked that standing-alone part of her brain and dragged it under. She was just her body now, no thoughts, no mind.

He popped his mouth free. The cold air hit her nipple, and more sensation crashed through her. She arched, gasped.

"God, you're beautiful," he muttered. "Let's see if I can make you do that again."

He pressed his mouth over her other breast, rocking her like she'd been thrown in the ocean. His arm slipped under her back, and he held her against his mouth.

Her body closed around him, arms and legs clinging to him while he suckled her and ran his tongue over her breast. Air rushed in her throat and lungs, dizzying her.

More, she *needed* more. She needed him *all.*

She grabbed at his belt, her fingers slipping off the tightly cinched leather.

His mouth left her breast, and he pressed his body against hers through their clothes. His voice in her ear was as harsh as her own gasps. "Birth control?"

Her heartbeat pounded in her throat and ears. *"Wha-what?"*

"Are you on the birth control pill?" he asked, his voice desperate. *"Tell me the truth."*

His sounds finally resolved into words. "No. I'm not in a relationship right now, so I'm not."

"I suppose not being in a relationship is good," he muttered again, his voice hoarse. "At least I can have you with my mouth."

"You don't have to—" Nicole panted. "I'll be fine. You don't have to—"

"Fuck, yes, I'm going to have you. You're too beautiful.

You're too sexy. Unless you say no, I am absolutely going to make you scream my name."

"*Kingston*—"

"Yeah, like that, only *louder*."

"But I'm not on—"

"I won't do anything that might get you pregnant. I don't want that either, yet. Just lie back and enjoy it. Close your eyes like a good girl. You're so wound up. Relax and *feel* me touch you."

Nicole let one of her arms drop to the side.

"That's a good girl. *Relax.* Let me touch you. Let your whole body unwind, open yourself, and let me touch you."

One of her legs dropped to the side of him, but with her knee up.

"We're on the fifth fairway at Pebble Beach. You can hear the Pacific crashing on the rocks to the right of us. We're alone. Nobody can see us. It's just you and me out here. *Feel me.*"

Cool air touched her stomach as he unbuttoned her shirt, and his warm mouth followed the chill toward her navel.

She touched his hair, silky between her fingers, and stretched to feel the back of his neck and shoulders.

"Mmmm, that's right. *Touch me.*"

The waistband of her pants loosened, and then the fly unzipped as his tongue slid down her stomach.

Was he—

His hands curled around her open pants top and wrestled the fabric down, leaving her lying on her back and exposed as he moved to strip them entirely off her. The plastic grass of the golf mat prickled her bottom.

The vulnerability of being naked from the waist down and her shirt hanging open shamed her, but Kingston rolled right back between her legs and pressed his mouth on her.

His tongue slipped between her folds, licking and rubbing inside.

Pleasure cascaded through her, and she arched and almost scooted away from the overwhelming rush.

The bright sun shone on the video screen above her, and birds cried, and the ocean crashed on the rocks below.

He wrapped his arms around her thighs and sucked on her, every caress with his tongue and lips wrapping her, compressing her inside until she was mindless, writhing, and then pulses of absolute bliss slammed up her body, waves of ecstasy caressing every muscle as she strained, her heel slipping on the plastic grass as she gasped.

Kingston gentled his mouth, keeping the caresses going, until her brain was pulverized and she nearly rolled backward.

And then he was crawling up her body, gathering her wretched and wrung-out form against his strength while she clung to him, clutching his shirt in her fists, pressing her forehead against his chest as she rasped for breath.

He asked, "You okay, there?"

"Oh my God." Nicole could barely force the words out of her spasming throat. "*Yes.* I mean, other than I think I died. But yes."

His chuckle echoed in his chest under her ear. "Good."

The shivering in her limbs settled, and then she was aware that he'd done something for her but hadn't had anything.

After pulling on her pants but not buttoning up her shirt, Nicole rolled over and laid on Kingston's chest.

His *massive* chest, now that she was up there.

She said, "Your turn."

"Oh, my little engineer. You do not have to balance the equation."

Nicole grabbed his arms and pinned his wrists above his head. She locked her elbows so he was wedged in place. "What if I want to?"

Kingston casually lifted one of his arms from where she held him down, his biceps rounding as he flexed his arm, moving her whole body and all her weight backward, and he scratched the side of his nose before he stretched his arm back where'd she put it. "I'm not going to say no."

Okay, he'd made his point that he was stronger and could escape any time he wanted to.

She ducked her head and ran her mouth up the side of his neck, the evening stubble of his beard rough against her lips. The last dregs of a warm cologne like whiskey and leather scented his skin, and his shirt collar was exquisitely soft against her cheek.

His slight exhalation and stretch underneath her were sexy as heck. His heavy muscles tightened under his clothes like he was winding like a spring.

"There are chairs over by the computer," he said, his voice rough. "I could sit there."

"I like you here," she whispered near his ear and nibbled down his neck.

"Yeah, but—" His soft groan as she unbuttoned his shirt made her smile. "It might be easier on the chair, with you on your knees."

She slipped a hand under his shirt, which was so amazingly soft that it must be silk. His trousers were cloud-soft like they'd been knitted out of kitten-tummy fur. "Do you have back problems?"

"No, but—"

Nicole pushed his shirt aside. A tiny bumblebee was

embroidered in gold thread near his waistband, and she shoved his undershirt up to reveal his cobblestone abdominal muscles and heavy pectorals.

A flap and a hook covered his pants' button, and she was working her way through the layers of enclosures and prying the button through the buttonhole when his body moved under her hands, and then his arms wrapped her waist and she was airborne.

"Hey!"

Her head was hanging down his back as he caveman-carried her the few yards—holy cow, he was strong like she hadn't weighed more than a piece of fluff when he'd picked her up and flung her over his shoulder—to the couch and chairs grouping and then slid her down the front of his body, a hard, bumpy ride. She landed in a heap at his feet where he was sitting, knees spread, on the couch.

He looked down at her as if from a throne, his eyes hooded, and said, "It's up to you."

Nicole slid her hands up his legs and almost—*almost*—stood up and walked away because he'd taken over, but his muscular thighs under her palms felt like a marble statue of Hercules.

He was really, *really* gorgeous. As an engineer who considered design as much art as science, she wanted to admire his form.

With her hands, and with her mouth.

And with her body, but she needed the Pill for that.

She went back to work on getting his pants undone.

The fine fabric was so soft that it caught in her calluses, and even the zipper worked smoothly like a properly designed machine. These were some expensive clothes he was wearing.

Underneath, his black boxer-briefs covered his erection, and she pushed everything down to release him.

Oh, jeez. There was *a lot* of him.

Okay, she'd just do her best. Nobody ever complained about a blow job.

"Good girl," Kingston said as he watched her from above, adjusting the angle of hips on the couch.

Nicole smiled up at him, licked her upper lip, and then ran her tongue over the head of his thick arousal and sucked that massive shaft into her mouth.

She peeked just in time to see his eyes roll up, and he threw his head back, arching his back off the couch, flinging his arms out to the side, and hanging onto the back like he was going to fall off the Earth. *"Fuck!"*

That was gratifying.

His hardness filled her mouth, and she rubbed her tongue over the thick veins coiled on the sides. As she pushed down, taking more of him until he bumped into the back of her throat, his fingers threaded into her hair.

His natural male musk filled her nose as the blunt end pushed into the back of her throat, choking her. She gagged a little and wrapped her fingers below her lips because she *couldn't* take him all.

"Fuck, yes," Kingston groaned.

Up and down, his thin skin moving like velvet over the steel core under her hand and lips.

Every time his cock hit the back of her throat, he arched, a muscular undulation under her other hand resting on his flat stomach, and he moaned like she was destroying him. She caught him looking at her, watching her, his blue eyes intense, almost glaring, and then a wave rolled up his body and he closed his eyes for a moment before staring at her again.

Yeah, this was—this was *fun.*

Kingston's fingers clenched in her hair, and he panted, "I'm close. I'm getting *close.* Watch out. If you don't want— *Fuck!"*

Inside her mouth, he throbbed, his rigid flesh pulsing, and salt flooded her mouth.

She sucked him down, sucked as he continued throbbing and gasping, and then his fingers tightened in her hair and held her on him. *"Fuck. Fuck yeah, Nicole."*

His hand fell away from the back of her head, and his whole body dropped, limp. "God, you're *amazing.* I don't think I can *stand."*

Nicole wiped the corners of her lips with her fingers and crawled up his body onto the couch to rest beside him. "Yeah, I know."

"I didn't know that a blow job on the fifth fairway at Pebble Beach was on my bucket list, but I can die a happy man now," he panted, clutching her to his chest and dropping a kiss on the top of her head.

She chuckled and pushed herself up. "Yeah, me, too. So, are we going to finish the golf?"

He covered his eyes with the back of his arm. "Give me a minute. Tell the foursome behind us to play through if they're done watching the show."

Nicole laughed out loud.

Kingston tucked himself away, and then he grabbed her and snuggled her down in the crook of his arm. "I don't think I'll ever look at a golf simulator the same way again."

"We can always fire up Augusta National and give new meaning to Amen Corner."

A jolt rolled through his body, and he clutched his chest. "This could be a really long night."

"We could get locked in here tomorrow night, too."

He ran one finger down her cheek, inspecting her like he was marveling at a really good design. "No, I want to take you out to dinner and then back to my hotel for a long, *long* night."

Her whole body quivered.

His smile grew. He ran his hand down her curves from the swell of her breast to her hip. "I can hardly wait."

Nicole smiled at him until her grin felt forced and then like a dead and rigor-mortissed Cheshire Cat.

They couldn't just roll over and fall into an orgasm-induced sleep because *all her techs* would walk into the building and the golf simulator room the following day and find them asleep on the floor in a mortifying state of dishabille.

She rolled off the couch and stood up while buttoning her blouse. "So, are we going to finish playing Pebble Beach, or what?"

15

EXCALIBUR

KINGSTON MOORE

Kingston's head was still spinning as he staggered to his feet, buttoning his shirt.

This woman was a handful, that was sure, and he should be wary. He wasn't at Sidewinder Golf to find a one-night-stand.

Or a girlfriend.

Indeed, Nicole was the head engineer and an essential component of Sidewinder Golf, the company, the investment.

This interlude was a terrible idea.

And he could hardly wait to take her into bed the next night. He was going to absolutely *ruin* other men for her.

That plan's stupidity was plain to him even while he finalized the details.

Supper first, definitely.

Wine.

Dessert.

His bed.

Maybe his ties. He'd packed four.

Even though he'd only booked the trip for three days.

But that was tomorrow.

Today, they were playing Pebble Beach on the golf simulator.

He laughed and balanced himself. "I think I still need to tee off."

She huffed a chuckle. "Yeah, I think you got teed off all right."

He laughed again out loud, a sound he didn't hear often come out of his throat, and walked over to his bag to select the big, long driver.

Even his driver seemed lighter as he stood in position over the ball and striped it dead-center down the fairway.

Getting off seemed to be good for his golf game. He'd have to remember that.

When Nicole stood over the ball to take her next shot, she was still grinning, still relaxed, and she hit her shot much better than before, too.

Getting off was good for everybody's game.

Convenient.

They played the spectacular vistas of Pebble Beach, marveling at the views of the ocean that stretched to the distant horizon and the sea birds calling and flying overhead.

After the first nine holes, at the turn, Kingston asked Nicole, "Got any other interesting new golf clubs over in the rack?"

"Nothing to speak of," she said.

Ah, there it was again, her non-answer that was as suspicious as hell. "You don't have an early mock-up of the Excalibur or the Vorpal Sword in that rack somewhere, perchance?"

She watched him again, her dark eyes gazing steadily into his, and he felt like he was being sized up.

"Come on," he said, smirking and trying to be charming. "I won't tell anyone."

Nicole bit her lip, her brain-gears grinding, and then she walked over to the wall of clubs.

Yes. She was hiding something.

He watched her delicate form, a lithe, curved silhouette in the dark recesses of the room, as she fiddled with the golf clubs in the bags on the stepped racks.

Her dark braid swung down her back as she twisted, looking in different golf bags and examining tags on clubs with the flashlight of her cell phone.

Wrapping her long, silken braid around his fist, controlling her, had damn near pushed him past his boundaries. He could have tormented her into a yes. He could have held out until she'd begged him to take her despite her not being on the BC pill.

But Kingston had boundless depths of self-control. In the gym, he pushed himself to carve his body into exactly the form he wanted, to optimize his VO2 max, and he ate to produce a minimal body-fat percentage. Not the dehydrated striations of bodybuilders or Method actors, but a strong, robust physique that could handle anything and would never fail him.

He could lift a car off someone if he had to and run a marathon distance to get help afterward.

But when Nicole had had him on the floor, when she'd been stripping his clothes while he'd been on his back like a turtle, he'd felt his control slipping away.

And thus, he'd stood up and taken it back.

If she'd ended things there, that was the risk he'd had to take.

Had to.

"Are you bringing me a club?" he asked.

Her voice came to him through the dark room. "Just a minute. I'm—I'm thinking."

She dawdled over at the racks for a while, half-pulling clubs from bags, regarding them, and then letting them slide back.

On the far end, she kept touching one, tapping it, but not taking it out.

Kingston stopped the game timer on the simulator and watched as she stewed about golf clubs.

Nicole walked back, her eyes sparkling, triumphantly holding up a golf club. "Okay, we'll try this one. It's special. Right-handed, regular-long, correct?"

A brittle shard near his heart melted a little. "Yes."

Her eyes squinted on the ends, so coquettish, and she held the very long golf club as if she might snatch it back from him to play keep-away. "It's the Excalibur."

Kingston's heart jumped. "The prototype?"

She nodded, the soft little tendrils of her hair around her face bobbing in her enthusiasm. "An early prototype. I've still got some refining to do, especially in the marketing aspects of the design. But this is—this is *it*. This is the concept. This is the idea that the final model will be made from." She grinned up at him "I love my job."

Nicole held it out to him on her open palms with both hands.

He half-expected her to bow like a maiden of the lake, presenting a sword to a knight before sending him off on a holy quest.

Kingston carefully took the club from her hands with both of his, because this was a rare gift and a measure of her trust.

Even in the dim light, watery holograms shimmered on the shaft and the top of the club head. "It's beautiful."

"I used Japanese steel-folding techniques to strengthen the metal at the top of the club head."

"It's like art." It might be just a mock-up, not properly glued together. He didn't want to take a full roundhouse swing and have the club head fly into the rafters and rattle around up there like a pinball. "Can I swing it?"

"It's fully functional. You can hit balls with it if you want to."

"Oh, I want to." He smiled at her. He'd meant to leer a little, maybe a wolfish grin, but the breathlessness in his chest at standing with her in the dim room, receiving what she obviously considered precious, made him serious. "I don't want to damage it."

"Just handle it gently, but it's tougher than it looks. It's pretty close to the final design. If it can't handle normal use, it wouldn't be a very good golf club."

"So if I hit a ball and it shatters—"

"Then it's back to the drawing board, literally. It has to be more than just pretty."

"How much force can it take?"

"We haven't performed those tests yet. We need to get closer to the composition of the final materials. Heck, I don't even upload the specs to the main intranet until it's closer to finalized."

He swung it a little more. "Everything should be uploaded to the company's intellectual property database as soon as it's conceptualized in case we need to defend the patents in court."

Nicole shrugged. "I can work on them better if I keep them private, without the lawyers poking around in everything and messing up my work. Everything is on my hard drive. Joe knew about it and said I could."

Kingston held the club gently as he walked back into the

simulator and prepared to tee off at the tenth hole, a punishingly long, straight par-four to a green surrounded by sand and ocean.

Playing a new driver on the tenth hole of Pebble, especially one that was an entirely new design for a golf club, was sheer lunacy, but Kingston wouldn't let that stop him.

Well, it was just a simulator. Maybe he'd gotten wrapped up in it.

He set a golf ball on a tubular range tee and backed off to take a few long, slow practice swings.

The Excalibur club was so exquisitely balanced that it felt like a silk rope in his hand, whipping back and forth. "Is this a stiff flex?"

"Yeah." When he glanced back at Nicole, she was watching him closely and called out, "Is it okay if I video you?"

"Sure," he said.

"It hasn't been swung by anyone with a *good* swing," she said. "Just techs, and you know, they're fine. But I want to see what it can *really* do."

Excitement trickled through him. "You want me to put it through its paces?"

"Sure," she said with a grin. "Knock it out of the park."

He swung the club in long arcs, feeling the break point and how the club responded to him, then stepped up to the ball and shot it off the tee like a bullet. *"Wow."*

When he looked back, Nicole was holding up her camera and grinning.

"That was an extra thirty yards and dead-center," he told her.

"Yeah," she said, lifting her eyebrows like she'd tricked him with magic.

"This thing *can't* be legal."

"It is. Well, it *should* be. It's not ready for production, so we haven't submitted it to the PGA yet."

"This will sell *a million* units," he said, admiring the rippling metal on the shaft in the simulated sunlight.

"A million units isn't Sidewinder's business model. We'll sell a hundred units to the *right* people and make the other million die of envy."

"Right," Kingston said, watching the aqua and silver ripples on the club head.

This magic club could save Sidewinder and Last Chance, Inc., but he needed to sell more than a hundred golf clubs to do it.

16

THE CENTURIAN CARD
NICOLE LAMB

The next morning, the doors unlocked with a click, and scores of employees walked into Sidewinder Golf to find their uptight head engineer and that nosy new guy sacked out on the couches in the front lobby.

Nicole sat up and rubbed her eyes in the glaring morning sunshine streaming through the glass walls.

Across the coffee table on the other couch, Kingston rolled up and glared at the people crowded around them. "Show's over. Back to work."

Everyone laughed.

Nicole demanded of the crowd, "What are you guys looking at?"

"You got locked in the building last night, didn't you?" Arvind asked, his thick eyebrows rising.

"Yeah, what about it?"

He spun and addressed the crowd. "Who had this week?"

Morgan was swiping on her phone. "I've got the spreadsheet. It's Caitlin Moffett. Caitlin! You won!"

Nicole watched in disbelief as her very own lab tech jumped around like she was on springs and 'shrooms. "I won! I won! How much was the pool?"

Morgan told her, "Six hundred. Congratulations!"

"What the hell was the bet?" Nicole yelled at them.

They all started laughing again at her, and she started figuring out ways to fire each and every one of them.

Arvind explained, "You're always working late and the last person to leave, and you cut it close at least twice a week. Heck, you said you'd heard the lock-down buzzer go off on Monday while you were in the parking lot. You were obviously going to get locked in here eventually. We just had a pool for how long it would take."

Kind of like the betting pool she'd put fifty bucks in, but that was for when Arvind was going to get locked in the copy room because he'd left his ID in his desk again and wouldn't be able to badge his way out.

Or the twenty-dollar-ante pool for whether Morgan or Meagan would hook up with either Ben or Andy. At least two of that double set of matched pairs on the sales team were going to couple up at some point.

There was a lot of wagering going on at Sidewinder. Nicole's inability to maintain a work-life balance was probably fair game. "Okay, back to work, you slackers!"

Caitlin, who should've been counting her winnings instead of sticking her nose in where it didn't belong, ignored her and asked, "How'd the new guy get locked in here, too?"

Because they'd been flirting in Nicole's office instead of watching the clock.

"Hi, again. Caitlin, isn't it?" Kingston interrupted them. "After your demonstration of fiberglass content in golf shafts, Nicole told me about other golf club manufacturing specifications, and I lost track of time. My fault. However, I made a deal with Nicole for the lab tour and lectures, so I'm on the hook to buy pizza for lunch for the research lab today."

Nicole watched her lab techs shuffle back and forth with excitement at the prospect of free pizza for lunch. Indeed, recent college grads were always looking for free pizza.

Kingston poked around in his wallet and pulled out a credit card. "Who wants to make sure that the pizza lunch happens? I'm going back to my hotel to shower. Nicole?"

She stretched her arms overhead, a jiggle going through her body. "Sure, I'll probably be back in the lab by ten. I can deal with getting lunch for these guys."

Kingston tossed his credit card on the coffee table between the couches. He must've moved over to that other sofa sometime during the night, probably because Nicole had explicitly told him that she didn't want those guys sneaking up on them in the morning and finding them sleeping *in flagrante.*

She picked up the plastic card from the table and turned it over, looking at it to see if she could discern any sort of information about him from the personal expression of his credit card.

Weirdly, it wasn't the green or metallic version of an American Express like all the other ones she'd seen. It looked like he'd dipped a perfectly good card in ink, dark gray and onyx covering the plastic, maybe like it had been made out of black-hued tungsten instead of silver or gold.

She checked her thumb to see if the ink had come off, but it hadn't. "Huh, I've never seen an American Express that's dark like this. Are you sure this is a real credit card, not some promo thing?"

Kingston stood up, stretching his arms over his head and throwing his head back. "It should work fine."

The image of Kingston throwing his head back while sitting on the couch upstairs whisked through Nicole's mind, and she blinked to get rid of it before she blushed. "Okay."

The crowd began to disperse, turning their backs on Nicole and Kingston as they made their way to the hallway behind the hostess's desk and then toward the elevators and stairwells.

Nicole risked a glance at Kingston.

He was smiling at her. "Don't forget I have to buy *you* dinner tonight, too. That was part of the deal for the expanded tour of the lab."

"Oh, I don't know. I'll have to think about it."

"Think about dinner? You have to eat."

"Yeah, but—this is fast. I need to think about it. I'll get back to you."

Nicole fled.

Actually, she *tried* to flee.

She grabbed her backpack on the floor, swung its laptop-heavy weight around her back to her shoulder, and trotted for the door.

Kingston beat her there with his long legs and easy gait and stood just marginally in the way. "You promised to go out to dinner with me."

"No, I extorted dinner from you for a lab tour. There's a difference."

"Then let me pay off my debt. Most blackmailers are particular about being paid promptly."

"I—*um*—how about tomorrow night?" Nicole asked him. She could think and cancel if she needed to. "Tomorrow's Friday."

That she didn't want to stay out all night on a work night is what she *didn't* want to say.

Kingston nodded solemnly. "Ah, yes. Tomorrow works better with my schedule, too."

A quiver raced along her nerves. "Great."

17

HYPOTHETICALLY

KINGSTON MOORE

Kingston's phone had been ringing off the hook since five o'clock in the morning because that was eight in the morning and the start of working hours in Connecticut.

A few hours earlier, he'd delicately extricated himself from Nicole's limbs tangled around him while they slept and moved to the other couch for propriety's sake, but he hadn't wanted to answer the phone and wake her up.

It was just those guys from Last Chance, Inc., anyway. He'd missed the Thursday morning standing meeting and hadn't called in, so they'd assumed he was dead.

He called Jericho Parr back from his rental car as he drove back to his hotel through the desert xeriscapes and emerald-velvet golf courses and talked at the windscreen. "Sorry, I missed the meeting."

"You run off and disappear like we're not even going to notice. Of course, we notice when you're missing," Jericho's voice said. "It was concerning that you turned the plane around and headed right back to California like there was an emergency, and then there was no word from you. Everything okay?"

The other three guys were the only people in the world who might check in on Kingston to make sure he hadn't fallen off a cliff or dropped dead in the middle of a round of golf. "Yeah, I'm working on my golf company for the wager, so I'm not supposed to say too much."

"Oh, sure. You know that The Shark is probably asking for advice from everybody he knows, right?"

"We could ask other people, in theory, just not each other."

"It doesn't seem fair that Gabriel Fish can ask any of his close friends for advice, and we can't ask each other."

"Assuming Gabriel Fish has close friends, as opposed to contacts or assets."

"Or marks. Anyway, in general terms, do you have any hypothetical questions?"

Right, because what was The Shark going to do, tap their phones? "Let's say I have a high-end golf club manufacturer that I bought for pennies on the dollar because the owner snorted all available cash reserves and leveraged customer deposits on this year's deliveries for the same."

Jericho's reaction was pained. "*Oh.* So you need to let people go, at least half of the staff, to start with. Maybe seventy-five percent. But the first thing you'll need to do is slash your costs down to the bedrock."

Kingston sighed. "Yeah, I know."

"How do the balance sheets look?"

Yes, Jericho was the king of Microsoft Excel. Nothing existed unless it was on a spreadsheet. "Cash flow is negligible. For the next year, all deliveries of any current hypothetical inventory will fulfill pre-paid orders, not count as revenue."

"You need to deliver those orders that people already put money down on because you've got to strike the red off the balance sheet, but you need to put a new product out there."

"Yeah," Kingston said.

"Yeah, you need a new product," Jericho mused. "And the problem is, it's got to be a blockbuster. I mean, it's got to be a product that everyone and their dog is clamoring for *right now*. You need a hundred thousand people, maybe twice that, to pre-pay for it by the end of the year. *Pre-pay,* so the money is in the books for *this* year."

"That's what I thought, too."

"Do they have a product like that in development, theoretically?"

"I suspected they did when I bought the company, hypothetically."

Jericho's voice sounded strangled. "You bought a company *for the bet* that may destroy us all, and you didn't *know* if they had a blockbuster in dev or not?"

"But I think they have one. I was swinging it last night, and it's like fucking magic."

"I hope you know what you're doing, Kingston. If you don't, you'll take all of us down with you."

After Kingston hung up with Jericho, he called the jet management company and changed his return flight from Friday morning to Saturday afternoon.

Surely, none of the other guys would need the plane that weekend.

18

ICEBERGS AND DEATH VALLEY IN AUGUST

NICOLE LAMB

Nicole was showered and back in the lab by ten o'clock because engineering school habits die hard. Face time in the lab was important.

When she walked through the front doors, a guy was kneeling, rewiring the security system.

She asked MEREDITH, "What's that about?"

"They're changing the security system, so we'll have a code to get out of the building if we work late. *Finally.*"

"Oh, cool."

That was quick.

At lunchtime, Nicole made the rounds of her lab, negotiating the pizza menu.

She used one of the lab computers to place the delivery order, and Arvind walked by while she was typing the digits of the strange-looking Amex into the website.

Arvind screeched to a halt behind her. "Is that a Centurion card?"

"Whatever that is," she grumped.

"No, really." Arvind plucked the credit card from her fingers.

"Hey!"

"*This is a Centurion card.* I've never seen one of these before. Whose is it?"

"Kingston Moore, the new sales guy."

"How the hell did the new sales guy get a Centurion Amex?"

"Is that a good thing?" she asked.

Arvind's mouth dropped open at her naiveté, which he did at least once a week. Nicole didn't care about brands and status symbols enough. "It *means* his net worth is more than a million dollars, and he probably charges at least half a million every year on his Amex account."

"It's probably a corporate card. The sales guys have to do a lot of entertaining. Maybe they're expecting him to put the entry fees for the golf shows on it. Those can be like ten or twenty grand per show."

Arvind was still marveling at the card like it was a Faberge egg. "I kind of want to take a picture of it. You don't see these things too often."

Nicole popped out of her chair and snagged the card from his fingers. "We will *not* be taking pictures of Kingston's credit card number."

"Yeah, fine," he sighed. "So what did you two do in here all night?"

Nicole thought about cold things. Icebergs. Liquid nitrogen. The absolute zero kelvin of deep space.

Her face burned anyway. "Talked about golf, mostly."

His eyebrow raised. "That's a lot of time to just talk about golf."

"We also ate everything out of the downstairs vending machines for supper."

"Oh, that's why the old guard sales guys were cursing this morning, because they eat the Pop Tarts for breakfast."

"I also had him swing the Excalibur prototype in the golf simulator. Kingston has a really good swing. While we didn't have anything else to do, I thought maybe we should see what it looked like in the hands of someone who knows how to play golf."

Arvind chuckled. "What, you don't think my hacking around a golf course counts as a proper trial?"

"Not in the slightest. Anyway, I videotaped him swinging it."

They stood shoulder-to-shoulder and watched the vertical video on her phone.

Nicole tried not to sigh at Kingston's athletic swing as he crushed the ball down the simulator.

"Wow, that is a good swing," Arvind said. "What's his handicap?"

Meaning the standardized rating for golf proficiency. "I don't know. He didn't say."

"It's low. I'll bet it's under ten. Maybe under five," Arvind said. Lower is better in golf handicaps. "And he likes you."

Her face started burning like Death Valley in August again. "No, he doesn't. We just talked about golf."

"Did you see the way he turned around and smiled at you? That is the smile of a guy who likes you."

A smile was a smile was a smile. "Are you sure it isn't the smile of a guy holding a really good golf club?"

Arvind frowned and went back to the video, scrolling it back and forth until he repeated a one-second clip about three times. "Look here. He was holding the club, but he turned around, then saw you over the top of your phone, *and then* he smiled. You were the one who actually took this video, right?

Nicole scowled at him. "Yeah. It's my phone."

"He was smiling at *you.*"

Nicole scrolled the video back and forth, watching Kingston smile at her over and over. "Are you sure?"

Arvind waggled one shoulder at her. "Trust me, I know what it looks like when a guy smiles at you because he likes you."

As the lab sucked down the free pizza over the noon hour, Nicole opened the table for information they'd gleaned from other departments about how the venture-capital takeover was being received.

Arvind started with, "Nobody likes these terse emails flung down from on high. It seems like they're just molli-fying us to lure us into thinking nothing will happen before they drop the hammer and half of us are gone."

Caitlin nodded, her orange curls flipping as she nodded. "That last memo was ominous. Everybody thinks layoffs are coming. Nobody wants to be last into the job market. Early birds. Worms."

"Has anybody found out anything more about this venture capital group?" Nicole asked.

Within minutes of the takeover, they'd found the obvi-ous: that Last Chance LLC was incorporated in Vermont but had an office in Connecticut, that it had been in business five years, and some guy named Jericho Parr was somehow associated with it.

But the easy internet trail had stopped there.

Last Chance, Inc. was not a publicly held company, meaning they had issued no stock market shares that were trading around. Since no public documents were required, they'd managed to keep most of their dealings private.

"I looked into their recent acquisitions," Arvind said. Arvind's Google-fu was spectacular. He could dredge anything out of the internet, often by semi-shady means like calling people on the phone, not admitting he wasn't the

FBI, and asking questions. "They recently purchased a regional country club and a national tee times booking app, and then they bought us. The only thing in common with all their purchases has been golf."

"That's weird," Nicole said. "Does anybody else think that's weird?"

Caitlin lifted her lip like she smelled something suspicious. "It's weird. Most venture capital firms specialize in a sector, not a theme. So, you'd expect a particular venture capital company to buy a bunch of banks, but not a bank, a marketing company specializing in banks, and a piggy bank manufacturer."

"Right," Bobert said. Bobert specialized in calibrating the lab machines. He was always tinkering. "It's not even vertical integration like a meat packing plant, a pet food manufacturer, and a website that sells pet food. It just seems like random golf businesses that don't fit together."

Nicole nodded. "Something is fishy with these guys. Okay, *without* a show of hands, how many people in the lab are willing to sign cards? Selma?"

Selma tapped printed-out spreadsheets, squaring them. "Twelve are willing to sign cards, first round."

Two of Nicole's lab bunnies didn't want to get involved. Interesting. Not that she would have any work-opinion about it. "Okay. That's a good start. Caitlin, did you talk to Meagan and Morgan?"

She nodded. "Meagan and Morgan and the two young guys are in. The two old guys won't even hear of it. They muttered something about driving prices up, which is exactly our business model, but okay."

Nicole rolled her eyes. "Yeah, but I suppose we had to approach them. We wouldn't want them to feel left out. Arvind, accounting and business operations?"

Arvind's small smile looked very pleased with himself. "Everybody's in, every last one of them."

"Perfect. Good job, Arvind." Nicole turned to the guy at the end of the table. "Matthew? How about legal?"

Matthew rolled his eyes so hard he might have sprained his eyeballs. "The lawyers and paralegal don't like it and are quibbling that there has to be a loophole somewhere, and they want to wait. They think we should see what Last Chance's next move is."

Nicole rolled her eyes. "I checked with my dad. There isn't a loophole anywhere. It's sewn up tight. McIverson? How about the stragglers?"

McIverson preferred to go by their surname for a reason no one knew. "Afifa, Molly, Maia, Elliott, Fortunato, and Rainbow-Supreme are all in."

"Okay, that's over fifty percent of the workers here, even without the legal department. We only needed thirty percent. I'll arrange for those signature cards to be printed and file the petition," Nicole said.

She stood and braced her arms on the table and glowered as well as she could glower at her friends. "This Last Chance, Inc. venture capital company may own Sidewinder Golf, but that doesn't mean they can push us around."

19

THAT SLOW ELEVATOR
KINGSTON MOORE

Kingston stood at the receptionist's desk Friday morning, leaning on the high top and chatting with the lady back there while he waited for Nicole.

He *itched.*

That was the only way he could think of to describe it. Not an itch in a particular region, certainly not his nether regions, but his whole body *itched* because Nicole was still upstairs, somewhere in her lab with other people, other *men,* and he was down here on the ground floor talking to this receptionist instead of to her.

Finally, a slam of a fire door from the hallway behind the reception area, and Nicole emerged from the back areas of the building and stood beside him. She said, "You don't have a sales meeting or anything today, do you? That was Wednesday."

"You showed me the new Mojave set the other night," Kingston said. "I just wanted to look at the Mojave set again."

"The Mojave set. Do you want to look at the Mojave set again?"

"Yes, the Mojave set."

"Okay, let's look at the golf clubs, the Mojave set."

He followed her past a pot full of cacti to the elevator with the utmost decorum.

Nicole said, "You could've just told her you'd come back for your credit card from yesterday."

Kingston flinched. "I didn't even think about the credit card."

He waited until the doors slid away and followed her in as if golf clubs were the only thing on his mind.

In the elevator, the itch turned into a jitter, turned into a compulsion.

Even though Joe Flanagan had told him there were no security cameras in the building, he checked the corners of the elevator, which were typical squared-off corners. No black globes lurked to spy on them.

Yep, safe.

Nicole squinted up at the corners, too. "We were wondering in the lab, what's your handicap, anyway?"

Kingston grabbed her hand and spun her like a ballerina, pushing her up against the wall with her arm stretched over her head. Her mouth made an O, but her dark eyes were smiling. He said, "Probably my distractibility."

He kissed the heck out of her, crushing her softness against his body and finally seeing the appeal of a decrepit elevator that inched up the shaft to the third floor.

When the doors finally ground open, they were both standing separately, though Kingston took one last surreptitious swipe at his mouth with the back of his hand in case he had any of her lipstick on himself.

Phenomenal.

Later that afternoon, Kingston was in a meeting with the other sales staff, where Meagan and Morgan were putting on a presentation comparing and contrasting Sidewinder's golf clubs for when he started selling them at trade shows the week after next.

His ostensible boss, Gia Terranova, glowered in the back corner of the darkened conference room, watching him. Joe Flanagan had mentioned that she hadn't liked having a new sales guy foisted on her, considering hiring and firing the sales and marketing staff entirely her responsibility.

It had been. Half this sales staff would have to go, and Gia Terranova was on the chopping block. Sidewinder wouldn't need most of its managerial-level personnel.

Morgan and Meagan were going to make the cut, though. Their numbers and knowledge about the products were the best on the team.

The two old guys snoring on the other side of the table were definitely out.

The two young guys, Ben and Andy, didn't know they were competing for the one last spot.

Ben was playing some sort of game on his phone. Andy was dozing off.

Maybe Sidewinder only needed two salespeople.

Half the research and development people would have to go, too.

Not Nicole, of course. Her creativity and rigorous design expertise were both essential to the company.

Kingston smiled and nodded through the meeting while he texted Nicole. *Where should I pick you up tonight?*

Numbers and a street name appeared.

A thrill at seeing her address sizzled through him like he was a stalker.

She asked, *What time should I be ready?*

I'll pick you up at seven.

He nodded at Meagan, who was talking about the pros and cons of the older Timber Rattler line of golf clubs.

Per Joe Flanagan's notes, orders for the Timber Rattler line had declined precipitously when the Massasauga line had gone into pre-sales. Joe had planned to discontinue the Timber after the summer.

Or Kingston could cut some corners on materials, order a million sets to be shipped via a fast boat, and have Timber sets in retail stores by mid-July.

Retail stores would leap at the chance to have Sidewinder clubs in their stores immediately available for purchase. The tactic of hand-selling individual units went out with the horse and buggy. Sidewinder needed to be profitable *soon.*

Kingston checked his watch.

Three forty-five.

Three hours and fifteen minutes until Nicole would be in Kingston's car and on their way to supper.

The meeting dragged on *forever.*

20

A GUY IN FINANCE

NICOLE LAMB

When Nicole went on her date with Kingston, the first thing she became absolutely convinced of was that Kingston was *rich*.

Not like he was being pretentious or flashing C-notes around, but like he was *wealthy*.

His rental car was a BMW with a model number starting with an M.

She didn't know what kind of watch was on his wrist because she had no clues other than Apple Watches, but the brushed steel casing and sapphire blue face with three inset little dials for the date looked ridiculously expensive.

Arvind would probably know what type of watch it was.

Kingston's clothes she'd touched yesterday had not been scratchy polyester or wrinkly cotton. They'd been—smooth. Soft. Silky. Not like something you'd buy at TJ Maxx.

Also, Kingston was not staying at the La Quinta Inn, where Sidewinder put up all the other regional salespeople. His hotel was a little farther down the coast towards San Diego and called Aviara, but even non-materialistic Nicole knew what the Four Seasons logo meant.

A colossal fountain stood in front of the grand Spanish colonial building, and a concierge walked right out of the lobby and called Kingston "Mr. Moore" as he opened his door.

Yeah, with the Spanish tile floors, real potted palms at the peak of health, and expansive windows overlooking the immaculate golf course, it was ritzy.

All of this added up to the fact there was no reason on God's green Earth that Kingston Moore should be working as a junior sales guy at Sidewinder Golf.

Maybe Joe knew something terrible about Kingston and was blackmailing him into working for the company, playing on his connections.

Maybe Kingston knew a terrible secret about Joe Flanagan and was milking the company for all it was worth. Maybe that Centurion Amex thingee was a corporate card, *a Sidewinder Golf corporate card,* and Kingston was draining the coffers as they spoke.

Maybe something had happened and Kingston was down on his luck but still had high-society tastes, and Joe had hired him because they were friends.

But *something* was up. Kingston didn't fit in. He was outlier data, a jolt in the pattern.

Also, Nicole didn't fit in at the restaurant.

When she'd been deciding what to wear before Kingston had picked her up, she'd put on her best date dress, which hadn't seen the light of day for eight months. Yet even in California, land of the casual, she felt underdressed in this high-ceilinged, bustling restaurant.

She didn't have a proper purse, either. Nicole wasn't a purse kind of girl. She'd brought her backpack with her wallet, a cell phone charger, her toothbrush, yoga pants, and a tee shirt just in case (and not in case of *yoga*), a pack of Plan B and a strip of condoms, and her work laptop.

Kingston had looked askance when she'd flung the hefty backpack into his backseat, but she'd just shrugged and climbed into the car while he'd held the door for her.

The other women at the other tables all had trapezoidal or crescent-shaped bags of smooth leather hanging on their chairs. Their hair was highlighted and glowing, flowing around their shoulders instead of plaited in a fresh braid. They all wore gauzy pastel dresses and strappy stilettos because it was spring, while Nicole's best dress was black, and her heels were medium at most.

Nicole shoved her backpack under the table by her feet to hide it.

The string quartet-type music was just loud enough that they and everyone else had to raise their voices to speak.

For the next problem, the menu didn't have prices on it.

She'd heard about such a thing but never seen it. She'd had to guess the cheapest thing on the menu without any data, which was disturbing. She eliminated beef and seafood and picked something else.

But the biggest problem by far the whole evening was that it became more apparent that Kingston Moore was not *just* a nice guy.

Nicole had dated a few nice guys. A fun guy. A couple of surfer dudes.

But Kingston wasn't a *guy*.

She was beginning to understand the difference between a guy and a *man*.

Kingston was a man, a sober, serious, responsible man.

Not to say he wasn't funny. He cracked clever little jokes that didn't hurt anyone, mostly self-deprecating that stopped before they became fishing for compliments. He didn't laugh too loudly or look around to see who was looking at him.

And he was looking at her.

He asked Nicole questions, and he listened.

He asked if she'd always wanted to be an engineer.

Nicole said, "I cycled through the usual doctor-lawyer-ballerina phases, but I was really good at math. Being good at math means people tell you that you should be an engineer, so I am. Did you always want to be in sales?"

He chuckled. "Sales isn't something most people aspire to. It's something that people fall into for a variety of reasons. Some people like the challenge of convincing other people to do something, maybe against their will. I just like people to have better golf clubs, so they play better golf. Good golf clubs make people happy."

Nicole sat forward and leaned over her chicken and risotto. "That's one of the reasons that I accepted the job offer from Sidewinder Golf after college. It's benevolent to want to help people be better at something they enjoy. It's wholesome."

He poked his steak and lobster, plus an extra side of potatoes and another one of mushrooms, and asked what she liked to do other than work.

"I like to go to the beach. I didn't do enough of that kind of thing during college, so I'm glad I stayed in California. But I'm also trying to be self-sufficient as far as fruits and vegetables are concerned. I live in an apartment, so there's no way I could grow grains or anything to be truly self-sustaining, but I have a bunch of gardening towers on my balcony where I grow at least half of what I eat. A lot of zucchini. And salad."

He grinned at her. "You're a prepper."

She held up one hand to stop him right there. "I prefer

prepping enthusiast. Have you ever considered what will happen with climate change? We need to start preparing now. Maybe that's because I'm an engineer and can see the engineering challenges coming, but everybody needs to do their part. Have you thought about it?"

He shrugged. "Maybe I'll buy a compound in the Northeast Kingdom of Vermont and ride it out."

Yeah, he had money. "But not everybody can do that."

He nodded. "True. Why didn't you work for a nonprofit if you're concerned about climate change?"

She scoffed, "Got to make some money to pay off my student loans. I had one offer from an NGO, but the salary was half that of Sidewinder's."

He asked about her family.

"Oh, you know, not a lot to tell. My dad is a minor-league lawyer working cases that matter to people, not corporations. My mom teaches third grade. My younger brother is majoring in information technology at Fresno. What's up with your family?"

Kingston smiled and shrugged. "Nothing to speak of. What's your favorite movie?"

And so on.

All the time, his electric blue eyes watched her.

Steadily like a camera, like she was the star, not like being spied upon.

Relentlessly like a predator, but like a lion, not a snake.

Fascinated, like a lover, attentive without accusation.

His slow smiles and tidbits of truth revealed with his eyes wide open fluttered into her heart.

"Where did you work before Sidewinder?" she asked.

A calm blink before his answer. "Mostly in finance."

"Oh, no. You're a meme," she told him. "You're a guy in finance, trust fund, six-five, blue eyes."

He tilted his head, his smile turning quizzical. "How'd you know about that?"

The joke had fallen flat and turned into fluster. "It's just a social media meme about the kind of guy that some women want. There's a silly song about it."

He was holding his recently refilled wineglass but not sipping it. "But how'd you know about the trust fund? A little internet research?"

"Good Lord, you have a *trust fund?* I didn't know that." Yeah, she'd figured out he had money somewhere, though. Family money like a trust fund made perfect sense. "I was just singing the internet meme. You said finance, and the rest of it was pretty obvious. The, um, six-five, and the—*um* —blue eyes."

Really amazing blue eyes.

"Ah, just a song, then." He sipped his wine.

A second bottle of wine arrived and was uncorked.

Before Nicole let the waiter fill the glass, she asked, "Um, am I driving tonight?"

His blue eyes were a little brighter from the wine. "If a ride is needed, the hotel can supply a chauffeur and car."

"They will?"

The waiter nodded subtly at her.

"The La Quinta sure doesn't offer that," she grumbled.

"And that's why I stay at the Four Seasons," he said, nudging his wine glass toward the waiter, who refilled it with a gracious smile. "I can just stagger back to my villa after supper, but you have a decision to make, my little engineer. Would you like dessert here, or shall we take a stroll around the pool and order room service from my place, where it's quieter?"

People chattered, their voices raised above the violins playing, silverware clinking, food slurping, and kitchen pans clanking, and a nervous shiver shook Nicole from the inside out. Words like *now-or-never-now-or-never* pinged around her head.

Nicole sniffed the air in and said, "Quieter would be nice."

Kingston lifted two fingers into the air. "Check, please."

"But we just opened this bottle of wine."

He shrugged. "We can take it with us if you're enjoying it. We can order dessert through room service, too."

"Oh." She scrambled down her leg and grabbed her backpack from the floor. "Let's go halfsies."

He chuckled again. "Of course not."

The waiter brought the bill, and Kingston signed it. He didn't put down that Centurion card or anything, he just *signed* it, like his name itself was money. "And send the bottle of wine ahead of us?"

When they stood, Kingston held out his hand and raised one eyebrow.

"I—what?" she asked.

"Your backpack, I'll carry it. It looks heavy."

"I can—it's okay."

He stood with his hand out, and his voice was lower. "Your backpack."

She handed it over.

Kingston slung one strap over his shoulder, picked up his wineglass, and gestured toward the exit.

"We can't take the glasses," she whispered.

His raised eyebrow and squinted smile told her otherwise. "It's all within the hotel. Housekeeping will take them in the morning."

Oh, right.

Nicole picked up her wineglass and, after he gestured again, led their way between the chattering people around white-draped tables toward the arched exit and the hotel lobby.

Outside, the April-night air was cool on Nicole's arms and bare shoulders as they strolled around the pool, her high-ish heels clacking on the cement, and then down a sidewalk along the golf course. She sipped her wine as they walked, feeling stupidly decadent in a pretty dress strolling along a gorgeous fairway in the twilight as the stars came out, a little buzzy, with a handsome man carrying her bag.

He said, "San Diego is so beautiful. It makes me wonder why I live in Connecticut."

A breeze coasted through the trees. "Are you from there?"

"Scranton, Pennsylvania, originally."

"Here in the West, most people are from somewhere else, but I'm from Oceanside. I've never been to Pennsylvania."

"A lot of mountain ranges and forests between towns, as I remember."

"Were your parents from there? Mine are from Colorado."

As she took a few more steps through the gathering night, Nicole wondered if he'd heard her, but he must have. Except for the whispering leaves on the trees around the path and cars hissing in the far distance, the rhythmic clap of their footsteps was the only sound in the night.

Warmth in her palm, and his hand closed around hers as they walked.

He slowed and stopped, then tugged her hand to turn her toward him. As she looked up to see what was happening, his dark silhouette was already bending, and his lips brushed hers.

The darkness, the quiet, the intimacy of the seclusion closed around them, a secret moment for a soft kiss.

His gentleness stole her breath. Yes, the wine and the anticipation swirled in her blood. If he'd grabbed her and thrown her up against a tree, she would've ripped his clothes off and jumped to wrap her legs around his waist, but this slow kiss, the taste of wine in his mouth, the warmth of his body traveling through the cool night air as if their clothes were already in a pile at their feet, the sweet fragrance of night-blooming jasmine and the scent of soap and masculine cologne from his body that was almost touching hers kindled a delicate but deeper fire.

He released her hand and stroked the underside of her jaw.

Nicole reached up, holding onto his shoulder and then the back of his neck for balance as the kiss lingered, and then they parted.

"How far is that villa?" she asked.

"Just at the end of the sidewalk, past these trees," he whispered.

"Let's go."

21

DESSERT
NICOLE LAMB

Nicole toddled along with Kingston, holding his hand again, for the last few yards until they got to a ground-floor suite in a two-story, four-plex villa, where he used his phone to activate a keypad beside the door and let them in.

Inside was a house.

On the other side of the wide living room was a dining room and a small kitchen, and then a door to a bedroom stood ajar.

Nicole was attuned to floor plans and square footage, having just moved apartments. This part of the hotel suite was definitely half the footprint of the entire house she'd grown up in. Depending on the bedroom, she guessed the suite was at least fifteen hundred square feet.

For a hotel room.

For one person.

Yeah, Kingston was used to nice things.

Their open bottle of wine was sitting on the coffee table with two fresh glasses, plus one slice of apple pie and a tri-striped serving of the triple chocolate mousses she'd mentioned while they looked at the menu. "When did you order this?"

"I wrote it on the bill."

"Sneaky," she said, grinning.

"I've been called worse."

He locked the door and slid her backpack down a chair back to its seat. He fiddled with his phone, and soft music began playing from speakers.

"Neat trick," she said.

He tossed his phone on the chair by her backpack. "Dessert?"

"Sure."

Silverware had been folded into white napkins beside their desserts.

The cream-colored couch was a nest of softness she sank into, a velvet-covered hug.

Yeah, the La Quinta paled by comparison at every turn. Nicole wasn't even staying here, and she was getting spoiled.

Kingston landed beside her on the couch and reached for the two desserts, holding them out to her. "You mentioned the mousses, or you can trade me for the apple pie."

"You don't have a preference?" she asked him.

He shrugged. "I like dessert."

She took the crystal cup of triple chocolate mousses and, following his lead, dug in.

They were smooth, heavenly, and rich, kind of like Kingston.

After his first bite of pie, Kingston raised his eyebrows and seemed pleasantly surprised, and he forked off a bite and held it out to her. "Want to try this one?"

Nicole leaned over and, rather than taking his fork out of his hand or maneuvering her spoon to somehow take the bite off his fork, she wrapped her lips around the bite of apple pie.

Which was kind of familiar for two people just getting to know each other, last Wednesday night notwithstanding.

She looked up and saw the darkness expand in his blue eyes like secret thoughts taking over his mind.

Looked like she hadn't made a faux pas.

She slid her lips slowly backwards off the fork, taking the apple pie with her, and chewed.

It was a really impressive apple pie—tart, juicy apples in a perfectly crisp and flaky crust.

Again, something about the La Quinta, and she could get used to this.

She scooped up a bite containing some of each of the dark rainbow in her cup and held her spoon out to him, looking him straight in the eyes. "Trade?"

Instead of leaning over to take the bite from her hand like she'd done, he set his pie plate aside and slid her spoon from between her fingers. Closing his eyes, he sipped the mousses off the spoon, his lips precise to not smear the chocolate foam all over himself.

Some guys would have been gross and tongued the spoon like an audition, but not Kingston.

Besides, he didn't need to audition. She'd already seen his work, and he was totally hired any time he wanted.

He handed the spoon back to her and looked her directly in the eyes. "Spectacular."

Nicole's breath quivered in her chest, and she didn't look away from his intense gaze. "I'm glad you—I'm glad you liked it. Do you want more?"

His word was almost a gasp. "*Yes.*"

Nicole got the dessert cup out of her lap and onto the coffee table as Kingston launched himself at her.

He scrambled across the couch, grabbing her wrist and pulling her toward him, his mouth crashing down on hers in a deep, insatiable kiss.

Finally!

Nicole kissed him and wound her arms around his neck, dragging herself up to stand on her knees.

But he pressed her backward while still kissing her, crawling over her, until she was lying with her back was pressed against the couch.

Kingston straddled her and curved one arm under her back to drag her body up to meet his. His other arm was braced on the arm of the couch above her head, caging her while he kissed her. She was a prisoner of his body and helpless and a hundred percent *there* for it.

He broke off, and his eyes were unfocused with the wine or passion. "I have been restraining myself all evening. For *days*, really. I am obsessed with you in a manner I didn't know I could be. I *need* you. "

The choke in his voice sounded desperate.

Hunger for him cramped her arms and legs as she wiggled, trying to press her body more tightly against him. "I have a Plan B with me," she said. "And a condom. Must be a condom."

"Yes." He ducked his head. His mouth warmed her throat under her jaw. "Look, if I'm doing something you don't like—if you want me to stop or slow down—Fuck, we should have had this conversation earlier. I can't even think. I can't even form words. Just—use traffic light colors, okay? Red for stop. I'll stop. *I will.* Yellow for not-that or slow down or something. And it's all fine. Just *tell me.* Got it?"

Passion raged through her head like a hurricane, but his ominous tone got through. "What do you want to do to me?"

His growl was feral. "I want to fuck you until you're

mine. I want to twist your body and take you every way. I want to own every part of you until you can't even think of anyone else. *I want.*"

The thick muscles of his back under her hands, his warmth surrounding her, and the caress of his mouth on her neck short-circuited her brain so hard that she could barely use her tongue and her mouth to make words. She wanted to taste *him,* feel *him* in her mouth and the back of her throat, grab handfuls of him with her palms.

"Green," Nicole panted. "Please, *green.*"

His kiss on her shoulder where he'd shoved her neckline aside turned into a bite, raking his teeth over her skin. It didn't hurt. It was just more *intense.*

Intense was the word. Everything about Kingston was suddenly intense. His fingers curving and digging into her waist. His breath rasping in his throat. The wildness in his eyes as he pushed himself up to shove her dress up her body and over her head.

Kingston glanced down her body, seeing the black lace bra and panties she'd chosen for him, too. He bit one side of his lower lip, looking at her like he couldn't stop, and with a deep breath that bowed his back like a bull, he dived to press his mouth to her throat again.

She raised her arms, but he didn't finish pulling it off her. Instead, he twisted one side of it, pulling the stretchy knit fabric tight like a tourniquet around her wrists, locking them together.

Nicole was getting an idea about what Kingston was into in the very small part of her brain that wasn't drowning in the flood of sensations, which was telling her to keep a lid on everything, but to heck with that. She was along for the ride. She'd never done anything like that, but she'd never felt anything like *this.* The hunger escaped her with a moan.

Kingston raised his head a little, glaring at her from where he'd been mouthing her neck, but with a half-smile. He twisted his wrist, tightening her dress around her wrists. "You like it?"

She nodded, even if her eyes stretched a little wide.

He hovered over her, staring right into her eyes. "Are you afraid?"

A lot could go wrong in situations like this. Nicole nodded again.

"But you aren't saying stop," he said. "You aren't saying red."

She shook her head.

"Good girl," he said, his voice low, and he held her dress wrapped around her wrists as he dipped back to kiss down her throat toward her bra.

A wisp of coolness floated through the storm in her body, soothing that rasp of fear.

He dragged his arm out from under her and caressed her curves up her body, holding the swell of her breast as he dragged his thumb over the top of her bra.

Passion blanked her again, raging through her as she wanted more, *more*.

When she was arching into his hand, he flipped her bra cup aside, pinched her nipple in a tweak of pain that lanced through the storming pleasure, and then covered her with his hot mouth, running his tongue around her and sucking hard.

She was a wiggling mess, writhing under where he'd pinned her arms down with his hand and her legs together with his thighs. Every time she twisted, her thighs rubbed together, *almost* stimulating that part of her that ached with need.

He did the same thing to her other breast, the hard pinch of pain before his mouth, and she cried out this time.

His mischievous smile at her cry terrified her, but his mouth covered her, soothing and sucking, and the pleasure swamped her in a wave.

Kingston sat up, still watching her like he was hunting her, and moved one of his thighs to part hers before swooping down to ravage her mouth again.

His muscular thigh pressed between her legs, a rough push, and her hips lifted to ride the pressure that only tightened, tormenting her more. It was closer, *she* was closer, but still not deep enough, not *hard* enough. The *lack,* the *hunger,* was driving her out of her mind.

"Please," she whispered.

His voice was lower than she'd ever heard him. "Tell me green."

"Green!" she whimpered. "Green, I told you green, *please* green."

"Good girl," he growled again.

This time, the soothing was stronger, that her wanting had pleased him, that her surrender was what he really wanted.

He reared back, still holding her hands twisted up in her dress on the arm of the couch because he was so tall that he could reach all of her, and lifted her thigh to bend her knee beside his hips. Slowly, as he watched her like a wolf and she watched him back through her eyelashes of her nearly closed eyelids, he ran his hand down the inside of her leg and under the lace leg band of her panties, gently swiping over her swollen clit.

Exquisite pleasure attacked her, compressing her inside, but it was one touch, barely a stroke, then too long and she was falling, and then another.

It was too little and too much, keeping her from riding over the crest but not allowing her to breathe. Her breath choked in her throat as she tried to push down on him, but his hand pinning her wrists prevented her from bearing down on him.

"Please!" she cried out.

"Oh, no. Not yet," he said. "I have barely started with you."

"Then—then—*please!*"

Her brain wasn't making words.

He flicked her clit again, another wave of sensation through her that verged on pain except that she craved more-more-*more.*

His fingers slipped lower, pushing inside her, a deeper rub that she tried to arch against, but his touch was just a little too slow, withholding what she was craving.

"So wet," he whispered, dragging his finger out and circling her clit with slipperiness.

A thicker fullness invaded her, a stretch.

"That's it. Take my fingers," he said.

A deep movement inside her, and the pleasure inside her amplified like a tornado.

"You like it when I curl them, when I stroke you inside."

He wasn't asking her. He *knew.*

The weight left her wrists and the pressure withdrew, and she was empty and cold and crazed lying on the couch. She almost sobbed.

Kingston was standing beside her, stripping his shirts off over his head, and he was *ripped,* swollen muscles braided under his skin that flexed as he threw his shirt and under-shirt on the floor and unbuckled his belt.

Nicole didn't move her arms from above her head where he'd tied them, but she watched him because getting an eyeful of that hard, muscular manflesh was electrifying.

Yeah, *that* man was the man who wanted her.

He shoved his trousers off with his shoes and socks and was on her again, lying on her, crushing her with his weight and the heat of his skin against hers.

More. She needed *more.* Not just on her but *in* her.

His knee shoved between her legs again, parting her thighs, and he reached beyond where her hands were to the side table drawer.

A ribbon of condoms floated over her head as he sat up, and he ripped open the top one and slapped it over himself. "Say yes again. *Say it.*"

"*Yes,*" she said, wiggling to move down as if that would help. "*Green. Yes.*"

He grabbed her knee with one hand and crammed her leg up against her stomach, holding her open.

The vulnerability scared her like he was holding a knife to her stomach, but he crawled backward and pressed his mouth to her again, his wet tongue circling her clit and then penetrating her.

Her whole body came off the couch, reaching for that orgasm that he was withholding and they both knew it, and then he did it again.

Kingston crawled up her and held himself while his body pressed her leg against her stomach, and he began to push into her.

She'd *known.* She'd had his thick and long erection in her mouth and throat, and she'd run her hands up and down it, and yet she squirmed as he slowly pumped into her, filling and stretching her until she thought he was going to tear her in half, and yet there was *more* of him.

He kept going, withdrawing and invading, filling her

harder and deeper with himself as she whimpered, squirmed, trying to reach for the orgasm she was hanging over the precipice of, and yet there was *more* of him.

And then he *finally* pressed his hips against her, the ache of fullness and need consuming her.

"Fuck, yes," he ground out, throwing her dress to the floor and freeing her hands. He braced himself on his elbows around her head and moved inside her, friction inside and against her clit. "Take it all. Good girl. *Take it all.*"

She was a butterfly pinned to a board, helpless but to writhe as he took her.

Every stroke was a higher shove, the intensity crushing her as he moved in her, and then with a few rough shoves against her, the pressure detonated. The wave of pleasure charged up her spine to her head, and she bucked as he stroked into her, each pulse grabbing her and tossing her *higher, again* and *another one,* another crest of ecstasy under she was exploding and throbbing with each deep thrust and she was *gone* in the void.

His arms were around her, holding her, keeping her from dying, she thought.

Holding her climax at bay for so long had nearly destroyed her, and she wanted him to do that *again.*

"You're okay," he told her.

"Oh, God. Yeah, I'm *better* than okay," she gasped, sucking air into her lungs because she'd forgotten how to breathe. "*Wow.*"

"*Good.*"

His low tone didn't suggest exhaustion. Indeed, it sounded more like a confirmation.

"Did you—?" she asked.

"No. I'm just getting started."

22

DRAGON
KINGSTON MOORE

Kingston pulled out of her with a smooth stroke and picked her body up, flipping her over and draping her limp form on the back of the couch.

Her pretty ass was bare to him, teardrops of soft feminine flesh that yielded when he grabbed her hips.

Fuck, he loved a pretty ass. He'd been watching Nicole's backside all night, when she'd bent over to put her backpack in the back seat of his car, when she'd walked ahead of him. He was wound up like an engine in the red zone by her smooth, plush hourglass outline and the cling of her silky skirt to her skin.

A gasp like "Oh!" escaped her lips as he watched how his hands grabbed her hips.

He leaned over her shoulder, staring at her. "Say it again."

"Yes," she whimpered, closing her eyes. "Green."

The way she surrendered to him was the hottest fucking thing. He was a monster, and she, the sacrifice.

He hadn't even conceived of the words that had tumbled out of his mouth earlier until the press of her skin had evaporated his boundaries. She fascinated him, every movement, every word. He wanted to possess her and take her world into his.

He spread her knees and angled her hips back, then pressed himself inside her core again, working himself inside her to the hilt with slow pulses until he was sheathed inside her, his hips pressed against that pretty, yielding ass of hers.

He didn't want to hurt her. He knew he could because he was too big, too strong. She was a kitten in his grasp, and the drive to take her could wipe that from his consciousness.

Nicole occupied all his attention, from his beauty-appreciating frontal lobes to his bestial brain stem that demanded he empty himself in her, impregnate her and pass on his genes like an oak tree seeding the world if he could.

But he ran his hands over her shoulders, her arms, her breasts and back, stroking her, his palms and fingers grasping her flesh and releasing, slipping over her scalp through her hair that had come undone and curtained her shoulders, and finally over her stomach and down her belly, slipping between her legs, rubbing over her clit with each surge inside her and then pressing in her stomach to compress her channel and G-spot against his cock.

She jerked in his arms, writhing against his body, her breath quickening as she tightened inside.

He grabbed her with both arms, holding her body against his chest as he thrust into her. Her head dropped back on his shoulder as she arched, straining as she came again.

Her pulses ran over his cock, *fucking incredible.*

He rose higher in his head, the wildness swirling in him like madness. His hips jerked, an undeniable animal urge and a downhill runaway train and then a moment of bliss, expansion into nothing, he was a wavelength flowing through the universe, and collapsed back into himself.

His body throbbed in release, relief like diving into cool water after a lifetime of his skin on fire.

He was clinging to her as she flopped limp against the back of the couch, his arms wrapped around her, thighs blocking her in.

Slowly, the world fell back into place, reassembling into order.

He wasn't standing aloof like an oak tree in the forest scattering acorns to the winds.

Nicole's sweet scent, the velvet of her skin, the sharpness of her gaze, and the intensity of her work were transmuting him.

He hadn't just been touching her, feeling her soft feminine skin for the eroticism of it.

The last man to touch every inch of her skin had been *him*.

It was possessive, the outward manifestation of *Mine*.

He didn't want to stand separate and alone like a tree.

He wanted to hoard her like a fucking dragon.

23

AFTERMATH
NICOLE LAMB

Nicole rolled her forehead on the back of the couch, sweat dripping from her temples.

That second one—second *series* of orgasms—had wrung every last molecule of energy out of her body. She didn't have a joule to spare.

Dear God. Dear all the gods. Dear every saint and angel. Kingston had done things to her she'd never felt before.

She had no brain. No braining. No thinkie, no arms-moving, nothing workie.

Nicole could only gasp for breath.

His lips pressed against the back of her neck, her shoulder. "My God, you're incredible."

"Right back at you," she mumbled.

His hands still roved her skin, but lightly, raising goosebumps as he brushed her arms, even her thighs and calves.

He pulled away from her, an ache and her last bit of strength, and she started to collapse sideways on the couch.

His arm caught her, lowering her gently into the cloud of cushions. "Wait here."

Softness settled over her, warmth.

Kingston was gone for only seconds, and then the steel of his arms curved under her back and legs and lifted her against his chest.

She curled into his chest, resting her cheek against his shoulder.

"It's okay. I've got you."

Yeah, he did.

He took her to the giant glassed-in shower—only high-end hotels had showers as big as a walk-in closet—and washed her body, her arms and legs, every finger, every toe, her back and her neck, kneeling and lifting her thigh to clean between her legs, while she stood trembling like a fawn.

Maybe it was the wine catching up to her, maybe eating the chocolate mousse had caused a sugar crash, perhaps he'd taken her body and her soul, but she was a zombie.

His hands and a soft towel swiped the water from her skin, and then she was in the bed sliding between the silky sheets, his naked chest and legs warming her.

One sigh, and she was gone into the night.

But she was sure as heck back the next morning with the sunlight streaming through the gauzy drapes.

Waking up in bed with a man she'd known less than a week would be weird if Kingston weren't laying on his back, eyes closed and dark eyelashes feathering his sharp cheekbones, snoring softly.

Should she get up and do her makeup or something?

Maybe just use the facilities.

She slithered out from between the sheets, flowing off the bed like water, and then padded into the bathroom.

Yeah, she'd been sleepy the night before, but she'd accurately assessed the quality of the fixtures in there. Brushed steel glowed softly, and the floor and shower enclosure were toasty golden stone. Nicole didn't do rocks.

After the basics, she caught a look at herself in the mirror.

Raccoon eyes.

Oh, jeez. The shower hadn't removed her mascara, just slopped it down her face. She worked with the washcloth and the hotel's microbottle of hand lotion to get it off because the mascara was obviously hydrophobic and needed an oil-based solvent.

Yep, it came right off and moisturized her under-eye area, too. *Natch.*

A knock on the bathroom door.

She swathed herself in one of the giant hotel bath sheets and opened the door. "Good morning?"

Kingston was wearing gray sweatpants and a smile.

And yep, it was like he was smuggling a python through customs. The tubular outline was proof he was definitely an Abrahamic religion *member.*

Or, you know, his parents were. Or whatever. *She could see the ridge.*

She'd already known that from the golf simulator, but yep, in case she'd needed confirmation.

He leaned on the door jamb with one arm, and muscles popped out of his arm and torso.

It would be uncouth to whip out her phone, take a picture, and post it, right?

Yeah, very unserious.

He asked, "Everything okay this morning?"

She stepped forward and wrapped her arms around his hard, toned waist, hugging him. "Yeah. Everything's great."

Wow. Really, wow. She hadn't thought that through.

His arms dropped around her, holding her against him,

and he laid his head on the top of hers. "Stay for a while? Breakfast, at least?"

"I could eat."

"Good."

He rocked back and forth, still holding her. "I know I'm supposed to wait three days, but I'm not leaving until Sunday. Let's go out tonight."

The games Nicole was supposed to play seemed childish. "I'd love to."

His arms tightened around her. "Good."

The silence was a little long, so Nicole joked, "The villa just happened to have a strip of condoms in the nightstand's drawer, huh?"

He chuckled. "I stashed them all over the place, just in case."

"Oh my God, no," she laughed. "There are condoms hidden all over this hotel room like Easter eggs?"

He lifted her head with one finger under her chin. His eyes were darker with the sunlight shining in the window behind him, and his smile turned predatory. "Want to hunt for them?"

"What'll happen when I find them?"

His hand trailed down her waist to her hips, and then he palmed a handful of her backside. "Try it and find out."

24

TEMPTATION

KINGSTON MOORE

Nicole found the strip of condoms between the coffeepot and the sugar bowl on the kitchen counter first, so Kingston tossed her up on the countertop and had her there, which was just the perfect height to drive into her with her legs folded up as she braced herself on the cabinets.

Being tall was great. Sure, the world was made for pint-sized people, but he'd always had the high ground.

First, he lifted her onto the counter, spread her legs, and kissed down her thighs, but when he got to the top of her right thigh, he bit her, *hard,* and sucked her wounded skin into his mouth, marking her. Her gasp and moan sounded more sexy than pained.

She'd feel that deep bruise all week, a bit of soreness, of hurt, when she crossed her legs.

And then he tongued her until she was squirming on the countertop, nearly falling off, and drilled into her until he made her come so hard she was a limp little doll again.

His limp little doll with pink-blushed cheeks and dark glazed-over eyes.

She insisted she was okay this time, so he watched her stagger off to the shower, weaving over the Spanish tile on the floor to the bedroom.

If he played his hand right, he could have her until noon the next day, Sunday, and—

Oops.

Kingston grabbed his phone from beside her backpack on the chair and called the jet management company's emergency scheduling number. "Hey, I need to change my reservation from today to two o'clock tomorrow afternoon. Maybe three. Four, if you can swing it."

"We can do a red eye at seven."

"Perfect."

After changing the flight, he found his charger and plugged in his phone because the battery was gasping.

Her backpack was on the chair, too. Maybe she'd brought clothes he should take into the bathroom for her?

Or maybe he should tell her to walk around the hotel room buck naked so that every time she found another roll of condoms—

He picked up her backpack by the top loop, intending to shove it through a crack in the bathroom door to Nicole.

The backpack was heavier than if it contained only clothes, unless she had a set of plate mail to go with her sword collection, maybe.

Her laptop was in there.

The heft and stiff plate on the back of it was definitely a laptop.

Nicole had mentioned more than once that she kept all the essential specs and data for her prototype golf clubs on her work laptop.

The specifications for all the clubs that Sidewinder Golf

manufactured were in the computer inside the backpack that he was holding.

Nicole did not have intellectual property rights to these designs. She was a salaried employee of Sidewinder Golf. Before Kingston had set foot in California, he and Morrissey Sand, and other of the Last Chance, Inc. guys, had poured over the documents associated with the business, including the boilerplate contract that all employees signed.

Any product or idea that Nicole generated while employed by Sidewinder Golf and any golf-related product for three months after the termination of her employment at Sidewinder belonged entirely to Sidewinder Golf.

Anything she did at Sidewinder was standard work for hire. Unless she had brought those designs with her, and the production timeframe suggested that she hadn't, Sidewinder owned all the intellectual property she had produced.

This work laptop was owned by Sidewinder Golf. Everything on it was owned by Sidewinder.

And Sidewinder Golf was owned by Kingston.

Ergo—

Assuming this was her work laptop, nothing personal should be on it. From what she'd mentioned about being unable to stream TV in the walled garden, there probably *couldn't* be anything personal on it.

The bag dangled in his hand like a dead rabbit held by its ears, the hunter staring at the prize and trying to determine whether it would be worth the hunt.

Joe had given him the master password, and he could access the computer because he was the owner.

Kingston had every right to open this laptop and find the specifications for the Timber Rattler golf club line, the Excalibur, or any other club she was designing.

Opening this computer and taking those specs might be the one act he could do to save Sidewinder Golf and as many their jobs as possible.

And he might be able to win the bet to save Last Chance, Inc. and his and his friends' investments in it.

Losing Last Chance's capital base would break up the company and, Kingston was sure, their lifetime friendships. They could try to rebuild, sure, but sucking four hundred million dollars out of the capital fund would cripple Last Chance. They'd have to liquidate so many assets at fire sale prices, not recovering what they'd spent.

He couldn't lose those guys. They were all he had.

Had Gabriel Fish known that losing would ruin all of them when he'd offered them the bet? Was that the point?

Kingston knew he should open this bag and confiscate Nicole's designs.

Pragmatically, he should have no qualms about taking the computer he owned out of this bag and inspecting the intellectual property he also owned.

He held the bag at arm's length until his shoulder shook.

From the bathroom, Nicole yelled, "Hey, Kingston? Could you toss my backpack in here? I have some yoga clothes and my toothbrush in there for absolutely no reason."

He laughed as he handed her the backpack through the cracked-open bathroom door, but prying his fingers from the handle took an act of will. "Here you go."

"Thanks!"

25

SATURDAY
NICOLE LAMB

Nicole didn't think she was falling in love because falling in love had to take months or years to happen. Love was the accumulation of shared experiences, common ground, and trust.

Kingston had been in her life for only a few days, so this was just twitterpation, or maybe that he was really good at batting for the home run, so to speak, or that he was drop-dead gorgeous with his highly symmetrical, testosterone-carved features and genetically recessive blue-eye trait.

That was just science.

This magnetic feeling of needing to be in the same room with him, craving to touch him, the urge to very precisely draw her eyeliner and lipstick so he would look at her, too, wanting to know more *and more* about who he was and what he thought, that wasn't *love*.

That was just, like, hormones or something.

And then, there was the *tall* thing.

Tall was a thing. Everybody knew it. *Tall* was scientifically proven, as much as psychology and sociology are sciences, Nicole chuckled to herself.

Physics was science.

Even when the pop singer sang that the guy she liked was tall and handsome as hell, she'd said he was *tall* first.

And Kingston was tall. Six-five, he'd said. A mountain of a man.

And Nicole was definitely up for some mountain climbing.

But that wasn't *love.*

The few times Nicole had caught feelings for a guy had been weeks or months into dating him. A lot of guys hadn't made it that far. They were nice enough, fun to hang out with or sleep with, but they hadn't lasted.

This thing with Kingston was new and exciting. It wasn't love.

Nicole slipped on her yoga pants and hurried back to the kitchen to meet Kingston, dressed in gray sweatpants and a blue tee shirt, sipping coffee while he was talking on the phone.

He covered his cell phone with his hand and turned to her. "It's a friend of mine, Morrissey Sand. He's a lawyer, so he can't say anything short. Grab a cup of coffee. We'll order room service for breakfast, but this might take a few minutes."

Nicole found sturdy ceramic mugs in an upper cabinet and poured herself a cup of coffee while Kingston talked on the phone.

Saying that he "talked" was an overstatement. His answers to his Morrissey friend were monosyllabic, some more grunts than language. Some of the few more elaborate sentences he said were:

"Yeah, okay."

"I didn't know. How could anyone know?"

"There's no way those numbers make sense. I went

through the spreadsheets with Jericho." *Pause.* "Yeah, the guy could be sued for hiding it during the deal, but it's too damn late now."

"Yeah, it's dire. What did you expect me to say?"

"Yeah, I know you can't say more, but I get it, dammit. How's your wager going?"

She didn't mean to eavesdrop, but he knew she was sitting right there on the bar stool, spooning too much sugar into her coffee. She wasn't lurking. He could've told her to wait in the bedroom or gone in there himself and shut the door.

When Kingston hung up and strolled over to where Nicole was ruminating over what she was overhearing and sipping coffee, his mouth was set in a firm line.

"Everything okay?" she asked.

Kingston sighed and scratched the back of his head, one eye squinting. "It's fine. Nothing that can't be worked around."

Nicole clinked her spoon as she stirred her coffee again. "It sounded serious."

Kingston turned to the coffeemaker. "Yeah, it was serious."

"It didn't sound like you were talking about golf club sales."

"It was about some finance deal."

"You said last night that you had been in finance but weren't anymore."

"Once you're in tight with some of those guys, they don't let you go," he said. "They're gregarious. Everything has to be discussed in a meeting, even when it shouldn't be."

"You said you're from Connecticut, right?" she asked him.

Kingston freshened up his coffee and stirred more sugar in. "I'm from Pennsylvania."

"But you're living in Connecticut."

He ran his hand through his dark hair. "Western Connecticut. Practically New York."

"Is your finance friend in Connecticut?"

Kingston stared at his coffee. "Yeah."

His tone hadn't sounded like he was talking to a friend. He sounded sort of like when he'd been talking business with the other people on the sales team, but even more serious.

Nicole was an engineer, so she was good at math. Tricky math problems were just puzzles that, once you saw the connections, were easy to line up and figure out.

She was good at making those connections.

And she saw the path linking Kingston to Last Chance, Inc., the Connecticut-based venture capital firm strangling Sidewinder and endangering her friends' jobs.

Asking Kingston about his connection to Last Chance would be like pricking the iridescent soap bubble around the previous night and that morning, allowing the grime into this private space they'd created.

She—*might*—never see him again, or at least never see him in the same light.

Working at Sidewinder these last few years and forming genuine friendships there had been her whole life. They were her friends. They trusted her.

The slithering around their feet might be fog, or it might be a snake.

Nicole said, "You know, the venture capital company that bought Sidewinder is based in Connecticut."

This time, Kingston shrugged. "They're incorporated in Vermont and have an office in Connecticut."

"Connecticut's a small state."

He nodded. "Compared to California."

"Do you know the people at Last Chance?" she asked him.

Kingston finished taking a long sip of his coffee and lowered the mug. "I know guys who work for them. That's how I got this job. Connections."

Not *just* connections. *Too many* connections.

Kingston living in Connecticut and having that conversation with a finance guy in Connecticut about a deal, a bad deal, were just too many coincidences. "Last Chance got you the job at Sidewinder."

His voice was quieter. "Yes."

"And that's how you had Joe Flanagan on your contacts list, because our new owners gave you Joe's number."

"Yes."

Nicole very gently and carefully set her mug on the coffee table and stared at the blue-painted swirls on the white ceramic. "You aren't spying on us for them, are you? Listening to our meetings—like the sales meetings and our employee meetings about the change—and telling the new owners what's going on?"

"I'm not a spy. I'm not some low-level grunt reporting what you say to a boss at Last Chance, Inc. Indeed, I'm not telling anyone at Last Chance *anything* about what's happening at Sidewinder."

That last part had an angry ring, a frustrated energy that said he was telling the truth but that more truth was hiding behind it.

But it was the truth.

Okay, Nicole was pretty sure Kingston wasn't a spy.

But—

"So, you obviously aren't just a sales guy. Everything

about you says you're not just cannon fodder to take to the summer golf trade shows. Why are you really at Sidewinder?"

Kingston sucked in his lower lip and bit it while regarding his coffee.

That much introspection before an answer might be due to deception or incoming bad news, and Nicole braced herself.

Maybe she shouldn't have asked.

"Last Chance, Inc. gets its name from its mission," Kingston said. "It's the last stop for companies before bankruptcy. They buy companies for pennies on the dollar and turn them around, or they don't."

Her breath choked her. "How much of a chance do we have?"

"Not good," he said. "Flanagan withheld information about an additional lien on Sidewinder's business operations."

"So there's another outstanding loan? Can't Last Chance just pay it off? That's what venture capitalists do. They're just a big pot of money that pays things off."

It sounded stupid even when she said it. Vultures were not charitable.

"Last Chance overpaid for Sidewinder. Sidewinder is farther in the hole than it was purported to be, and they'll have to work harder to get out of the hole and return it to profitability." He looked up at her. "This is really bad, Nicole."

"So, that's your job, to evaluate Sidewinder, then? You're like the trauma surgeon, seeing how bad the damage is?"

He shook his head. "It's my job to turn Sidewinder around, to do anything necessary to get the ledgers in the black by the end of the year."

"You can't flip companies around to making a profit like that," Nicole scoffed. "Businesses are like aircraft carriers. Changing the direction of that much mass takes a lot of energy. I don't care about the operations side, and even I know that."

"We have to," he said. "It's not an option or a hope. Sidewinder must make a profit by New Year's Eve, or everything falls apart."

"But venture capitalists invest money in companies," she argued. "They don't just close them."

"If Sidewinder doesn't turn around, Last Chance will try to sell the company for whatever they can get for it. They'll likely just close the company and sell the equipment."

"I knew it. When a VC bought us, I knew Sidewinder was going down. Maybe I should have taken that job at EB. Nuclear war is always a growing sector."

"A large profit by December is the only way to save it."

"It's not possible," she told him. "Not with our business model. We're a luxury brand, selling a few units for high markup. I mean, you'd have to double our sales *and* price sets of clubs for a hundred thousand dollars each. No one's that dumb, even golfers."

Kingston huffed a sarcastic chuckle. "Yeah, a few billionaires would be dumb enough and have the poor taste to buy gold-plated golf clubs, but most billionaires aren't stupid. The materials cost would eat into the profit, anyway."

"But you have a plan to save Sidewinder Golf, don't you?" Nicole asked. "That's why they sent you. *Right?*"

He frowned. "I'm in sales. I wasn't lying about being the new sales guy. I am an employee of Sidewinder Golf, on the HR org chart, and drawing a salary, but there will have to be changes."

"You mean cuts," she said. "People are going to lose their jobs.

"Not necessarily." Kingston frowned at his coffee. "I need to see all of your prototypes and the designs. Basically, I need your computer."

Panic grabbed her throat, and her ribs and stomach caved in, whooshing all the air out of her lungs. "But they're not ready yet."

"I need your plans, Nicole."

The command in his voice was unmistakable.

"But they're not *ready*. There are mistakes that I haven't figured out yet. The steel might not be the right composition. They might shatter into shrapnel the first time you hit a ball with them. The ball might just flop off the tee and go nowhere. *They aren't ready.*"

"I need a mirror of your hard drive on the company's servers in an hour."

The soap bubble had well and truly popped, and Nicole had to fight to preserve Sidewinder Golf. "I can't do that, Kingston. As far as I can see on the company org chart—and I looked—you're the new sales guy, not my boss. I'm not turning over my designs and prototypes."

26

AIRLESS

KINGSTON MOORE

When Nicole Lamb walked out of Kingston's suite at the Four Seasons, she took the air with her.

Her backpack with everything stuffed inside after her shower was lying on the chair again, and she snatched it by the top handle as she walked by.

Her slip-on trainers were sitting by the door, and a wiggle of her ankles sucked them onto her feet.

The door slammed after she was gone.

She hadn't looked back. Kingston knew because he watched her all the way out the door.

And then he was standing alone in an overpriced hotel villa that he'd rented for the rest of the weekend, his plane reservation not until the following evening.

What was he supposed to have done, allowed Sidewinder Golf and Last Chance to go down in flames by *not* demanding that she give him the designs?

He should've just taken them. Her computer with the specs and prototypes had been sitting right there in that damn chair.

They were, by all legal accounts, *his.*

Throwing the ceramic cup against the wall and splattering coffee over the plaster would not change anything, no matter what violent instincts rose in him. He longed for Neanderthal days when a burst of violence would solve the problem of the tribe being hungry or the cave being invaded by man or beast.

Instead, he sipped his coffee and concentrated on the breath filling his lungs and leaving him. Filling his lungs and leaving him.

Just like Nicole.

Just like everyone in his life.

27

RYDE AND OTTO

NICOLE LAMB

She'd been so stupid.

Ever since she had met Kingston Moore, he'd been wheedling for the designs for the next set of clubs and prototypes.

In retrospect, his ploy should have been obvious.

First, he'd tried to trick her into telling him about the prototypes and future clubs she had designed, even buying the free pizza for the lab.

When that hadn't worked, he'd tried the honeypot tactic, as spies called it.

But Kingston Moore wasn't a honeypot. More like a beef pot.

It didn't matter what kind of pot he was. Nicole had not fallen into his trap.

And she wouldn't. She knew what he was after now. Some guys might've been just after a piece of tail, but Kingston had pursued something far more important to Nicole.

He'd been after her creativity, her art.

There was no reason on God's green earth why a junior salesman should want prototype designs for clubs that didn't exist, that he couldn't sell. Even if he was working on commission, which the sales team sort of was because they had a base salary but also got bonuses based on their numbers, he couldn't sell designs that weren't being manufactured yet to consumers.

Nicole stood in the covered driveway outside the hotel's lobby, and a battered Honda Accord skidded to a stop in front of her. A pink neon sign in the front window read *Ryde*.

The passenger window rolled down, and the guy inside asked, "Ryde for Nicole Lamb?"

"That's me."

She tossed her backpack in the backseat and climbed in after it.

"I'm glad you waited," the driver said. "Sorry I was a few minutes late. I was hoping you would be waiting because those Otto Rideshare drivers have been hacking our site and intercepting our rides. I got your address that you're going to right here." He rattled off her apartment address.

"Yeah, that's it. Why are they doing that?"

"One of our software coders left in a huff a few months ago, and he stole the code for our ride management software and sold it to Otto, and now they're hacking our system and stealing all our business."

"I'm so sorry. That's terrible," Nicole said, automatically commiserating. "It's terrible that he would betray your company like that."

That scum had stolen designs and sold them to the competition.

And with that, a blast of cold air washed down Nicole's back more frigid than any air conditioning.

Kingston might be in sales, all right.

He might be trying to get her prototypes and designs to sell them to the highest bidder, like rival golf club companies like Titleist or TaylorMade.

And she'd almost fallen into his trap.

28

CONFESSION TIME

KINGSTON MOORE

Kingston made it into Last Chance's office in Stamford, Connecticut, with ten minutes to spare before their Monday morning all-hands-on-deck meeting.

After disembarking the redeye flight that had landed in White Plains only a few hours before and a quick shower at his apartment, he'd hightailed it in to attend this meeting.

First, there was a general summary of Last Chance's current business operations and status, a list of sad-sack companies with sound fundamentals upon which Last Chance was performing institutional CPR.

Most of them were doing well. That wasn't a surprise. Last Chance had an eighty percent recovery rate for businesses they chose to invest in.

That was a phenomenal success rate. Most VC firms with similar business models averaged a fifty percent or less survival rate for companies they picked up.

After the meeting, Kingston didn't move to stand up like normal, and none of the three other guys did, either.

Jericho Parr, a sunshine golden boy who sat at the head of the table this week, was staring at his hands spread on the ebony conference table. "It's April. We are into the second quarter of the year. We need to know how we are doing."

He didn't have to say he was talking about Gabriel "The Shark" Fish's poison-pill wager.

Kingston warred between telling these guys the truth and desperately not wanting to let them down. "The business I bought for the bet is a dud. The owner didn't disclose a lien on the business operations at acquisition. It's farther in the hole than we thought, a lot farther. It's worse than the Hospilala Pharmaceutics."

Everyone winced. Their only saving grace for that bad apple was that they'd disposed of it immediately instead of wallowing in their bad investment, trying to turn it around.

"Morrissey reviewed the new information," Kingston said. "He'll discuss the legal aspects."

Morrissey Sand, the quiet one of the group, the one most likely to give nonfiction books for Christmas presents, paused before he spoke. "Kingston did his due diligence. I looked it over. The previous owner committed fraud by not disclosing a lien on the business operations. We have a basis to sue him. If we do, I don't think we'll recover our costs if for no other reason than this guy, Joe Flanagan, is likely to declare bankruptcy by the end of the week. He is succumbing to a cocaine addiction."

All of the guys shifted in their seats, uncomfortable. That kind of bad-faith negotiation is always a risk in business.

Kingston's tone turned particularly dry. "We didn't realize that his addiction was quite so advanced that he would lie about his business in a sale, probably to get more money for drugs. We should consider adding a tox screen to our standard acquisition procedure."

There, it was out. Kingston had not deceived his friends.

"In the meantime," Morrissey said, "I'll be looking over what legal and accounting measures can be brought into play to mitigate the damage to Kingston's wager. It doesn't seem fair in the spirit of the wager that fraud should be a variable."

Mitchell Saltonstall stared at his water glass like it might grow a snake head and bite him. "And do we expect Gabriel Fish to agree to such a change in the wager rules?"

"Of course not," Morrissey said. "He'd be a fool if he did, but maybe we can use it as a negotiating position on other points."

Ever the math guy, Jericho said to Kingston, "Well, you can always increase your total percentage profit by increasing your final net, even though you are not going to benefit as much from a lower denominator."

Kingston nodded, even though that was impossible, too.

Morrissey tapped the papers in front of him, aligning the edges. "Okay, guys, good meeting.

The other two guys murmured encouragement before they left Kingston alone in the conference room to think over his strategy for Sidewinder Golf.

Well, there were a couple of ways to save Last Chance, Inc.

If they couldn't win the bet and lost nearly half a billion dollars, they'd better make damn sure that Last Chance could absorb the loss and not go bankrupt.

If Sidewinder was a lost cause, Kingston should concentrate on Last Chance's other assets.

Even as Kingston thought of it, he disregarded the idea.

Nothing was ever a lost cause.

There was always another day, another route, another fight to win the prize.

He had a month before returning to California for the strategy meeting before the first trade show, so he needed to hustle and make some money.

29

GIA TERRANOVA
NICOLE LAMB

Monday morning, Nicole stood outside Gia Terranova's office, waiting for Gia as she rolled in carrying two four-cup-holders stacked with venti-size lattes and a long, pink doughnut box perched on top.

"I need to talk to you right now," Nicole said.

"No, you need to get my office door for me right now," Gia said, the over-tall stack of breakfast swaying like she was spinning plates on sticks. "Damn, I hate performance review season when your direct reports get to review you, too. Gone are the days when managers terrorized everyone else with performance reviews. The whole world is turned on its head."

Nicole took Gia's badge off the top of the doughnut box and swiped her door.

The lock buzzed and turned green, and Nicole flattened herself out of the way.

Gia completed her circus act and set the coffees and doughnuts on her desk. "What is so all-fire important that it elicits this much emotion on a Monday morning?"

Nicole stared Gia straight into her mahogany brown eyes. "Kingston Moore is an industrial spy. I don't know if he's directly working for one of our competitors like Titleist or planning to sell our prototypes and future designs to the highest bidder."

Gia leaned back with her hands against the desk and tilted her head sideways. "You must be joking."

Nicole had thought she'd sounded crazy, too. "Look, there was this Ryde driver who was telling me about how Otto is stealing their customers by hacking their website, and it got me to thinking."

"Look, honey, I'm sure your designs are phenomenal, but other companies aren't trying to steal them."

"I don't know why he's trying to do it, but something very fishy is happening with that guy."

"I'll agree, but he's not working for someone else."

"What do you mean?" Nicole asked her.

"Before Kingston Moore came on the scene, I was the absolute queen of sales because I am phenomenal at it," Gia said with a deadpan expression. "Our only limitation for how much money this company can make is its manufacturing. If you got me ten times as much product, I could move that volume."

Oops, Nicole had started a rant. Everyone knew not to start one of Gia's rants.

"I hire the salespeople. I fire the salespeople. I give the bonuses. I dock pay. I decide the trade show schedule. I decide which country clubs we send reps to for personalized events."

Yep, a rant. Nicole listened and nodded.

"I am a fucking *monster* in this industry. I am a *legend*. The day I say I want a change of scenery will be the day twenty other luxury brand golf club manufacturers will be down that front door and beg on their knees to hire me."

Nicole sidled into one of the chairs in front of Gia's desk because she didn't want to be on her feet for however long this would last.

"And yet, one day I get an email—*a fucking email*—from Joe Flanagan that tells me this Kingston Moore guy will be showing up for work tomorrow and he's on my team, and then the company gets sold to some rich VC assholes who also tell me that Kingston Moore will be reporting to me, and there's nothing I can do about it. What *the hell* is going on with this company? *What is the world coming to?*"

Nicole nodded and waited, but it seemed like Gia had run out of steam.

That was quick. Gia must have had a big weekend.

Nicole asked, "But he is just a sales guy, right?"

"Yeah, his title is rookie sales representative, he's paid like a rookie sales representative, and he's going to trade shows to work the booth like a rookie sales representative, starting next month. It's like he's got someone protecting him. You know how important connections are in this business."

"Okay, but there's still something weird going on with that guy."

Gia squinted at Nicole." Did you sleep with him?"

"What! *Why?* Why would you ask me that?"

"Because in that sales meeting on Wednesday, you guys were eye-fucking each other like dogs in heat. Good for you. You keep nailing that beast. It's good for the circulation."

No, Nicole wouldn't.

30

FIRST WAVE
NICOLE LAMB

Nicole was in the lab, watching a fabricator carve a hunk of folded steel into part of the head of a golf club.

Sparks sprayed as the robot, in a glass box, applied its needle and cut away all the metallic shreds that were not specified by the computer-drafted design.

Her Tyvek suit, protecting her clothes and skin, itched a little on her bare arms underneath. Late April was short-sleeve season in Southern California.

She could have worked in her office while the program ran, but when she was alone, her eyes tended to get wet as her mind wandered back to that lost weekend.

Which was stupid. She hadn't fallen in love with Kingston. She knew that love takes time. Love takes attention and effort.

This yearning to see him, to know he was okay, to laugh with him over supper or at Pebble Beach in the golf simulator—

—to touch his strong shoulders, to feel his body move in hers—

—that wasn't love.

It was just—*interest.*

Or estrogen.

Maybe it was libido.

So Nicole sat on a metal stool and watched the face of the second-generation Excalibur golf club take shape beyond her safety glasses and behind the glass, and she willed her burning eyes not to drip.

Over on the next row of bench tops, Caitlin muttered, *"Oh, shit."*

Nicole prairie-dogged to peer over the shelves and between the machines. "What happened? You okay?"

Accidents are always a problem in engineering labs. It's a good thing humans come with extra fingers.

"Last Chance sent an email. Layoffs start Monday," she said.

Arvind checked his phone, which was lying on the bench. "I got it, too. This looks like an informational email, not a specific one for me. Is that what you got, Brax?"

"Yeah, it's just information and numbers. Ten percent layoffs are what they're saying."

From the other side of the metal shelves stacked with tools and metal ingots, Caitlin sucked in a breath.

Nicole asked, "What is it?"

"I got a second email," Caitlin said, her voice quivering. "I'm in the first wave of layoffs."

Over on the other side of the lab, Rainbow-Supreme said, "I got a second email, too."

Nicole checked her own phone.

She'd received just one email, the one with information. Not a layoff notice.

"Anybody else?" she asked aloud.

The machines whirred and squealed, but no one said anything.

That asshole.

Kingston Moore was narking to Last Chance, Nicole just knew it. He'd been really interested in what job everybody did in the lab, information he'd exchanged for free pizza.

That free pizza had cost Caitlin and Rainbow-Supreme their jobs.

"Sorry, folks," she said. "I wasn't informed ahead of time that this was going to happen. I got the same info email that you did. To heck with those venture capitalists."

Everyone nodded.

Nicole announced, "It's time we did something about this."

31

THE STAIRWELL
KINGSTON MOORE

I n the warmer air of mid-May, the Last Chance company jet landed at the John Wayne Airport in Santa Ana, California, at seven o'clock Monday morning, a red-eye flight in the wrong direction.

Kingston's customary BMW rental was waiting for him on the other side of the airplane hangar, so he arrived at Sidewinder Golf HQ two hours later. Even wealth can't solve the problem of SoCal traffic.

The first waves of regret didn't hit Kingston until he had paced past the front admin's desk with a cheery "Hello!" and was heading toward the elevator in the back of the building.

The last time he'd ridden in that elevator, he'd had Nicole in his arms and up against the wall, kissing the living daylights out of her.

He only had to go to the second floor, to the larger conference room for today's pre-trade show meeting.

That slow elevator was crap.

Kingston turned right and headed for the stairwell.

Two flights of stairs joined each floor, and he was

between floors when the metal fire door directly above him clanged shut and footfalls joined his on the staircase.

Sidewinder Golf had over fifty employees. The chance that the person up there was her was less than two percent. That was just statistics.

Kingston continued running the stairs, his leather-soled dress shoes tapping like eighth notes.

The footsteps above were light, delicate, and his heart sank just as Nicole turned the corner.

She stared down the stairs at him, her hands clutching both the handrails, her dark eyes full of shock.

Her presence was a gust of wind that blew back Kingston's hair and stung his eyes.

"Hi," he said.

Nicole spun, her ponytail on the back of her head whipping around her shoulder, and she fled up the stairs.

Kingston watched as she disappeared and waited for her to slam the door on the landing above before he resumed his trudge up the stairs.

Yes, running into Nicole Lamb was inevitable, but why did it have to be so damn soon?

He was quiet in the meeting, his mind returning to the shock in her dark eyes and furtive retreat. A few quick comments about sales figures and population dynamics kept him from being sullen, but his fingers, which caressed Nicole's hips and breasts, twined on the table in front of him.

32

THE DOWNSTAIRS BREAK ROOM
NICOLE LAMB

There were no Snickers in the lab techs' break room, and Nicole wanted a darned Snickers bar.

It had been a long, really long day, and no matter what she did, the materials specs wouldn't line up right. Just freakin' frustrating.

Thus, a Snickers would soothe her soul.

Kingston Moore was in the building. The sales reps had had a trade show in Dallas the week before, and the orders taken had been astronomical. When Nicole had hunted through the company intranet to see which clubs were being ordered, Kingston had sold half of them.

Half.

He'd sold more than Meghan and Morgan put together.

That was crazypants.

Huh, maybe he really was a sales guy.

She rode down the elevator because at least the elevator had no corners where Kingston Moore would randomly pop around, and then there he was, standing on the stairs below her with startled blue eyes, broad shoulders, and his big hands clutching the handrails in a slim cut suit that accentuated his long legs.

Nope, didn't want to run into him again unexpectedly.

And alone.

Kingston was probably cloistered in the second-floor conference rooms with the rest of the sales department, running the post-mortem with the manufacturing coordinator to deliver the massive order to the customers.

And she did want a Snickers bar. M&Ms just weren't cutting it that afternoon.

Nicole rode the pokey elevator down to the first floor.

The floor and walls jiggled the whole way, and she sighed a little as it passed the second floor without stopping.

Okay, she was on a quest for a Snickers bar, and she ducked into the break room to pillage its superior vending machines.

Kingston Moore was sitting at one of the round tables, the one she'd crawled across to kiss him because *of course* he was.

Papers littered the table. A laptop was open in front of him, which he glared at as he sprawled in a chair like he was accustomed to a big executive chair and a wide desk.

He looked up, his lips parted like he'd drawn a breath. "Nicole."

"I just want a Snickers bar," she said, plodding across the room to the machine she knew was always stocked with them.

"I'll arm wrestle you for one."

She paused, swallowing, before she tapped her credit card on the reader. "I'll just buy myself a candy bar."

"I'm not a corporate spy," he said.

She couldn't get over how he'd demanded her designs like he had a right to them. "Okay."

"I wasn't up to anything."

"There were layoffs. Caitlin Moffett and Rainbow-Supreme are gone, and a lot of other people."

"That's rough. Trimming a company down is brutal."

"The lab feels empty."

"I imagine it does."

"You're still here."

"Different department. I'm a sales guy."

Nicole tapped the code for the Snickers into the keypad. "You're pretty good at sales. I saw the numbers."

"It was a good trade show. Can we talk?"

The Snickers bar dropped, and she fished it out of the tray. "I'm working on iterations of a design right now. I don't have time to talk. I just needed a snack."

"Nicole, please."

She turned around to flee, but she caught a glimpse of Kingston out of the corner of her eye.

He was leaning forward at the table, his eyes intent on her, a piece of paper crumpled in his fist.

"Let me explain," he said.

Nicole retreated, making it to the door. "Send me an email."

'I will," he said, his gaze never leaving her.

"Okay."

33

AN EPISTOLARY INTERLUDE

icole,

I was brusque in our discussion about your designs. I overstepped, and I'm sorry.

I'm just a sales guy, trying to save the company any way I can. I know you value Sidewinder, and I do, too.

Your designs are beautiful, and powerful, and more people deserve to use them. Sidewinder is being elitist, hoarding the designs and only allowing the richest, most connected people access to them.

I wanted more people to see what I see in you because you're amazing.

Sincerely,
    Kingston

KINGSTON,

BULLHOCKEY.

WHATEVER,
    Nicole

34

THE COPY ROOM
KINGSTON MOORE

Kingston was walking down the utilitarian hallway on the second floor of the Sidewinder building in late June, when Southern California became incrementally warmer than its standard daily high of seventy-five degrees and the locals thought the sky was raining fire, when he saw Nicole Lamb disappear into the copy room.

He hadn't seen her during his three previous trips to Sidewinder Golf after he'd emailed her and she'd rejected his entreaty.

The fault might have been his because he hadn't gone up to the third floor to try to see her in her lab or office, but she might also have been avoiding him.

Probably both.

The front lobby was carpeted with deep, plush carpeting and furnished to impress investors and buyers, and the lab was equipped for engineering marvels.

The second floor, however, was where legal and accounting languished unloved and walked on a floor of industrial tile. Fluorescent bulbs flickered unflattering blue light from the dropped ceiling, turning lawyers and CPAs ghastly as they haunted the corridors.

Nicole was a ghost slipping through the door to where the copiers were corralled, her white skirt fluttering inside just as the door closed.

His legs sped to a half-run. His hand reached, desperately grabbed and caught the door.

Kingston hurried inside, dodging into the over-warm room after her. "Nicole!"

She whipped around, spinning in the small space not taken up by the beast of a copier, shelves stacked with office supplies, and one geriatric fax machine, even though the copier and most of the printers in the building could also fax. *"Oh."*

His soul writhed in his body, spewing stupid confusion. "I know you're mad at me—"

"Then why are you following me?" she demanded, hands on her shapely hips.

In a white sundress.

His little engineer was a feminine flower, and Kingston thought his heart would explode.

"Just the last few steps," he said. "I didn't even know you were on the second floor. There's a sales meeting in late September to start pre-planning for the show at the Javits Center in NYC. It's going to be a huge show."

"Yeah, well, I'm just making a few copies."

She turned back to the copy machine, a behemoth that came up to her shoulders, dropping a sheaf of papers in the feeder.

"I just wanted to explain—"

Her words were clipped when she spoke, "I'm not interested in your reframing of what you said."

"There are things I can't tell you."

"Then you shouldn't."

"I didn't want them to have to lay people off from Sidewinder. I want to help the company."

She spun back to face him. "You *never* should've asked me to give you my designs. I don't know what game you're playing, but I will not be a part of it."

Kingston lolled his head to the side in frustration, his brain so busy coming up with retorts that he did not see his hand reach forward. "Nicole, that's not what I meant."

His fingers grabbed hers.

Their hands were joined, linking them together, a bridge and a bond.

Nicole didn't pull away.

Her fingers tightened around his.

Passion is anger and passion is sex, and the energy can channel either way.

Kingston dragged her toward him.

When she slammed into his chest, he wrapped his other arm around her, caging her.

Nicole grabbed the collar of his shirt to rise up to her toes, closed her eyes, and her head tilted back.

His mouth crashed down on her, kissing her and sucking her breath into his mouth until his head spun. He let go of her hand and reached out to steady himself on the copier, but she stumbled with him, ending up with her back pressed against the mammoth machine while it pounded out pages with rhythmic clanks and howls.

She was kissing him back, her arms around his neck, her breath quick in his ear as he ran his mouth over her neck to her shoulder.

Her curves under his hands were a cherished memory, tinged with regret.

Longing made him desperate.

She bit his neck, a spark of pain that jumped his nerves, and her hands insinuated between their bodies to find his belt.

"I don't have a condom," he growled. *Cried? Growled.*

"I'm on the Pill," she said, her voice cracking.

"You weren't."

"In case you came back," she said, her whimper sad and needy at the same time.

In case Kingston came back.

He all but attacked her, his body shoving hers against the hot copy machine, and she yanked at his suit belt until it was undone. He flipped her skirt over his hand and grabbed that luscious, teardrop ass of hers.

His palm filled with rough lace and tender flesh.

The need to see those panties—white? Her skin tone?—was a dart in his mind, but his body's roar to take her swamped his thoughts.

He moved his hand around her thigh and slipped past the leg band, slipping his thumb into her slippery folds and rubbing through the sexy parts of her until she was hanging on his shoulder and gasping.

Then he shoved her panties to the floor, and she shook them off her pretty ballerina shoes.

Kingston was standing back, giving her room while she fumbled with his belt until it jangled loose under his suit coat, and he took his hand off of her sweet little bottom to jerk his shirttails out of the way and undo his pants' hook and fly. "You're sure?"

"God, yes," she groaned, bracing her elbows on the copy machine.

He hooked his hands under her armpits and lifted her right off the floor.

"Oh!"

Carrying her lightness over to the wall was easy, and she wrapped her legs around his waist when she got the idea.

He wrapped his hand around the back of her skull and slammed her against the sheetrock. His little engineer's brainy brain had to be protected, but the rest of her was his for the ravaging.

Her body sank over his, taking him in with a slick press upward, and he ground into her and crushed her between his oversized body and the wall, surging into her in time with the rhythmic thump-thump-thump of the copy machine.

She was tightening inside, holding onto his neck and keening near his ear, her breath higher with each whimper.

His own release was impending, his body on fire from her touch, her softness magnetic.

Nicole seized in his arms, her body rigid as he ground into her, and he was experienced enough to know to keep doing exactly *that*.

Her breath was caught in her throat, not breathing, and then she gasped and clutched his neck, her body throbbing inside.

The mind-consuming urgency *to have her* grabbed him, and Kingston thrust up into her as his soul expanded into the bliss and nothingness, and then his balls pumped into her with each throb of relief.

Dear God, he hoped she really was on the Pill, but he couldn't have stopped unless she'd told him to.

After he'd held her, told her what a good girl she was, with soft skin and a pretty ass he liked to squeeze, she got worried about how long they'd been in the copy room and bent to retrieve her pink lace panties from the floor.

Pink.

"Leave them," he told her.

"What?"

He kept his voice low. "Leave them there."

"But I have to—"

"You should leave the copy room first so people won't see us coming out together. Go."

Nicole peeked out of the cracked-open door. "Okay. The coast is clear. Give me five minutes."

She swished out the door, her fluttery white skirt escaping as the door closed.

Kingston picked up her panties, such a delicate scrap of pink lace, and folded them precisely before stuffing them into the breast pocket of his suit as a pocket square.

The Javits Center meeting would start in just a few minutes.

When he went to leave, the doorknob wouldn't turn in his hand.

Odd.

He jiggled it.

Nothing.

He rattled it longer and pounded on the door. *"Hey!"*

Finally, Gia Terranova, his erstwhile manager who watched him too closely and asked pointed questions about his employment history that had nearly tripped him up on more than one occasion, shoved the door open from the other side. "What are you doing in the copy room?"

Ben, the young sales associate who had narrowly survived the first wave of layoffs, not that he knew that, stood behind her to better observe Kingston's plight.

He swiped some of the copies off the tray. "Getting the handouts."

"The handouts are already in the conference room," Gia said. "What have you got there?"

He looked down at the paper in his hand.

Not copies of handouts, but spreadsheets that someone had remotely printed.

Tables and tables of numbers.

Dammit.

"Why must one badge oneself *out* of the copier room?" Kingston demanded.

"When Hammerhead installed the internal security badge network, they put the lock on the wrong side of the door because that's what Joe wrote down."

'That's *ridiculous.*"

"Yeah," Gia said, holding her hand at her shoulder like a waiter with a serving tray.

Ben fished around in his wallet and slapped a twenty into her hand.

"You were wagering on it?" he asked them.

Ben cocked his head at Gia. "We paid off HR to not give you a badge because you were 'non-local,' to bet on how long it would take for you to get stuck somewhere."

"And my getting stuck in the building after hours wasn't the endpoint of the bet?" he asked them, just to cause trouble.

Ben's sharp glance at his manager told Kingston everything. "Hey! Yeah, it should have been!"

Gia's face scrunched like she'd stubbed her pinkie toe.

Kingston strolled back to the sales meeting, enjoying the thought of Nicole somewhere in the building, maybe in her office, sitting in her office chair, flustered because she wasn't wearing panties.

Absolutely titillating.

Back at the pre-planning meeting for the NYC golf show at the Javits Center, Kingston sat at the back of the table.

Nicole walked into the conference room with her white skirt fluttering around her bare bottom.

The moment she saw her pink lace panties in his breast pocket like some depraved sociopath's trophy, her eyes grew on her face, and a blush bloomed over her throat and cheeks.

Kingston kept a demure smile on his face while Nicole blushed furiously during her presentation.

Meghan, Morgan, Ben, and Gia didn't notice a thing, probably.

With a languid move, Kingston crossed his legs. He did not allow his face to show that he was suffering from a raging, unremitting hard-on that threatened to give him blue balls at the thought of bending her over that table, her bare ass in the air and pussy naked to him, and taking her right there in that damn conference room.

His throbbing blood pressure almost gave him a migraine.

35

NICOLE'S OFFICE
NICOLE LAMB

Nicole was in her office, sitting on her desk and sharpening a long, steel katana with a whetstone, stroking the round stone along the edge and ruminating on the metallurgy of the forged blade-style irons she was planning to design next.

Kingston stepped inside and closed the door behind himself. "We didn't actually talk about what happened." He glanced at what she was doing. "Do you want to put that back on the wall?"

She laid it aside but didn't hang it up with the rest of her collection. "Nah."

He smirked at her with a jump of his dark eyebrows and a half-smile. "Interesting."

Nicole leaned back on her arms as he approached, his long legs taking only a few sauntering steps across the room. A Sidewinder employee badge with a photo of his chiseled face was clipped to his suit jacket's breast pocket.

A white lace pocket square might be tucked in there later that day, and her face heated.

Kingston leaned over her, his arms braced around her,

and he looked down between them at the pale blue dress with a fifties-style circle skirt she wore.

When he looked up, his eyes were alight.

Yeah, she would've had to tuck the skirt around her legs if she'd had to don Tyvek coveralls to enter the lab, but the paperwork and CAD work had built up to where she'd known she would be stuck in her office all day.

And Kingston was still in town. The heat in his gaze had scorched her when she'd worn the white sundress the day before.

Afterward had been fun, too.

Even though she was still mad at him, and didn't see him as forever material, and suspected much.

She asked, "Did anyone see you come in?"

"No one was in the hall. I don't think anyone saw when I badged myself into the engineering area's back hallway."

"Good. Let's keep it that way."

"On the down-low. How exhilarating."

The drop in his voice that sounded almost like malice made her skin heat, but she answered honestly. "I don't want anyone to know about us yet. I need to think about what to tell them."

Arvind and a few other lab people had noticed her red eyes for weeks.

Finally, their gentle probes had broken her down. "I have terrible taste in men," she'd told them. "If I like a guy, that's a huge waving red flag. He's either a cheater or a thief."

She didn't want to explain to them that nothing between her and Kingston had been resolved, and yet everything was back on.

He leaned toward her, and his warm breath trickled over the skin of her shoulder and throat. "Our little secret."

Dear Lord, the scent that puffed out of his collar was like dark caramel, freshly cut wood, and something dark and masculine that made her want to bury her face in his neck and inhale forever.

She closed her eyes as his hand caressed her curves. "Did you want to talk about—"

His lips moved on her neck. "If you want to talk."

No. No, she didn't.

He drew her dress strap down over her shoulder and cupped her breast, running his thumb over her peak through her dress. "I'm staying at the Four Seasons Aviara again," he murmured against the top swell of her breast. "Spend the weekend with me. We'll get a bottle of wine, sit on the beach, and talk this weekend."

"Okay."

They didn't talk.

All weekend.

Kingston had to go back to Connecticut on Monday. He said he was needed at a meeting Back East. He couldn't stay.

THE NEXT MONDAY, Nicole was eating lunch in the downstairs break room with Meghan and Morgan when Afifa from HR walked in, carrying her lunch box, and sat with them.

After the usual chitchat, Morgan yawned and stretched, looking around the break room at everything except Afifa. "I wonder when that supposed second round of layoffs is coming."

Meghan shot Nicole a look and rolled her eyes.

Pressuring Afifa seemed wrong. If Afifa knew something, she probably wouldn't have been able to tell them.

Even so, the lower-level HR associates probably weren't in the know.

"So, Morgan, how about this heat wave?" Nicole asked. "Eighty-three, today."

"Oh, it's all right." Afifa waved her fork with a bite of red-flecked chicken in the air. "I don't know anything. I don't know when or if there will be more layoffs. For the first wave, Human Relations received an additional email at the same time everyone else got theirs, detailing the packages we were to offer, and that was all. That is all we have heard."

"So that's the only email you've ever gotten from our Last Chance overlords?" Nicole asked her.

"Oh, no. We get emails daily, just not about layoffs."

All three of the other girls leaned toward Afifa.

"Do tell," Nicole said.

"Just routine business emails or asking for information," Afifa said. "I just admit, it would be good to put a face to such interrogating emails."

"Like *what?*" Nicole asked.

Afifa rolled her large, dark eyes. "Benefits and compensation packages. Where our 401K is managed. Passwords for the intranet so they can go hunting for clues, I guess. And then last week, out of the blue in the afternoon, a phone call *demanding* that Kingston Moore—the new sales man, you know?"

Nicole joined Meghan and Morgan in nodding.

"—*demanding* that Kingston Moore be issued a badge immediately, that *day,* that *hour,* as if we had been remiss."

"Were you—remiss?" Meghan asked her.

Afifa shrugged. "Gia paid me twenty dollars to tell him he couldn't have a badge because he was a remote worker."

"Oh," Nicole said. "Was there a bet?"

"Of course, there was a bet, which I got in on. I won an

additional ten dollars after he was locked in the copier room last week after over a month but less than three."

Oh, Kingston probably hadn't caught the door after—

She hadn't even thought about—

Nicole's cheeks warmed.

"And it was odd," Afifa said. "The man on the phone said that Kingston Moore should have *all-access,* meaning his badge should open every door in the building. Odd."

"Every door?" Nicole asked.

"Yes, and his name was odd, Morrissey Sand, like the desert."

That's who Kingston had been talking to on the phone that day. Nicole asked, confirming, "Morrissey Sand?"

"Yes."

"Odd."

Kingston had said he had friends at Last Chance, and Gia Terranova had told her Kingston had someone powerful protecting him.

And that guy's name was Morrissey Sand.

Huh.

36

NEW YORK CITY
NICOLE LAMB

onths went by, months of stolen moments, criminal glances.

Trysts in supply closets, locked offices, the stairwell, his car in the parking lot, and now that they could stay after hours without getting locked in until the following day, with her bent over the second-floor conference table.

When Kingston told her what to do in a dark, sexy voice, his eyes intent on her, Nicole did it, whatever he wanted, any way he wanted, and she didn't want to say no.

Maybe it was the scientist in her, but she just wanted to see what would happen.

Maybe it was an addictive adrenaline rush of getting away with it.

Maybe it was a dopamine craving because he positively reinforced her obedience with mind-blowing orgasms to the point where she worried about her brain cells dying.

Or some serotonin because she was happy around him.

But surely it wasn't oxytocin.

It wasn't *love*.

Because it was just sex. It was hot, seductive, obsessive, toe-curling sex, but love required more.

If it was love, she was on a fast track to getting her heart broken again, so it couldn't be love.

Finally, one night when Kingston had taken her away for the weekend to a resort in Carmel by the Sea where no one from Sidewinder would discover them, he asked her as they lay in bed, sweat covering their bodies, "Come with me to New York for the Javits Center trade show."

"We can't travel together to hang out at a work event."

"Why not?"

"Everyone will know," she whispered in the dark.

"No one will find out, I promise," he said, his voice rough. "Let me show you New York City. It's brilliant."

Sometimes he had a British accent, which was crazy, of course. He was born in Pennsylvania and now lived in Connecticut, but he did say he'd lived in London, Paris, and other places that West Coast Nicole had never been to. "I don't know, Kingston."

"Come, my little engineer. Let me take you to a Broadway show and supper at beautiful restaurants. Come see my life."

"You sure live high on the hog for a small-time sales guy."

"Oh my sweet, I do nothing small."

Nicole put in for PTO, which was readily granted because she had four months saved up from the last few years.

The following Friday after work, Nicole picked up her backpack and roller bag from home, made sure her neighbor had a key to water the plants, and waited outside her apartment in the heat for Kingston to pick her up in his dark gray M-something BMW rental car.

She'd never seen anything Kingston actually owned. He flew to California and rented a different car every time, running the gantlet from medium gray to black, though they were all BMW M-class models. He stayed in various villas at the Four Seasons for each trip.

Everything Nicole had seen of his was a temporary rental, not even a long-term lease.

His clothes fit well, though. From the beginning, that first night when they'd gotten locked in and played Pebble Beach in the simulator, his clothes had been made of tailored fine cloth, and his shoes and belts had been soft, rich leather.

His credit card was black.

But that wasn't—solid.

Kingston's car slid to a stop in front of her, putt-putting from its tailpipe.

As always, he stepped out and trotted around to get her luggage. "I told you not to wait outside. I'll park and come to your door."

She dumped her backpack in his backseat and climbed in. "I'm fine. It's a nice day."

He laid her roller suitcase in the trunk along with his roller board suitcase and garment bag. "Suit yourself."

"When we get Back East, are we going to your house first? Maybe for the weekend?"

"We'll land in White Plains, but a car will take us into the city. I want to get started on showing you the Big Apple."

"But you'll need to do laundry."

He smirked. "I had clothes sent ahead to the hotel. I'll have the hotel dry clean these suits for the week, too."

"Oh. Okay."

A thought kept wriggling around in Nicole's head: Kingston walked into her life, a visitation, but she never really entered his. He knew her work friends. She'd even taken him to a get-together with a few of her high school friends at a bar, where he was gregarious and curious, asking questions about them and her.

But not answering many questions.

He never answered questions about himself in any real depth.

Other than the fact that he knew a guy or some guys at Last Chance, Inc., and he'd gone to boarding school for junior high and high school, she only knew some biographical data about him.

Even this trip to, supposedly, his home turf wasn't to his home, whatever that might be.

They were going to a city near where he lived.

A car service would pick them up from the airport and take them to a hotel in New York, where they would do tourist things for a few days, and then she would fly back home.

Connecticut wasn't a stop on their itinerary.

Was Nicole worried that Kingston Moore had a wife and kids in a big house in Connecticut, and she was an unwitting side piece?

No.

Not a lot, anyway.

But she felt like she was circling his periphery and wasn't near his heart.

Mulling over what-might-be wasn't good for anyone.

This trip was supposed to be fun as he showed her around New York, the capital of the world, a place she'd never been.

He held the door for Nicole, and she scooted into the car.

When he'd walked around and got in the driver's side, she asked, "So we're not going to Connecticut at all?"

He smiled a confused frown. "Why do you want to go to Connecticut? There's nothing to do in Connecticut. The eastern half of the state has some beaches, although Rhode Island is better for beach time."

"I just—I don't know—I want to see where you live. You've seen my apartment. You've slept over in my apartment."

"I don't even have any plants for you to meet. I'm never there. If I were in Connecticut any less, I'd stay in a hotel and establish residency someplace with lower taxes."

Not California, then. "That seems—fiscally strategic."

"You'll love New York. I got us tickets to *Wicked* tomorrow night."

"And tonight?"

"Dinner reservations, and then *we'll* be wicked."

A little thrill ran over her arms and down her back. "Yeah, that does sound good."

They talked about Sidewinder, movies, and the weather after that, Kingston dodging traffic on the freeways and Nicole along for the ride. The traffic was normal for Friday afternoon traffic, a boiling white-water river of vehicles.

Kingston was a good driver, Nicole had decided some months before, just assertive enough in Southern California traffic so that they didn't get sideswiped by the crazy people, but not aggressive enough to make it any more dangerous.

When they'd gotten caught in a jam after a Chargers game let out once, Nicole had mentioned something to him about how crazy the traffic was that day, and he'd just shrugged. "I drive in Boston, and I travel to Delhi. Nothing scares me."

They talked so much that Nicole barely noticed that

they had missed the exit to the airport. "Hey! Wasn't that the John Wayne exit?"

"We'll take the next one."

"Oh, I'm sorry. I shouldn't have been talking so much and let you drive. Now we have to go around the long way."

"We didn't miss the exit," he said. "We're going in the back way."

"I didn't even know there was a back way into John Wayne."

"We're not going to the commercial terminal. I booked us out of the FBO."

"What's an FBO?"

"Fixed-based operator. You'll see."

And then, Nicole had the weirdest airport experience of her entire life.

Nicole had flown before. She'd been to all the states on the western seaboard, plus other western states for trips with friends, school trips, and family vacations. She'd learned to ski in Colorado as a kid and wasn't a fan. *Too cold.* She'd been to Cabo with friends and definitely was a fan of Cabo. Art and culture weren't any farther than Los Angeles or San Francisco at most. She lived an hour or two from Disneyland, Knotts Berry Farm, and Universal Studios Hollywood. Las Vegas was a long car trip or a short plane hop away.

How far do you really need to travel when you live in California?

But that day, Nicole learned that an FBO is a private airport terminal.

When Kingston drove up to the very front of the building and parked, an attendant came out, asked his name, and drove the rental car away with their luggage in the trunk.

Nicole lifted her hand like she could catch the retreating car. "My backpack was in there!"

"They'll put it on the plane," Kingston told her.

"It's fragile. It shouldn't go in the hold. It's my carry-on."

He glanced down at her, amusement crinkling his eyes. "You brought your work laptop, didn't you?"

"I'd feel weird without it. Besides, this is a work trip for you because you have to do the show. I might as well noodle on designs while you're at the Javits Center all day."

He shrugged. "The hotel suite comes with a thousand-dollar credit at the spa that someone will have to use up while I'm at the trade show."

"Well, I didn't say I would work the *whole* time."

The building was essentially a lounge with a few discreet ticketing and information counters tucked away near the floor-to-ceiling windows overlooking Costa Mesa.

As soon as they walked in, a man wearing a navy blue uniform that was not Air Force but kind of close approached them, holding a silver tray with drinks on it. "Hello again, Mr. Moore. I assume this is Miss Nicole Lamb?"

"Yes, indeed," Kingston said, taking the two glasses off the tray and offering the champagne glass to Nicole. "Mimosa?"

Nicole loved mimosas. "Yes, thank you."

The guy who'd approached them said, "I'm Vasily, and I'll be your point of contact today. Your plane should be leaving shortly. I'm afraid I'll have to ask Ms. Lamb to show some identification, as it is her first flight with us. If you'll just follow me to the counter—"

And they walked toward the counter where there was no line or even people milling around. A similarly uniformed lady smiled at Nicole as she glanced at Nicole's offered driver's license and typed quickly into the computer. "Excellent, and thank you, Ms. Lamb. Your flight will be leaving in about fifteen minutes. If you'd like to help yourself to some hors d'oeuvres, the brunch buffet is against the wall to your right, or you can order from the waitstaff."

Kingston squired Nicole over to the buffet. When she dithered, uncertain about all this, he grabbed a plate, tossed some flaky pastries, and led her over to a hightop table. "Do you want coffee?"

"Oh, I had a cup before I left home. I'm fine."

"That's not what I asked. You usually have three cups before noon at Sidewinder."

"If it's not too much trouble—"

Kingston flagged down a waiter who practically tire-screeched as he stopped beside their table. "A caramel macchiato for the lady and a cappuccino for me, please."

The plane was a small, silver jet, and the seats inside looked like the leather-clad loungers Nicole had only seen when she'd passed through first class to get to the normal-people part of the plane.

Once they were on board and settled in seats so luxurious that Nicole almost fell asleep immediately, a flight attendant wearing the now-familiar blue uniform offered them yet more mimosa.

Nicole lifted it off the tray and fixed Kingston with a pointed stare. "This is a private airplane."

Kingston was sipping his mimosa and raised one eyebrow over the rim of his glass. "Why, yes. Yes, it is."

"Are you flying private every time you come into the office from Back East?"

"Not always."

"But enough to where they know you by sight."

Kingston set his mimosa on the table between their chairs with a rueful smile. "The plane is serviced by a flight management company. I booked the plane for today. Vasily and the desk attendant looked up my ID before we arrived at the airport and were looking for us. I've never met Vasily before."

"And yet, that doesn't happen when I fly Southwest to Las Vegas for the weekend with friends."

His amused smile irritated her as he picked up his champagne again. "No, I suppose not."

Nicole leaned forward, her elbows on the table and her hands clasped as if she were staging an intervention like back in college when she'd been a resident assistant in the dorms. "Look, Kingston, I know you're a big shot and bringing in good amounts of money for Sidewinder—I mean, *great* sales numbers—but Sidewinder is having cash flow issues. I don't know if you noticed, but ten percent of the staff was laid off, and everyone thinks more cuts are coming. Maybe we could have flown on a regular airplane. Maybe you should be flying on regular airplanes all the time."

He shrugged and vaguely gestured to the airplane's fuselage with his champagne flute. "It's not coming out of Sidewinder."

"Then where is it coming from? Do you have a sugar mommy or something? Or a sugar daddy? I won't judge."

"No, no. I am not trading 'services rendered' for private flights."

Though Nicole sort of was, but she wasn't going to look at that too closely.

"Another business venture I'm associated with provides private flights," he said.

She squinted at him. "Do you have a second job?

Because I think your contract with Sidewinder says you can't do that."

"Yes," he said slowly, drawing it out. "A second job. *My* contract with Sidewinder doesn't forbid it."

He was bringing in an extraordinary amount of sales. Nicole had peeked again that week, and his numbers had remained astounding and had increased.

Anyway, Nicole was R&D, and this seemed like an HR or Sales department problem. "I guess that's okay, then."

"Indeed, and rather than discuss employment contract details, how about we discuss what activities we will be partaking in this weekend?"

He smiled that sultry smile at her, half-smirk and half-fire, and Nicole suddenly wondered just how many mimosas he was going to ply her with on this rather long private plane flight, and to what end.

Three.

It took three mimosas until Kingston chaperoned a very giggly Nicole past the air hostess who studiously avoided looking up at them into the private plane's lavatory, where he sealed his hand over her mouth as he spun her around, flipped her sundress up to her waist, and angled himself inside her with one slick thrust.

The way his demeanor changed from charming and good-natured to darkly commanding took her breath away.

His growls in her ear from behind as he ground up into her, his muscular arm encircling her waist, his cologne's dark musk, his finger between her legs massaging her clit, and then his teeth sharp on her shoulder avalanched her into an orgasm that shook her so hard she couldn't see.

Maybe her reaction wasn't so much adrenaline or serotonin, but Pavlovian.

When she was a limp octopus afterward, her limbs

dangling like ribbons in a breeze with Kingston still hard inside her, he growled in her ear, "You are *mine* for the week, my little engineer."

"Yes, please," she whimpered.

"On the way back, I'll book a flight without a cabin staff and with a locked-door pilot. I'll bend you over and make you orgasm so hard you *scream*."

Against all odds, her body managed one last pulse of ecstasy. *"Yes, please."*

And her mind stopped thinking, for just a while, about how the new sales guy could summon up a private plane and fly her to New York.

37

THE BACCARAT

NICOLE LAMB

Flying east over the North American continent, coast to coast, ate up the hours as they flew against the sun's path.

After four hours of airtime, a sumptuous lunch that was definitely unlike any standard airplane food that Nicole had ever been served back in steerage, plus two lattes later, they landed at seven o'clock at night in White Plains, New York.

As Kingston had said, a waiting car drove them, their luggage, and her backpack into New York City, through the squared-off maze of Manhattan, to a building that seemed to be encased in gold-glowing crystal. Dark marble slabs jutted out over the doorways above the sidewalk.

Instead of a pumpkin magicked into a stagecoach, this was a chandelier transformed into a skyscraper.

The chauffeur held the door for Nicole as she got out.

Kingston met her on the sidewalk, casually buttoning his suit jacket.

"Who stays in a place like this?" she asked. "Celebrities? Kardashians?"

"Celebrities tend to stay at the Mark or the Carlyle. This is quieter."

They went inside the hotel lobby, dark wood paneling the walls contrasted the crystal-encrusted chandeliers hanging from the ceiling, frosted crystal candlesticks on coffee tables, and a crystal chessboard. As Nicole went by, she picked up a pawn, which was sharp glass and heavy in her palm.

She put it down quickly.

The answer as to who stayed in a place like this occurred to her.

Money.

Probably *Old Money.*

But definitely *A Lot of Money.*

Wealth.

Wealthy people with so much money that they didn't want to stay where the celebrities did because they did not desire to be seen.

At the desk, the attendant smiled serenely at the two of them. "Welcome to the Baccarat Hotel. Mr. Moore, how lovely to see you again. And you'll be staying with us for a week?"

After their phones had been keyed to open the suite, a bellhop led them up to a crystal-encrusted suite. Inside, every surface held a crystal candy dish or votive lamps, and matching bathtub-size chandeliers like glass-scaled Cthulhu-dragons dripping with frosted glass daggers hung over the dining table, living room sitting area, and king-size bed in the bedroom.

"What did you say the name of this hotel was?" Nicole asked him.

"The Baccarat. Yes, just like the crystal. It's very French, but the service and the spa are incomparable. And the food, of course. We have an hour before our reservations downstairs."

"Do you bring all your mistresses here?"

"Of course not. One takes one's mistresses to the RH Guest House. Very discreet. No photos allowed."

She turned and stared at him. "That just rolled off your tongue."

He laughed. "I was wondering whether you'd catch it."

"Do you have a mistress? Is it me? Am I the mistress?" She made it sound like a joke.

He walked over to her and smiled down at her, placating her. "You're not a mistress. I'm not married and never have been. Even relationships have been few and not recently."

She squinted up at him. "That's what all the married guys say."

His expression softened. "Did someone say that to you?"

"Oh, once." She flipped her hand like she was flipping off nothing that mattered. "But it was a few years ago, and I don't want to kill him anymore. Mostly."

His eyes took on that blue-fire devilish sparkle. "Is that why you started buying medieval weapons a few years ago? To murder this knave who dared treat such a beautiful woman so badly?"

Um, *yeah,* it matched up, but she hadn't thought of it that way. "Well, I started buying them when I graduated and passed the PE exam, so I had real money for the first time. *That's* why I started collecting them, not to kill that other guy."

She had bought that first steel dagger quite soon after she'd figured out Jackass Face was a cheater and dumped him hard.

Weird. Huh.

"Tell you what, if we ever run into him, I'll kill him for

you." Kingston lifted her hand and brushed his lips against her palm, then her wrist. "I would never want you to soil these beautiful little hands with blood."

Lethal violence seemed excessive, probably, at least practically. "You would?"

He looked up from her wrist, almost vampiric as he gazed at her, and his voice was lower. "Try me."

She knew he was kidding, or at least being chivalric, but she was turned on.

Which was probably why he'd said it.

He straightened and lifted her chin, kissing her. "Do you want to be late for our supper reservations?" he whispered.

"That seems rude," she whispered back.

"Then we'd better hurry." He grabbed her hand and lifted it over her head, twirling her away from him like a ballerina to face the bedroom. "Go."

She began walking away through the living room populated with exquisite vases and cut-crystal bottles, and she passed a wet bar with glass shelves loaded with amazing glassware, wine glasses with blue crystal bowls and silver stems and highball glasses like ice sculptures.

White velvet upholstery as soft as a puppy's tummy invited her touch, and the dark walnut wood kept everything from becoming eye-blindingly ethereal. Even the sconces on the wall were covered in crystal: crystal drops, crystal scales, and crystal-beaded shades.

Nicole knew she was gawking but couldn't seem to stop. "Kingston?"

"Yes, my little engineer?"

"I brought some sundresses and that little black dress that I wore to our first date, but maybe we could go somewhere a little more casual? I don't think my on-sale finds from TJ Maxx will cut it here."

He walked over to her again and stared down at her, a small, fond smile lifting one side of his mouth. "You could be dressed in a tattered bathrobe and bunny slippers, and I would still find you beautiful."

Her body warmed under his gaze. "I appreciate that, and that's lovely, but other people won't. It's not fun being underdressed."

"Wear that sexy black dress tonight. It is perfectly appropriate for the hotel restaurant. If you would like some other clothes, we can pick up some other dresses for the rest of the week if you want."

"I'm an Oceanside, California girl. I know more about surfboards than haute couture. Seriously, ask me if I'd rather have a F-One Mitu Pro Bamboo board or a Jimmy Lewis Stiletto because the answer is it depends on what kind of waves you're going to ride."

He tilted his head and then ran his hands down her arms. "A whole new dimension to my little engineer. I like it. But more to the point, they have professional shoppers at the hotel. We can arrange for someone to make appointments and escort you to boutiques who will know exactly how to put you together. Would that be acceptable?"

"I suppose. I feel like I should know how to buy a dress because I'm a girl, but I suppose even an engineer doesn't know everything."

He walked over to the wet bar along one wall and poured himself one finger of whiskey. The crystal highball glass caught the setting sunlight streaming in through the windows. "I'll arrange it for tomorrow morning and afternoon. I have a quick meeting, anyway."

"Is that where you get your suits? You have a hotel personal shopper like that who takes you around?"

The glass was almost to his mouth, and he mentioned, "I

have a tailor in London," and slid the whiskey into his mouth.

"*You do?* Does Sidewinder sell that many golf clubs in England?"

The whiskey must've caught in Kingston's throat because he coughed a little before he said, "Scotland. I tend to travel to Scotland, where wealthy golfers from all over the world go. I stop in London on the way."

"Oh. That makes sense."

"Let's hope so. All right, dinner reservations in just over forty-five minutes. I'll take this bathroom and clean up."

"I can wait until you get out of the shower."

"All these suites here have two bathrooms. Toddle along, my little engineer."

Nicole toddled along, and she did her make-up as carefully as she'd ever done it, trying hard.

Supper was perfect, just like always, with Nicole casting glances around them and Kingston looking at her.

The high floor of the hotel looked down on the sparkling diamond and ruby strands of Manhattan traffic in the black velvet night.

The Grand Salon restaurant glowed with twinkling crystal.

Blood-red drops studded the white-crystal chandeliers, and topiary spheres covered in gem-red roses, from basketball- to beach ball-size, stood on tables, sweetly scenting the air.

This menu had prices, *high* prices, prices for the salads like Nicole would have paid for a whole *nice* meal including drink, tax, and tip.

She tried ordering a watermelon and tomato salad, but Kingston wouldn't have it. "Do you want vegetarian, fish, chicken, or beef?"

"I'm fine. We ate on the plane," she insisted.

"Six hours ago. We ate on the plane six hours ago. I won't force-feed you, but I distinctly heard your stomach grumble when we walked in. I was wondering if I should have had room service waiting."

"Oh, no. No, I'm fine," she reassured him. "I just don't need a meal like this one."

He cocked his head and stared hard at her. "Like this one, how?"

"Like—" She leaned over the table at him and whispered. "—*these prices.*"

Kingston snorted mildly. "Stop looking at the numbers. Get what you want, or else I'll order the Wagyu Steak Frites for you. That's what I'll probably get. I know you like a steak occasionally."

That was just a downright threat.

The Wagyu was the most expensive thing on the menu, of course. She could have taken six people out to eat at her favorite Mexican restaurant for the same amount of money as just one order of the Wagyu.

He looked over the top of the menu at her, and his voice lowered. "Tell me what you want to eat."

Nicole took one more glance at the menu, but she'd already been eyeing what sounded good. "The cavatelli with shrimp."

It wasn't the cheapest thing on the menu, which would have aroused his suspicion, but it was less than half the price of the Wagyu.

And it sounded good.

"Excellent choice."

He signaled to a waiter and ordered for her, then added the Wagyu for himself, and then he spoke a bunch of French that Nicole didn't catch.

When the waiter was gone, Nicole said, "You really ordered the Wagyu beef."

"Proper Wagyu beef is an excellent dish. The chef here does it exceptionally well. You should try a bite."

The waiter was back with a napkin-draped wine bottle, which he twisted the cork out of with a champagne-distinctive *pop,* and then poured the pale wine that sparkled like the crystal around them into the flutes beside their plates.

It was yummy.

After their salads—the summery watermelon and definitely heirloom tomatoes were exceptional and slightly spicy from red chili—she tried a bite of his beef.

The Wagyu steak was exquisite, tender without being mushy, earthy and meaty without being too strong, and the sear was almost sweet on her tongue.

Nicole's eyes popped open.

She didn't think she'd ever be able to eat a regular ol' ribeye again.

Kingston was watching her, his fork held in the air between them.

"Yeah, it's good," she said.

He casually switched their plates.

"No, no, no! I didn't mean that! It was just a really good bite. I'm sure I'll like the pasta and shrimp, too. That's what I ordered."

"You will eat," he said quietly, forking a bite of her pasta into his mouth.

And then he looked at the plate with the slightest raised-eyebrow surprise. And then he ate another bite, this time with a shrimp, and made a little " Hmmm" sound.

Yeah, okay. Nicole was outfoxed.

She ate the insanely good Wagyu beef fillet with its fantastic crisp-outside, fluffy-inside steak fries, and a lemony herb sauce that somehow, *impossibly,* made it all even better.

This meal would probably be the best food Nicole would ever eat in her life, so she tasted and chewed every bite, noting how this bite was a little more rare and tender, that one was a little more crisp, and so on.

Her tongue absorbed every flavor out of the food, savoring it.

Kingston's smile at her was too knowing as she tucked the last bite of steak fry in her mouth, biting down on the fantastic potato goodness.

Around the fry, she demanded, "What?"

He shook his head and went back to his shrimp. "Nothing. Just glad you enjoyed it."

"That obvious?"

"The Wagyu is known to be good. I don't think anyone would disagree with you."

"It was a really good steak."

"I just hope I can make you moan like that later tonight."

Oh, dear God. "You're joking."

"Mostly."

"Are you sure you're not the oldest child? This sort of thing is exactly how I keep my younger brother in his place. I mean, not with S-E-X-Y jokes, but you know, keep him humble."

Kingston didn't flinch. "I'm not an oldest child."

"What are you, then, birth-order-wise?"

He looked up. "Ah, the dessert menus."

"Oh, I couldn't," Nicole protested, both because of the meat and potatoes she'd eaten but also from mentally adding up the bill from the salads and the shrimp and the Wagyu-flippin'-beef and the several bottles of champagne and the who-knew-what-else. "I'm stuffed."

"Just a bite," Kingston said. "Sorbets, maybe? We could share."

The menu said the sorbet was only eight bucks. "Okay."

"Great." To the waiter, "We'll split the Summer Sundae."

Which was *thirty-four bucks,* not the single scoop. "Whoa!"

He still spoke to the waiter and lifted the champagne bottle half-out of the silver ice bucket. "And another bottle of this in the room, and we'd like the candlelight turndown service."

"Yes, sir." The waiter looked between Nicole and Kingston, and then he angled his body forward, asking, "Special occasion?"

"Just for us," Kingston told him.

"Ah. I'll bring the sundae and arrange the rest."

Kingston turned back to Nicole. "You'll love the strawberry yuzu sorbet in the sundae. Trust me."

And she *did.*

And the Alphonso mango sorbet.

And the creamy sauce— "What is this?"

"Coconut cardamom caramel," Kingston told her.

"Okay, *wow.*"

And the teeny fruity sandwich cookies were amazing, too.

"Mini macarons," Kingston clarified.

And more champagne.

The napkin-twisted *pop* made her head spin and her mouth water.

Nicole liked champagne, sure enough, but each bottle tasted a little different, a little sweeter, tarter, or citrus-y-er.

"You're going to have to carry me upstairs," she told Kingston.

His smile, a little fuzzy from the champagne, sharpened. "Promises, promises."

"Yeah, well, word to the wise, put pressure on my tummy at your own risk. I have overindulged on *everything.* This is too much."

Later, she would believe the champagne made her say it. And him.

Nicole sighed. "Look, Kingston, I have to ask, are you maxing out your credit cards to stay at places like this, and at the Four Seasons in SoCal, and the plane, and that resort in Carmel, and the sporty rental cars?"

He smirked a tad and glanced up at her. "Don't worry about it."

Nicole continued, her voice low so the richie-riches around them wouldn't hear her. "We can eat at a taco truck because I know all the good ones in Oceanside and Carlsbad, and you can crash at my place when you're in SoCal. You don't have to take me to fancy places. You don't have to do all this." Her breath caught, but she pressed on. "I like you for *you.*"

She saw the moment her words hit him.

He froze.

Kingston had just reached for his tall glass of champagne and was on the verge of lifting it, and he froze.

His watch was half-peeking out of his shirt cuff, which was just a half-inch of pristine white below the dark sleeve of his suit jacket, and it twinkled like the crystal around them.

Two quick heartbeats later, he lifted the glass and sipped, then set it down.

The base of his crystal glass rang as it tapped the bread plate.

Kingston looked up at her slowly, his blue eyes so still

that Nicole had an intuition flash that she was about to be broken up with, but he said, "I love you, my little engineer. You have absolutely enthralled me. Be reassured, I am not 'maxing' out my credit cards, but I would, to give you anything you wanted. I am all too aware that I am teetering on the brink of destroying everything I have because I would rather lay it at your feet than do what must be done."

38

CANDLELIGHT
NICOLE LAMB

In the elevator, Kingston spun Nicole around again, pressing her back against the wall in an echo of a moment months before, but this time, his kiss was gentle, savoring, and she was wet-plaster flat against the wall as she gave herself up to him kissing her.

When they'd been sitting at the table, Nicole had drawn a breath to say it back to him, but Kingston had already stood up and holding out his hand. "Come."

"Kingston, I—*wait.* I'm trying to say—"

"Upstairs," he said, still smiling. "Now."

Her resistance was washed away by his words, the champagne, and her whirling thoughts.

Through the lobby, "Kingston, wait. Stop."

"Keep walking."

And she did.

Because he told her to, and he'd conditioned her to, she thought later.

In the elevator, her heart was full to bursting, but he kissed her so thoroughly but gently, that her soul hungered for him and her body was ravenous—

Her mind lived only for the touch of his lips, his hand pinning her wrist to the wall above her head, his other hand on her waist, steadying her.

Yeah, this was what it was like to swoon.

A wave of his phone at the door, and they were inside the suite, candles burning *everywhere.*

The flickering candlelight caught and rebounded and sparkled in the crystal and in the air, exquisite and glorious to even Nicole, who was stumbling as Kingston lifted her in his arms like he was a knight and she was a lady and carried her to the bedroom.

"Are you too drunk on the champagne?" he asked, his mouth against her neck as he lay her down on the wide bed.

"Only in a good way," she said, sighing at the shimmering chandelier above the bed with only the tiniest filaments glowing in the bulbs. "Not too drunk at all. Are you?"

"Not too much," he whispered, his words shivering against her skin. "And only for you."

The candlelight and his words enchanted the last bit of rationality from her mind. "Oh, Kingston. Please, I love—"

"Not now," he said, covering her mouth and sealing her words inside. "Later."

She tugged his hand away. "You're not letting me speak."

"I know, but not now," he told her. "Not yet. Think before you say anything. You need to think about *everything* before you do it. Think about this. Think about *me.*"

She *was.*

And she *did.*

Her mind was filled with him, this moment, the sensation of his body as he shed his clothes and hers, and their skin slipping together.

In the flickering ambient glow of the candles, his body was strong and beautiful, wrapped with muscle and sinew, languid in movement like she was, his mouth slow like trickling water over her breasts, down her stomach, between her thighs.

Kingston licked her slowly, first over her folds, then deeper, parting her. The roughness of his tongue drove her to heights, to arch and wind her fingers into his hair, to gasp as he rubbed through her.

When she writhed, almost crying out, he crawled up her body, his dark hair messy over his forehead and his eyes glazed with desire, and he lifted one of her legs over his broad shoulder and filled her, so hard, so thick inside, that her body was pushed farther toward the brink.

He lay down on her, covering her body with his, and wrapped his arms under her shoulders, holding her as they moved together.

Each surge of Kingston's body into hers crested her higher, decimated her mind and her will further until she was crying out, begging him, dying for him. He drove harder into her, and she was shattered into shards and candlelight, holding him while he trembled, his breath harsh on her throat.

He gathered her against his chest, holding her, the world still spinning.

Nicole cuddled into his warmth, trying to sleep because unconsciousness would be the perfect end to this night, but midnight in New York was only eight o'clock in California.

She whispered, "Kingston?"

His arm curled, rolling her more tightly against him. "Yes."

Candlelight still washed over them like the glow from faerie lights. "This was beautiful. Amazing."

"I'm glad."

"Kingston, I lo—"

"Don't say it now." His voice lowered, but she could hear his smile in it. "Don't make me spank you."

"This emotional edging is kind of hot."

He chuckled. "Okay."

"Fine." She slithered sideways and ended up lying on his chest, her arms folded under her chin and staring into his amused eyes. "Then tell me something."

"Like what?"

"Anything. Something *real.*"

"Real. That's a tall order."

"Real," she said. "Tell me about your family."

He shifted her off of him and started to roll toward the side of the bed. "I've got a better idea. We have a bottle of champagne in the next room, and the ice is surely melting."

"Kingston!"

His head dropped before he turned and looked at her over his strong shoulder, a mild smile softening his face. "Yes?"

"This is—" She tried to come up with the right word. "This is scaring me. We've been—whatever this is—this off-and-on thing—for a while. For four months. We seem to be moving forward—traveling together, spending weekends together—but there are vast tracts of unknown territory in you. When I ask you about some things, it's like I come to a barrier, a wall, and it's absolute."

He nodded. "Boundaries."

"Okay. I—*okay.*" Nicole was from California. Everyone she knew had been in therapy at some point. "I understand boundaries, but this doesn't feel like boundaries. This feels like you're hiding things from me, a lot of things. It feels like *bad* things."

He turned around on the bed, sitting with his long legs

crossed and the covers pulled up to his waist. "Please stop asking."

Worry for him warred with fear for herself.

Nicole had terrible taste in men.

She knew this. Arvind and some of her high school friends had joked that they should vet any possible boyfriends before Nicole started seriously dating them because she always fell for the wrong guy.

The wrong guy had bad secrets, like a wife, kids, a house, and an actual dog, a Pomeranian.

The wrong guy devastated her heart and her soul. Craig had broken her soul because he'd lied to her, and he'd cheated on his wife *with* her. He'd made her into a home-wrecker, a cheater, too.

A smarter woman would have seen the red flags waving from the ramparts, but Nicole had had her eyes on the fairy tale castle.

Until Craig's wife had called Nicole's cell phone and called her a cheating scum.

And after Arvind had done a little internet stalking for her, Nicole had texted Craig that it was over and never seen him again, not when he'd said he could explain, not when he'd called her a dumb bitch and she'd known what she was doing.

Because she'd been in love.

Falling for another guy who wasn't who he said he was would be stupid.

"I need to know what's going on with you," she said.

Kingston blinked and looked up at the ceiling, breaking eye contact with her. "I don't want to end the night like this."

"Like *what*?" she demanded.

39

VULNERABLE
KINGSTON MOORE

Placating her was Kingston's foremost thought.

Nicole was right. They weren't boundaries. They were walls, and they were there for a reason.

Don't say it. Please don't say it. Please don't utter it, ever.

The world is a finite place, a means to an end that were ends to the end, ideas and connections and people and worlds that die.

The words like broken teeth that had come tumbling out of his mouth at the end of supper were all the pain he could withstand.

No more, he silently begged her. *No more.*

"This isn't fair, Kingston. I've let you into my whole life," Nicole said, her dark eyes haunted. "You've invaded where I work, my friends I hang out with, heard my thoughts, and know my dreams. I've offered to take you to Sunday dinner at my parents' house, but you always have to fly back to Connecticut on Sunday afternoon."

"Yes," he said. It was all true.

"But you are an enigma wrapped in a mystery locked in a secret box."

"You know some things," he said.

'I know you went to boarding school and have some friends from there. You're good at golf, and you've golfed a lot of places. You have some mysterious connection to Last Chance, Inc., and you've said you're not a spy for them."

"Yes."

"But there's a black cavern beyond that. I'm beginning to feel like I must be a chatterbox if I've talked so much all this time that you haven't been able to get a word in edgewise to tell me anything."

"That's not true."

"I'm beginning to think I've screwed up *again*, that the reason I don't know anything about you is because you're a cheater or in the mafia or something."

How often had she used the word *cheater* to mean the worst betrayal she could think of?

That cad had destroyed her trust.

Kingston wasn't the right guy to mend it.

He kept his breathing calm, and his racing mind slowed. "You want to be let into my life more."

"Yes!"

"I'm not a cheater," he told her, catching her gaze with his. "I told you I'm not married or in a relationship with anyone but you. I meant it."

She nodded, but tears lined her dark eyes in the candlelight.

Kingston half-rolled and leaned over the edge of the bed, the mattress sagging where he was reaching, and grabbed his trousers on the floor to get his phone.

The time on the face read one o'clock, Eastern Time.

He tapped the phone icon and then the top on the recent-call list, putting the call on the speaker.

Nicole watched him, looking from him to the phone, her worry widening her eyes.

After the ringing, a man's rasping voice. "Hello? Kingston? You okay?"

Kingston said, "Are you in the city yet for the Javits Center golf show this week?"

"I was planning on catching the train at ten tomorrow morning," he said, his voice low. *"This* morning, I mean. Do you know what time it is?"

"Sorry about the time. I'm still on a West Coast schedule. You want to have lunch tomorrow?"

"Uh—sure?"

"There's someone I want you to meet," Kingston said, looking straight into Nicole's eyes.

She blinked, and her luscious lips dropped open a little.

"Yeah, whatever. Okay. I'm going back to sleep, Skins. Text me where and when." *Click.*

Nicole raised one eyebrow. "Skins?"

This, Kingston could tell her. "My high school nickname was Skins. I discovered the gym during my sophomore year of upper school and played rugby on my school's travel team. You know, *murderball.* I bulked up early, and people noticed I was always on the 'skins' team during pick-up games of absolutely anything because I was fifteen and wanted to show off."

The funny little light he loved returned to her eyes.

"Rugby. Nickname. And lunch with a friend of yours."

"Yes."

She sat back on the bed a little. "Okay, *for now.*"

"I need to text Morrissey to tell him where our reservation is."

Nicole looked off, and her head bobbled oddly as she asked, "Morrissey? Like Jim Morrissey?"

"Morrissey Sand."

"Oh, okay."

Kingston texted Morrissey, *Rao's, noon. DONT mention Im Last Chance. Just a sales guy at Sidewinder, but you know me from boarding school. You helped me get job at SG. *Not kidding.**

NOTHING about my parents etc.

40

LUNCH WITH MORRISSEY
NICOLE LAMB

The next day at noon, Nicole sat across a round table from Morrissey Sand.

Kingston sat between them and had introduced them, but he seemed a little distant, like he knew they weren't there to talk to him.

Morrissey's pale blue eyes didn't miss a thing, from her ringless hands when they shook to her cheap sundress from two years before. He watched how she awkwardly scooted in the chair Kingston held for her and fumbled with the thick menu.

Calculating. That's the word that came to Nicole's mind when she looked at his dark hair, loose and framing his face, and cold eyes: *calculating.*

All her mistakes and secrets rose in her mind, and she wondered if Morrissey Sand could pick them right out of her gray matter and examine them. "Hi, it's nice to meet you."

Morrissey's gaze raked over her like he was quantifying everything from her IQ to her cup size. "Likewise."

After they'd ordered, Morrissey said to her, "So you asked to meet someone who knows him."

"Well, yeah." Way to put her on the spot. "I didn't think he'd tell you that, though."

"Kingston knows it's best to tell me how to behave."

She wasn't going to be passed around Kingston's friend group like a hot potato. "Otherwise, you might try to pick me up?"

"No. Otherwise, I might discuss coefficients of restitution with you the whole time and not get around to answering your real questions."

"Are you an engineer?" she asked him, suddenly leaning in.

"Lawyer," Morrissey said. "But my undergraduate degree was in physics."

"That's an interesting combination. Why?"

He shrugged. "I didn't want to get a graduate degree in physics or math and end up working in the evil mines for Goldman Sachs."

"So, you're a venture capitalist instead," she said.

His sharp glance at her was gratifying, and an amused smile tugged at his lips. He turned to Kingston, "I like this one."

An opening. "Are *you* Sidewinder's new owner?"

"I'm a partner at Last Chance, Inc.," he said. "Last Chance owns Sidewinder Golf."

"So you do own it."

"One of four. I only occasionally consult on the project."

"Then who's the owner?"

"Last Chance."

Nicole kept her gaze level, but inside, she was rolling her eyes so hard that she saw her own brain. "And who owns Last Chance?"

"Jericho Parr, Mitchell Saltonstall, myself, and a silent investor," Morrissey said.

Nicole looked askance at him with a tilt of her head and a stare from under her eyelashes. "Silent investors are always shady."

His prim smile was pressed and small. "I couldn't agree more."

"And who's making the decisions for Sidewinder?"

"We're all on the hook if Sidewinder fails."

"But there's one owner who's in charge."

"Yes."

"The silent one."

Morrissey drew the word out, but he was still smiling. "Yes."

"Can I meet the owner?"

"He's shy."

"So it's the silent investor, who isn't so silent if he's making decisions for Sidewinder."

"I'm afraid I'm not at liberty to discuss this matter further."

Yeah, this guy was a lawyer, all right. "Do you often meet Kingston's dates?"

"Not often," Morrissey said. "Only once, five years ago."

"And what happened to her?"

This time, the sharp glance was at Kingston before Morrissey answered Nicole. "It didn't work out."

"Because—"

"Because she was too immature to let Kingston have his quirks. Everyone who grows up in boarding school is a bit— *odd*. We're overly reliant on our friends, and none of us had proper parental figures."

Kingston's fork clattered on his plate. *"Morrissey,"* Kingston said, his low hiss a warning.

Nicole glanced at Kingston. His face was immobile as stone, eyes locked on Morrissey.

Morrissey waved him off and turned back to Nicole. "Michelangela was the younger sister of our friend from boarding school, though she attended day school in Naples rather than boarded at Le Rosey. It wouldn't have worked out unless Kingston wanted to join the mafia."

Kingston coughed into the glass of water he'd been drinking. "*Morrissey,* the *restaurant* we're in."

Morrissey waved him off. "But the breakup was several years ago and amicable, which is good because otherwise ol' Skins here might've died in a car bomb."

Being cussed out suddenly felt less threatening than other possibilities. "Michelangela isn't going to take offense if Kingston starts dating someone else, is she?"

Morrissey chuckled. "She's rabidly in love with someone her brother considers more suitable. And then there was Emily Saltonstall."

Kingston scowled at him. "Jesus, Sand. Don't make that into something gross."

"You were the one who dated the girl when you were twenty-four, and she was only sixteen."

Kingston rolled his eyes and turned to Nicole. "Emily is the younger sister of Mitchell Saltonstall, also of Last Chance. She has Down's Syndrome. Mitchell took her to every dance at her school, but when she was sixteen, she insisted that she wanted a *real* date. I got her a wrist corsage and played gallant knight for an afternoon. Her dad *drove* us to the dance and picked us up."

"And then he ghosted her," Morrissey said.

"Jeez, I knew I should've asked Jericho to meet Nicole." He turned to her. "Emily thought I was *too old* and got a boyfriend from her school for the next dance."

"Aw, that's sweet," Nicole said.

Morrissey tweaked Kingston's ear. "Yes, *so sweet.*"

"Please don't," Kingston said. "He'll never shut up about it."

Nicole watched them squabble like siblings.

Kingston had let her meet someone who truly knew him. Found family rather than genetic, but family nevertheless.

She asked Morrissey, "Who else has he dated? And did it end horribly?"

He laughed, but it was a sardonic chuff. "No one he's ever brought home to meet us, so I can only assume it was something tawdry and embarrassing. You're a breath of fresh air."

Jump in now. "But he's never been married or anything?"

"Dear Lord, no. All four of us are confirmed bachelors, I'm afraid, in the new sense of the word, meaning we haven't found women who love us more than their peace. We're too wrapped up in our work at Last Chance to be decent husband material."

Opening. "You said Kingston didn't work at Last Chance."

"I did."

"But you said the four of you."

"The four of us from boarding school. Kingston wasn't in a position to comfortably finance a stake in Last Chance, even with his trust fund. Thus, the silent investor is our fourth. But Kingston is more my brother than anyone else in the world."

"So Kingston works for you?"

Morrissey steepled his fingers and looked over them at her. "No, Kingston doesn't work *for* me. He's an employee of Sidewinder Golf. He's my childhood friend who I trust to go into companies that are *highly at risk—*"

Morrissey's pointed squint at her conveyed the serious-ness of being *highly at risk.*

"—and improve their bottom line by beefing up their sales figures fast. He's saved several companies from a quick liquidation after we became aware of fraud during the sale, like Sidewinder. He seems to think Sidewinder is worth saving, though I can't figure out why for the life of me. The math doesn't math, if you catch my drift."

His drift was that Nicole and all her friends might be unemployed next week if Morrissey Sand stopped listening to Kingston.

Morrissey continued, "Kingston's good opinion is the only thing standing between Sidewinder and my recom-mendation. That, and some magic golf club that he insists will change everything if it ever gets out of R&D." His stare pinned Nicole to her chair. "You wouldn't know anything about a magic driver, would you?"

She swallowed hard just as the waitress settled a round dish of pasta with garlic-fragrant red sauce in front of her. "Sidewinder's research and development group is meticu-lous, and it shows."

"Yes, well, let's hope R&D releases those magic clubs to commercialization sooner rather than later, for all our sakes. All the owners at Last Chance are getting antsy about seeing the turnaround, and the situation is becoming dire."

The copious pasta carbs and then main dishes soothed the tension as they ate, and by the time Morrissey left for his next meeting an hour later, he seemed fine. "Lovely crossing swords with you. I'm not often kept on my toes."

When he was gone, Nicole turned to Kingston. "He's intense."

Kingston sawed another bite of his meal. "He had a Bloody Mary or two with breakfast on the train. That was happy-drunk Morrissey. You should see him when he's sober."

"Well, those Last Chance guys had better not be holding their breath for me to release the Excalibur driver and the Vorpal irons. They're *months* away from release, maybe a year or more."

Kingston's voice sounded like he was choking on his lemon chicken. "Months? *Still?*"

Nicole folded her napkin and tucked it under the side of her plate. "Yeah. I mean, signing off on them wouldn't be right until they're *perfect*. You don't build a reputation like Sidewinder's by slapping together some cheesy clubs and tossing them onto the market for quick cash."

"Yes, but these clubs have been in development for well over two years. The situation is serious."

"Rushing things is never the right decision," Nicole said.

"So you won't release them for commercialization anytime soon."

"I *can't*," she told him.

41

SAVING SIDEWINDER
KINGSTON MOORE

Nicole was asleep in the bed beside Kingston, her breath light on her pillow.

But Kingston couldn't sleep.

Above the bed, the Baccarat chandelier caught the twinkles from the city outside the glass wall, and he watched sparkles play through the hanging crystals.

He'd been a success as a man that day, squiring his little engineer around New York, showing her the Rockefeller Center in a private tour and then taking in *Wicked* that night, which she'd loved. His lady was happy and happily exhausted, unconscious beside him, her skin as velvet as rose petals under his fingers that night.

The air conditioner turned on, whispering cool air across his face and into his hair.

His mind replayed the conversation between Nicole and Morrissey, which he'd observed nearly in silence.

Morrissey hadn't exactly lied to Nicole, but he'd skirted the truth as only a lawyer could and then misdirected her into a conversation about Kingston's few relationships. The absolute truth was that Kingston didn't bring women home to meet his friends.

None of them did, particularly.

But Morrissey's most pointed comments had been directed straight at Kingston, even though he'd supposedly said them to Nicole.

We're all on the hook if Sidewinder fails.

Yes, they were. The end of the bet with Gabriel Fish was just over three months away, when the value of the companies would be tallied and the winner determined.

Kingston carefully rolled over, the sheets cool under his hip and legs again.

Nicole didn't stir, her sighing breath unchanged.

Morrissey had said, *We're overly reliant on our friends, and none of us had proper parental figures.*

A double-edged comment the size of a two-handed broadsword.

—My childhood friend who I trust to go into companies that are highly at risk—

Yes, Kingston was the hero who saved companies by jousting with the dragons of insolvency and inefficiency. He raised them from the dead like a mage.

Kingston's good opinion is the only thing standing between Sidewinder and immediate closure.

It was.

And Kingston's opinion *was* the only thing saving them, not logic or business sense, because—

The math doesn't math.

Morrissey was telling Kingston he was fucking it up.

If he'd said that during the meeting with Jericho and Mitchell, they'd have known what a fuck-up Kingston was. Morrissey had let him save face, but he was telling him his real opinion of Sidewinder Golf.

The math doesn't math.

Morrissey was right. It didn't.

Sidewinder was a failing company circling the drain if you calculated the math using only the scheduled products and employees Sidewinder had.

Last Chance was shoveling good money after bad into the company.

For any other business deal, Kingston would have insisted they terminate Sidewinder immediately. It was a money pit.

A gaping, sucking chest wound of a money pit.

Morrissey, Jericho, and Mitchell were relying on Kingston to win the damn bet.

Jericho was the spreadsheet king of fundamentals who could lay down a solid ROI for decades.

Mitchell found hidden value in companies and utilized it with creativity that was unseen in usual business dealings.

Morrissey and his legal skills could rip apart a business plan or a contract and analyze it like an equation, understanding exactly where the most minor loopholes could be exploited.

But Kingston was the sharpshooter business guy, the assassin, the one who could spy long-range business deals like he had a sniper's scope, the one who made the thousand-fold deals on the regular, the one everyone thought had *the chance* to win the bet.

And he was fucking it up.

Kingston knew it. He'd admitted it to Nicole the night before.

I am all too aware that I am teetering on the brink of destroying everything I have because I would rather lay it at your feet than do what must be done.

But he didn't think Morrissey and the guys knew it.

In his stupor, in his romantic detachment from reality, he'd lost track of time.

And time was running out.

Kingston had delayed as long as he could, longer than he should have, waiting for Sidewinder's bottom line to change.

It hadn't.

Liquidating Sidewinder would result in a loss, which meant there was no way he could win the Shark's bet.

Kingston rolled off the bed, landing on the floor with his toes, and pulled on his pants and the fluffy hotel robe wadded up on the floor.

Pressing the bedroom door closed so he didn't wake Nicole up was simple.

Pulling her laptop computer out of her backpack on the coffee table and logging in with his all-access administrator account and password was easier still.

He stood, paced.

Kingston splashed thirty-year-old Macallen into a cut-crystal highball glass, sharp against his fingers and palm, from one of the standing wet bars and sat in the living room on one of the velvet couches, warm in his robe.

The smoky scotch burned his tongue and throat like his soul was on fire.

Kingston had every right to do this. He *owned* Sidewinder Golf and every scrap of its intellectual property. Nicole's standardized contract specifically said that all golf-associated products, prototypes, ideas, schematics, or knowledge were treated as work-for-hire. Thus Sidewinder Golf owned *everything* she came up with.

He settled her laptop on his legs and his fingertips on the keys.

His teeth grated in his jaws, molars clenched against molars, straining.

Her filing system was organized and straightforward, an engineering schema, not a businessman's schemes.

The folder labeled *Experimental Designs* was obvious, and the subfolders *Excalibur Driver, Vorpal Irons,* and *Khanda Putter* held specs, CAD drawings, spreadsheets, and metallurgy data.

He uploaded all of them to his owner's private vault in Sidewinder's cloud storage service and texted Morrissey.

No more delays. Get the Dali Manufacturing plant on the line. I reserved space with them in April. We're cranking out a whole new line in time for the Vegas PGA Show in December with deliveries before Christmas.

We'll call it the Legendary line.

And we're expanding. The Rattler line will go into retail big box stores. Dali should be able to start making them this week. And fuck the slow boats. We need them for October when people start buying Christmas presents. Put them on planes.

We're going to destroy Titleist and TaylorMade's market share.

Even though it was after two in the morning, Morrissey's text came back immediately.

Atta boy.

The first part of winning the bet was in motion.

Kingston just needed to draft a memo for Sidewinder to go out next Monday on his own company laptop, which he had also brought on the week-long trip to New York.

Nicole's whispered voice behind him asked, "Kingston, what are you doing with my computer?"

42

BETRAYAL
NICOLE LAMB

Nicole had been standing in the doorway from the bedroom for over a minute, wrapped in the Baccarat Hotel's over-floofed robe, watching Kingston stare at the screen of her laptop.

It was definitely *her* laptop.

The desktop image behind the open folders was a pink and lavender high fantasy illustration of swooping dragons and maidens with swords.

When she'd eased the bedroom door open, a green uploading progress bar had just finished and then disappeared.

When she spoke, Kingston's shoulders slumped before he twisted on the couch and looked back at her, his blue eyes wary.

With one step closer, she could see that her Experimental Designs folder was open, and the subfolders with all her plans, specs, and ideas had new green checkmarks beside them, showing that they had been backed up in cloud storage instead of *only* residing on her hard drive.

He'd stolen them.

He'd stolen everything.

She couldn't even talk, couldn't accuse him of what they both knew that he had obviously just done.

If she opened her mouth, she might vomit on the hotel's expensive rug.

If he denied it, she was going to grab the nearest froufrou crystal candlestick and heave it at his head.

To save them both from that, Nicole walked over, plucked her laptop from his unresisting fingers, and slapped it closed. Grabbing her backpack, she stalked back into the bedroom, yanked her frilly pink pajama bottoms over her bare butt, and jammed her feet in the hotel slippers.

With a quick swipe in the bathroom, her birth control pills, toothbrush, and a few of her favorite cosmetics fell into her backpack. She crammed the laptop in the rear compartment made for it.

The sweet little sundresses in her luggage and even her favorite LBD were garbage. She would never wear them again, so she walked out of the bedroom and through the living room toward the suite's front door with just her backpack.

"Nicole!" Kingston called after her.

Her throat was choked closed, and she couldn't answer.

"*Nicole, wait!* I can't book the plane with less than twelve hours notice."

She kept going, the slippers slapping the thick rugs and dark walnut floor and her heels as she half-ran. "I'm going to the airport."

Running footfalls behind her, and Kingston caught up to her, snagging her elbow and his fingers. "Please don't leave."

"Take your hand off of me," she snarled at him, and he let her go. "I don't want to hear your rationalizations. I gave you a chance when I shouldn't have, and you threw it away."

"You heard Morrissey Sand. I've been dancing around the subject for months, but without a huge change, Sidewinder will self-destruct. This is the only way to save the company and everyone's jobs."

"You're trying to save your own reputation as the guy who saves companies, but you're going to destroy Sidewinder if you put those designs into production. *They are not ready yet.*"

"Failure is not an option. I *have* to do this."

"I don't care what you do, but leave me alone. Don't talk to me at work. Do not try to contact me. I am *done* with you."

Nicole marched out of the suite and didn't look back, even when she heard the door click closed behind her.

She caught the elevator down, stewing and replaying the scene in her head the whole way. She should've told him to go to Hell.

A bellhop met her when the elevator doors opened to the lobby. "Mr. Moore has instructed us to arrange a limousine to safely take you to JFK. I cannot recommend that a young lady such as yourself walk the streets of New York City alone after two o'clock in the morning. We are working on getting you an airline ticket to the John Wayne airport. Or would you prefer LAX?"

The barrage of information ricocheted around Nicole's head. "First available, please. San Diego is also fine. Thank you. I have my credit card here. I'll get it."

"Mr. Moore instructed us to put it on his account. There are often six a.m. flights to the West Coast. We'll see what we can book you on. In the meantime, we have a private VIP lounge where sensitive guests can wait if needed. You're welcome to it."

He led her to a discreet door on the lobby's back wall.

Inside was a lounge with couches and a TV high above a mini-bar with alcohol and snacks.

"Can I get you anything to eat or drink or anything to make you more comfortable?"

Service at the Baccarat really was impeccable.

The rage leaked out of her body because this very nice man was not to blame. "No, thank you. I appreciate your help."

The bellhop's slight smile was purely professional. "It happens all the time, ma'am. Please do not hesitate to ask if I can do anything to make these moments more comfortable for you. I can even collect additional items from the room while you wait."

"No, thank you. There's nothing up there I want anymore."

"I understand. Please rest here, and we will have more information about the car service and airplane tickets soon."

Within an hour, a black car drove Nicole through the shockingly empty streets of New York City to JFK airport, where the United desk asked her for her driver's license and then handed her a first-class plane ticket to San Diego.

No, she had no luggage to check.

The security lines were short, and the hotel slippers were easy to slap into a bin on the conveyor belt.

The hotel robe was too fluffy for the X-ray machine to see through, and a very sympathetic TSA agent patted Nicole's shoulders with the backs of her hands and looked under the robe's cowl collar before waving her through.

Crying in first class seemed absolutely ridiculous, so Nicole held it together during the eight-hour flight to San Diego, the Ryde car trip back to her apartment, and until she set her backpack on her threadbare couch.

The time was only one o'clock in the afternoon, and she needed to water her plants.

She connected the engineering marvel of rubber tubing to her kitchen faucet and spooled it outside to the tall towers overflowing with plants, and she took care of them.

As the water dribbled into the black potting soil warmed by the California sun, the gaping hole of loss swallowed her.

43

OOPS

KINGSTON MOORE

onday was set-up day at the Javits Center golf show, and Kingston had been working the cavernous main expo room for three hours with the movers, ensuring the booth was perfect.

This show was Sidewinder's first mega booth, an enormous tent at the end of a row like an English king's battlefield palace. Tables, couches, pamphlets, and three walk-in closet-sized golf simulators had to be perfectly placed.

At lunch, he'd left the Javits to work in his suite for a few hours, catching up on emails about his other three Last Chance project companies he was working on, too, because there was no rest for the wicked. His kingston-moore@lastchanceinc.com email inbox was burgeoning with questions, notes, data spreadsheets, and bad news.

He spent hours dealing with the accumulated problems.

As he plowed through those, the sun finally reached the West Coast, where Nicole and the others would doubtlessly, hopefully, be rolling into the lab by nine in the morning.

The chandeliers above dripping knife-edge crystals, glassware-laden glass shelves lining the walls, and cut-crystal candy dishes standing on the coffee table at his knees sparkled rainbows in the LED lights like Kingston was sitting inside a massive, shattered glass heart.

At his direction, the hotel staff had packed the dresses and things she'd left and shipped them to her address in Carlsbad.

With them gone, the last of her sweet jasmine and vanilla perfume had dissipated, and the suite smelled like liquor and New York City car exhaust.

Finally, he was done with his Last Chance business after neglecting it all weekend.

Time to do what must be done at Sidewinder.

The first email memo was easy.

He logged into Outlook and clicked into his special anonymous email for managing Sidewinder that he now thought of as his "silent partner" account, last-chance-c-suite@lastchanceinc.com, and typed out the email announcing the next round of layoffs two weeks hence.

The tone was terse, but it didn't need to be flowery. The best way to give someone bad news was to be clear and quick about it. Drawing out the suspense or giving people false hope was cruel.

Kingston was many things—a liar, a traitor, a thief, unworthy of trust—but not cruel.

He sent it and then logged into his Sidewinder email account, checking to make sure it had gone through to the company's emails because sending out the layoff notices without a warning shot was a dick move.

Yes, his *October Layoffs* email had hit his Sidewinder inbox.

Good.

He switched back into Outlook and his Last Chance email account, copied and pasted the April employment termination email from a Word docx in the Last Chance server's cloud, changed the dates that people were going to be fired, copied and pasted the email addresses of the people he'd analyzed to be redundant, and sent it.

There.

Done.

Sidewinder Golf was thoroughly on track now, what with Morrissey having done him a solid yesterday by contacting Dali Manufacturing in China and starting the tech transfer process.

The mass production of the Rattler line had already begun, and the sets would be available in giant golf retail stores like Cox Sports and Golf Universe by Halloween.

The prototypes of the Legendary line would be crafted and shipped by plane within two weeks. With a simultaneous submission to the PGA for compliance certification, they'd be taking orders for Excalibur drivers, Vorpal iron sets, and Khanda putters at trade shows for delivery starting at Thanksgiving.

The price was going to be legendary, too. He wasn't holding back on the zeroes.

The Legendary line wasn't going to be just a luxury item. It would be a status symbol, the must-have for every golfing billionaire. No gaudy diamonds or gold on them, either. Nope, the Legendary line would be sleek titanium and steel, understated and tasteful, quiet old-money rich like no-logo baseball caps that cost five grand or outdoorsy coats that cost twenty thousand dollars.

If you knew, you knew.

He'd market them to royals and Vanderbilts, not insecure nouveau riche slobs that flaunted their gauche froufrou so disdained by those who had taste.

Indeed, an email from Dali confirming receipt of the

designs and specs was in his inbox. His gaze swept over it, noting that the delivery dates were correct.

And then he slammed his email shut, slammed the door behind him, and slammed the car door of the hotel's courtesy vehicle to take him back to the Javits for the afternoon.

He might have to move hotels to the Four Seasons or the Intercontinental. Something about the Baccarat was making Kingston's chest feel heavy and giving him a sinus headache.

44

THE SECOND WAVE

NICOLE LAMB

Monday morning, Nicole was back at work at Sidewinder, hanging out in the lab, swathed in white papery Tyvek like a mummy, and hiding her red eyes behind scratched plastic safety glasses.

Everyone had noticed her, said hello, hovered for a moment in case she wanted to process her emotions, and then went off to do their work.

Machines hummed and clanked, and keyboards clicked around the lab.

Arvind had double-swiveled at her when he'd shuffled in. "I thought you were out for the week."

Oh, trust Arvind to poke the grumpy boss-beast.

She couldn't be chipper, so she kept her voice level. "I changed my mind."

Her words came out grim, dang it.

"Well, good," Arvind said, "because I've got a problem with face deformation on the new women's club, the Cascabel."

The Cascabel driver was their new women's low swing

speed driver with a thinner face for more spring when the club hit the ball.

They were running out of good rattlesnake names for their clubs, however. The Cascabel was a South American rattlesnake, along with the Marajoan and the Rupunini.

Rupunini.

No matter that Nicole thought it was a cool name, marketing would not like that one.

Pickin's for names were getting slim.

Within a few years, they were going to have to expand their nomenclature to the rest of the pit viper snakes. Nicole was looking forward to designing a driver that would be named the Copperhead. Excellent name.

"But the Cascabel isn't due for production until next summer," she said to Arvind, confused.

"Yeah, but I've got some data that calls into question whether we should be using our usual glue formulation to attach the driver's face to the body of the club. The face must be thin to get that bounce at low speeds. The failure rate is too high."

Changing glue formulations from their standard recipe would add months and millions of dollars to the club's development. "Oh, no. Let me see."

Every phone and computer in the lab simultaneously beeped or chimed in a flurry of delivered emails like they were living inside a pinball machine.

Everyone looked up, worried eyes meeting through plex-iglass visors or goggles before reaching for their devices.

Nicole's phone screen opened to her glove-thumbed passcode, and a new email at the top of her inbox from last-chance-c-suite@lastchanceinc.com.

The subject line read, *October Layoffs.*

Way to break it gently, buddy. Could that silent investor be any more callous? No wonder no one spoke his name.

As she read the email about the impending second wave of layoffs at Sidewinder, her trembling turned to anger.

Twenty-five percent cuts this time, which meant two or three *more* of her people would be gone.

More pings chimed through the lab.

No more emails showed in Nicole's inbox. "Who got the second email?" Nicole asked the room.

"I did," Selma said, dark eyes narrowed behind her round glasses and visor.

"Who else?"

Arvind raised his eyes from his phone. "Me."

Bobert, the guy who calibrated all their equipment so that it worked, raised a blue-gloved hand.

This was insane. These cuts would make it impossible to do her job.

Last Chance was cutting off the feet and wings of the goose that laid the golden eggs.

"We're not taking this lying down," Nicole said.

The white-clad people turned toward her, facing her with their visors and safety glasses surrounded by their clean suits.

"Lab work is canceled for today," she announced. "I have the boxes of cards in my office. Only eighty-five people are left in this company, and the Last Chance management is offsite. We can walk around the offices and do this out in the open."

The lab techs were swiveling to look at each other, to gauge the reaction of the herd for flight or fight.

"The whole sales team is at the big golf show in New York," Selma said.

"Meghan and Morgan can join when they get back. Ben was wobbly anyway."

And Kingston Moore could take a long walk off a short roof of a New York skyscraper for all she cared.

Really.

"We only need thirty percent of the eight-five employees to sign to be recognized, which is twenty-six people," Nicole said. "The more we get, the better it looks, though. Let's degarb and get those signatures. *Let's go.*"

After they'd all stripped off their rustling paper over-suits in the changing room and the others had marched off to her office to get the cards, Arvind whispered to her, "I was worried today might be your last day."

"Those venture capitalist jerks can't lay *me* off," she said. "I would never answer another question about the dev projects, and then they'd be screwed."

"I was worried you were going to resign because of—you came back early from your—paid time off."

Yeah, Arvind was sharp. "Yeah, well, maybe that would have happened, but not now. I'm going to stay *right the hell here* and *fight* these jerks."

"Ooo," Arvind said. "You said hell."

"Yeah." Nicole grinned at him as she fluffed her hood-flattened hair and re-slicked it back into a ponytail. "I *did.*"

Arvind glanced at his phone again. He was degarbed, so Nicole could see a quizzical frown dip his eyebrows. "That's strange."

"What?"

He showed her the second email.

45

UN-IONIZED

NICOLE LAMB

"No way," Nicole said, sitting in her office chair as her entire lab, accounting, and legal department filed into her office.

Arvind and the other traitors must have narked to the rest of the office about the secret back hallway to get into the lab office corridor, which meant the rest of the staff were going to sneak in and raid the vending machines up here, too.

"This was your idea," Afifa said to Nicole. "I wouldn't have even thought of it."

"I am in research and development," Nicole insisted. "I researched and developed this, and then I handed it off. Someone else needs to market and sell it to Last Chance, Inc. There is no flippin' way I'm going in there with their representative, whoever that is."

The lies stuck in her throat. She knew *exactly* who would be in that room, and she didn't want to see him.

Selma braced her hands on Nicole's desk and leaned over it at her. "Look, I don't care if you need to strap on one of these swords or whatever, but screw your courage to the sticking place and go in there and fight for us."

"Don't quote Shakespeare at me. Shakespeare isn't going to work."

Selma turned to the other twenty people in the office. "Anybody else going to go in there and negotiate for us?"

Nobody uttered a dang word. *Cowards.*

Finally, Arvind said, "I can't. English isn't even my first language."

"You were born in Irvine. You can negotiate as well or better than I can."

"No, I can't. I really can't. I have anxiety."

"You call anxiety a 'white-people problem.' Besides, I'm an engineer. Engineers are notoriously bad at talking to people."

"You're not," Afifa said.

Arvind reached over, grabbed her hand, and tugged, making her bend over to not be pulled out of her chair. "Come on, boss. We need you."

"Any of you can do this. *Selma,* I nominate Selma. You were pre-law for a while before you went into materials science."

"I changed my major because I can't talk in front of people," Selma told her.

"Plus, she's on the reduction in force list. It'll look like she's just trying to save her skin instead of speaking for the group," Arvind said.

Nicole glared up at Arvind. "Conveniently, that lets you out, too."

He grinned at her. "Yup. Up and at 'em, tiger. Let's go."

That's how Nicole found herself propelled at the head of an overeducated and very ruly mob walking down the staircase, their shoes echoing on the cement like herds of horses thundering through the desert.

Afifa told her, "We put their delegation in conference room two because it's the larger one."

"Delegation? I thought it was one representative!" Nicole hissed at her.

"Too late to back out now," Arvind muttered, shoving her through the conference room door and closing it behind her.

Three men sat on the other side of the conference table.

Morrissey Sand.

Some guy she didn't know.

And as she'd absolutely expected, Kingston *doggoneit* Moore.

Her heart clenched just breathing the same air he was.

Nicole looked him right in his bright blue eyes. "Fancy meeting you here, *silent partner.*"

Kingston's shut-tight expression didn't change. "It's good to see you."

"Aren't you supposed to be at a golf show in New York City?" she demanded.

He looked down at his hands lying on the conference table.

That conference table. *Right there,* where his hands were resting, in the *middle* of that long side of the table.

Yep.

He said, "We're flying back this afternoon. I'll be at the show for Friday and the weekend."

"On *Last Chance's* private plane."

"Yes. The plane is Last Chance's private plane."

"Yeah. Huh." Nicole turned around and shoved the door open, startling Arvind and twenty other people lurking out there.

She grabbed Selma by her wrist and yanked her inside. "If I have to negotiate with these jerks, you have to take notes. We need a record of this meeting."

Selma scooted around and sat at the far end of the table, half-sideways, her thumbs at the ready on her phone. "Okay, I'm video-recording it."

Kingston's gaze followed Nicole as she stomped into the room and sat across the table from the three stupidly handsome men.

She tried not to look at Kingston. Every time she did, flashes of him laughing with his head on a white pillow, walking with her barefoot on beaches with his hand holding hers, and that obsessed sharpness in his blue eyes when he took off her clothes dominated her thoughts.

Her body dissolved with longing, wanting to drift across the table as mist and touch him.

"Thank you for coming, Ms. Lamb," Kingston said.

Nicole ignored that and glanced at Selma. "Attendees at this meeting are Nicole Catherine Lamb, designated representative of Fairways and Greens Un-Ionized."

"I thought you formed a union, and this was a union negotiation," Kingston said, frowning at the paperwork littering the table in front of him.

"It is. Unionized and un-ionized are spelled the same way. Since the union started with the engineers and scientists in the lab core, its name is a science joke."

"So it was you," Morrissey said, unsmiling. "I am not at all surprised."

"We'd been talking about a union before Last Chance bought Sidewinder. You guys have to state your names for the record."

Morrissey regarded her with his pale blue, almost gray

eyes. "Morrissey Sand, attorney at law and partner at Last Chance, Inc."

The other guy on the end said, "Jericho Parr, partner at Last Chance, Inc."

Kingston didn't take his eyes off Nicole. "Kingston Moore."

"And your position," she told him, her jaw barely moving.

Then he looked down at the table. "Partner at Last Chance, Inc."

"Yeah," Nicole said. *"Partner."*

"Wait," Selma said, pointing her finger across the table. "He's not our new sales guy?"

"No," Nicole told her, "and he never was. He was on our payroll somehow, but he was a viper in our midst. He was spying for Last Chance the whole time."

"It wasn't like that," he said.

"You thought you were so cool, playing undercover boss while deciding who would lose their jobs, but you made some mistakes."

"The email account for the second email," Kingston said. "I figured it out that night, but it was too late."

"Yeah, once you sent the second email from your Last Chance partner account, *kingston moore* at last chance inc dot com, the ISP made it easier to trace you as a partner. We had info in fifteen minutes."

"I was careless." Kingston looked straight at her. "I was distracted."

"And then you made another mistake," Nicole said. "You sent those layoff emails on Monday, but you didn't file the paperwork with HR to lay people off until yesterday afternoon, Wednesday. We filed our union paperwork with the state Tuesday morning, and the IFPTE recognized us that afternoon as a chapter."

"The International Federation of Professional and Technical Engineers is a union for scientists," Morrissey said, nitpicking. "The admin, accounting, and legal staff wouldn't be covered."

"Sidewinder has been declared an R&D and materials science company for union purposes," Nicole told him. "Our other staff is covered by the same union. You don't want to negotiate with five different unions, do you? Because we will totally talk to each other."

"No," Kingston said. "We accept Fairways and Greens Un-Ionized as the union representing Sidewinder's employees."

"And that means you have to negotiate in good faith," she told them.

"We know labor law," Morrissey said, his tone sharp.

"Looks like you didn't get your Bloody Mary this morning," Nicole said to him. "I was reading it into the record."

Kingston quietly placed his hand on the table in front of Morrissey, who rolled his eyes. "Nicole, let's negotiate in good faith."

"Okay," she said. "First order of business: layoffs. No layoffs until January at the earliest."

"We can't delay it that long," Kingston said. "The second round should have been in July, and I delayed it for no good reason. This company is falling apart. If we don't reduce costs now, Last Chance will have to liquidate Sidewinder."

"Threatening to close a company when the workers join a union violates the National Labor Relations Act. We will report any unfair labor practices to the National Labor Relations Board, and to reiterate, we are recording this meeting."

Morrissey muttered, "She's right."

"Sidewinder's finances have been precarious," Kingston said to Nicole, "and that's a generous way of describing them, for *years*. We aren't closing to avoid unionizing. We might have to close the company because even one more hit would mean insolvency."

"The NLRB won't see it that way," Nicole said.

Morrissey said under his breath to Kingston, "The absolute last thing Last Chance or Sidewinder needs is an NLRB investigation."

Kingston interlaced his fingers and leaned forward. "Sidewinder has to be solvent *now*. Last Chance has been pouring money into it, hoping for a miracle turnaround that didn't happen. The situation is desperate. The layoffs are necessary."

Something wasn't making sense. "Why did you think 'a miracle' would happen when you bought the company? It's been puttering along with the same cash flow for years."

The other guy, Jericho Parr, spoke up. "We were misled by the former owner on two fronts. First, he didn't disclose a lien against the company that we discovered only after the sale."

"That's not our problem. Sue him for fraud," Nicole said.

"It's too late for that and won't fix the bottom line," Jericho said.

"And what was the other thing?" she asked.

Kingston said, "Joe Flanagan said that several innovative new products along the same line as the Scimitar Edge lob wedge were ready for commercialization."

"No, they weren't," Nicole scoffed. "You know that. They're not even close, and they sure as heck weren't close to commercialization in March."

He nodded. "We were misled."

"Well, you shouldn't have been misled. You should've done a site visit or asked R&D about anticipated release dates, not just taken Joe Flanagan's word for it."

"Did you take a vacation in early March?" Kingston asked her.

"Yeah. My college friends and I go down to Cabo every year for spring break. We never got to go while we were in college because we were studying for midterms."

The three Last Chance guys eyed each other.

Kingston said, "My site visit was the first week of March. We met with a white guy named Bode Shultz."

Nicole rolled her eyes so hard she thought she might sprain her eyeballs. "Bode was let go two weeks after I got back because he couldn't do the work. He was a Level-Three Technician and a suck-up. A real sucker for people in authority. He would have said anything Joe told him to."

Kingston leaned back in his chair and pressed his fingers into his eyes. "Sorry, guys."

Morrissey clapped him on the shoulder but spoke to Nicole. "All right, Joe Flanagan's fraud isn't your fault, but now it's all our problem. What are we going to do *now?*"

They were tag-teaming Nicole, and she didn't have any backup. Selma was curled up in the chair like someone might hit her with a club, but she held her phone steady to capture everything that was said.

"Okay," Nicole said. "No matter what has happened in the past, we need to negotiate in good faith now. So, there are no layoffs, and Kingston has to delete the specs and plans he stole off my laptop."

Jericho raised an eyebrow. "What?"

Morrissey shook his head. "That wasn't stealing. Trust me, I'm a lawyer."

"No, Kingston *stole* them," Nicole said, raising her voice because she was *right*. "They were *my* thoughts, *my* plans, *my* ideas and experimental models, and he *stole* them."

"That laptop itself and all intellectual property you

produce during your contracted employment are the sole property of Sidewinder Golf, and we own Sidewinder Golf," Kingston said evenly. "I recovered intellectual property that was not uploaded to the company's cloud servers as your contract specifies it must be."

"You didn't have the right!" she gasped. Stealing them was *such* a violation.

"I did, and I do. Morrissey looked over your contract and our purchase agreement with Joe Flanagan. You should retain counsel if you need the work-for-hire sections of your contract explained to you."

"That's not fair," she said.

"I'm sorry, but it's generally the way business works. We pay you a salary at risk to develop ideas, and the company then owns the patents on those ideas. If you want to go it alone, you have to start your own company."

"Maybe I will," she said, refusing to acknowledge that her nose was burning inside.

"Anything you wrote down, tested, *or thought of* while under contract is Sidewinder's property," he said gently. "In another situation, if you quit a job and immediately started a competing company with a novel idea, your previous company would sue you for the patent, and they'd win easily. I've seen it happen."

"That's not fair," she said, feeling her best ideas slip away.

"I'm sorry it happened that way," Kingston said, "but they always were company property and should have been in the cloud backup. I asked you to hand them over more than once."

"*You* were a random new sales guy."

"I'm going to use them to save Sidewinder. They won't be forgotten. You will be credited on the patents and marketing materials. It would be great for the company if you were the face of R&D for promo."

Nicole shouldn't be whining about her own petty problems, anyway. This negotiation was for all of them to save people's jobs, not her own grievances. "In any case, this is a union negotiation. I reiterate our demands: no layoffs."

"We *have* to cut staff," Kingston said, leaning forward and bracing his arms on the table.

"Fine," Nicole said. "I'm the highest-paid employee at Sidewinder, even more than the lawyers. I'll quit. You don't even have to offer me a package. That'll cut the bottom line."

Kingston literally blinked. "You can't."

"Absolutely, I can. I can find a job and start next week. I'll go build nuclear war machines. Probably not at Electric Boat in Connecticut, though. Maybe I'll go to Virginia."

"Of all the top talent we need to retain, *you* are at the top of the list," Kingston said.

"Hire someone else."

"Nicole, you designed those clubs. No one else knows them like you do."

"So you need me," she said, verifying.

"Yes," Kingston said. "I need you."

"*Sidewinder* needs me," she said.

"—Yes."

"Then that's my price. No layoffs, and I won't quit for thirty days."

"A year," Kingston said.

Morrissey said under his breath to Kingston, "Final tallies are December twenty-eighth."

That was weird. "Two and half months," she said. "Thanksgiving."

"Six months," Kingston said. "No layoffs, and *no one* quits until the end of the year. Full staff."

"First, you want to get rid of a bunch of people. Now, you want to lock everyone into their jobs."

"You will personally stay for six months," Kingston said, "which is March of next year, and this whole company goes on wartime footing until New Year's. We make sure the Rattler line inventory is delivered to the big-box retail golf stores by Halloween."

What on God's green— "The what? We can't manufacture big-box retail quantities of the Rattler line in a month *and* deliver it. That's crazy-talk."

Morrissey asked him, "How much of an investment will Last Chance have to put up for that?"

"That's the deal," Kingston said to Nicole. "If we can't cut the denominator, we have to increase the numerator by *a lot*. Every employee has to pull their weight and then some. I'm not talking about going to China and working on the assembly line—"

A chill passed over her spine. "It's Dali Manufacturing, isn't it? You retained *Dali.*"

He pressed his lips, then said, "They have the capacity. No one else does."

"They're going to swipe our intellectual property. *Your* IP, as you insist, because it's not mine, it's *yours.*"

"It's our *only* shot at the company surviving. That's what it's going to take to save Sidewinder Golf. The Rattler line goes to retail, and the Legendary line becomes our high-end, and I mean *very* high-end, line that goes on order *right now* with delivery by Thanksgiving."

Jericho looked across to Morrissey, who wore a shocked scowl like he'd seen a zombie company shamble across the table, and he asked, "A new elite-level line going into production, *too*? How much is *that* going to cost Last Chance?"

Nicole stopped short, the word *Legendary* echoing in her head. "You want to call it the Legendary line."

Kingston sighed. "It's a great name. If Sidewinder's marketing department doesn't love it, they don't know what they're doing."

"And the prototype names, the Excalibur, the Vorpal irons?"

"And the Khanda putter. We're keeping your names. We can make great golf clubs to live up to them, but it will take *work*. To avoid layoffs, we have to make *both* those things happen at the same time."

"I'm telling you right now, that timeline is insane," she said. "The only reason we got the Scimitar Edge out so quickly was because everything went *perfectly*. There were no snafus, which never happens."

"We need it to happen again."

"You're delusional."

Jericho's spreadsheets rattled as he sorted through them. "We didn't account for a mass-market product *and* an elite-level product going from dev to commercialization. The start-up costs for *two* product lines are going to be astronomical."

"If those Rattler clubs need any modifications for mass manufacturing—" Kingston said to Nicole.

"Oh, they will. They *definitely* will."

"And if there are changes needed for the Legendary line as we're commercializing them—"

"I'll say it again. *Those designs aren't ready.*"

"—you *need* to be here to work on those changes. Six months. Please, Nicole. Sidewinder can't live without you."

His voice choked in the last part of his sentence.

Nicole looked up at him.

Kingston was staring at her, his blue eyes wider, vulnerable, and he was half-leaning on the table. "It will be a challenge like no other. You'll probably never see anything like it again in your professional life."

"Yeah," she said, frowning at her fingers knotted together. "It would be."

"I will personally buy you any sword you want in the whole damn world if we pull this off. I will ask the King of England if he will sell us the knighting sword he uses at investitures, King George the Sixth's Curtana, and I will buy it for you."

"You don't know the King of England," Nicole said, her tone hopefully conveying her obvious dubiousness.

"I know people who do," Kingston said.

"Who?" Jericho asked him.

"That alumnus who teaches that one-credit pragmatic world politics seminar in the summer every other year," Kingston told him. "Arthur Finch-Hatten."

"Oh, yeah," Jericho said. "That guy. There's a rumor that the *real* reason he—"

"But Nicole," Kingston turned back to her. "I need you to stay."

"Seriously, George the Sixth's Curtana," she said.

"I will *try,* but I will get you *anything* you want."

Six months of passing him in the hallways, sitting in meetings at this conference table, and trying to figure out whether she should take the elevator or the stairs to avoid him were going to be torture. "Okay, I'll stay for six months, with a *contract* for zero layoffs until the end of the year."

Jericho spoke up, tapping a printed-out spreadsheet covered with green and red flowing numbers. "With the caveat that the Rattler line must be *delivered* to retailers by Halloween, and the Legendary series beginning delivery to pre-orders by Thanksgiving. Otherwise, the numbers don't work at all. The math doesn't math, and we need to close Sidewinder *immediately* without notice." He glared at Kingston. "Because we need to stop throwing good money after bad, bet or no bet."

Bet?

"But it's a chance," Kingston said, looking straight at Nicole. "If we pull together, we can save Sidewinder."

Selma was staring over her phone at Nicole and nodded.

"Yes," Nicole said. "It's a chance. We agree."

46

BOY COOTIES
KINGSTON MOORE

K ingston took over Joe Flanagan's old office at Sidewinder Golf and signed a short-term lease on an apartment through the end of the year.

Drudgery filled his days, a far cry from when his heart had lifted at walking into the glass-fronted building.

Meetings that included Nicole were the hardest. He was pretty good at keeping his face perfectly composed, quiet and businesslike, but he was burning inside.

She appeared as composed as he was, casually reciting numbers as she flipped through slides and ignoring him better than he would ever be able to ignore her.

After the meetings ended, she grabbed her laptop and scurried out of there as if she had more secret golf club designs on her hard drive to hide, or maybe she just didn't want him getting his paws on it again.

Boy cooties.

Or maybe she didn't want him to betray her again.

That was probably it.

When she left the room, her dark ponytail twitching and her black and white sundress skirt fluttering as she ran out the door, his arm cramped with wanting to lift his hand to reach after her, to explain to her that he was saving Sidewinder Golf for her.

Yes, there was Gabriel Fish's infernal bet and Last Chance, Inc.'s money pouring into Sidewinder, but his heart knew all that was secondary.

He'd blurted out the truth at the restaurant at the Baccarat Hotel, that he was neglecting what he knew he should do to lay the company at her feet. The layoffs were needed to make Sidewinder profitable.

And he knew he was doing it again, but he couldn't stop.

Watching his hands pack his suits into suitcases and zip his golf clubs into their travel case felt like a ghost riding a meat skeleton, but he didn't stop. Running Sidewinder from his office at Last Chance in Connecticut would have worked just fine, yet he'd boarded Last Chance's plane, flown over the farmland and mountains of the continent, and settled in California.

Being near Nicole was addiction and agonizing withdrawal at the same time.

He scanned her every move, analyzing the set of her sweet lips and waves of her graceful arms for an invitation, but nothing ever came.

As the glowing red dot from her laser pointer manically circled digits and traced graphs on her PowerPoint slides, as her skirt hem floated as she turned back to the data she was presenting to the room full of managers, he wondered what kind of panties she was wearing—Lace? Silk? Pink? White? —And how they would look as he hooked his finger around the ribbons around her hips and dragged them down her curvy thighs to her ankles.

With his hand spread on the conference table in the dark, he swore he could feel the heat from her breasts lingering in the wood from when he'd bent her over the edge, holding her there with his hand clamped around the back of her neck, and taken her.

Just a few days before, he'd walked out of his office to see her standing at the door to the copy room, holding a stack of papers and badging herself inside, the pale blue hem of her sundress still waving around her knees.

Longing had choked him so hard that he'd retreated back inside his office and waited until she'd gone inside.

So when he emerged from his office that day in mid-October, looking at his watch to check the time and the unchanging San Diego weather outside the windows, he was preoccupied with ship travel times and the weather in the middle of the Pacific Ocean.

Golfer Magazine had sent a questionnaire about the Excalibur's availability for pre-orders at golf shows. Marketing's description of the driver had seemed staid. Kingston needed to swing the real thing a few times to describe it for the magazine, so he headed up to the golf simulators on the third floor.

He badged himself into the dark simulator room, and the sweet scent of jasmine and vanilla perfume set his blood on fire before he even looked up.

47

A SIMULATION
NICOLE LAMB

The Excalibur driver didn't sound right when it hit a golf ball.

At least, it didn't make the correct sound when Nicole hit a golf ball with it.

The manufacturing prototypes from Dali had arrived via FedEx the night before, and the changes they'd had to make to the club for manufacturing might have messed it up.

Not that it mattered. By spring, just in time for next season, a thousand knock-offs of the club were going to litter the retail golf stores like every drug store's generic Advil, and no one would buy the overpriced real thing.

Nicole lined up another shot with the chubby-headed club, her hands choked down on the grip so far she was nearly holding the club's shaft.

A description she refused to giggle about.

This was golf. This was serious business.

Right up until you remembered it was a game that people wagered stupid amounts of money, betting who could hit a rock into a hole with a stick the fastest.

She tried smacking the ball again.

Tink.

Golf clubs should not go *tink.*

The golf ball smacked into the simulator's screen and dropped to the Astroturf mat, while the virtual ball continued into the blindingly blue sky above the ocean churning on the rocks below.

And a proper golf club striking a ball should make a bright metal-on-ceramic *click,* not a sound like ice cubes dropped in a whiskey class.

At the Baccarat Hotel, when Kingston had poured himself a drink at the minibar in the suite, the diamond-clear ice cubes bouncing in the crystal glass had rung out a *tink* like that.

Her worry over the sound wasn't aesthetic or even marketing. The metal itself had a resonance it shouldn't have, which meant energy was being lost instead of being transferred to the ball, so the ball wouldn't fly as far, and that was indicative of a design flaw.

And she was going to figure out what the heck was wrong with it.

Assuming that the problem wasn't operator error, which it might be.

Nicole still wasn't very good at golf.

Nicole was barely adequate at golf.

Most people who play golf as badly as Nicole did quit.

Which meant the problem might not be within the club but how she was hitting the club.

So, there might not be a problem with the Excalibur. In the hands of a good golfer, a person with enough strength and height to smash this men's-length club the way it should be smashed, there might be no *tink.*

The club might produce a proper bright metallic *click* like a splatter of sparks, like it was supposed to.

Nicole kept hitting the club, trying to figure out whether *it* was the problem or *she* was, and so she didn't look up when the door to the outside world clattered closed somewhere beyond the computer and couches.

She lined up a new ball.

Tink.

Darn it.

Footsteps had stopped behind her, and she didn't even bother to look up because the languid saunter of expensive leather shoes and fresh wood on the thin carpeting had already told her who it was.

"Did you need something, Kingston?" she asked without looking up from the golf ball on the unnaturally green plastic grass in front of her bare toes.

His voice was even and steady, as if he were perfectly in control of his emotions. "I was going to hit a few balls with the Excalibur manufacturing prototype, but I see you beat me to it."

"This is the regular men's length. The long shaft is over in the racks."

"Thank you."

The footsteps walked away, and Nicole sucked long, slow breaths through her nose, trying to calm her fluttering heart.

Adrenaline was the worst thing for golf. Some pros took beta-blockers to regulate their heartbeats as performance-enhancing drugs.

Hitting the ball in that state wouldn't give her any usable data.

Nicole backed up, letting the golf club fall to her side as she stepped away from the ball.

The next simulator's projector whooshed as it initialized, and it cast light into the whole room.

Heck, Kingston had a fantastic swing. In the interest of science and for the good of the company, Nicole should just walk over there and see what sound *his* golf ball made.

Her feet seemed glued to the plastic-prickly fake grass mat under her soles.

Besides, she could listen from over here. It was pretty obvious that when he swung the club, it made a loud—

Crack.

Even accounting for Kingston's much higher swing speed, that didn't sound quite right either, or was the simulator wall between them absorbing some of the sound waves?

Nicole fidgeted, tapping the golf ball back and forth with her too-heavy club.

Crack, and then Kingston made a descending, dissatisfied hum.

Nicole charged around the barrier between the two simulator bays. "You heard it, too. Didn't you?"

Kingston glanced up at her, and fear wormed into Nicole's heart that maybe he hated her.

The flatness in his blue eyes was so different from the warmth and humor that had been there when they were together that Nicole stopped walking.

Maybe his anger at her refusing to hand over the design for the clubs that may very well save Sidewinder from bankruptcy had turned to straight-up distaste.

Kingston looked away and stared at the head of his golf club on the ground next to a ball. "This driver doesn't sound quite like it did that night you and I were locked in here."

"I had to make some changes for manufacturing, and I don't think Dali is producing the same quality as our in-house, hand-crafted prototypes were."

His voice was that same emotionless monotone. "Why was the original design changed?"

"Because there's no way we could make a thousand Excalibur golf club heads on site, which is the goal you set, by Thanksgiving with the old process. There's just no way. Even if we had a hundred blacksmiths pounding on them night and day, it still wouldn't have worked. It had to be mass producible."

Kingston turned the club upside down and examined its fat head and striking surface. "So it's not the same."

"It couldn't be and meet manufacturing deadlines. I'm trying to figure out how to bring the specs closer to the original design before six o'clock tomorrow night, which is when they start work in the morning in Dali. If we can email the new specs and they can cast another one right away and airmail it, I'll have time to look at that one before we finalize the design for the PGA submission."

Kingston nodded. "That's excellent business sense."

"Can I hear you hit it just a few more times? Arvind is analyzing the coefficient of restitution and other specs in the lab, but sometimes hearing its sound gives me more clues as to what is wrong."

Kingston's flash of a glance at her held a shred of humor. "Kind of like the sound of a really good sword in battle?"

"That luxurious swish as you murder your enemy," she quipped back.

His low chuckle made her homesick for joking around as they lounged between cool sheets. "Again, remind me not to be alone with you in your office when you're sharpening your katana."

"The last time didn't go so badly for you."

His glance at her was wary, but as he inhaled and his

shoulders rose, his whole body seemed to swell as he stepped toward her.

What the heckers was she doing?

But she didn't step backward.

Instead, she stepped *toward* Kingston, her freezing body gravitating toward a fire.

In two more long-legged strides, he was reaching for her waist and the back of her head, and his mouth crashed down on hers.

Nicole grabbed his shoulder and cricked her arm around the back of his neck, and she didn't so much melt against Kingston as whip her arms and one leg around him like a vine trying to climb a tree.

As his lips plundered her mouth, he ran his hand from the back of her knee up her thigh to her hip, and his thumb hooked around the string bikini band of her panties.

He mouthed down the side of her throat, sucking and nipping to her shoulder left bare by her sundress. He'd wrapped her ponytail around the fist with his other hand, pulling her head to the side so her skin was stretched taut under his teeth.

He murmured against her skin, "What the hell are you doing to me?"

In reply, Nicole tightened her arms and legs around him, pushing herself against the thick ridge in his pants.

Her body was famished for him, and like an unfed vampire, she wanted to wrap her lips around any part of him she could.

But Kingston slowed down, kissed the side of her neck with one last slow suck, and then peeled her off of him.

He set her back, holding her shoulder tightly, and glared down at her. "This is a mistake."

Kingston walked out of the golf simulator room, leaving

Nicole panting and staring at the messed-up Excalibur driver lying on the fake grass under the projected image of a sky.

In the simulator, too, waves crashed on the black rocks below the cliff.

Kingston had also chosen Pebble Beach.

Nicole braced her hands on her knees and waited forever until her heart rate slowed, wanting to scream and cry as she stood alone on the fifth hole of Pebble Beach golf course.

After a while, she made her way back over to the lab where Arvind was glaring at a scientific instrument, his eyes squinting so hard that wrinkles folded his skin.

"I figured it out," Nicole said. "The metal is resonating like a crystal wine glass when it sings. It's setting up a standing harmonic wave when the club head hits the ball. That's what we need to fix."

48

A RISK HE'S WILLING TO TAKE
NICOLE LAMB

A week later, Nicole was sitting on her desk and sharpening a pretty little falchion, a short, single-handed, single-edged sword she'd bought from a master blacksmith in Nevada, when Kingston stalked into her office, a piece of paper crumpled in his grip.

He slapped her door closed behind himself. "They rejected it."

Only one thing could upset him this much, and she set the falchion aside on her desk near her thigh, almost resting the blade on the bright yellow fabric of her sundress spilling across her desk blotter. "The PGA? Was it the Excalibur or the Vorpal irons?"

"The Excalibur. The Vorpals passed, but it was right on the number, just like you said. The Excalibur didn't."

They could still sell the Excalibur, of course. Any company could sell any golf club it wanted to any golfer who would buy it, but professional golfers could not use it in PGA Tour events. Even most nonofficial tournaments, like country club championships, wouldn't allow it to be used in play.

Good golfers wouldn't buy it.

"Let me see the letter," she said.

He handed the paper to her and began pacing back and forth in her office, one hand running through his dark hair.

Nicole read what the Professional Golfers' Association of America had written in their letter, which Kingston had evidently printed from an email.

The paper rattled in her grip. "They said we could resubmit. If we get the prototypes there within two weeks, they'll rerun the tests and might change the rating."

"But can you? Is there anything we can do to change the design so that it will pass and yet still be as good as it is now?"

"We can try. At the very least, I can promise that we will try. We'll work night and day until the deadline if we have to."

Kingston stopped pacing, but he was still looking at the ground, and his hand was still clutching his hair. "I want you to know that I appreciate how hard you have worked for Sidewinder Golf. You could have just phoned it in these last few months and ensured we would fail."

"If I wanted Sidewinder to fail, I wouldn't have formed a union. I would've quit, and everybody else would've eventually seen the writing on the wall and followed me out the door."

"Nevertheless, I appreciate your loyalty."

Nicole looked down at the falchion beside her leg and shrugged. "I love my job."

"I know you do," Kingston said, his voice choking. "I know this company and making people happy with better clubs is important to you."

"Sure beats making weapons to blow up the world."

"I'm trying to save Sidewinder, too," he said.

"I know, Kingston. I know you're trying everything to save it."

"Because it's important to you,"

"And because it's a company and there are people here who depend on it, your real business, Last Chance, has been pouring money into it and needs to make a profit."

He looked up at her, a grim set to his mouth. "I miss you."

The shift of the conversation from Sidewinder to them was an earthquake under her legs, and she grabbed the desk just in case it wasn't a metaphor because that was California, but the trembling was in her heart.

"I am sorry I didn't come clean about who I was earlier," he said. "Because even though it gave me the information I needed about the company, I lost you over it. I would do anything to change the fact that I lost you."

Words jumped out of her mouth before she could edit them. "I miss you, too. So much. I don't want you to lose me."

He was across the room before she'd finished saying that, and his lips swallowed her last word. His kiss was starving, almost violent, shoving her back across the desk until he grabbed her around her waist and dragged her against his chest.

The door was closed but not locked and they shouldn't do anything while the office was full of people coming and going and any one of them might open her door and walk in to ask her a question and just start talking—

The frustration lingering in her body from a week before roared back, and she opened her mouth and tangled her tongue with his.

His hand was already under her skirt again, dragging her panties down her legs and dropping them to the floor before pressing a finger roughly inside her, pumping into her as he massaged her clit, and then she was squirming against his hand, trying to get more.

He growled against her throat, "You're already wet for me. You were thinking about me fucking you on this desk the minute I walked in."

Nicole was gasping as she rode his hand, her body already clenching because, no, she'd been thinking about him the whole time she'd been sharpening that sword, methodically and mindlessly running the whetstone up the hard length of it and hoping he'd walk into her office and leave with her panties as a pocket square.

Her mind was off-line. Her thoughts about everything were gone, and yet she needed to say, "Just so you know, I'm still on the Pill."

"I don't care. I'd have you anyway," he growled, his head near her ear.

"No, you wouldn't. You have too much self-control."

Kingston stared right into her eyes as rivulets of pleasure ran through her, his fingers stroking her inside, and the ends of his blue eyes narrowed in what might have been anger. "I would take you every time I could, and if you got pregnant, I would buy a big house in Connecticut and fuck you until you'd had ten babies to fill it up."

"Ten?" she laughed as she gasped, thinking he was joking. God, she wanted him to *never* stop.

The grit in his voice sounded like he was on the edge of rage. "Twelve."

"That's excessive."

"I'm excessive," he told her, the edge of his voice finally breaking as his words ground out between his teeth with her body impaled on his fingers. "I am absolutely the kind of man to take a pretty girl and hide her away from the world if she'll let me. I would protect her and our children from *everything*. I would never let *anything* happen to them."

"You're joking."

"Try me."

Kingston unbuckled his belt and opened his fly, shoved her back to lay on the desk with her knees folded up to her shoulders, and then he rammed himself into her.

Nicole's back arched off the desk at his possession of her body. She hated that she needed him so much, that her anger was secondary to her need for him to touch her.

Kingston reached past her head, grabbing the other side of the desk for leverage with both hands and railed her, his hips bucking as he stroked into her, his body grinding up against hers.

His body dragged inside her again, his hips grinding against her clit with each stroke, and words fled, and her body spun and twisted like a spring, torquing with pressure, until it broke and she broke and waves of pleasure reverberated through her, wiping out her memory and who she was and all the reasons she had to be angry.

Kingston rammed harder into her, his body jerking like he was out of control, and then he let go of the desk and grabbed her with both of his arms under her back and held her against him as he pulsed inside her, his cheek against hers, his ragged breath on her shoulder, the muscular hardness of his body heavy upon her.

Nicole's eyes burned, and she wiped wet streaks away from her temples with her palms before he saw them.

As his breath smoothed, Kingston turned his head and kissed her neck, moving back to her mouth, and he kissed her slowly, tenderly, with his thumb on her cheekbone and his fingers woven into her hair that had fallen out of its ponytail.

His voice was a murmur against her lips. "I missed you."

She rested her hand on his cheek. "I missed you, too."

He held her, kissing her, until he slipped away and tucked himself back in his pants, buckling his belt.

Nicole struggled to sit up and smoothed her skirt down over her knees. "What if I didn't want to be locked in a house in Connecticut with twelve babies?" she asked him.

"Fourteen. You'd have to fight me a little on it, just to make sure you really wanted it, which is too bad." His voice dropped to that sexy lower register. "Because I would've loved keeping you like a little doll to take whenever I wanted."

"I studied really hard in college because I want this to be my life," she told him.

"College should open opportunities, not lock you onto one engineering track the rest of your life. It might be fun to be my little fuck toy for a year or so while you wait for the noncompete clause in your contract to expire, and then start your own company with all the ideas I know you have but never wrote down."

Okay, if this guy could actually read her mind and see all the other golf designs in there, this was going to get creepy.

Because she had more ideas, a lot of them for golf clubs and a lot of other things that could make the world a better place.

Kingston laughed. "Don't confirm or deny anything. The look on your face is answer enough."

"Well, now I can't say anything, can I?"

He grabbed her pink silk panties off the floor, folded them, and tucked them into the breast pocket of his suit coat.

Like a serial killer's trophy. "I'm going to run out of panties if you keep doing that."

"That is a problem. If you're walking around this building in flirty little sundresses without any panties on, I won't ever get any work done."

"I'm serious!" But she couldn't help but laugh, which totally destroyed the prim effect she was going for.

"Good point. Saturday morning, I'm taking you shopping for new lingerie. You can model it for me in the dressing room. Maybe I'll fuck you with your hands against the mirror so you can watch me take you."

As an engineer and self-professed workaholic, Nicole had never known what it was like to be "working for the weekend" until then because it seemed like Saturday morning could not arrive soon enough.

49

ABOUT THE BET

NICOLE LAMB

Two days later, Nicole was standing in the mostly unoccupied corridor door outside Kingston's office at six-thirty at night, holding her handwritten notes of three possible changes they could make to the Excalibur prototype to both make it compliant with the PGA's parameters for club design and yet still magic on the golf course.

Chickenscratch writing and equations in blue ballpoint littered the pages.

His door was cracked open, a puff of air-conditioned air wafting through the vertical opening.

Men's voices, heated with argument, rambled and talked over each other inside.

She pushed the door open just a little bit more with one finger, not wanting to knock and disturb them, but Kingston had told her to print out all the possible ideas the lab had come up with and bring them to his office right away, and it had been almost fifteen minutes.

As the door opened a little more, she recognized Morrissey's sardonic tone as he and Kingston argued on a video call app.

"Yeah, Skins, you might be able to save that worthless dog of a company if you keep pouring money into it, but you're not going to win the bet with it. We should have liquidated Sidewinder as soon we realized Flanagan had committed fraud, and you could've run Last Chance's portfolio while the three of us worked on our wagers."

"Sidewinder still has a shot. I'm telling you, these clubs are magic. They will revolutionize the golfing industry."

"Nothing revolutionizes the golfing industry. Nothing revolutionizes *any* industry."

"These will."

"Look, you shot your shot with Sidewinder. It wasn't a bad idea, but it didn't work out. It wasn't your fault that Flanagan lied about the lien and their product pipeline. Just admit to yourself that you lost the bet, and then we can move on and double-down on our wagers that actually have a chance to win against Gabriel fucking Fish."

Bet? They'd said something during the union negotiations about a bet.

Nicole eavesdropped harder.

"Just because Sidewinder isn't going to win the bet doesn't mean we have to throw it out. It can still turn a profit for Last Chance."

"Even if Sidewinder had a possibility of turning a profit, your time would be better spent on the rest of our portfolio," Morrissey snarked. "Nobody thinks any less of you, Kingston. It was part of the strategy."

"Yeah, I know, but—"

"Jericho's safe bet will get us a decent percentage gain with an easy-win institution. Mitchell's job is to take a left turn with his business and multiply it to be worth several-fold over what it was before. Your job was to shoot for the moon with a high-risk, high-reward bet, and you did. *But it was high-risk.* It's not your fault it didn't work out."

"And what was your role in the strategy, Morrissey?" Kingston asked.

"I'm a lawyer. I was never going to do as well as you business types, so my job was just not to screw up too badly and make it look like I tried. Just close that time-suck down and get back here to Connecticut, where you can be useful."

"We signed that union contract. We can't just bail on Sidewinder."

"I wrote an escape clause in that contract if profits fell below a certain point. They've *always* been below that point by Jericho's accounting. Wrap it up, Skins."

A heavy sigh from Kingston shook Nicole's world. "I'll look at the numbers."

"You're not banging that California biscuit again, are you? You can't let a hot lay cloud your judgment. This is business, and the wager is serious business. If we lose, it's going to ruin us."

"*—it's going to ruin us,*" Kingston chanted along with Morrissey. "I know. I have heard that threat so often that I cannot stand hearing it anymore. If Fish wins the bet, I will sell off anything I have left and be a beach bum in Mexico."

Nicole wasn't sure whether she was insulted or complimented at being called a California biscuit and a hot lay in less than a minute.

"You have been in California too long," Morrissey said. "It's time to come home to the East Coast where people are serious. Get rid of Sidewinder, and I'll send the plane to bring you home."

A mouse clicked, and Kingston swore a blue streak.

Nicole slapped open Kingston's office door and barged in. "What the heck was that about a *bet?*"

Kingston looked up from where he was sprawled in his office chair, his eyes looking upward as if a problem had barged into his office. "Close the door, my little engineer. You're telling everyone in the hallway our business."

She swung the door closed behind her, and it rattled in its frame. "Did you buy Sidewinder on *a bet?*"

"It doesn't matter if I did."

Her fears were too close to the surface. "You're going to close the company, aren't you?"

He toyed with a pen on his desk. "If you were listening long enough to hear about the bet, then you heard me tell him I won't close Sidewinder."

She marched across the office at him. "It sounded like Morrissey Sand is your boss."

Kingston stood, and his desk chair skittered away on its wheels. "We are all equal partners at Last Chance. They can't make me close Sidewinder if I refuse to."

She leaned on his desk and stared into his eyes, not looking away because she thought she'd saved Sidewinder, and now he was telling her she hadn't. "What *can* they do, then?"

Kingston's jaw clenched. "If they take a vote, they can cut off funding to Sidewinder."

"So that's it." She flipped her hand at the door, indicating the rest of the building. "People's lives and livelihoods are at stake. I can't believe you destroyed people's lives on a *bet.*"

Kingston skirted the table, grabbed her, and shoved her up against the wall, his hand diving under her skirt and grabbing the side of her panties. "Let's cut to the end. You're going to be mad at me for something stupid I did, and then

I'm going to fuck you until you can't remember why anymore because I am so obsessed with you that I can't keep my hands off you, but we never get anything resolved."

Nicole put her hands on Kingston's broad chest and shoved him, and he stepped backward, hands splayed at his shoulders. She said, "Then we need to talk instead of—*that.*"

His blue eyes were the hottest fire, and he was breathing hard through his nose as he stared at her. "I am a fucked-up man. I know that. But I'm doing my best to save Sidewinder for you."

"*Bullhockey.* It was for a *bet* because you decided to take people's jobs and lives and roll dice with them."

"That was how it started, but not how it will end."

Nicole strode over to his desk and grabbed her notes that she'd dropped when he'd grabbed her because she wanted him to, but now she needed her notes.

And she needed him *not* to have them. "Morrissey said the union contract had an escape clause that you could activate any time because our profits are below an arbitrary line. That contract and those negotiations were not *in good faith.*"

"The union negotiations didn't change the fact that Sidewinder is a money pit."

"But it's *your* money pit. If you want these design changes for Excalibur—and there's one that I *know* will work and solve our problem with Dali stealing our IP—then I'm scheduling another union negotiation for eight o'clock tomorrow morning. If we can come to an agreement, I'll give you these plans."

"And if not?" he growled.

"Then I'm done, and you can tell Morrissey that you shut down Sidewinder just like he wants you to."

"That's *my* intellectual property," Kingston said, pointing to the papers in her hand. "You're still employed here by your work-for-hire contract. I don't have to negotiate for *anything*."

To heck with it. The equations and specs were all in her head.

Nicole slapped her papers on his desk. "Then good luck stealing this one because I wrote it *by hand in Old English*. And if I quit, I'm not obligated to *translate* it for you. Eight o'clock tomorrow morning, Conference Room Two, buddy."

And she walked out.

If she'd thought he wouldn't show up the next morning, that he'd let Sidewinder fall apart, her heart would have been breaking as she stomped through the cheap-carpeted hallway under the tube lights in the ceiling.

But he wouldn't.

Kingston Moore was too stubborn to throw Sidewinder into the fire.

She was counting on it.

50

AN OFFER

KINGSTON MOORE

P art of Kingston wanted to slap a closed sign on Sidewinder's front door and have the locks changed overnight because he was a damaged, stubborn man.

If Nicole didn't want Sidewinder to survive, Kingston didn't need to work this hard to save it.

And jeez, she *had* written her whole set of papers in Old English, weird letters and double-flipped-p's and crossed-d's and all.

Þæt mægen of hengan is to
hæh. An forð geworht cyrcle of
isen wile lædan þæt mægen.

NEVERTHELESS, Kingston walked past the crowd lining the hallway and into Conference Room Two at precisely eight a.m., finding Nicole Lamb sitting primly on her side of the table.

Two other women flanked her, all of them wearing business suits.

The same woman was down at the corner of their table, holding her camera flat but watching Kingston walk in.

Looks like Kingston was outnumbered this time.

He shut the door, but the long windows on both sides of the door showed the crowd of employees milling around out there. They weren't plastered to the glass like zombie Halloween decorations, but they were out there, pacing, talking, waiting.

As he took his place across from her, she shrugged as if to say that she didn't know how they got there, raising the shoulders of her black business suit jacket.

He'd worn a dark blue Dior suit, so both of them took the occasion seriously. Last time, she'd worn a sunshine yellow and white striped sundress, and he'd barely been able to concentrate.

He'd deliberately not tucked a pocket square into his suit jacket's breast pocket.

She'd already looked at the empty space twice.

Let her make of it what she would.

"Okay," Nicole said. "Let's get started."

The woman on the end raised her phone and touched something on her screen.

Nicole announced, "Fairways and Greens Un-Ionized and the management of Sidewinder Golf is now meeting for good faith negotiation and being video-recorded," and she stated the date and time.

They did the identifying thing again. Kingston did not quibble on calling himself a partner.

After Nicole stated her name, the other two women on her side of the table declared that they were Gail Stein, attorney-at-law and Sidewinder legal department, and Becca Jamison, CPA and accounting department.

"Fairways and Greens Un-Ionized has a proposal," Nicole started, reading from a prepared statement. "You have stated that Sidewinder Golf is insolvent."

Kingston sighed. "Technically, yes."

She looked up at him, her dark eyes serious. "And what does that mean, *technically?*"

"If you look at a simple balance sheet, revenue in, expenses out, EBITDA, etc., Sidewinder is deeply underwater and a foolish investment."

"Then why have you been shoveling money into the money pit?" she asked.

"Because that's not the only way to value a business. You will miss the best investments if you only look at red and black ink on a balance sheet. Growth is the most important indicator. I am always more interested in the product pipeline. Every company is only as good as its next product."

She kept watching him with her dark eyes. "So you believe in the company."

Kingston looked right back at her. "I believe in Sidewinder's pipeline. I believe in the brilliance of its forthcoming products."

"Tell me about *the bet,*" Nicole said, her voice flat and raspy.

He inclined his head and opened one hand, a gesture of embarrassment. "So, it all started last New Year's Eve when my three best friends and partners at Last Chance and I got roaring drunk, and there's this other guy named Gabriel Fish—"

"I don't want to know the tawdry details. I want to know the conditions and dates."

His little engineer was nothing if not pragmatic. "All five of us are to buy a golf-related business."

"And that explains Last Chance's weird golf-related buying spree."

She had done her homework. "We work to increase its value. Results will be tabulated this December twenty-eighth for reveal on New Year's Eve. Winning will be based on a calculation of net increase in value."

"And what do you win? Bragging rights? Have you done all this to us for *bragging rights?*"

"A hundred million dollars ante, each. Winner take all."

All three women rolled their eyes as they should.

Nicole asked him, disbelief lacing her voice like poison, "And you *made* this bet?"

Their frustration was only a fraction of his own. "There was alcohol involved. A lot of alcohol. And a watertight, unbreakable contract that we all somehow signed."

Gail Stein, the attorney wearing a conservative dark gray suit that Morrissey would've called a court suit, leaned forward. "If you were inebriated, no court would uphold the contract."

Kingston held up one hand to stop her because they did not need to get into the weeds of this ridiculous situation. "We signed. There are no loopholes. Trust me on this one. We are on the hook."

"And you can't just go buy something else?" Becca Jamison the CPA asked. "Especially considering Joe Flanagan obviously committed fraud when he suckered you into buying us."

"Unfortunately, the company for the wager had to be declared at the time of purchase. Otherwise, we all would've bought ten companies and put forward the one that did the best. At least, that's how Gabriel Fish would have played the game."

Gail the lawyer bobbed her head as she looked at the ceiling, perhaps admiring the trap Kingston had been caught in.

Nicole just shook her head like she was secondhand embarrassed for him.

Which was probably kinder than he deserved.

"Now that the situation is on the table, what are we here to discuss?" he asked.

Nicole read from the paper in her hands, "In exchange for a commitment from Last Chance, Inc. to fund operations at Sidewinder Golf through—" Nicole conferred with the lawyer and accountant beside her and then said, "—through the end of the year, we offer three things."

"I'm listening."

Nicole's eyes flashed up at him again, less angry, more wide and honest. "I am ninety percent sure that I have a fix for the Excalibur driver. We will make the face of the driver even thinner—"

Kingston winced at her idea as even he saw the problem with it. "But that will make it *more* bouncy, *more* outside of the PGA's limitations."

Nicole continued, "—*and then* we will craft an additional structure, like a strut, to be glued inside the club head to reinforce the face plate, which we can tune to *exactly* the PGA's upper limit, making it the absolute springiest club on the market while increasing forgiveness for mis-hits. Every pro will rip off their left leg for it. It'll win all the long-drive competitions."

Air stroked across Kingston's tongue and down his
throat as he couldn't repress a gasp. The brilliance of it was
astounding. *He* wanted the club *right then.*

He could sell a club like that for whatever he wanted,
any price he could name.

"The additional support is small," Nicole continued.
"For a very minor startup cost, we can manufacture it in-
house. We could make a thousand struts in a week. The
custom part would then be shipped to the final
assembly plant where they glue the club head together
in Texas."

His little engineer was flipping brilliant. "Dali would
never see the new part."

"They won't know it exists, and they certainly won't have
its specifications. I also formulated a new glue that inte-
grates into the strut itself. If any other company tries to cut
the club head apart to reverse engineer it, the support will
disintegrate as they try to take it out. It should buy us at least
three, maybe five, years as the magic golf club everyone
wants."

Kingston spread his hands on the table. "Amazing."

"If they try to manufacture a generic version of the
design of that driver head without the reinforcing strut
inside, the club's face will collapse after hitting about twenty
shots. It will be like hitting a golf ball with an empty beer
can on a stick."

He could feel a grin growing on his face. "Devious. *I
like it.*"

Kingston did like it. As a matter of fact, he *loved* it.

With the Rattler line of club sets already in transit for
the big box stores, the Excalibur and Vorpal lines would be
the cornerstone of Sidewinder's turnaround strategy.

If Kingston could sell a thousand Excalibur-plus-Vorpal

sets at ninety grand apiece, Sidewinder would add ninety million dollars to its bottom line.

Sidewinder would be highly profitable by the end of the year, a long black number for the profit-and-loss spreadsheet for Gabriel Fish's wager.

His moon shot might work.

Nicole grinned back at him and looked back at her paper. "Second item: union members will pledge to remain with the company, barring unforeseen individual decisions."

"Agreed," Kingston said, the clause just like the previous contract.

"Third, *if you lose the bet,* on January first, the union will purchase Sidewinder for the amount of its operational debt from Last Chance, the previous purchase price Last Chance paid to Joe Flanagan, and a reasonable interest rate, becoming at that time an employee-owned business. We will assume all previous debt."

"The purchase price was one hundred thousand dollars, plus assumption of debt," Kingston told them.

"*What?*" Nicole yelled, half-jumping out of her chair. "Joe Flanagan sold us for *a hundred grand?* That's *it?* I could have put that on my credit card!"

"That's why Sidewinder was a moonshot. If we sell pre-orders for a thousand Excalibur and Vorpal sets, plus the expected Rattler profits from the golf retail stores, the expected return is thirty thousand-fold our initial investment. *That* should win the bet."

"I can't believe he sold us to you for such a *pittance.*"

"That's how bad the debt is. Flanagan financed the retrofit of this building with your labs and bollocks amount of equipment, golf simulators, the million-dollar couches in the lobby, and all the other depreciating assets in here because he didn't have the cash on hand. Just the interest payment every month is insane. He should have rented the equipment and re-invested profits."

She lifted her hands off the conference table between them like it was fire, which it was. The table and every other piece of furniture and lab equipment were literally burning cash. "That's crazy."

"Sidewinder doesn't own the building, either. This structure is rented. You'd be better off walking out *en masse* and starting a new employee-owned company without the debt."

"But the non-compete and work-for-hire agreements in the contracts," she said.

Kingston shrugged. "If Sidewinder goes bankrupt, there won't be an entity to enforce them. You can do whatever you want."

Nicole flopped back in her chair and tapped the notes before her. "We were making this deal, though. We already made you the offer."

"Don't make the deal. Reneg on it. When we write the contract I'll take to Last Chance, add a clause that says the union can back out on January first for a one-dollar penalty." He leaned in. "Let Last Chance finance Sidewinder through the end of the year before you back out."

She tapped the papers in front of her again. "But if we buy Sidewinder, it will give you a lot of money to save Last Chance if you lose the bet."

"It's *business*. You shouldn't take our position into account."

"But you told Morrissey Sand that you were ruined if you lost the bet."

Kingston barreled ahead. "Here's your plan: if I lose the bet, or if all of us Last Chance guys lose, you should all quit. Walk out on this turkey. Let Sidewinder burn. The banks will repossess everything."

"But everyone would lose their jobs."

He kept talking. "In a month, offer the banks to buy Sidewinder's lab equipment, inventory, and product lines for ten percent of what Flanagan owed on them. *Ten percent.* The banks will do it. They've already taken the loss in the repossession."

She frowned. "That doesn't sound legal."

"It's legal. Corporations do it all the time. The bank has insurance for failed loans, and those insurers have re-insurance. And if the re-insurers fail, the government bails them out. Your tax dollars at work."

Her frown turned into a scowl. "That's a racket."

Now, she was understanding. "Negotiate with the building's owner to take over the lease from *that* point forward, which will be a good deal on their end rather than trying to find a new tenant, costing them time and money. You'll start your employee-owned business in a much better financial position. You could immediately rehire Caitlin Moffett, Rainbow-Supreme, and all the others."

Nicole looked up at him, her dark eyes wide. "You didn't have to tell us this. You could have taken our money and walked away."

Kingston didn't let his gaze waver, just looked into her eyes as if he were giving her his soul. "You didn't have to devise a fix for the Excalibur. You could have let Sidewinder fail and offered a union buyout when it was in ashes."

"Yeah, I know, but I didn't want to watch it burn."

"So we won't let it burn, my little engineer. Let's fix the Excalibur, win the bet, and rule the world together."

Her slow smile was more gratifying than he'd had any right to expect. "Yeah."

Kingston accepted the union's offer, and they shook on

it. Nicole's small hand was cool in his, and their eyes met across the table.

Gail Stein said that *she'd* write up the contract for them to sign, the insinuation being no more sneaky clauses from Morrissey Sand.

The lawyer, the accountant, and the woman recording on her phone filed out first, grinning like their mouths were tied to their ears. The crowd of employees lurking in the corridor started cheering even before any details were divulged.

Nicole caught the door and closed it behind them, leaving just the two of them in the conference room.

Kingston leaned against the short end of the conference table and, aware of concerned faces peering in the windows on both sides of the door, assumed a casual expression. "Yes? Did you forget something?"

"No, you did," Nicole said.

Where she was standing with her back flush against the door, the people outside couldn't see what she was doing.

She reached under her suit skirt and wiggled her hips like a pouncing kitten, and her white lace panties dropped to her ankles around her stiletto heels.

Kingston held on to the table edge with both hands as all the blood left his brain.

She held them out to him. "You forgot your pocket square."

He held out his hand for the crumpled ball of white froth and tucked it into his suit's breast pocket, fluffing the lace without displaying what they were to the crowd outside. "Why, thank you. Very much."

"My office, three o'clock," she said, a naughty smile on her lips.

Kingston was not going to survive until then.

51

THE PGA SHOW IN VEGAS
NICOLE LAMB

The Sidewinder Golf booth at the early December PGA Golf Show in Vegas was a mini-castle cut from dark blue canvas.

One giant simulator in the middle, the size of a two-car garage, displayed the fifth hole at Pebble Beach, and smaller simulators on the sides held windows to other parts of that golf course.

Meghan and Morgan stood at the entrance, blonder and bubblier than all the showgirls in Vegas, instantly analyzing and sorting golfers as to whether they should be shown the more economical Rattler line of clubs, available for order at a slight discount compared to Golf Universe or Cox Sports, or whether they were high rollers who should be given access to prototypes from the exclusive Legendary line and then evaluated as to whether or not they deserved a space on the pre-order list.

Although "pre-order" was only a marketing term, now. Excalibur drivers and Vorpal iron sets had started delivering a week before Thanksgiving, on budget and ahead of schedule.

Rattler sales in retail stores were exceeding expectations. Sidewinder was profitable.

Nicole walked among the golfers in the Sidewinder booth, as anonymous as a country club waiter, watching how people responded to the Excalibur and Vorpal irons.

Their shocked exclamations were gratifying. She'd made the right choice.

The one gross slob of a billionaire tried to neg her clubs to Kingston, saying that he had played with better clubs and his new brand of golf clubs was going to be the best in the world, and thus he was refused a spot on the coveted waiting list and shown the door, sputtering the whole time.

His swing was awful, anyway. He probably cheated his friends at golf.

Kingston was still playing sales guy, which became funnier every time Nicole saw him do it.

How had she ever thought that this man who was obviously wearing a custom-tailored ten-thousand-dollar suit and, when he wasn't playing a role, had the reserved manners of royalty was a newbie hawker of sporting equipment?

Last Chance's jet had picked Nicole up that morning for the half-hour hop to Las Vegas, so in the afternoon, Kingston took her to a suite at the Four Seasons, a serene oasis away from the jangling slot machines and thick cigarette smoke of the Strip.

When they walked in, Nicole had noticed the distinct lack of a casino and smoke. "I can't believe they don't just have a few slot machines around here."

He'd raised an eyebrow at her as he opened their door via an app. "Would you rather stay somewhere with slot machines?"

"Oh heckers, no. This is lovely."

Kingston had booked them into the Stadium View Panoramic Suite, a descriptive name rather than an obscure one named after authoritarian figures, which also over-looked the red rocks desert, afire with the last of the winter's scarlet sunset.

Nicole turned to Kingston. "This is great."

"You deserve it after working like hell the last couple of months. I still can't believe I found you sleeping under your desk."

She shrugged. "Yeah, well, I love my job. And it was just like in engineering school. I slept under my table at the library and on the couches in the design labs more times than I can remember, waiting for pieces to be fabbed so I could start the next step of the process."

His fond smile tickled her. "Nevertheless, it was above and beyond, and it worked."

"Says the guy who sold more golf clubs than the rest of the sales staff put together."

It was Kingston's turn to shrug. "It's not hard when the clubs sell themselves."

"Really, how did you do it?"

His sly side glance made her start laughing even before his confession. "I went to a billionaire's boarding school for high school. I called my friends and told them I had a magic golf club. The *anciens Roséens* were climbing over each other to pre-order for the full amount."

Nicole cracked up. "Connections, again."

"It wouldn't have worked unless the clubs were that good, so you can stop laughing. Also, I ordered supper in."

Nicole trailed off laughing at him and grabbed her chest in relief. "After all the peopling today, room service sounds fantastic."

He smiled. "I thought you might find it so."

Supper arrived on silver-covered carts and was served in the suite's dining room.

Las Vegas sparkled in the darkness outside the floor-to-ceiling windows.

The long table was set for eight.

Nicole sat at one end, and Kingston sat beside her, at her right hand.

When the waiters removed the silver domes from their dinner, revealing what Kingston had ordered, Nicole looked up from the steak and thick fries on their plates. "You didn't."

"Wagyu steaks," Kingston replied. "And this time, I get to enjoy it, too."

With her first bite of the tender meat that practically melted on her tongue, she knew it was as good as at the Baccarat Hotel in New York City. "Phenomenal."

"I'm glad you like it," he murmured.

She pointed to the steak with her knife. "My dad would love it, but he would try to throw it on the grill out on the back deck."

Kingston's smile held a genuine joy in it. "While it is not traditional, I would bring Kobe steaks to see how they would taste grilled over hardwood like your dad makes, but only if your mother makes the au gratin potatoes."

"You know they're from a box, right?"

He shook his head. "She does something to them."

"Yeah, she stirs in some sour cream, but they're from a box."

"I don't care. As far as I'm concerned, your mother's au gratin potatoes are the pinnacle of potato."

"I will be sure to tell her you said so."

"Oh, I think she knows. When we were there for Thanksgiving, she sneaked a frozen casserole dish of them to me as we were leaving. I ate them every night for a week."

Nicole dropped her jaw in mock outrage. "You didn't share?"

"You ate those potatoes every week of your life growing up. Yes, I hoarded them like a desert rat defending his grain."

"I guess that's true," she conceded. "You were deprived of box-mix au gratin potatoes your whole life, going to your fancy Swiss boarding school."

He nodded. "Le Rosey did not serve box-mix au gratin potatoes. The dorm mothers would've swooned at the lack of Emmental cheese."

This was it. This was the opening. He'd met her parents a dozen times and never said anything about her going to meet his family anywhere. "So how did a kid from Pennsylvania end up at a billionaire boarding school, anyway? Are your parents rich?"

Kingston paused, sawing off another bite of steak and then resumed. His studied movements seemed deceptively casual. "My parents and my older brother Stephen died in a car accident when I was ten."

The urge to grab and comfort him flashed through Nicole's brain, but his lack of reaction to what he said slowed her down. "I'm so sorry."

"It was a long time ago."

"Jeez, Kingston. I'm still so sorry."

Kingston stared at his food, but his knife and fork had stopped moving. "I didn't have much extended family. My mother had an older brother, a confirmed bachelor in the old-time sense of the word, a lawyer who'd done very well for himself. He wasn't interested in raising a kid, even a ten-year-old who literally had no one else, but he didn't let me go into the foster system, either. That definitely would've been a worse life."

Nicole reached over, took his knife out of his hand, and folded her fingers around his.

"I think he sent me to Le Rosey because it was on another continent and they had school-vacation residency packages. I didn't return to the States until after graduating high school. He died while I was in college and left me a significant amount of money, some of which is still in trust until I turn thirty-five."

And that was the trust fund remark from their first date at the four seasons in San Diego.

His fingers tightened around hers. "And that's my whole life. I met the three Last Chance guys at Le Rosey. They've been the closest thing I have to family ever since. They come from more money than I do. To put up the money to start Last Chance with them, I liquidated almost everything I had and borrowed against the trust fund for the buy-in."

No wonder he was flailing so hard to win the bet. "Oh, wow."

"It's been a good investment. Last Chance has been the opportunity of a lifetime for someone like me. We were making money hand over fist until one stupid night when we got drunk or were roofied. It was probably drunk, though. We all learned to hold our liquor very well at boarding school, and we might have an inflated sense of what it is humanly possible for a liver to do."

"And so this one bet—" she said.

"And so this one bet could destroy all of us. I was not kidding about leaving it all behind to be a beach bum in Mexico, except that I know that I would get bored in about six months and want to rebuild. That's been the whole theme of my life: everything is taken away from you, and then you rebuild. As long as I am alive, I will rebuild."

Nicole wrapped her other hand around his, too. "If everything falls apart, I'll be there with you."

"I couldn't ask you to do that. You're set for a great life. You have a fantastic family, and no matter what happens with the damn bet, I know you will change the golfing industry, either with Sidewinder or its employee-owned successor."

She rolled her eyes, but she kept her hands tightly around his. "I don't want to talk business right now."

"Remember when you were going to allow your union and your friends to buy Sidewinder as is, and I told you it was a bad bet and you should run?"

"For someone who believes that it's just business, you kind of screwed yourself on that one," she said.

"Well, I'm going to do it again. I am a bad bet. Even with Sidewinder's moonshot paying off, I would lay money—"

"I thought we agreed that you wouldn't make any more bets."

"—I would lay money that Gabriel Fish has something truly nefarious up his sleeve. I believe there is a seventy-five percent chance that no matter what kind of numbers we throw down, Gabriel Fish already had a million-fold business opportunity and suckered us all just for the fun of it. I am about to lose every bit of money I have ever earned and go bankrupt."

Nicole started patting his hand, the despondent direction this conversation was taking made her nervous. "Oh, don't talk like that. It'll be fine. We'll figure out something, and we'll make it fine. Like you said, you always rebuild."

Kingston slid off his chair and kneeled beside her, still holding her hand. "And that's why I am warning you that marrying me is a terrible idea. Financially, it would be the worst decision you could make. You are a beautiful, brilliant woman, my little engineer, and any man would be the luckiest man in the world to have you. If I really wanted to prove my love for you, I would introduce you to my billionaire and royal friends and let one of them marry you, but I'm selfish."

Shock was slamming into Nicole's frontal lobe so hard she could barely breathe and far too hard for her to say anything.

"I love you more than I could ever tell you. You are life and hope and love and already more family than I have felt since I was ten years old. Even though it's a terrible idea and I'm advising you to say no and find someone worthy of yourself, I'm asking you to marry me."

He pulled a black velvet jewelry box from his pocket and flipped the lid open, revealing a hunk of crystallized carbon bigger than anything Nicole had ever seen. "Oh my God, Kingston!"

"It's all right to think about it. Every time there was a huge conundrum at Sidewinder, you came up with a solution better than anyone could have ever expected because you took the time to mull it over. Maybe we need to return to California so you can sharpen your swords and think about it."

Nicole reached into the box, plucked the diamond ring out, and stuck it on her own finger. "Yes!"

Kingston raised an eyebrow at her. "That quick?"

Nicole grabbed his hands because he was still kneeling on the thick carpeting beside her chair. "With you, I've always known it was right. When you said you loved me on that trip to New York, I was ready to say it back right then, and I still don't know why you didn't want to hear it."

His slow blink wasn't an answer.

She kept talking. "I don't have to think it over. I don't have to write out the equations and do the math. Every time you touch me, it feels right. You're right, and I know it. So, yes, Kingston. I want to marry you because I love you."

Kingston was on his feet, lifting her in his arms and cradling her against his chest. "I love you, my little engineer," and strode for the bedroom.

She laughed and slung her arms around his neck. "Supper?"

His growl was fierce. "It can wait."

He tossed her on the bed, shucked his suit jacket and shirts, and crawled on top of her, his body warm and overwhelming.

"Kingston, we can have supper—"

"Can't wait," he said, methodically stripping her clothes from her body. "You're *mine* now, and I must have you."

She was plucking at his waist, trying to unbuckle his belt because hands on her skin and his mouth on her throat fogged her mind with rabid desire. "Okay, *fine*. If you *insist*."

His hands—so big, so rough—caressed her body. Her breasts and nipples, he led to his mouth, sucking and then raking his teeth over, and he squeezed her bottom and legs in his grip.

His ring was heavy on her hand, a new weight to get used to.

Nicole was limp in his grip, swallowing sensations as he gave them to her. Her skin was a canvas for his hands pinching and massaging and for his mouth on her.

Kingston crawled backward, his mouth trailing down her stomach, and she grabbed at his shoulders. "Where are you going?"

But he'd already parted her legs and, with a devilish

glance up at her from between her knees, kissed the inside of her thigh, then higher, then *higher.*

He licked within her folds, spiraling his tongue over her clit, a pleasure so intense that Nicole was already gasping. "Kingston—"

"Lay back and take it," he growled between swipes of his tongue. "Quickies in the office against the copy machine or on your desk aren't nearly as fun as a long," *lick,* "luxurious," *lick,* "love-making where I can take my time and do whatever I want to you."

She reached down, trying to drag his shoulders up and his body over her. *"Please."*

"Not yet, little engineer."

He sucked on her, his mouth dragging pleasure through her body until tension spun lower, compressing, squeezing. "Kingston!"

Deeper inside her, filling her but not enough, and a press inside to lift her within, harder against his tongue.

Ecstasy ripped through her, a blinding rush of heady pleasure that left her gasping.

When the world stopped whirling, her fists clenched the sheets, her feet cramping from the strain. "Oh my *God.*"

Kingston hovered above her, his knees bracing her apart, his face inches from hers. "We're just getting started."

He pressed inside her even though she was still quivering, and he bit his lip. "God, you're so wet. So tight."

His invasion was sensory overload, the orgasm still reverberating in her bones as he moved slowly, his slow presses against her clit at the top of his strokes a spark that sent the energy surging through her body again, and again, and again.

She was keening, begging him to keep going, crying for

relief, but he kept her at those peaks, an unrelenting, drowning rapture.

"I love you, my little engineer, my Nicole," he whispered, the words falling into the waves surging through her.

Hours later, maybe months, he stroked faster, urgent, crashing into Nicole as she clung to him, and *still,* he wrung surges of mindless bliss from her spent body.

Kingston curled around her, his naked body warm and strong, and Nicole gasped as she held onto him, still floating and spinning.

His lips pressed her forehead, her temples. "You're everything to me. You're my whole world."

She clung to him. "You're mine, too. I will be your little doll in a house and fill it with babies if that's what you want. Just—this—*wow.*"

His voice was quiet near her ear in the dark. "My parents and Stephan told me they loved me before they got in the car. I stayed home alone while they went to church, because I had a cold and didn't want to go."

Nicole slithered her arms up and around his neck, holding him. "I love you, and I'm not going anywhere."

"I didn't know why they didn't come home. The next morning, I went over to a friend's house. His mother fed me breakfast and learned what had happened from the police. I stayed with them until they found my uncle, who picked me up the next weekend. Two weeks later, I was at Le Rosey."

She tightened her arms, trying to make up for his whole life. "Oh, Kingston."

His arms wrapped around her, tucking her head under his chin. "That was the last time someone told me they loved me."

"Oh, Kingston," she said, trying to love and hold him hard enough.

"I barely remember them," he said. "I keep going over memories—my mom holding me when I had strep throat one time, my dad and Stephen throwing a football with me —trying to keep them, but even those are fading like they're just memories of the real memories."

Nicole entwined her legs with him. "I'm your family now. We all are. We'll make new memories, and I love you."

His arms seized her more tightly, holding her, and she held him back, never letting go.

He whispered, "We're in Las Vegas. Marry me *now. Right now.*"

She pulled back to look at him, finger-combing his hair away from his face. "You're a part of my family now, and my parents would be *so mad* if we eloped. Nope, we're getting married for real, with our family and my friends and your friends and my cousins and everyone around us, not some Vegas quickie wedding with no one else around."

Nicole stared straight into his blue eyes. "You have a family now. Get used to it."

52

UN-IONIZED II

KINGSTON MOORE

On the Wednesday before Christmas, Kingston stood at a makeshift podium of three stacked cardboard boxes with a clipboard taped to the top because he wasn't going to spend anymore of Sidewinder's or Last Chance's money on a single-use grandstand.

"Okay, settle down, settle down. The sooner we talk about this, the sooner we can eat lunch."

Couriers holding pizza boxes filed in through the front door at the other end of the lobby, stacking scores of hot boxes on the receptionist's desk.

Nicole Lamb was in the front row, her right ankle crossed over her left and her left hand crossed over her right, his big engagement ring prominent on her ring finger. She was smiling at him, which sent a flush through his entire body.

Sidewinder's seventy-some employees were looking at each other, nervous about what he was going to say but slightly reassured by the presence of pizza that it wouldn't be too bad.

Bad news is usually disseminated from management to employees late on Friday afternoons, so the rabble won't have time to discuss it before they go home. Good news traditionally hit on Monday mornings.

"Okay," Kingston said as the chatter died down. "From how you guys have been ripping me for the last month, word of the bet seems to have leaked to the general population."

Laughter. A lot of laughter. Kingston smiled even though he was cringing inside.

"We won't know the outcome of the wager until January first, when I will be sending an email as soon I know anything, but I do know a lot about Sidewinder's state of affairs. Sidewinder golf has gone from sucking money like the La Brea tar pits sucked baby dinosaurs down to their deaths to now being extremely profitable."

A smattering of applause.

He glanced at Nicole for strength and then proceeded. "And as we don't know the wager's outcome, Sidewinder's ultimate future is still up in the air. But we know exactly how much money is in our accounts, which means I can feel confident declaring a New Year's bonus."

Nicole was grinning. She'd known what was coming.

"Due to the odd circumstances of the bet with Gabriel 'The Shark' Fish, the bonus will be paid on New Year's Day and equal to fifty percent of your current salaries."

Shock.

Gasps.

Nicole laughed, and the joy was contagious. Laughter spread through the room as people fanned themselves and turned to each other to confirm that what they'd heard was real.

Kingston couldn't help but laugh with them. "We are a

family here at Sidewinder, and family takes care of family. Now let's eat pizza!"

The crowd flowed toward the receptionist's desk and the pizza boxes, and Kingston threaded his way through the people slapping his shoulders and thanking him to find Nicole, who hugged him around his waist.

Someone shoved a slice of supreme-topped pizza in his hand, and he folded it in and took a bite off the end, his arm around his fiancée, happiness surrounding him and looking forward to a barbecue that coming weekend and his wedding on Valentine's Day, two months hence.

No matter what, Kingston had people around him who loved him, a family, and the love of his life under his arm, and a really good slice of pizza in his hand.

Everything was perfect.

53

THE NARRAGANSETT CLUB
NICOLE LAMB

N icole was trying so hard not to complain, but—
"*Why* is it so *cold?*"

"Because it's Connecticut. Actually, we crossed over into Rhode Island," Kingston said, walking beside her.

"Why does anyone live where the air hurts their face?"

"Spoken like my favorite little California girl. We can return to the car, and I'll drop you off at the door. I offered."

"No. I'm fine. I'm tough."

She was not tough. Nicole was, at best, a complete wimp when it came to the frigid wind blowing off the ocean that had been slate-gray earlier in the afternoon and was now pitch black except for the whitecaps of waves roiling in the light spilling out of the clubhouse at the Narragansett Club on New Year's Eve.

She'd been afraid she would slip on ice. Somehow, there was ice on the ground, outside, like the ice that built up in garage freezers, but it was *outside*. "There's snow on the beach, just like the song. *Snow* should not be on a *beach.*"

"New England might as well be on a different planet than California."

"Please reassure me again that we're going to live in California."

"We will live in California."

Nicole clung to Kingston's arm as she shuffled over the frozen gravel, the toes of her snow boots barely visible peeking out of the puffy coat that went down to her ankles. "You got my bag out of the trunk, right?"

"Yes, my little engineer. I brought your bag with your shoes and hairstyling implements for after you remove the hat and muffler once we get inside."

"I'm trying really hard not to complain."

"And you're doing a smashing job of it," he said, laughing out loud into the night.

Despite the snow tire-like treads of her boots, her feet kept slipping out from underneath her every time she took a step, and he caught her. "I'm sorry, but I don't know how to walk on this. Wha—*what?*"

Kingston swept her up into his arms, carrying her easily as he marched over the snow toward the front of the country club's clubhouse.

"How are you not slipping and falling down?"

"I grew up in Switzerland. The weather here may be wilder than in the Alps around Gstaad, but ice is ice."

As they approached the clubhouse, the front doors whipped open, and people were right there to take her coat and help her out of the boots before one of them led her downstairs into the ladies locker room to freshen up after her perilous fifty-yard trek across the parking lot.

Whipping her curling iron through her hair and refreshing her makeup didn't take very long because she was a California girl, and she trooped upstairs to rejoin the party just ten minutes later.

A bonfire was crackling a dead tree inside a room-sized fireplace, and she sidled over to that side of the group where Kingston was standing.

Jericho Parr, the third guy at the initial union negotiation, was there with his fiancée, as was the new guy, Mitchell Saltonstall, with his bombshell fiancée.

After the introductions, Kingston looked up and around. "Where's Morrissey?"

"He said he was on his way and had someone for us to meet."

Mitchell Saltonstall laughed. "Did we all get engaged this year? All of us?"

Kingston looked over the party, effortlessly searching above the crowd with his ridiculous height.

Sometimes, Nicole still felt two feet tall next to him.

"And more importantly, where's The Shark?" Kingston asked.

Jericho frowned. "Nobody's seen or heard from Gabriel Fish for months."

"That's weird."

Mitchell Saltonstall turned and looked at the doors. "Yeah, really weird."

WHAT COMES NEXT?

The series continues in *Sand Trap!*

Morrissey Sand is the most cynical, least romantic, grumpiest CEO in Last Chance, Inc.

There's no way he'd take a chance on gambling, the lottery, or love while sober.

When his old school chum's little sister needs job as his assistant, he can't refuse, and she's a blast of motherfucking sunshine.

What's a grump to do when a ray of goddamn sunshine won't leave him alone?

Go here to see if *Sand Trap* is available yet!
https://blairbabylon.com/books/sand-trap/

Sign up for my newsletter to get an email when *SKINS GAME* is up for pre-order and released!

Go to
https://blairbabylon.com/emailbx
on your computer's browser.

BUT WHAT SHOULD YOU READ NEXT?

The next book in the Last Chance, Inc. series is
SKINS GAME,
but I've got lots for you to read in the meantime,
and they're ALL in
KINDLE UNLIMITED!

If you haven't read any other books in the Billionaires in

Disguise (BID) universe, I recommend that you start at the beginning with *WORKING STIFF,* the very first book chronologically in the BID saga.

From USA Today Bestselling Author Blair Babylon, a thrilling romantic suspense tale about a Hollywood lawyer to the stars with a royal secret!

INCLUDES YOUR FAVORITE TROPES:

- ✓ Friends to Lovers
- ✓ Secret Royals
- ✓ Over the Top Romantic Suspense
- ✓ and always, Thrillers that Bang!

WHEN ROX WAS HIRED, **she told her smoking-hot boss Cash that she was married,** *but she's not.* Now, three years later, she's kind of accidentally living with him, and he's being a perfect gentleman, *dang it.*

Everybody in the office said that Cash was a heart-breaker, that he'd bump her and dump her, so Rox decided not to become a statistic. She went out and bought herself some rings of the finest cubic zirconia so that she could work with Cash, who was several inches over six feet tall, emerald-eyed, ripped, gorgeous, his tailored suit clinging to his athletic body, sporting a British accent, and *loaded.*

It had seemed like such a good idea at the time.

But now, three years later, she and Cash have become friends. They travel together for work often, and they're the best of buddies.

When Rox gets thrown out of her apartment, Cash

insists that she come live with him until they can find her a place because that's what friends do.

Now, even though everyone insists that Cash never goes after married women, something about him has changed. There are little touches, little slips, and Rox is more and more tempted to tell hunky, gorgeous Cash that she never was married.

And then he'll take her and break her, and then he'll walk away, and then she'll lose her job, and she still hasn't found a place to live.

And yet, every time he looks at her with mischief in his dark green eyes, every time they're teasing and it somehow turns into tickling, every time she swats at him and somehow ends up in his arms, she wants so much to risk everything.

What's a working stiff to do when she falls in love with her friend, the boss?

Get WORKING STIFF now to start reading the Billionaires in Disguise series!
https://blairbabylon.com/books/working-stiff/

And there are chapters for you to read right here!
Turn the page to get started!

RED FLAGS

Rox was standing in Cash Amsberg's corner office in the law firm again, listening to him rant, *again.*

If he hadn't been so damn sexy, she might have had to put a stop to this. But he was, so she just ranted along with him.

It was kind of their thing.

At least Rox wouldn't get fired from this law firm for being a "hothead." She wasn't a hothead. She was a Southern belle with a fiery temper, a tradition harkening back to the founding of Virginia. She would have done well in bygone eras, stamping her foot beneath her flowing hoop skirts and cursing like "Fiddle-dee-dee!"

Except for maybe that last part. Rox enjoyed a good cussin' when the situation called for it. Not that the situation called for it too often. But sometimes, she went *biblical* on people who desperately needed to be told that she would smite them and salt the Earth.

Cash Amsberg pointed to a sentence in the contract,

stabbing at the thick sheaf of paper with his finger. "What the bloody hell could Monty mean by this section? He must have known we would strike it off. It's not even a negotiating point. There's no way we would let Gina Watson sign this. Why would he even suggest such a thing?"

They were standing on the same side of Cash's mahogany desk. He leaned over the contract, bracing both hands on the edge. Windows broke open the walls on two sides of the room. The afternoon California sun blazed in, glaring on the scarlet design of the Oriental rug covering most of the floor. Cash's enormous diploma from Yale Law School hung above the couches at the back end of the office.

Dark bookcases packed with leather-bound books lined the other two walls. The books were mostly for show because the law firm had done all their research via Lexis-Nexis for years, but Rox had caught Cash reading the hard copies late at night sometimes, rubbing his eyes.

He ran his hand through his hair, a sign that he was perilously close to losing his cool. She'd only seen him do that a few times, once when a Taiwanese film director had insisted that Cash play golf with him. Cash had appeared to be in good humor and had shot a perfectly respectable ninety-two, but he had returned to their hotel and ranted about *The Damned Scottish Game* for half an hour. Rox had laughed at his tantrum until he started chuckling about how his ball had gone into the water three times on the seventh hole.

Rox flapped her hands at her sides, narrowly missing Cash's broad shoulder. "I cannot believe that he would even try such a dick move. That's why I put a red flag sticky on it, so you would see that part first. Does he think we're *redneck* idiots?" She emphasized *redneck* with her Southern accent to camp it up.

Cash scowled. "He must think we're idiots. He must think we're *all* idiots, every *one* of us, if he thought no one here would catch this." Cash's upper-crust British accent made them sound like the King of England conversing with a redneck colonist.

When Cash got all heated up like this, he literally got hot under the collar, and the subtle cologne that he wore—sandalwood and cinnamon and vanilla—crept out of his sharp designer suit and crisp white shirt. She tried not to lean in to catch a whiff, but she could just smell it when he was having a good rant. She could almost taste the vanilla on her tongue, as if she had her mouth pressed to his neck.

"This is one of Valerie's contracts," Rox reminded him.

Cash ran a hand through his hair. "Surely Monty doesn't think that Valerie wouldn't have caught this. Was he counting on her illness throwing us in such disarray?"

"This came in the very morning that Val had her stroke. I don't see how Monty could have known that that was gonna happen. He's still an asshole of the first degree, both for thinking that Valerie and her paralegals would miss this *and* for trying to do this to Watson. I mean, these frickin' autobiography rights have nothing to do with the movie. It's just a jackass rights grab."

"This is egregious," Cash muttered, his British accent turning more clipped. "Monty has gone senile or something. Call Patty. Mention it in passing. See what you can get out of her."

Patty was Monty's paralegal at his law firm. She was in Rox's lunch bunch of girls who ate meals and went to movies together sometimes, mostly chick flicks. Rox went with them when she could escape from workaholic Cash, who liked to work through meals, and nights, and other appointments.

He shook his head. "Perhaps she can give us some insight into his thought processes, such that they are."

Rox refrained from rolling her eyes and nearly sprained an eyebrow from the effort. "I don't think Patty is going to do any industrial spying for us, not after you didn't call her the next day, *or ever again.*"

"She didn't care," he said, waving his hand to dismiss that.

"Oh, I *assure* you, she *cared,*" Rox told him.

Cash raised an eyebrow at her. He seemed genuinely puzzled. "Did she?"

"Oh, yeah." Rox had heard from Patty about what an asswipe her boss was for weeks, and Rox hadn't disagreed, not when she knew that ghosting was Cash's favorite *modus operandi* to end relationships. He took women out on a couple of dates, screwed them a few times, maybe kept up the appearance of something that was becoming substantial for a few weeks, and then dissipated into thin air, *poof.* He became unreachable, untextable, untouchable. As far as the women could figure out, he might as well have turned into a ghost, even if they worked in the same office and saw him every day.

Which was one of the many, many reasons why Rox would never date him.

One of many, many, *many* reasons.

Other women looked far, far up at Cash's brilliant, intense green eyes, the dark blond streaks in his auburn hair and his pale scruff of beard, and the hard lines of his cheekbones and jaw line.

They dropped their panties even before he took off his perfectly cut suit and silk shirt to reveal his broad, rounded shoulders, those chiseled abs like cobblestones on his flat stomach, and the deep vee of his obliques that pointed below his tight boxer-briefs.

They were lost before he whispered to them in that cultured, sexy accent and far before they saw the top-of-the-line Mercedes Maybach that he drove to his rumored enormous, manicured estate in the foothills. No one had ever been there, but everyone said that his house was huge without any evidence whatsoever.

Yep, Cash was several inches over six feet tall, emerald-eyed, ripped, gorgeous, his tailored suit clinging to his athletic body, sporting a British accent, and loaded.

Shockingly, women swooned over him.

Even after he ghosted on them, every admin and paralegal and client in the office still flirted with him. When he walked by their desks, they pushed their boobs together with their elbows and smiled up at him, blinking rapidly.

The one time he got a little bit of road rash on an elbow playing basketball on the roof of the parking structure, they fawned over him and brought him cookies the next day to raise his spirits, even though he had laughed the whole thing off at the time.

But not Rox. *Never.*

The afternoon sun heated the corner office, and Cash had already taken off his suit jacket and rolled up his sleeves, baring the strong ropes of muscle on his forearms, the rough hairs on his tanned skin, and his tattoos. On his right forearm, above his wrist on the inside, three shields surrounded some kind of a triangular Celtic knot thing. It was small, maybe three inches across. The orange shield that pointed down at his hand had a white figure on it like a stylized lion rearing up with extended claws. The other shields were blue with three crowns and a red and white diamond checkerboard.

On his left arm, ink trailed tendrils of black fire all the way down to his wrist.

He glared at the Watson contract as if the paper had offended him.

Other women might fall across his desk, hike up their suit skirts, and let Cash screw them face-down on the green blotter.

But three years ago, the other women in the office had warned Rox about Cash.

Manwhore.

Ladykiller.

Heartbreaker.

He was a walking, waving cluster of red flags.

And Rox had been fresh meat.

At first, she had assumed that he wouldn't be interested in a chubby, dumpy, short, brunette Southern belle such as herself, not in an office swarming with slim California blondes.

When he had walked by her desk at ten o'clock that first morning, Rox had suppressed the gasp that had sucked into her mouth and through her body.

When he turned his head, gazing into her soul and her heating chest and her very cells, she gripped her mouse like she might fall off her office chair.

She had wiped beads of sweat off the mouse afterward where she had clutched it.

Stunning, she thought later, when her brain had rebooted. He was *stunning.* Looking at him made the world stop.

No wonder he could get away with loving 'em and leaving 'em.

"Why?" Rox had finally asked Melanie, one of the beautiful-blond admins. Rox could tell Melanie apart from the rest of the herd of golden beauties by the strawberry high-lights in her hair. "Why would women have casual sex with him if he's just going to dump them like that?"

"Well," Melanie had mused, and her smile turned senti-mental and vague. "He's never a jerk about it. There's never a fight. There's no drama. He never calls a woman a slut afterward, ever, or says anything bad about her to anyone, as far as we can tell, and we all talk a *lot*. He won't even confirm or deny anything. And he's," she cleared her throat, "attentive."

Rox frowned. "Like, he listens to you?"

"Yeah, that, too." Melanie twiddled with a piece of paper on her desk and wouldn't look at Rox.

"You mean that he told you that he loved you?"

"Oh, no. He's not mushy at all. A good time is had by all, but he doesn't lie about what's going on. He doesn't talk about 'love' at all."

"But there's something else," Rox prompted. "He's *attentive*—"

Mel cleared her throat. "In bed. I mean, *you know*. He's *good* in bed."

Rox shrugged, wanting to reach over and snatch that shredded paper away from the blonde. "A lot of guys are good in bed."

Mel glanced up at Rox, her blue eyes serious and direct. "Not like him."

Rox had tugged her sundress lower on her thighs the whole afternoon that first day, but after that, Rox had worn professional-class suits, either skirts or pants, but definitely suits, and wedding rings.

Since then, in the three years that Rox had worked with Cash as his paralegal, he had humped and dumped at least fifty women, and those were just the ones she knew about for sure. The actual number was probably higher.

He didn't seem to have a "type," either. He liked the skinny-willowy ones and the shortie-curvy ones, the pale redheads and the delicate blondes and the gorgeous raven-haired, the porcelain-skinned and the golden-tanned and the polished obsidian-hued, the nubile nineteen-year-old interns and the silver-fox lady partners, and all the women in between.

Cash even sent out discreet, non-threatening sexual feelers to the seven lesbians who worked at the law office, just in case any of them were actually a little more toward the center of Kinsey scale than they had previously thought themselves. One was. For two and a half weeks, Ginger declared herself bi-for-a-guy, which is not the usual meaning of that term but she owned it. She got along with Cash better than any of the other women, afterward.

Rox had watched them all traipse into Cash's bed and then out of his life.

All the admins stared at Cash with weepy doe eyes. All the other paralegals teared up or blushed when they saw him stride through the office. The women attorneys were businesslike and courteous to him, but their glances turned sharp when he wasn't looking.

The clients, however, still flocked to him, flirted with him, and went for round two in record numbers.

And then he ghosted them again.

The actresses didn't seem to care much about his retreats. They were used to ninety-day shoots, so to speak.

The models probably didn't have the attention span to notice his absence.

And, for some unholy reason, the guys in the office *loved* him. You would think that, with Cash sopping up all the available women, that the men would be competitive or derogatory, but they were all bestest buds with him. He was a great guy, always up to go have a beer with, or to watch a game with, or to be on a league team with.

He charmed them, too.

But Rox was the only person in the office who could *work* with him.

Now, after three years, every time Rox went in for quarterly evaluations with the senior partners, her paycheck fattened, just by her suggesting that she might be looking at other, less tempestuous law firms. They couldn't let her leave, not with just about everyone else emotionally unable to work with Cash.

Some of the women threw themselves at him, hoping for another taste. He usually accepted their offers, but the ghosting came sooner the second time or the third.

Some of them stared at the floor and mumbled around him, stealing glances at his chest or lower, but dodged when he came too close, unwilling to go through it again.

It was a matter of concentration and efficiency, really. The women imagined his hands taking the sheaves of paper from their fingers for hours, imagining a brush or a touch, and failed to get the damn work done.

And so Rox made out like a proverbial bandit.

She had bought herself an awesome sports car last month even though she knew she *should* be saving for a down payment on a house, and she grinned just thinking about the drive back to her apartment.

But sleep with beautiful, brilliant Cash Amsberg?

Never.

And he had never hit on her, anyway. Not even once. Not even a little bit.

Not in any serious way. He joked around a lot.

But she could tell that he was just joking. It was pretty obvious.

Cash wasn't particularly a chubby chaser, anyway. Not only could he have any woman whom he wanted, he actually had them *all,* one after another.

"Well, talk to Patty anyway," he said, poking the Watson contract again. "See if she'll do it for you."

Rox flicked the red plastic tag hanging onto the margin of the page. The sparkling stones in her wedding rings caught the afternoon sunlight streaming through the windows and threw spangles over the office for a moment, illuminating the heavy desk and running down Cash's bare arms.

He saw the glitter on his arm, tracked the points of light to her rings, and shifted his weight away from her.

There was only one type of woman that Cash Amsberg was not interested in.

He did not hit on married women, not even once, not even a little.

Rox said, "Fine. I'll call Patty and see if she wants to grab a drink after work today."

Cash said, "We appreciate you taking one for the team."

And that was the *only* way that Rox was going to take one for the team of Arbeitman, Silverman, and Amsberg. "Yeah, whatevs."

Cash smiled at her, his lush lips sliding apart over his straight, white teeth, and his green eyes sparkled with humor. "Thanks, work-wife. Have I told you that I love you today?"

That time, Rox let it happen, and the muscles at the corners of her eyes strained from her epic eye-rolling. "I'll bet you say that to all the girls."

He laughed, his broad shoulders lifting. "Only you, Rox. You're my rock."

"Yeah, the ball and chain holding you in this law firm. If it weren't for me, you would probably be the Chief Justice of the Supreme Court by now, writing learned opinions about which of the lawyers arguing the case in front of you was better in bed, the redhead with the fake boobs or the black woman with the low-cut top."

He was laughing harder now. "Surely I'm not so bad as all that."

"Worse. You'd probably have all the lawyers, the women ones anyway, in your chambers in some sort of a horrible orgy on your huge law desk, and then they'd all kiss and make up and dismiss the case. It would be the only Supreme Court session where absolutely no decisions were handed down, and you would go down in history as the Screw It All Court."

Casimir fell backward onto the couch, his long legs splayed, both his arms wrapped over his stomach and giggling helplessly. *"Stop."*

"All right, fine. But seriously, at least with me, you get the work done."

"Yes, I can trust you." He leaned forward, resting his elbows on his knees and shaking his head. "Now, did Bessie from Universal send us the DiCaprio contract yet?"

"Yep. Got it this morning." She waved her phone, indicating email.

"When can I see it?"

"Soon as I read it and flag it."

"This evening, then?"

"Not if I'm gonna be pimping Patty for information about Monty."

He shrugged, his white shirt sliding over the thick

muscles of his chest and arms and straining around his tight waist. "Come back afterward. We can get delivery from that new Thai place around the corner and go over it."

Rox waggled her left hand at him, letting the cubic zirconia stones in her rings catch the sunlight again and trying to flash the spangles in those brilliant green eyes of his. "I've got to see my own husband sometimes. I'll check out the file before I leave so I can look at it when I get home."

The law firm's draconian security system didn't let them access files from outside the office unless they had been checked out, a stupid process involving speed-typing security codes.

"Oh, *Grant.* Leave your husband, Grant, for me, Rox. I'll take you to Fiji for our honeymoon."

They played this game a lot, too, sometimes every day. "Never. He's six-foot-seven and a blond-bearded Norse god."

Cash mused, stroking the soft hairs of his short beard, "Last week, you said he was six-three, two seventy-five of pure muscle, and a Latin lover."

"Grant is all things to all women," Rox said, her chin held high.

"Is he coming to the office volleyball tournament this weekend? We could use a guard, if he really is that tall."

Yet another opportunity for Rox and all the other female staff to view Cash with his shirt off, displaying his rippling abs and black tattoos, always an impressive sight. A tribal-looking tattoo illustrated the left side of his body. A swirl of black fire on his round pectoral muscle spread into flames that reached over his shoulder to his back, trailed down his left arm all the way to his wrist, and slid over his rippled stomach to duck into his waistband.

Rumor suggested that the ink ran down the cut vee of

his belly, over his hip, and to the middle of his thigh, but Rox had not seen that much of his skin.

"No," she said, blinking. "He's busy working on his screenplay, and that's taking up a lot of his time. One of the series that he does stunts for is going to start shooting next month, so he has to get his script done because choreographing the stunts gets in the way of his writing. He gets really sore from being beaten and blown up all day. And he's thinking of auditioning for 'American Obstacle Course Warrior' this year."

Cash frowned. "I saw one of their contracts. It was reprehensible. Don't let him sign anything unless we look at it first."

"Josie Silverman always looks over his contracts."

He nodded. "Josie is good. All right, then. But come back to the office tonight."

And spend yet another long night curled up on those couches under Cash's diploma, feeding each other with chopsticks or plastic forks, battling legal wits and cracking jokes, while she watched that beautiful man harmlessly flirt with her, that gorgeous man who was so delicious on the outside but poison when tasted?

Not if she could get out of it.

Rox said, "I need to spend a little time with my actual husband instead of my work-husband."

Cash laughed. "Tomorrow morning, then?"

"You'll get it when it's done. You know that Bessie will try at least one thing like this," she tapped the red flag in Watson's contract, "for her studio. Maybe she'll try to tie Leo down to a fifty-year right-of-first-refusal clause or something."

Cash shook his head. "Why do we always play these games? It's going to end the same way."

Rox glanced at him, wary, but the seriousness in his green eyes meant that he was talking about the movie studios' contract shenanigans. She said, "I couldn't say, Cash."

He pushed off the desk, his biceps pumping under his shirt, and ran a hand through his gold and bronze hair. "Until tomorrow, then. What would I do without you?"

Rox lifted her nose in the air as she walked away. "Wither away and die, I s'pose. Good night, Cash."

She went back to her own office, a much smaller, interior room. The only window was beside the door and looked down a corridor between cubicle dividers. None of the other paralegals had a separate office, instead working in the cubicle farm in the center room, but Rox got whatever she wanted from HR.

She sucked in a deep breath.

It was exhausting, sometimes, being around him, knowing that she *shouldn't,* knowing that she *must not,* and waiting for a touch or a glance from him that never came.

THE CRAZY CAT LADY

A fter an entirely non-enlightening supper with Patty the night before, Rox went home, slept, and was getting ready to leave for the office the next morning, standing in the entryway of her single-bedroom apartment.

Yes, nine hundred square feet of shag carpet and Craigslist furniture were all hers.

Well, hers and her three fuzzy roommates'.

She had uploaded the DiCaprio contract to the office cloud, ready to print it out and hand it to Cash when she got there after flagging it last night. For some reason, Cash liked to go over a contract at least once in hard copy, reading the actual pieces of paper with her notes typed in little bubbles in the margins. Pointing and yelling at the contract was easier to do with a stack of paper.

Paper was much more dramatic when thrown against a wall, too. A thumb drive just went *plink* on the plaster and dropped to the carpet. So unsatisfying.

Rox trotted over to the door, adjusting her blouse and suit jacket, which she was of course wearing even though it was almost eighty degrees Fahrenheit out there already. Suits hid her lumpy pudge a lot better than some of the slim sundresses that the other girls wore, anyway.

Luckily, her new car had fantastic air conditioning and that new-car smell.

On the table near the door, one of her cats had squeezed himself into Rox's purse. His long, ginger-blond fur and sumptuous gut overflowed her bag, and he swished his bushy tail and blinked his one good eye up at her. His chewed-up ears, long since healed, swiveled toward her while he purred, thrilled with himself that he had wedged himself inside it once again.

She scratched his head, feeling the lumpy scar tissue, and ran her hand down his back, careful to go easy on the hard pebble where someone had shot him with a BB during his homeless kittenhood. "Pirate, we have discussed this. I need my purse."

He purred more loudly and blinked his yellow eye at her.

"Come on." She slipped her hands around him—her fingers running through his cottony fur—and grunted when she lifted him out of the bag. "You need to diet, mister. You and me, both."

She had been working a lot the last few years, staying late and getting into the office early, and working through meals. Back home in Georgia, she would have been considered pleasingly plump. In body-obsessed Los Angeles, Rox was constantly aware that she was always the chubbiest one in the room.

Rox carried Pirate over to one of the three cat beds in the middle of the room where the sunlight shone most brightly during the day and lowered him into the nest. Hand-crocheted kitty afghans lined each bed. The one in Pirate's bed looked a little shredded. She should buy some yarn and whip him up a new one.

Speedbump and Midnight sprawled in the other beds, stretched to suck up the morning sunlight. Pirate sniffed and poked around before he settled.

Yep, three cats.

When you volunteer at an animal shelter, accidentally adopting cats is an occupational hazard.

It was a good thing that she volunteered at the no-kill shelter the next town over. They needed her help more than the local shelter, and if she had volunteered at the local shelter that euthanized a lot of their strays, Rox would have owned three hundred cats.

Hiding even these three beasts from the super could be a hassle.

Behind the cats, her living room was smothered in pearl pink velvet and lace, just how she liked it. Rose potpourri fumed flowery scent from every tabletop.

Rox might wear dark, tailored suits to work, but she went full-blown girlie-girl when it came to her own space. One of the guys she had dated last year, Robbie, had loved it, saying that it was like being invited into a lady's bedchamber where no man had ever entered, only to ravish her.

Robbie had been fun, but it hadn't quite worked out. They had drifted apart amicably after a few months.

She went back over to the little table by the entryway and called goodbye to her cats as she fished around her purse for her keys. They thumped their tails, ready for their fully booked day of eating and sleeping while she earned the money for the kibble and cat litter.

Just before Rox left, she slipped on the wedding ring set that had been lying in a blue bowl on the table beside a larger bowl of lemons and oranges. The cubic zirconia glittered in a stray sunlight shaft, and the thin gold plating shone.

She had bought the rings for herself during her lunch break on her first day of working at Arbeitman, Silverman, and Amsberg, after hearing that Cash Amsberg the Heartbreaking Superman was repelled not by kryptonite, but by diamonds.

Cash might be a male slut, but he didn't touch married women. He didn't even flirt with them. It was like he shut it all down. His flirting with Rox was just friendly banter, like girls do with their gay guy friends. It's just all in good fun.

He didn't mean anything by it.

She didn't want to have her heart broken like all the other women in the office. They had all assured her that Cash would come for her and that she would love every minute of it, until suddenly, he wasn't there anymore.

Rox fell apart when people left her like that, like they didn't give a crap about her and just walked into oblivion.

She wasn't going to go through that again.

And so, since her husband "Grant Neil" had not existed, Rox had invented him.

She had assured Cash and anyone else who would listen, yes, she was married. Her husband was a stuntman for several of the television studios, but he wanted to get into screenwriting and directing. He did a little modeling on the side. And maybe his music would take off for him.

So, yeah, "Grant" was a ridiculous mashup of all the Hollywood wannabe clichés and thus utterly believable. No one had even questioned his existence for three whole years.

Despite the fact that no one had ever seen him.

A friend of hers, an agent, had found a suitable headshot of a hot model/stuntman for Rox to use.

Really hot.

You could see ripply abs under his tight, black tee shirt. She had folded under his real name, Lancaster Knox, and wedged it into a frame for her desk.

Rox liked to stare at pretend-Grant and imagine that he was, indeed, her lawfully wedded husband. Sometimes she drooled.

And for three years, Cash hadn't turned that sexy glower on her.

Yeah, thank goodness. She certainly didn't want the hot, ripped British lawyer coming on to her.

She slid the cheap rings onto her left hand, scratched her cats on their heads one last time, and opened the front door to leave the apartment.

Three cats.

She was twenty-seven and unmarried, not even dating anyone, and enmeshed in a workaholic office so she couldn't even meet any guys who might be prospects.

Yep, it was official.

At what point had Rox turned into a crazy cat lady?

She was pivoting on her heel away from her door as it was slamming toward her, when a piece of paper taped under the door's knocker fluttered in the breeze.

The two words at the top, bold and in all-caps, read: *EVICTION NOTICE.*

Oh, shit.

A box was bolted over the doorknob.

If that door shut, she couldn't get back in.

Her cats.

Rox kicked the crap out of the swinging door. It banged

back against the wall, and she threw herself through the doorway.

The door bounced and punched her in the arm, but she shoved it and rolled inside before it could slam shut.

The door closed, but she was inside the apartment.

She sat up, panting.

Her three cats looked over at her from their beds, vaguely amused at her antics. Pirate yawned, showing three long fangs.

"Oh, my God," Rox said. "What am I going to do?"

She couldn't leave them there. That lock was bolted on. Once that door shut one more time, she wouldn't be able to get back in. They would be trapped until the super came and—

Rox didn't know what he would do. Toss them out into the landslide-prone hill behind the building? Throw them in the pool?

Take them to the local animal shelter where they would be considered unadoptable because they were old and ugly, where they would be immediately slated for a lethal injection?

At least they were all healthy now. They might have a week or two before they were put down for overcrowding. Or maybe three days.

Fuck, no. She would not, *could not,* abandon them like that.

Okay, it was only six-thirty. She needed to plan. Rox needed to calm down and plan.

First of all, she wasn't behind on her rent at all. She had automatic withdrawal set up for the first of the month, and the rent had been deducted on schedule on the first. She had checked. She always checked.

Rox needed that eviction notice. She needed to know *why*.

She just had to make sure the door didn't close while she did it.

From growing up in the South, Rox understood that the solution to any engineering problem lay in shoe glue, bailing wire, or duct tape.

A fat roll of extra-strength, silver tape was wedged in her kitchen junk drawer. She pried it loose and marched to the door.

Like Hell she was going to get locked out of her own apartment.

Rox might be a paralegal, but her daddy was an engineer. Anything that is worth engineering is worth *over*-engineering.

The duct tape cracked as she ripped a long length off the roll, and she wadded it into a sticky ball before she shoved it against the side of the door, binding the bulge in place against the latch by winding layers and layers of duct tape around the knobs on both sides of the door. She did the same with the hole in the strike plate, mashing the gluey tape to the wall. So what if it peeled off some paint? If she was getting evicted, she probably wasn't getting her deposit back, the thieves.

Luckily, Rox knew a few lawyers. She would take those jerks to court and get her damn deposit back later. Right now, she had to get everything she could out of this trap, starting with her cats.

She glanced behind herself.

Pirate, Speedbump, and Midnight were limp in their beds, basking in the morning sunlight, oblivious to the fact that they had almost ended up back in kitty jail.

And maybe death row.

Rox bound the duct tape more tightly around all the parts of the door lock, wedging the door open with her feet and yet still standing back inside the apartment. The door looked like it had grown a silver tumor by the time she was done with that part.

She stood inside her apartment in the entryway and let the door slam closed.

The heavy security door bounced off the duct tape, and sunlight shone off the mound of tape through the open crack.

Good.

Rox wedged the door all the way open by jamming a butcher knife under the bottom of it and proceeded to secure another ball of duct tape into the hinges so that it couldn't swing even partway closed. Winding the duct tape around and around the hinges, gumming them up but good, calmed her down a little.

When there was no way that damn door could possibly swing shut, she swiped the eviction notice off it.

Animals was written in the box for Violations. *No pets policy* was scrawled underneath. Boxes for *lease violation* and *deposit forfeited* and *endangerment of other residents* and *immediate eviction* were checked below.

Legal action was written in uneven letters, and *authorities called.*

All for three damn *cats?*

That was ridiculous. Rox wasn't hoarding goddamned cobras.

Pirate stretched and extended one paw, his claws gleaming in the morning sunlight like vampire fangs or hypodermic needles or something.

Seriously. How the hell were three geriatric cats endangering *anyone?* They'd had all their shots.

Even if they did look a little ragged.

Okay, she couldn't fight this right now. Cash or Josie would slap the apartment management company upside the head with a lawsuit for her soon.

But in the meantime, she couldn't leave her cats here, not with a permanent lock on her door stymied only by duct tape. Even a small knife would make quick work of it.

So she couldn't stay, and the cats couldn't stay.

Which meant that they all had to go together.

This part had to be done carefully.

Rox sidled over to her bedroom and violently shook the treats bag, nearly powdering the shrimp-flavored bits inside.

The cats ambled in after her, checking out each other, unsuspecting but more than okay with an unscheduled shrimp-treat break.

She slammed the bedroom door behind them and fed them the treats.

They didn't see her sliding the three cat carriers out from under her bed until it was too late.

HOMELESS

Three days later, Rox sat behind her desk, annotating yet another contract on the enormous monitor that threw blue light on the walls of the office, blazing even brighter than the sizzling fluorescents overhead. Her feet were baking, nearly steaming, but she didn't so much as wiggle her toes.

The picture of the very hot Lancaster Knox, model and stuntman, sat on her desk. She blew him a kiss.

A huge rubber plant blocked the tall window beside her door. A dark track in the beige carpeting led from the heavy pot to the far wall.

Over the thick leaves, Cash's face rose in the window. He grinned at her, pointing at the locked doorknob.

Couldn't that man ever text or email or call on the damn phone?

But he never texted unless something was horribly wrong. When they traveled, he showed up at her door at all hours of the night, holding documents to talk with her about. She had bought three pairs of travel jammies so she could open the door when he had had a brainstorm or just needed to talk to her in the middle of the night.

But today, she hadn't seen him coming.

Usually, that enormous plant stood beside her desk, and Rox could see Cash striding down the aisle lined with cubicles where the admins and other paras worked. His long legs covered the floor, and he grinned at everyone in the office he passed. The other women smiled at him, laughed at something, and a few fluffed their hair and inhaled deeply.

Considering that they were all nursing broken hearts about him, they sure got aggressive with the flirting whenever he walked through the cubicle farm.

She withdrew her feet from under her desk, found her pumps with her toes, and walked over to open the door.

As soon as she flicked the lock on the door, Cash poked the door open and started to walk into her office. "Rox? Did you receive the Killer Valentine contract?"

She stepped in front of him, blocking his way. He stopped short and blinked at her, looking far down from where he stood up there at six-feet-whatever. Confusion twitched his eyebrows downward.

She glared up at him and stepped toward him, crowding him back toward the door. "Yeah. Working on it," she said. "Let's talk in your office."

"But I'm right here," he said.

Rox put her hand in the center of his broad chest and pressed, intending to steer him out of her office. Even through his crisp shirt, his pecs rounded in toward his sternum. "Let's go."

He grinned down at her, his white teeth even and straight between his lips. "Don't worry, I won't take advantage—"

He paused, looking over her head.

Everyone was able to look over Rox's head.

He asked, "Is that a cat?"

"Nope. No cats in here. Let's go."

He side-stepped, peering around her, and her fingers slid across his chest to his muscular biceps.

He said, "That's a cat."

Rox slammed the door behind him, not to keep Pirate, Speedbump, and Midnight from running out the door but to keep anyone from seeing them or hearing Cash. "Look, I've had a little problem."

Pirate was peering around the corner of her desk with his one, good eye. His blond fur was rumpled on one side of his head where he had been sleeping on her feet. His ears— rounded on top from crumbling off due to frostbite and the stumps shredded from fighting—twitched toward Cash. He yawned, showing that he was missing one of his big canine fangs, too.

"It is a cat, right?" Cash asked.

"Um, yeah." Rox started figuring out some new lies, just in case he didn't believe the fifty or so she had already cooked up.

He asked, "You have a cat in your office?"

"It's a long story."

He squinted at Pirate. "What's wrong with it?"

"Nothing's wrong with him. He's perfectly healthy."

Cash frowned. "Is it one of those weird mutations that got turned into a breed?"

"He's not a Scottish Fold. He had a rough kittenhood."

"You can't keep a cat in your office."

"It's just for another day or two."

A black cat's face appeared above Pirate's blond head.

"There's two of them," Cash said.

"Um—" *Damn.* Rox needed a good lie about now. All the ones she had thought of seemed stupidly transparent.

Of course, right then, Speedbump sauntered around the other side of the desk and stretched like he was doing kitty yoga. His body arched so hard that the silver and gray stripes on his sides expanded.

Cash's lips parted, and his eyebrows pinched in the middle. "There's *another* one? How many more of them are there?"

"Three. Just three," Rox told him. "I call them the motley crew."

"It's like a cat clown car under that desk." He whipped his head around and faced her, his bright green eyes wide. "What's wrong?"

"Nothing," Rox said, a reflex that she couldn't have stopped. "I'm fine."

"No, something is wrong," he said, his British accent softening. He looked down her body to the toes of her high-heeled black pumps and back up to her face, searching.

"Really, it's nothing," she said.

Rox could see him winding up to lay out the facts of the case like the lawyer he was.

Cash pointed at the cubicle farm of admins outside her door. "Melanie or Sierra might decide to bring their cats to work. I wouldn't be surprised if Sunbeam or Daffodil were hiding hamsters in their desks. Not *you.*"

"It's nothing," Rox whispered because her throat was closing up.

He continued, "I can count on you to be professional in all things. I can take you to impromptu meetings with clients or other lawyers because I know that you'll behave impeccably and you're always dressed professionally."

Her hands twisted together in front of her, and Pirate

chose that moment to bonk his thick skull against her leg, begging for petting, because of course he did.

Cash said, "I can trust that you won't dress like a sexy vampire on Halloween or sport foil hearts in your hair on Valentine's Day. I can travel with you because I know that I won't find you naked in my bed as if we're on a nookie run on the firm's expense account, and we can get the work *done.* I force HR to give you whatever salary you ask for because I can't work with the other paralegals. They're all over me and the clients and the opposing counsel that I bring in. They're unprofessional. I *rely* on you. You're my rock in this office. You wouldn't bring *cats* to work unless something were terribly *wrong.* What is *wrong?*"

Her eyes burned. "Nothing."

"Bullshit. I call bullshit, Rox."

When he swore in that staunch British accent, it always made her giggle, and she gulped while she looked at the fluorescent tube lights on the ceiling and blinked.

"Rox?" His voice had softened.

When she glanced at him, the whole room swam from the water in her eyes.

"Are you *crying?*" he asked, panic rising in his voice.

"No. I never cry." Something dropped out of her eye and splashed on her cheek.

"*Roxanne!*" Footsteps clomped on the carpet, and Cash's horrified face blocked out the lights. His hands hovered near her shoulders but grasped the air. "Did Grant hit you? Was there an incidence of abuse? Did you have to leave him in the middle of the night?"

"No. He would *never.*" Really. He would never. The other figments of her imagination almost never hit her, either. She almost laughed at that.

"Are you *sick?*" Cash asked, his eyes horrified.

"I'm not sick. Why would I bring my cats to work if I were sick?"

"I don't know. Comfort? The thought worried me." Cash's shoulders lowered, and his hands dropped to his sides. "All right, whatever it is, you can tell me. No matter what it is, I'll help you."

He was standing really close to her. They never stood this close together. They stood shoulder-to-shoulder, sure, when they were going over paperwork or sitting at a table, negotiating a contract. On airplanes, they always flew first-class, so the seat armrests were solid all the way down to the cushions.

They never touched each other, though, unless it was absolutely necessary, and even then, as little as possible. It was one of the unspoken rules of their relationship that kept them friends, good friends, and nothing else.

The light scent of his cologne, sweet wood and delicious spices like cinnamon and vanilla, mixed with the warmth drifting out of his suit, even though he wasn't ranting.

They didn't stand this close together, ever, and Rox's forehead only came up to his chest, even though she was wearing heels.

If she leaned forward, she could rest her forehead against his chest.

His low voice was gentle, almost like he murmured to her, "We've been friends too long for this. Tell me what's going on."

She couldn't quite open her throat enough to talk.

He raised his hand beside her shoulder, and for a minute, she thought he was going to wrap his arms around her.

She should step back if he did. She should gently push him off of her and not let anything get out of hand.

Rox leaned forward two inches and rested her forehead against his shoulder.

It was ridiculous that the square inch of contact of her forehead against his suit jacket suffused comfort through her. She hadn't told anyone what was going on, and the isolation was the worst part.

She breathed in the subtle scent of his cologne and natural musk.

Her shoulder warmed, and she realized that, instead of wrapping his arms around her, he was stroking her shoulder and upper arm. He whispered somewhere near her hair, "Roxanne, tell me. I'll help you."

"Something stupid happened," she admitted.

He took a deep breath, and his chest expanded. She angled her head, and his suit brushed her cheek.

Cash asked, "Did you have an auto accident? Is there a legal problem, perhaps you panicked and left? I can help you with that. I'll bring the full power of this firm into play."

"Nothing like that. It's just—I got evicted from my apartment."

A pause.

Which lengthened.

He finally asked, "You live in an apartment?"

"I've really only been making good money the last couple years, and I was saving for a down payment for a house, but I bought the car."

"I don't need to know this." He shook his head and stepped back to peer down at her. Her forehead chilled. "Why would you be evicted?"

"They found out about the cats. The lease said no pets. And the eviction notice was effective immediately. They put a bolt on my door. I just took my cats and some clothes and left."

"You can't be evicted without due process. An eviction proceeding usually takes months, even if there is a lease violation."

Cash looked down at their feet.

Pirate leaned so hard against Rox's leg that her knee almost buckled, and his bottle-brush tail coiled around her thigh like a furry snake.

"I suppose I shouldn't ask why you even have cats, then," he said, "if the lease forbade them."

"I volunteer at an animal shelter on Sundays. These guys were so sad. They needed someone to love them. And I did. So I took them home."

"Even though your apartment had a no-pets policy."

"I figured that it was easier to ask for forgiveness than to get permission."

"I don't think you received either."

"Look at this little guy." Rox hoisted him into her arms, burying her fingers in his deep fur. Pirate tucked his forehead under her chin and purred hard. "He was so depressed, living in that little cage for months. How could I just walk away from him?"

Cash stared at the cat—at his ruined ears, the blank fur where his eye used to be, and the scarred pits where he was missing some of his yellow fur—and his eyebrows rose with skepticism. "I'll leave that to your judgment."

"I couldn't," she said, scratching him under the chin, and Pirate closed his yellow eye in happiness.

"And the others?"

"Same thing. They needed me."

A slow smile crept over Cash's face. "It would not have occurred to me that you would rescue three motheaten cats at some risk to yourself. You're a sweet person, Rox."

"I am not. You take that back." She set Pirate down on his paws. He sat and washed his flat face with a paw.

Cash watched the cat smear spit on his face. "So where have you been staying?"

"That's kind of the problem," she admitted.

"Oh?" His query was laced with wariness, and he began watching her more closely again.

"I couldn't find a hotel that took animals, and I swear to God, *all* my friends are allergic or have aggressive dogs or something."

Cash looked horrified again. "So where have you been staying?"

"I've been sleeping in my car and showering at my gym."

"In your *car?* You can't sleep in your car in *Los Angeles.* There are homeless persons, and vagrants, and criminals. It's not *safe.* You can't *do* that."

"I didn't have any other options," she said.

"Of course you did. You could have called *me.* I'm not allergic to cat hair—"

"It's actually the dander, not the hair."

"—and I don't have a dog to frighten them."

Rox fidgeted, digging her toe into the flat carpet. "But, you're a guy."

"Does not follow," he said, his eyebrows drawing farther down. That was lawyer-speak for something illogical or that he couldn't understand.

"I can't ask a *guy* if I can come sleep on his couch. It *implies* things."

"Gender propriety rules do not apply when you are *homeless.* This is *appalling.*" Cash ran one hand through his hair.

And yet she had no choice. There was one damn good reason why she hadn't told him. "And, you're *you.*"

"What on Earth is that supposed to mean?" he demanded.

"You're *Cash Amsberg*. You're *that* guy in the office."

His brilliant green eyes lit with anger. *"What guy?"*

"The guy. The guy who everyone has—you know."

He rolled his eyes and raised his hands. "Rox, it's *me*. It's *just me*. We travel together every month. I've certainly never assaulted you."

"Well, there was that one time in Japan that you dragged me into your room—" she mused.

"I carried you out of the bar on the night when you discovered sake. I held your hair back. That night was like the aftermath of a frat party."

"You took my clothes off." This was one of their comedy routines. They'd been through it a dozen times, but Cash was still ranting so much that he didn't recognize it.

He insisted, "It was an act of charity to take that vomit-soaked blouse off of you, and I got you into one of my tee shirts before I rolled you into the bed."

She was trying to repress a smile at his sputtering. "You stayed in my room when I was too drunk to give consent."

"I slept on the floor to make sure you didn't choke to death on your own vomit, and it was actually my room."

"That's still not consent."

"I have never behaved improperly or even suggested such a thing."

Cash was well into a good rant. His ears were even turning pink. Rox blinked hard, trying to get the teary crap out of her eyes.

God, he smelled good, like cookies and fresh lumber and something darker, masculine, and clean.

He demanded, "And where is your husband during all

this? Is he sleeping in his car, too? Or has he gone to stay with someone and left you out in the cold?"

It wasn't particularly cold in early autumn in Los Angeles, especially with three traumatized cats who had slept draped on top of her while she reclined in the passenger seat, but that wasn't the point.

Rox said, "Grant is on a month-long shoot in Thailand. He's been gone for over a week. He doesn't even know. I didn't want to worry him."

Cash's deep voice rose, along with his hands. "Good God, Rox. So you were alone, in your car, with three cats, and you didn't *call me.* I can't bear it."

"It didn't seem like the right thing to do."

His voice rose further. "Damn you and your bizarre Southern proprieties. *Get* your cats. *Get* your things. We're taking everything to my place so that you can concentrate on work the rest of the day, and then you'll stay in my guest suite until we can find a *proper* apartment for you that accommodates *pets* so this doesn't happen again. Do I make myself perfectly clear?"

He was so funny when he was outraged. Even though Rox saw it a couple times a week, it was still kind of cute.

And because it was cute, she provoked him further. "You're not the boss of me."

"I assure you, I am *actually* the boss of you," Cash said, still ranting. "I *am* your boss and you will do as I say and you will not sleep in your damned *car* even one more minute."

Cash paused, taking in the fact that she was grinning at his tirade, even though her eyes still burned a little.

He said, "Oh, I see how it is. *Fine.* Get these beasts packed up. We'll pick up some lunch while we're out. Have you been eating?"

Rox rolled her eyes at that. "I have money. I just couldn't find a place to stay."

"Then it's settled."

"It's just for tonight. I'll find someplace starting tomorrow."

"Fine, then. I'll be back in ten minutes to carry your things downstairs to my car." He turned to leave.

"I can drive myself," she insisted.

"My car is larger, and yours has been recently used as a flop for homeless people and unwashed beasts. It's not fit transportation."

She laughed at him that time. "You don't have to do this. I'm really fine."

Cash rolled his eyes, finally thoroughly exasperated. "I will brook no more arguments. *Pack up your cats.*"

"Okay, boss."

His shoulders relaxed as he finally simmered down, and she could see the snark building in him. He asked, "Also, you belong to a gym?"

Oh, a chubby crack.

Rox popped her chin up. "Yeah, I do. Where I take kick-boxing, and I will pound your skinny, arrogant, lawyer butt if you make a fat joke."

Cash chuckled. "That's not what I meant. You should try mine. It has an excellent juice bar with very good food service. The treadmills have desks. I often look at contracts on a laptop while I'm there. You might like it."

She rolled her eyes at that, too. "Dude, you have a serious workaholism problem. There's gotta be a twelve-step program for that."

~~~~~

Get WORKING STIFF in Ebook, Paperback, or Audiobook narrated *to start reading the Billionaires in Disguise series!*

https://blairbabylon.com/books/working-stiff/

A NOTE FROM BLAIR

Dear Reader,

Thank you so much for reading *SKINS GAME,* Book 3 of the Last Chance Billionaires saga. I hope you loved Kingston!

Leaving a review helps the author by letting other readers know that you loved the book!

Thank you also to Caitlin Moffett, who won the Romancing the Vote auction to have her name in this romance novel. The character is not based on her, but the character bears her name to honor Caitlin and her mom for their generous contribution to Romancing the Vote.

And thank you, dear reader, for reading *Skins Game.*

Love,

Blair

Before you go, there's so many more Billionaires in Disguise to love!

I write books described as "THRILLERS THAT BANG," which are suspenseful, plot-twisty thrillers with a hefty serving of spice.

If you're new to my books, the Last Chance series is part of the overall Billionaires in Disguise (BID) world. Each individual mini-series stands by itself, so look for the "Book #1" in each set. Some are collected in boxed sets, so keep an eye out for those collections. I've written over 50 books in the greater BID universe and have no intention of stopping anytime soon, so you have lots of books to fall in love with!

The chronological reading list is here at my website, https://blairbabylon.com/reading-order/ . Really, each of the mini-series can be read by themselves, so you don't have to worry about doing it perfectly. Don't forget that many of them are available in audio, read by Joe Arden, John Lane, Shane East, and more!

If you want to know when I publish a new book or have a sale, sign up for my newsletter at https://blairbabylon. com/emailbx .

I also have a Facebook reader group, Blair's Babes' VIP Room, where we have fun and talk about books. I hang around in there and answer questions. A couple of times per year, we have an "ABA," or Ask Blair Anything, but I reserve the right to waffle if there are spoilers for future books involved. I also do giveaways. My reader group gets the best prize boxes. We talk about a lot of books in there, and other authors drop in for their giveaways. It's a fun and positive place.

Make sure you're signed up for my **NEWSLETTER** so you'll know when I have a new book out! I often put pre-orders up for special, lower pre-order sales for 24 hours, and I'll let you know when's the best time to buy.

Newsletter subscribers also get FREE access to special epilogues and books that there's no other way to get.

Thank you again for reading.

Love,
Blair Babylon

All Blair's Books

Reading Order

Never Miss A Sale!

ABOUT BLAIR BABYLON

What order should you read Blair's Books in?

Go to Blair's Website: Lots of Fun News, Extras, Reading Order, List of Blair's Books, and More!
www.BlairBabylon.com

About Blair Babylon

Blair Babylon is an award-winning author who used to publish literary fiction. Because reviews of her mainstream fiction usually included the caveat that there was too much deviant sex in her novels, she decided to abandon all literary pretensions, let her freak flag fly, and write hot, sexy romance novels. She's having much more fun now.

www.ingramcontent.com/pod-product-compliance
Lightning Source LLC
Chambersburg PA
CBHW030547020726
47494CB00005B/1506